喚醒你的英文語感！

Get a Feel for English !

喚醒你的英文語感！

Get a Feel for English !

MP3 帶走到哪記到哪

大考 7000 字只有 1500 字要背！
電腦分析歷屆考題，

{ 把單字分為產出、認知、印象等三類，有些字根本不用背！
迎合大考趨勢，以語意單字為重點教學！
以歷年考題為單字例句，字彙&試題情境一起掌握！
3D 動畫、綠能環保、基因工程等命題新趨，搶鮮收錄！ }

改變一生的
大考單字課

編著：**陳超明** 教授

整理：**巫立文**

Vocab

貝塔語言出版
Beta Multimedia Publishing

IRT 語言測驗中心
Language Testing Center

一 劃時代的單字學習方式

任何語言的學習不外乎二部分：單字與句型文法。

而近年來，高中升大學的考題題型，對於文法的著重已逐步轉為對語意的瞭解。此一改變，相對地突現出同學強化自身單字能力的重要性。大體來說，國中到高中的六年課程，同學已累積大量英文單字數，然而，以強迫記憶學習而來的單字，即便記憶下來的字為數不少，久而久之卻不免從腦中流失遺忘。再者，研究後發現，個人記憶力的強弱與個人的單字能力並不見得成等比發展，因此，本書將採取不同於坊間單字書的學習方式，改以一種革新創新的單字學習法來幫助同學們有效並能長久記憶單字，收事半功倍之效。

二 單字學習時的三個層面

所有單字的學習皆需透過三個層面的整合連結才能達到最佳學習效果。

1、要能出口唸，唸出聲的單字才能進入腦子。

2、與考試閱讀或生活經驗相關，可以放在情境中使用。

3、依單字的重要性、使用性分層次去理解使用。

三 單字學習書的編輯方針

本書主要是針對大學考試而編。回溯歷年來，遑論是校內的考試、大學入學考試甚或是市面上的單字書籍，皆以大考中心於 1993 年，經由國外的語料庫以單字的使用頻率高低，篩選歸納而出的 7000 個單字為圭臬。然而在語言學習過程中，不同時空與資訊的變遷，單字本身在使用頻率上其實是會跟著時代而不斷變化。近年來，新的英文用語與使用方式每天都在推陳出新，而這些隨著時間潮流或不同知識閱讀所衍生出的單字，自然不在大考中心的 7000 單字之列。顯而易見地，大學考試考題也隨著時事及新知識在走，將近廿年前整理出的單字資料庫自然無法應付當今的大學考試所涵蓋的知識層面。有鑑於此，本書的編輯將完全針對現今的大學考試將單字及知識作全盤性的更新與整理。

四 本書的編輯主旨

✔ 從知識面建立單字素材，補足未來知識的單字

以科學的角度以索引軟體（concordancer）分析過去十年來大考單字測驗、綜合測驗、文意測驗、篇章結構、閱讀測驗等所出現的句子與文章段落，找出現今高中生閱讀時所需要用到的單字共有 4473 個，與大考中心的 7000 單字比對後，產生了 2527 個字的差距。不可否認，這 2527 個單字會被收錄自有其正當性，對於學習有所幫助。然而，我不免要呼籲的是，大考中心公布的單字裡，很多單字在現有的閱讀經驗與知識裡很少出現。此狀況下，大家不免質疑，我要花時間學習這些不會影響閱讀與知識吸收的單字嗎？舉例來說，全球暖化、綠能環保、氣候變遷、3D 動畫、基因工程、科普新知等相關的議題近年來頗受關注，與這些議題有關的閱讀考題在大考中出現的比例也逐年增加，這些新鮮字彙隨著新知識的萌生陸續出現在大考考題的單字中。但，這類字彙卻不在大考中心公布的 7000 單字之列。本書針對此缺失作彌補，將知識性的單字加以更新。也針對未來科普及人文社會新知的單字加以補足，以提升學生應付未來閱讀的挑戰。

✅ 單字與考試情境

　　學有用的單字必得從情境上學習而非一昧死背。本書將單字從各類文章中整理出來，但在語意用法及例句說明時，以大考出現的句子為主要範本，將單字學習與考試情境結合，對於熟悉這類單字在未來考試的用法上有很大的幫助。在考試情境中學習單字。將單字與實際的文章閱讀結合，是單字學習最重要也最有效的過程。

✅ 單字分類與分層記憶

　　根據 ETS 的統計，在語言學習過程中，約需具備 2000 ～ 3000 個單字的實力才能流暢看完並看懂一篇文章。實際上，並非所有的單字都必須背到滾瓜爛熟，都會拼寫，才能透徹瞭解文章的文意，有些單字僅是作為閱讀時輔助瞭解內容的工具而已。一般來說，高中生單字的學習，大抵依記憶的深淺度區分為三大類：

a. 實質產出類（Word for Production）：日常聽說讀寫與考試時會使用到的關鍵字。

b. 基本認識類（Word for Cognition）：有助於語意的瞭解，知道含意即可。

c. 背景資訊類（Word for Background Information）：可有可無的模糊單字，如專有名詞、動植物學名等。

五 關鍵的動詞與名詞

　　以上這些單字分類中，又以動詞、名詞及部分影響語意變化的形容詞、副詞，對於閱讀或寫作翻譯影響最大。如以下 100 學年度學科測驗的英文閱讀測驗：

It is easy for us / to **tell our friends** / from **our enemies.** / But can other animals do the same? / **Elephants** can! / They can **use** their **sense of vision** / and **smell** to / **tell the difference** / between people / who **pose a threat** / and those who do not.

In Kenya, / **researchers found** / that elephants **react** differently / to clothing / **worn** by men / of the Maasai and Kamba ethnic groups. / Young Maasai men **spear** animals / and / thus / **pose a threat** / to elephants; / Kamba men are mainly **farmers** / and are not a **danger** / to elephants.

將長篇的段落或文章分成語意的小單元（如上面以 "/" 將主詞、動詞及語意小單元分開理解），這時，大抵掌握標示成黑體字的動詞與名詞，整段的語意也就浮現了。

因此，本書再從四千多單字中，篩選出 1500 個關鍵的動詞、名詞與少數形容詞、副詞作為最後強化記憶與學習的突破點！

學習單字時記得要依循 Word for Production → Word for Cognition → Word for Background Information 的先後次序與熟悉度去記憶。而其中 Word for Production 大部分都是動詞與名詞，熟悉這些產出的動詞與名詞，尤其是動詞的用法，對於翻譯及寫作題型，幫助更大！

六 如何使用這本書

1. 從動詞著手，要記住每個動詞，依照書中所附的光碟，跟著唸出聲音，要複誦三次。
2. 研讀從閱讀篇章中所摘選的例句時，也跟著光碟唸一至兩遍。
3. 接著要再看此單字有關的舉例與補充，了解語意與用法，例如什麼時候要接介系詞、名詞、動詞加 ing 等。

4. 把課本闔起來，以回想的方式默記今天學到的單字。

5. 每天以至少要學三個單字為原則，且不只是要記住單字的拼法，要唸出聲、要學會如何使用。

七 結語

　　整體而論，本單字書除了為因應高中同學的考試而編纂，也顧及了日常的實用性，我們也增加了一些多益及全民英檢的關鍵動詞。

　　單字必須唸出聲才會進入腦子裡、才能在生活中使用，因此，每個字都附有音標。再者，為了讓同學能有效記憶單字，書中採情境式學習概念，將單字與日常生活與考試題目結合在一起實際運用，讓單字學習變得有意義好記憶。最後，更為同學將單字的重要性依類別區分出層次，以避免同學花費寶貴時間查字典記誦無用的單字。用此書來學習單字，單字記憶將不再是難事。

政大英文系教授　陳超明

CONTENTS 目錄

略語符號說明

- sth. = something（某物）
- sb. = somebody（某人）
- S = subject（主詞）
- V = verb（動詞）
- Ving = verb ending in –ing（動詞進行式）
- 主 = 主詞
- 受 = 受詞
- 補 = 補語

動詞篇

▶ ▶ ▶ **Verbs**

accomplish

adapt

abate

acquire

abandon

activate

abandon [ə`bændən]	放棄、中途停止、放縱；名詞作放縱解 英解 to discontinue

例 Their boat was badly damaged and they had to **abandon** their journey.

（91 學測）

他們的小船嚴重損壞不得不放棄之後的行程。

語意用法 人＋ abandon ＋受（人／物／地位）。

abate [ə`bet]	減少、降低、減輕 英解 to lessen

例 The sharp pain in my neck **abated** after a day.

我頸部的刺痛一天後減輕許多。

語意用法 主（事件或事物）＋ abate。

abhor [əb`hɔr]	厭惡、痛恨 英解 to detest

例 Most people **abhor** cruelty to animals.

大多數人痛恨虐待動物的行為。

語意用法 主＋ abhor ＋受。

abolish [ə`bɑlɪʃ]	廢止、革除（制度、法律、習慣） 英解 to cancel

例 Slavery wasn't **abolished** in the United States until 1845.

奴隸制度在美國一直到 1845 年才被廢止。

語意用法 主＋ abolish ＋受，此處為被動用法。

abort
[ə`bɔrt]

流產、夭折、退化
英解 not reach

例 Everybody agrees that a woman can decide whether to **abort** or not.
（95 指考）

大家都贊同女人有墮胎自主權。

語意用法 abort 表示終止某項計畫（如懷孕）。

accept
[ək`sɛpt]

接受、同意、應允
英解 to take willingly

例 I basically **accept** your plan, but I think it should be somewhat reworded.
（90 學測）

基本上我同意你的計畫，不過我覺得仍須重新用詞。

語意用法 accept ＋受＋ as ＋補，表示認定（說明、學說）為……。

accomplish
[ə`kamplɪʃ]

達到、完成、實現
英解 to achieve

例 The tools used for sculpting also affect when the task can be
accomplished.（97 學測）

用於雕刻的工具會影響作品何時完成。

語意用法 人＋ accomplish ＋工作，表示完成某項工作；此處為被動，task ＋ be
accomplished。

accuse
[ə`kjuz]

指責、指控、歸咎於
英解 to blame

例 Japanese companies have been **accused** of over-packaging.（95 指考）
日本企業被指責過度包裝。

語意用法 accuse ＋人＋ of ＋事，指責、指控某人某事；此處為被動，人＋ be
accused of ＋事情。

accustom [əˈkʌstəm]	習慣於 英解 to adapt

例 Only a few people worked with the whales so that they would not become too **accustomed** to human beings. (84 學測)

只有少數人與鯨魚一起工作，避免牠們習慣於人類。

語意用法 be accustomed to ＋人／事，表示習慣於某人或某事。

achieve [əˈtʃiv]	達成、實現、獲得 英解 to acquire one's goals

例 A plan is carefully designed to **achieve** a goal. (92 指考)

為了達成目標，周密構思了一個計畫。

語意用法 人／計畫＋ achieve ＋目標或工作。

acquaint [əˈkwent]	介紹、使瞭解熟悉 英解 to familiarize

例 I **acquainted** him with my new neighborhood.

我介紹他認識我的新社區。

語意用法 acquaint ＋人＋ with ＋事，表示讓某人熟悉某事；人＋ be acquainted with ＋事，表示某人熟悉某事。

acquire [əˈkwaɪr]	獲得、取得 英解 to obtain

例 They **acquire** the wolf's hunting skills of stealth, courage, and stamina.

(95 指考)

他們獲得狼狩獵時輕巧、勇敢以及耐力等技巧。

語意用法 人＋ acquire ＋技術、能力。

activate
[ˋæktəˌvet]

刺激使活動、使活化、使活潑
英解 to put in motion

例 She **activated** the machine by pressing a button.

她按了一個按鈕讓機器動起來。

語意用法 人＋ activate ＋機器或物品，表示人啟動某機器／物品。

adapt
[əˋdæpt]

使適合、改編、改造
英解 to modify

例 This impact forces a company to **adapt** its products in order to meet the needs of the local market.（94 指考）

這項衝擊迫使公司改造他們的產品以符合當地市場所需。

語意用法 adapt ＋物品＋ to/for，表示改變某些物品使適合市場或某些功能。

adjust
[əˋdʒʌst]

調整、調節、校正
英解 to modify

例 At Tsavo National Park, Zoe has been taught to **adjust** to life in the wild.（90 學測）

佐依在 Tsavo 國家公園學習調整適應野外生活。

語意用法 人＋ adjust to ＋環境或事物，表示人做某些調整來配合環境。

administer
[ədˋmɪnəstə]

給予、執行、管理
英解 to give

例 An intelligence test was **administered** to over 350,000 Dutch males when they turned 19 years of age.（94 指考）

超過 350,000 名荷蘭男性在步入 19 歲時接受智力測驗。

語意用法 administer ＋事＋ to ＋人，表示督導某事執行，此處為被動用法。

admit [əd`mɪt]	承認、許可、容納 英解 to confess

例 The university Susan is **admitted** to has been noted for making research in science and technology.（93 指考）

蘇珊進入的大學在科學技術的研究上聞名。

語意用法 admit ＋人／物，表示容納；admit ＋受＋ to/into ＋地方，表示容許進入某地方，此處為被動，人＋ be admitted to a university，某人進入大學。

adopt [ə`dɑpt]	收養、採納、吸收 英解 accept as one's own

例 We **adopted** two children whose parents were killed in an accident.

我們收養了二個父母意外喪生的孩子。

語意用法 人＋ adopt ＋人，表示收養某人。

adore [ə`dor]	愛慕、崇拜、很喜歡 英解 to love deeply

例 He simply **adores** his teacher, who is patient with students.

他很崇拜他那位對學生很有耐心的老師。

語意用法 adore ＋人＋ as ＋補，表示崇拜某人為……。

advise [əd`vaɪz]	勸告、告知、建議 英解 to counsel

例 His doctor **advises** him not to take his medicine with alcohol.

他的醫生勸他不要用酒配藥吃。

語意用法 advise ＋人＋ on ＋事物，表示忠告某人某事；advise ＋人＋ to V，表示建議某人去做某事。

affect
[əˈfɛkt]

影響、使感動、疾病侵襲
英解 to influence

例 Climate change may **affect** people's health both directly and indirectly.

（96 指考）

氣候變遷可能直接和間接影響人們的健康。

語意用法 affect ＋事物。

afford
[əˈford]

負擔得起、足以、提供、給予
英解 to be able to pay for st. without difficulty

例 Peter is now living on a budget of NT$100 per day. He cannot **afford** any recreational activities.（96 學測）

彼得現在每天的生活預算只有 100 元，不足以支付任何娛樂活動。

語意用法 afford ＋ to V，表示有餘力去做某事；cannot afford，沒有能力（金錢或時間）去做某事。

alter
[ˈɔltə]

改變、修改、閹割
英解 to change

例 Alcohol works directly on the central nervous system and **alters** one's moods and limits judgment.（97 指考）

酒精直接作用於中樞神經系統，進而改變一個人的情緒並限制判斷能力。

語意用法 alter ＋事物，表示改變某項事物。

announce
[əˈnaʊns]

正式宣告、聲明、通知
英解 to make public

例 After being introduced, he strode confidently to the lectern and **announced** his topic.（94 指考）

被介紹出場後，他自信滿滿地邁開大步走向講台宣布他的講題。

語意用法 announce ＋主題，表示發表某項主題。

| **annoy**
[əˋnɔɪ] | 惹惱、困擾、使苦惱
英解 to irritate |

例 The constant noise from the street traffic **annoyed** me.

街上交通持續發出的噪音困擾我。

語意用法 事物＋ annoy ＋人，表示可厭之事煩擾某人；如為被動，人＋ be annoyed，表示某人對某事厭煩。

| **anticipate**
[ænˋtɪsəˏpet] | 預期、預料、搶先
英解 to await |

例 Joseph's behavior is so unpredictable that no one can **anticipate** exactly what he will do.（92 學測補考）

約瑟夫的舉止相當難以預料，沒有人可以正確預測他會做什麼。

語意用法 人＋ anticipate ＋事情，表示預測某事。

| **apologize**
[əˋpɑləˏdʒaɪz] | 道歉、認錯
英解 to ask forgiveness |

例 The boy **apologized** to the teacher for his improper behavior.（85 學測）

這男孩為自己不恰當的行為向老師認錯。

語意用法 apologize to ＋人＋ for ＋事，表示向某人為某事而道歉。

| **apply**
[əˋplaɪ] | 申請、塗敷、適用
英解 to request |

例 He just needs to **apply** for a non-visa entry when he arrives at the CKS airport.（85 學測）

當他抵達桃園國際機場時，只需要申請免簽入境。

語意用法 apply for ＋事情，表示申請某事，此處為申請簽證。

appreciate
[ə`priʃɪ,et]

感激、欣賞、體會、增值
英解 to be thankful for

例 The Transportation Safety Administration **appreciated** Barnett's help and welcomed his suggestions. (92 指考)

運輸安全部門感謝巴奈特的幫助並欣然接受他的建議。

語意用法 人＋ appreciate ＋事物，表示感謝某事物。

approach
[ə`protʃ]

接近、靠近、方法、著手處理；亦作名詞用
英解 to near

例 The doors of these department stores slide open automatically when you **approach** them. (98 學測)

當你走近時，百貨公司裡的門會自動開啟。

語意用法 人＋ approach ＋物，表示接近某物。

argue
[`ɑrgjʊ]

爭論、主張、說服、證明
英解 to disagree

例 Fans of professional baseball and football **argue** continually over which is America's favorite sport. (94 學測)

職業棒球與橄欖球的球迷永無止境地爭論何者是美國的國民運動。

語意用法 人＋ argue over ＋事情，表示爭論某事。

arrange
[ə`rendʒ]

安排、配置、籌備、改編（音樂劇劇本）
英解 to schedule

例 To live an efficient life, we have to **arrange** the things to do in order of priority and start with the most important ones. (94 學測)

我們要過有效率的生活，必得依優先順序來安排事情，從最重要的事情做起。

語意用法 arrange ＋事情，表示安排事情。

arrest [ə`rɛst]	逮捕、制止、吸引、抓住；亦作名詞用 英解 to seize or hold a person

例 The drug dealer was **arrested** by the police while he was selling cocaine to a high school student.（94 學測）

這名毒販在販賣古柯鹼給高中生時被警察逮捕。

語意用法 arrest ＋人＋ for ＋罪行，表示以某罪名逮捕某人。此處為被動，人＋ be arrested。

assess [ə`sɛs]	估價（財產、稅金）、進行評估 英解 to evaluate

例 My father **assessed** how much it would cost to build a new house.

我爸爸評估了蓋一棟新房子需要多少費用。

語意用法 assess ＋事物，表示評估某事物的價值。

assign [ə`saɪn]	分配、指派 英解 to designate

例 Because of her high level of proficiency in both Chinese and English, Miss Lin was **assigned** the task of oral interpretation for the visiting American delegation.（95 學測）

由於中英文程度很好，林小姐被分配擔任美國訪問代表團的口譯工作。

語意用法 assign ＋人＋ for/to ＋工作，表示指派人任務。此處為被動，人＋ be assigned ＋工作。

assist [ə`sɪst]	協助、支持、參加 英解 to aid

例 My friend **assisted** me in moving to a new dorm.

我朋友協助我搬進新宿舍。

語意用法 assist ＋人＋ in/with ＋工作，表示幫助某人做某事。

22

assure [əˈʃur]	擔保、保險、使確信 英解 to guarantee

例 We are **assured** that we are destined to live happily ever after.（94 學測）

我們確信從此之後我們注定會過著幸福快樂的日子。

語意用法 assure ＋人＋ of ＋事／ assure ＋人＋ that ＋子句，表示向某人保證某事。此處為被動，人＋ be assured ＋ that ＋子句。

attach [əˈtætʃ]	貼上、附加、使附屬、查封、使喜愛 英解 to affix

例 The student **attached** a note to his report with a paper clip.

那名學生在他的報告上用迴紋針夾了張便條。

語意用法 人＋ attach ＋物＋ to/on ＋物，表示繫上、裝上。

attack [əˈtæk]	攻擊、抨擊、責難、著手；亦作名詞用 英解 to assault

例 If you want to keep your computer from being **attacked** by new viruses, you need to constantly renew and update your anti-virus software.（96 學測）

如果你想要避免你的電腦遭受新病毒的攻擊，你必須經常更新你的防毒軟體。

語意用法 物＋ attack ＋物。此處為被動，物＋ be attacked by ＋物。

attain [əˈten]	獲得、到達 英解 to achieve

例 One key factor to success is to have a definite goal first and then do your best to **attain** the goal.（87 學測）

成功的關鍵要素首先要具備明確的目標，接著就是全力以赴達成目標。

語意用法 人＋ attain ＋目標。

attempt [ə`tɛmpt]	試圖、企圖、嘗試;名詞亦當攻擊解
	英解 to try

例 I **attempted** to gain pride in myself by obtaining my father's approval or acknowledgment of my value as a person. (97 指考)

我試圖贏得自尊,獲得我父親認可與贊同我作為一個人的價值。

語意用法 人＋ attempt ＋ to V,表示試著去做某事。

attend [ə`tɛnd]	出席、前往
	英解 to be present at

例 All the students are required to **attend** the two-day orientation program so that they can have a complete understanding of the university they are admitted to. (93 指考)

所有的學生都被要求出席為期二天的新生訓練課程,幫助他們全盤瞭解他們所進入的大學。

語意用法 attend ＋會議,表示出席會議。

attract [ə`trækt]	吸引、引誘
	英解 to appeal to

例 They need those well-known ancient objects to **attract** people from all over the world. (93 學測)

他們需要那些眾所周知的古老作品來吸引世界各地的人們。

語意用法 attract ＋人＋ to ＋地方,表示將人吸引向某處。

attribute [ə`trɪbjʊt]	歸因於、歸咎於;名詞作屬性、特質解
	英解 to credit

例 I **attribute** Stephen W. Hawking's success to his talent and hard work.

我將史蒂芬霍金的成功歸因於他的天賦與努力。

語意用法 attribute ＋成功之事＋ to ＋人、事、物,表示將成功歸諸於某人、事、物。

| **avoid**
[əˋvɔɪd] | 躲開、避免、撤銷
英解 to bypass |

例 When there is a heavy rain, you have to drive very cautiously so as to **avoid** traffic accidents.（98 指考）

在豪雨中開車時，要格外謹慎小心避免交通意外。

語意用法 avoid + Ving，表示避免做某事。

| **behave**
[bɪˋhev] | 表現、行為舉止、檢點
英解 to act in a certain way |

例 Boys and girls **behave** differently because of biological differences.

（96 學測）

男孩和女孩的生物結構不同，表現出的行為舉止也不一樣。

語意用法 人 + behave，表示人的舉止行為。

| **betray**
[bɪˋtre] | 背叛、出賣、洩漏
英解 to commit treason |

例 However, she spied for the enemy and **betrayed** him.（98 指考）

然而，她暗中替敵人偵察並出賣他。

語意用法 betray + 人，表示背叛某人。

| **beware**
[bɪˋwɛr] | 小心、注意、提防
英解 aware of danger |

例 "**Beware** of the tiger" means that a tiger might attack you.

「小心老虎」的告示牌表示可能會有老虎攻擊你。

語意用法 beware of + 物，表示注意某物。

blame [blem]	責備、譴責、歸咎、詛咒；名詞亦作責任解 英解 to accuse

例 For the five highway deaths, the author **blames** a large heavy station wagon.（84 學測）

對於造成五人死亡的公路意外，作者歸咎於一輛大型休旅車。

語意用法 blame ＋事＋ for ＋原因，表示將某事歸咎於某原因。

boil [bɔɪl]	沸騰、煮熟 英解 to heat a liquid until it reaches the temperature of 100℃

例 My roommate **boiled** the water to cook the instant noodles.

我室友煮開水沖泡麵。

語意用法 boil ＋水＋ to V，表示煮水以做某事。

bore [bor]	使厭煩、無聊 英解 to make sb. feel tired

例 They were **bored** because the medical topics were not their daily concern.（94 指考）

他們感到厭煩因為醫療主題不是他們日常所關心的。

語意用法 人＋ be bored about ＋事，表示對某事感到無聊、厭煩。

borrow [`baro]	借入（錢、物品）、採用 英解 to receive a loan of st. with the promise to return it

例 If you want to **borrow** magazines, tapes, or CDs, you can visit the library.
（94 學測）

你如果想要借雜誌、影片或 CD，可以去圖書館找找看。

語意用法 人＋ borrow ＋事物＋ from，表示從某處借東西。

breathe
[bri ð]

呼吸、喘息、通風、散發
英解 to inhale and exhale

例 The astronauts can hardly **breathe** in a space suit.（94 學測）

穿著太空衣，太空人幾乎無法呼吸。

語意用法 人＋ breathe，表示呼吸。

broadcast
[ˋbrɔd͵kæst]

廣播、散佈、播種；亦作名詞用
英解 to send over the air

例 The president's speech will be **broadcast** simultaneously on television and radio so that more people can listen to it at the time when it is delivered.（97 指考）

總統的演說將會透過廣播與電視同時播送，讓更多人可以即時聽到這場演說。

語意用法 主＋ broadcast ＋事物，表示廣播某事；此處為被動。事、物 | be broadcast on television，表示某事物在電視轉播。

browse
[brauz]

瀏覽
英解 to look over in a slow, relaxed way

例 **Browse** through visions of the world as seen through a photographer's eye.

透過攝影師的眼睛瀏覽世界奇景。

語意用法 browse through ＋資訊，表示瀏覽、尋找某資訊。

burst
[bɜst]

爆炸、爆發、闖、突然出現；亦作名詞解
英解 to explode

例 Kevin **burst** into tears on the spot because his teacher punished him in front of the whole class.（92 學測）

凱文的老師當著全班的面處罰他時，他當場飆淚。

語意用法 人＋ burst ＋ into tears，表示突然流淚。

bury
[ˈbɛrɪ]

埋葬、隱匿、沈浸於
英解 to inter

例 Mark **buried** his pet yesterday.
馬克昨天埋葬了他的寵物。

語意用法 bury ＋人、物，表示埋葬某人或某物。

calculate
[ˈkælkjəˌlet]

計算、估算、打算、認為
英解 to do math

例 Howard **calculated** the calories of everything he ate during his participation in the diet program. （89 學測）
霍華德參與這項減食計畫的期間計算所有食物的卡路里。

語意用法 人＋ calculate。

cancel
[ˈkænsl̩]

取消、註銷、抵銷
英解 to call off

例 The outdoor concert was **canceled** because of rain. （85 學測）
戶外音樂會因雨取消。

語意用法 人＋ cancel ＋事情；此處為被動，事＋ be cancelled。

carve
[kɑrv]

雕刻、切片、開創
英解 to sculpe

例 It takes more time to **carve** with razor-sharp chisels. （97 學測）
使用鋒利的鑿子得花更多的時間來雕刻。

語意用法 carve with ＋物，表示以某物品來雕刻。

| **catch**
[kætʃ] | 捕獲、接住、感染 |
| | 英解 to grasp sth. in motion |

例 The carver must work fast in a cold environment to avoid **catching** cold.
（97 學測）

在寒冷的環境中工作，雕刻工作者必須動作迅速避免感冒。

語意用法 catch cold，表示感冒。

| **celebrate**
[ˈsɛləˌbret] | 慶祝、舉行儀式、頌揚 |
| | 英解 to do sth. special to mark an occasion |

例 The tower is built to **celebrate** the coming of the year 2000.（87 學測）
這座塔被建造來慶祝西元 2000 年的來臨。

語意用法 celebrate ＋事件，表示慶祝某事件。

| **challenge**
[ˈtʃælɪndʒ] | 挑戰、質疑、激發、盤問；亦作名詞用 |
| | 英解 to test one's abilities |

例 These changes **challenged** many of the traditional roles men and women were expected to play.（95 指考）
這些改變挑戰許多男人和女人被期望扮演的傳統角色。

語意用法 事物＋ challenge ＋物、人，表示某事物挑戰另一事物／人。

| **cheat**
[tʃit] | 欺騙、作弊；名詞作騙子、詐欺解 |
| | 英解 to deceive |

例 This information came from a very reliable source, so you don't have to worry about being **cheated**.（98 學測）
這消息的來源相當可靠，你不用擔心會被騙。

語意用法 cheat ＋人＋ (out) of ＋物，表示騙取某人的某物；此處為被動 be cheated。

29

cherish [ˈtʃɛrɪʃ]	珍惜 英解 to love most dearly

例 We have to find a way to live comfortably inside our bodies and make friends with and **cherish** ourselves.（94 學測）

我們必須尋求一種舒適的內在生活方式，與自己當朋友並珍惜自己。

語意用法 人＋ cherish ＋人、事、物，珍惜某人、事、物。

choose [ˈtʃuz]	選擇、做決定 英解 to select

例 He was born with so many talents that he couldn't **choose** a direction.
（99 指考）

他天生多才多藝，以致無法決定往哪個領域發展。

語意用法 人＋ choose ＋方向，表示選擇某方向。

circulate [ˈsɜkjəˌlet]	循環、流通、流傳 英解 to pass around

例 The smiles of the babies in the pictures greatly shocked the public and were widely **circulated** on the Internet.（95 指考）

照片中小嬰兒的笑容大大震撼了群眾，在網路上廣為流傳。

語意用法 circulate ＋物，表示傳布某項物品；此處為被動，物品＋ be circulated。

claim [klem]	主張、要求、聲稱、奪走（生命） 英解 to maintain

例 Typhoon Morakot **claimed** more than six hundred lives in early August of 2009, making it the most serious natural disaster in Taiwan in recent decades.（99 學測）

2009 年 8 月上旬的莫拉克颱風奪走了超過 600 條的生命，被視為台灣近十年來最嚴重的天災。

語意用法 主＋ claim ＋生命，表示奪走生命。

clarify
[ˋklærəˌfaɪ]

澄清、闡明、淨化
英解 to explain

例 It is necessary for you to **clarify** this point. We simply cannot understand it.（91 學測）

我們完全不瞭解你所說的，你有必要闡明重點。

語意用法 人＋ clarity ＋事件，表示澄清事件。

classify
[ˋklæsəˌfaɪ]

分等級、歸類、列為機密
英解 to categorize

例 The biologist **classified** that plant as a tree.

生物學家將那種植物歸類為樹木。

語意用法 classify ＋物，表示將某物分類。

cling
[klɪŋ]

黏、纏、擁抱、依戀、依附
英解 to hold closely

例 After the big flood, the area was mostly deserted, with only one or two homes still **clinging** to their last relics.（95 指考）

這個地區在大洪水過後一片荒蕪，僅餘一、二間房子仍緊緊黏附在地的遺跡。

語意用法 cling ＋ to/onto ＋物，表示黏住、附著於某物。

collapse
[kəˋlæps]

倒塌、瓦解、崩潰、衰退、衰竭；亦作名詞用
英解 to fall into ruin

例 These buildings **collapsed** in heaps of dust and sand.（94 學測）

這些建築倒塌成一堆堆的沙和塵土。

語意用法 物品或建築物＋ collapse，表示某物或某建築物瓦解、倒塌。

collect [kəˋlɛkt]

收集、聚集、收款、募款；亦作形容詞與副詞用
英解 to assemble

例 My brother **collects** stamps.

我弟弟有在集郵。

語意用法 人＋ collect ＋物品，表示某人收集某物品，此處為集郵。

collide [kəˋlaɪd]

碰撞、抵觸
英解 to crash

例 Two taxies **collided** on the street.

街上有二部計程車撞在一起。

語意用法 物＋ collide with/against ＋物，表示某物與某物相撞。

colonize [ˋkɑləˏnaɪz]

開拓殖民地；移居殖民地
英解 to send people to live in another area of land or country

例 By 1975 the red imported fire ant had **colonized** over 52 million hectares of the United States.（94 學測）

到了 1975 年，被引進的紅火蟻在美國國土的領域已經拓展到超過 5 千兩百萬公頃。

語意用法 人或物＋ colonize ＋地點，表示殖民或佔領某地。

combine [kəmˋbaɪn]

結合、混合、兼具；名詞亦作集團解
英解 to join together

例 Teachers either **combine** volunteer work with classroom lessons or make service work a requirement.（98 指考）

老師們要不是將學校課程與志工工作做結合就是要求做勞動服務。

語意用法 combine ＋物＋ with ＋物，表示把某物與某物合併。

commercialize
[kə`mɝʃəl͵aɪz]

使商業化、使商品化
英解 to change sth. so that making money is its main goal

例 Before it was totally **commercialized**, this was a nice quiet little town.

在它完全商業化之前，這是個安靜的美好小鎮。

語意用法 主＋ commercialize ＋物品，表示將某物品商品化。

communicate
[kə`mjunə͵ket]

溝通、交流、通訊、傳染
英解 to give information to others

例 Fireflies use their headlamps to **communicate**.（93 學測）

螢火蟲藉由身上發出的亮光相互溝通。

語意用法 communicate ＋訊息＋ to ＋人，表示傳達訊息給某人或溝通。

compare
[kəm`pɛr]

比較、相比、匹敵
英解 to look for similarities and differences between two or more things

例 My command of English cannot **compare** with her.

我的英文能力無法與她相比。

語意用法 compare with/to，表示與……相比。

compensate
[`kɑmpən͵set]

賠償、報酬、補償、抵銷
英解 to pay sb.

例 The insurance company **compensated** the woman for her injuries.

保險公司賠償這名女士的損傷。

語意用法 compensate ＋人＋ for ＋事情，表示因某事而賠償某人。

compete [kəm`pit]	比賽、競爭、媲美 英解 to vie

例 Packaging is a way to **compete** with Westerners in economy.（95 指考）
包裝是與西方經濟競爭的一種方式。

語意用法 compete with ＋人，表示與某人競爭。

complain [kəm`plen]	抱怨、控告、訴苦 英解 to whine or gripe

例 I can **complain** about the breakfast I had this morning or rattle on about friends and movies.（95 指考）
我可以抱怨我今早吃的早餐或喋喋不休講我的朋友和我看的電影。

語意用法 complain about ＋事情，表示向某人抱怨某事。

complicate [`kɑmplə‚ket]	使複雜、使惡化、使牽連 英解 to make more complex

例 His indecision **complicates** the situation.
他無法做決定讓情況更複雜。

語意用法 事情＋ complicate ＋情況，表示某事讓狀況變複雜。

compose [kəm`poz]	撰詩、作曲、組成、調停、使鎮定 英解 to create art

例 The whole area is **composed** of two parks located in two countries.
（97 學測）
整個區域是由分別座落在兩個國家的兩座公園所組成。

語意用法 某物＋ be composed of ＋組成成份，表示某物由某成份構成。

comprehend
[ˌkɑmprɪˋhɛnd]

瞭解、領會、包括
英解 to understand

例 Billy **comprehends** that he must improve his work, or lose the job.

比利瞭解自己的工作狀況再不改善就會失去這份工作。

語意用法 人＋ comprehend ＋ that ＋ S ＋ V。

compromise
[ˋkɑmprəˌmaɪz]

妥協、危及、姑息、和解；亦作名詞用
英解 to reach a compromise

例 I **compromised** with the manager, so I get the promotion I asked for.

我與經理達成協議，所以我得到我要求的升遷。

語意用法 compromise with ＋人，表示與某人妥協和解。

concede
[kənˋsid]

承認、讓步、讓予、容許
英解 to admit that sth. is true

例 The driver who caused the traffic accident finally **conceded** to the police that he had done it.

那名司機最後終於向警察承認這場交通意外是他造成的。

語意用法 concede to ＋人＋ that ＋子句，表示向某人承認某事。

concentrate
[ˋkɑnsɛnˌtret]

專心、集中、全神貫注；名詞作濃縮物解
英解 to focus one's attention

例 Don't worry about your grades. Just **concentrate** on your studies.（88 學測）

不要擔心你的成績，只要專注在你的學習上就好。

語意用法 concentrate on/upon ＋事情，表示全神貫注於某事。

| **concern**
[kən`sɜn] | 與……有關係、使關心；名詞亦作企業解
英解 to be about |

例 I am very **concerned** with the way you manage money.（95 學測）

我很關心你處理金錢的方式。

語意用法 concern ＋人，表示讓某人擔心。此處為被動，人＋ be concerned with ＋事，表示某人關心某事。

| **conclude**
[kən`klud] | 做結論、結束、推斷、締結
英解 to finish |

例 She **concludes** that this is indeed a table where rich people sit.（93 學測）

她做出一個結論，這張桌子鐵定是給有錢人坐的。

語意用法 人＋ conclude ＋ that ＋子句，表示總結、做結論。

| **condense**
[kən`dɛns] | 濃縮、縮短、凝結
英解 to shorten |

例 The author **condensed** his article from 10 thousands words to 6 thousand words.

作者將他的文章從 1 萬字濃縮成 6 千字。

語意用法 condense ＋物＋ from ... to ...，表示把某物從……濃縮成……。

| **confess**
[kən`fɛs] | 坦白、承認、懺悔、招認
英解 to admit sth. |

例 The criminal **confessed** his guilt in committing the robbery.

這名罪犯坦承犯了搶案。

語意用法 人＋ confess one's guilt ＋ in Ving，表示承認某件罪行。

confirm [kən`fɜm]	證實、確認、堅定、批准 英解 to verify

例 I called the airline to **confirm** my flight reservation a week before I left for Canada.（93 學測）

我去加拿大的前一個星期打電話跟航空公司確認我訂的機票。

語意用法 confirm ＋事情，表示確認某事。

conform [kən`fɔrm]	遵守、遵照、符合 英解 to obey legal requirements

例 Athletes also must **conform** to strictly controlled diets during their sports season to supplement any physical training program.（97 指考）

運動員在賽季期間也必須嚴格遵守飲食控制以應付每項體能訓練計畫。

語意用法 conform to ＋事物，表示遵循某事物。

congratulate [kən`grætʃə͵let]	恭喜、祝賀 英解 to praise for

例 They **congratulated** him on the success of the speech and asked him questions.（94 指考）

他們恭賀他的演說成功並問他問題。

語意用法 congratulate ＋人＋ on/upon ＋事情，表示就某事恭賀某人。

connect [kə`nɛkt]	連結、接通、聯繫、結合、連姻 英解 to join together

例 Built under the sea in 1994, the tunnel between England and France **connects** the UK more closely with mainland Europe.（97 學測）

1994 年，英法兩國間建了一座海底隧道，使得大英國協與歐洲大陸間的聯繫更加緊密。

語意用法 connect ＋物＋ with ＋物，表示將某物與他物連結。

| **consent**
[kən`sɛnt] | 贊同、允許；亦作名詞用
英解 to agree to sth. |

例 Her mother **consented** to her marrying David.

她媽媽同意她嫁給大衛。

語意用法 consent to ＋事情，表示同意某事。

| **consider**
[kən`sɪdə] | 考慮、考量、視為
英解 to think about sth. |

例 Although your plans look good, you have to be realistic and **consider** what you can actually do.（97 學測）

你的計畫看起來雖然很理想，你還是得注意現實面仔細考量實際上能執行多少。

語意用法 consider ＋ Ving，表示考慮做某事。

| **consist**
[kən`sɪst] | 構成、存在
英解 to be composed of |

例 Black tea preparation **consists** mainly of picking young leaves and leaf buds on a clear sunny day and letting the leaves dry for about an hour in the sun.（94 學測）

紅茶的製造主要是在晴朗的天氣摘採嫩葉與細芽，並讓葉子在太陽下乾燥大約一小時。

語意用法 consist of ＋事物，表示由某事物組成。

| **construct**
[kən`strʌkt] | 構造、建築
英解 to build |

例 Buildings have been **constructed** where they shouldn't have been.

（93 指考補）

這些建物被蓋在它們不該存在的地點。

語意用法 主＋ construct ＋物；此處為被動 be constructed。

consume
[kən`sjum]

耗盡、吃喝殆盡、燒毀、揮霍
英解 to use up

例 Hard candies take a long time to **consume** and are also a bad choice for Halloween treats.（96 學測）

硬糖除了得花時間吃完外，也是萬聖節用來款待孩童的壞選擇。

語意用法 be consumed by ＋物，表示完全沈溺於某物。

contemplate
[`kɑntɛm‚plet]

熟慮、凝視、打算
英解 to think about sth. seriously

例 The manager **contemplated** the decision for several hours.

經裡對於這個決定思量了好幾個鐘頭。

語意用法 contemplate ＋ Ving／事情，表示打算做某事。

content
[kən`tɛnt]

滿足；又作名詞與形容詞解
英解 to be satisfied

例 My friend **contents** himself with a cozy house.

我朋友那間舒適的房子令他感到滿足。

語意用法 人＋ content oneself with ＋事物，表示某人對某事物感到滿意。

contribute
[kən`trɪbjut]

貢獻
英解 to donate

例 Schools and parents also **contribute** to the rise in youth service.（98 指考）

學校和父母對於提升青年服務也有貢獻。

語意用法 人＋ contribute to ＋事情，表示對某事情有貢獻。

convey
[kən`ve]

表達、搬運、護送、護衛
英解 to carry from one place to another

例 When he cannot find words to **convey** his thoughts, painting helps him find the words to express himself.（99 指考）

當他找不到文字可以表達他的想法時，繪畫成了另一種幫他傳達的文字。

語意用法 convey ＋觀念或事物，表示傳達某些理念。

convince
[kən`vɪns]

使相信、說服
英解 to persuade

例 However, if you **convince** yourself beforehand that the pain won't be so bad, you might not suffer as much.（97 學測）

然而，如果你能事先說服自己沒有那麼痛，或許就不會覺得那麼痛。

語意用法 人＋ be convinced of that，或人＋ convince oneself that，表示某人信服。

cooperate
[ko`ɑpəˌret]

合作、協助
英解 to collaborate

例 The two **cooperate** as a team.（98 學測）

他們倆個相互合作就像一個團對一樣。

語意用法 人＋ cooperate with ＋人，表示與某人合作。

coordinate
[ko`ɔrdn̩et]

協調、調和
英解 to harmonize

例 They **coordinated** the colors of wall paint and furniture in their living room.

他們將客廳牆面與傢俱的顏色搭配得很協調。

語意用法 coordinate ＋事物，表示協調或調和某事物。

correspond
[ˌkɔrɪˈspɑnd]

相似、符合
英解 be similar, match

例 It also **corresponds** to the Greek verb meaning "gather" or "pick up."
（97 指考）

這個字相當於希臘語動詞裡的「聚集」和「拾起」的意思。

語意用法 事物＋ correspond to/with ＋事物，表示與某事物相符。

create
[krɪˈet]

創作、創建、致使
英解 to make sth. in a special way, usually with skill or artistry

例 The company **created** a new division in 1947 to handle overseas sales.

公司在 1947 年創立新部門來負責海外銷售。

語意用法 create ＋事物，表示創造某物；此處為被動 be created。

criticize
[ˈkrɪtəˌsaɪz]

評論、批判
英解 to evaluate art, music, theater, etc. as a profession

例 He didn't like to be **criticized** for being idiotic. （89 學測）

他不喜歡被批評很白癡。

語意用法 criticize ＋人、事、物，表示批評某人、事、物；此處為被動，人＋ be criticized。

crowd
[kraud]

擁擠、聚集、催促；名詞又作群眾解
英解 to form into a crowd

例 I hate **crowding** onto the bus every morning.

我厭倦每天早上擠公車。

語意用法 crowd into ＋地方，表示推擠進入某地方。

cure [kjʊr]	治癒、糾正、保存（食物）；亦作名詞用 英解 to make sb. healthy by using medicines and treatment

例 They can **cure** the common cold.（91 學測補）

他們能夠治癒一般的感冒。

語意用法 cure ＋疾病或惡習，表示治療疾病或去除惡習。

deal [dil]	處理、交易、發牌；名詞又作松木解 英解 to handle

例 Faced with this new situation, people have yet to find out how to **deal** with it.（91 學測）

面對這個新狀況，人們尚未找到處理它的方法。

語意用法 deal with ＋人，表示應付某人／與某人交易。

debate [dɪˋbet]	辯論、討論、思考；亦作名詞用 英解 to argue

例 The two parties **debated** the tax issue openly.

兩政黨公開辯論稅收議題。

語意用法 debate ＋議題，表示辯論某項議題。

deceive [dɪˋsiv]	欺矇、哄騙 英解 to mislead

例 Male fireflies may **deceive** females with false signals.（93 學測）

雄性螢火蟲或許會用錯誤的訊號欺騙雌性螢火蟲。

語意用法 deceive ＋人＋ with ＋事物，表示以某事物欺騙某人。

declare [dɪˋklɛr]	聲明、宣稱、報稅、斷言 英解 to proclaim

例 He **declared** his love to her in an email.

他透過電子郵件向她示愛。

語意用法 declare ＋立場或態度＋ to ＋人，表示對某人聲明自己的立場或態度。

decline [dɪˋklaɪn]	婉拒、下降、衰退；亦作名詞用 英解 to refuse

例 I had to **decline** Jack's invitation to the party because it conflicted with an important business meeting. （95 學測）

傑克的派對跟我的一個重要商務會議撞期，我不得不婉拒他的邀約。

語意用法 decline ＋事情，表示拒絕某事；decline ＋ to V，表示拒絕去做某事。

decrease [dɪˋkris]	減少；亦作名詞用 英解 to grow smaller in number

例 Smoking fewer cigarettes **decreases** the risk of cancer. （91 學測補）

少抽一點煙可以減少罹患癌症的風險。

語意用法 原因＋ decrease ＋結果，表示某項原因降低某項後果。

dedicate [ˋdɛdəˌket]	奉獻、獻身、致力、題獻 英解 to give completely

例 The monument has been **dedicated** to the memory of our Founding Father.

這座碑是為了紀念我們的國父。

語意用法 be dedicated to ＋人，表示奉獻給某人。

defeat [dɪˋfit]	戰勝、擊敗、使挫敗；亦作名詞用 英解 to beat

例 Samson might never have been **defeated** if he had kept the secret to himself. （98 指考）

參孫如果能守口如瓶或許永遠不會被擊敗。

語意用法 人＋ defeat ＋人、事、物；此處用被動 be defeated。

defend
[dɪˋfɛnd]

防禦、辯護、答辯
英解 to protect against attack

例 The army **defended** our country.
軍隊保衛我們的國土。

語意用法 defend ＋事物，表示保衛防禦某事物。

degrade
[dɪˋgred]

降級、降低品質
英解 to lower in the opinion of others

例 Don't **degrade** yourself by accepting such a poor job offer.
不要接受一份低薪工作貶低自己的身價。

語意用法 degrade ＋人（或事物），表示貶低或降低某人的價值、位置。

delay
[dɪˋle]

延遲、耽擱、延期；亦作名詞用
英解 to slow or stop for a time

例 I was **delayed** by a traffic jam on the freeway for about an hour.（85 學測）
我在公路上被交通阻塞耽擱了將近一小時。

語意用法 delay ＋ Ving/to V，表示延遲去做某事；此處為被動，人＋ be delayed，表示某人被耽擱了。

delete
[dɪˋlit]

刪除
英解 to eliminate

例 My brother might glance at my mail, have a laugh, and then **delete** it.
（95 指考）
我哥可能掃視我的電子郵件，笑一笑，然後刪了它。

語意用法 人＋ delete ＋事物，表示刪除某事物。

demand
[dɪˋmænd]

要求、請求、需求；亦作名詞用
英解 to command

例 It often **demands** even greater effort in adjustment since we are not quick enough to catch up with the new time schedule.（94 學測）
它通常需要更多氣力來適應，因為我們很難趕上新的時程表。

語意用法 demand ＋努力（effort）in ＋事情，表示某事需要努力才能達成。

demonstrate
[ˋdɛmənˌstret]

展示、顯示、證明、實驗說明
英解 to show

例 This can be clearly **demonstrated** by comparing the genes of chimpanzees and those of humans: the difference between them is just about 2 percent.（90 學測）
這一點可以清楚驗證，藉著比較黑猩猩和人類的基因，其中差異僅有百分之二。

語意用法 demonstrate ＋事件，表示論證或證明某事；此處用被動 be demonstrated。

depart
[dɪˋpɑrt]

離開、啓程、死
英解 to leave

例 The plane to Singapore will **depart** at 8:00.
飛往新加坡的班機八點起飛。

語意用法 depart at ＋時間，表示何時出發。

deposit
[dɪˋpɑzɪt]

存放、寄放、沈澱；名詞亦作保證金、存款解
英解 to place sth. valuable

例 I **deposit** my paycheck in the bank.
我將薪資支票存進銀行。

語意用法 人＋ deposit ＋錢或支票，表示將錢或支票存進銀行。

depress [dɪ`prɛs]	使沮喪、抑制、壓下 英解 to sadden

例 The loss of her job **depressed** her.

失去工作讓她很沮喪。

語意用法 事情＋ depress ＋人。

deprive [dɪ`praɪv]	剝奪、使喪失、免職 英解 to dispossess

例 The court ruling **deprived** him of his inheritance.

法院的判決剝奪了他的繼承權。

語意用法 事件（或事物）＋ deprive ＋人的某種權利或物品。

derive [dɪ`raɪv]	取得、導出、衍生、起源 英解 to obtain

例 The blue-and-green landscape used bright blue, green and red pigments **derived** from minerals to create a richly decorative style.（93 指考）

藍綠色景觀用源自礦物的亮藍色、綠色和紅色顏料創造出豐富的裝飾風格。

語意用法 derive from ＋物，表示源自於某物。

describe [dɪ`skraɪb]	描述、形容、描繪 英解 to explain

例 Will the genetic copies of a human really have "one mind" as **described** in this story?（91 學測）

人類基因複製真的會如同故事中所形容的連腦袋都一模一樣嗎？

語意用法 describe ＋事件，表示描述某事件；此處用被動 as described。

deserve [dɪ`zɝv]	應得、應受賞罰 英解 to warrant

例 All dogs **deserve** to look and feel their best.（96 學測）

所有的狗應受到最好的對待。

語意用法 deserve ＋ to V，表示有做某事的價值。

---

designate
[ˋdɛzɪgˌnet]
指定、任命、定名；亦作形容詞用
英解 to appoint

例 These islands are **designated** as natural reservations.（94 指考）

這些島嶼被指定為自然保留區。

語意用法 designate ＋物＋ as，表示任命、指定某物為……；此處用被動 be designated as。

---

desire
[dɪˋzaɪr]
渴望、渴求、願望；亦作名詞用
英解 to wish

例 The love we **desire** will come from all of the following actions.

我們渴望的愛來自以下的一切行動。

語意用法 人＋ desire ＋事物，渴望某事物。

---

destroy
[dɪˋstrɔɪ]
毀壞、毀滅、使無效
英解 to demolish

例 The existing mountain roads were **destroyed**.（97 學測）

現有的山路被毀壞了。

語意用法 人＋ destroy ＋事物；此處用被動 be destroyed。

---

detect
[dɪˋtɛkt]
查出、察覺
英解 to find

例 Girls are better than boys in their ability to **detect** sounds.（96 學測）

女孩子的聽力天生比男孩子強。

語意用法 人＋ detect ＋事物，表示識破、察覺出某物。

deteriorate
[dɪˋtɪrɪəˌret]

惡化、墮落、質量下滑
英解 to fall into bad condition

例 The custom had **deteriorated** to a point whereby the groom and his family had become very greedy. (98 指考)

風俗惡化到新郎和他的家屬都變得極為貪婪。

語意用法 事物＋ deteriorate，表示某事物惡化。

determine
[dɪˋtɜmɪn]

決定、裁定
英解 to ascertain

例 Recently a health survey was carried out in Taiwan to **determine** what people know about health. (91 學測補)

最近在台灣進行的健康調查測出人們對健康的概念。

語意用法 人、事、物＋ determine ＋結果，表示某人、事、物決定了某一結果。

develop
[dɪˋvɛləp]

發展、開發、進化、揭露、使顯影
英解 to cause to grow or expand

例 He **developed** a new form for creating his poems during the trip. (99 指考)

他在旅途中發展出一種創作詩的新體裁。

語意用法 人＋ develop ＋事物，表示某人發展某事。

devote
[dɪˋvot]

奉獻、致力於、獻身
英解 to dedicate

例 We are completely **devoted** to helping dogs enjoy a full and active life. (96 學測)

我們全心致力於幫助狗狗享有完整有活力的生活。

語意用法 人＋ be devoted to ＋ Ving，表示某人致力於做某事。

diagnose [ˌdaɪəgˋnoz]	診斷 英解 to discover or identify

例 Once your child is **diagnosed** with Attention Deficit/Hyperactivity
Disorder, it is important to let the school know.（96 指考）

你的小孩一旦被診斷出患有注意力不足過動症，重要的是一定要告知校方。

語意用法 diagnose ＋人＋ with ＋疾病，表示診斷出某人罹患某種疾病；此處用
被動。

differ [ˋdɪfə]	不同、意見相異 英解 to vary

例 Our new car **differs** from the earlier model in many ways.

相較於舊款，我們的新車很多地方都不同。

語意用法 differ from，表示與……相異。

differentiate [ˌdɪfəˋrɛnʃɪˌet]	區別、使差異 英解 to describe or show differences

例 One important purpose of the course is for the students to learn to make
sound judgments so that they can **differentiate** between fact and opinion
without difficulty.（93 指考）

這個課程有個重要的目的就是教導學生在毫無困難的情況下區分出事實與輿論的
不同。

語意用法 differentiate between ＋事、物，表示區分兩者間之不同。

digest [daɪˋdʒɛst]	消化、融會貫通、忍受、摘要；又作名詞用 英解 to process in the stomach

例 Mary is suffering from a stomachache and needs to eat food which is
easy to **digest**.（97 學測）

瑪莉正在犯胃痛，需要吃一些容易消化的食物。

語意用法 人＋ digest ＋食物。

diminish
[də`mɪnɪʃ]

減少、變小、削弱、貶低
英解 to less in force

例 Even the development of radio and television has not **diminished** the importance of printing.（83 學測）

即便電視與廣播蓬勃發展也未降低印刷的重要性。

語意用法 事件＋ diminish ＋結果，表示某事或原因減低某項結果。

disappear
[ˌdɪsə`pɪr]

消失、滅絕
英解 to vanish

例 If the rainforests **disappear**, many of these species will become extinct.
（96 指考）

如果雨林消失不見，很多物種也會跟著滅絕。

語意用法 人、事、物＋ disappear，表示某人、事、物消失了。

disappoint
[ˌdɪsə`pɔɪnt]

使失望、受挫、阻礙
英解 to sadden sb. by failing to meet their hopes

例 The boys were very **disappointed**, but there was not much they could do about it.（96 學測）

這些男孩們相當失望卻也無能為力。

語意用法 人＋ be disappointed at (about, in) ＋事，表示某人對某事感到失望。

disapprove
[ˌdɪsə`pruv]

不贊成、不准、非難
英解 to refuse to accept

例 Her boyfriend **disapproved** of her behavior.

她的男朋友不贊同她的行為。

語意用法 人＋ disapprove of ＋事件，表示不贊成某事。

disclose
[dɪsˋkloz]

揭發、透露、洩漏
英解 to divulge

例 The actor refused to **disclose** his marriage.

這名男演員拒絕透露他的婚姻狀況。

語意用法 人＋ disclose ＋事件，表示表明某事件。

disconnect
[ˌdɪskəˋnɛkt]

使脫離、分開、切斷
英解 to detach

例 John had failed to pay his phone bills for months, so his telephone was **disconnected** last week.（93 學測）

約翰的電話上週被斷線，因為他已經好幾個月缺繳電話費。

語意用法 事物＋ be disconnected，表示某事物被切斷。

discourage
[dɪsˋkɝɪdʒ]

使氣餒、勸阻、阻擋
英解 to dishearten

例 Bag-matching would delay flights and **discourage** people from taking airplanes.（92 指考）

行李比對導致航班延誤進而打消人們搭飛機的意願。

語意用法 人或事件＋ discourage ＋人＋ from Ving，表示阻擋某人做某事。

discriminate
[dɪˋskrɪməˌnet]

區別、辨別、歧視
英解 to see the differences

例 The expert **discriminated** between two periods of art.

專家區分兩個時期藝術的不同。

語意用法 discriminate between ＋事、物，表示區別兩事物；discriminate against ＋人，表示歧視某人。

disintegrate
[dɪs`ɪntəgret]

使破碎、使分解、使崩潰
英解 fall apart

例 The books were so old that they **disintegrated** when touched.

這些書非常老舊，一翻就散掉了。

語意用法 物品＋ disintegrate，表示某物瓦解。

dislike
[dɪs`laɪk]

不喜歡、嫌惡；亦作名詞用
英解 to not like

例 George Bernard Shaw and Winston Churchill apparently **disliked** each other.（89 學測）

蕭伯納和邱吉爾顯然不喜歡對方。

語意用法 dislike ＋ Ving，表示討厭做某事；dislike ＋人，表示不喜歡某人。

dismiss
[dɪs`mɪs]

打發走、解雇、摒除
英解 to send away

例 The company **dismissed** the employees.

這家公司遣散了員工。

語意用法 dismiss ＋人或念頭，表示趕走人或念頭。

display
[dɪ`sple]

顯示、展示、炫耀；亦作名詞用
英解 to show

例 A good speaker should **display** his learning to the audience in an enthusiastic way.（94 指考）

一個好的演說者應該對聽眾熱誠展現他的學識。

語意用法 人＋ display ＋觀念或想法＋ to ＋人，表示將觀念或想法展示給某人。

dispose
[dɪˋspoz]

排列、配置、處置、使傾向於
英解 to make

例 Once used, the bags are sealed and stored for the flight back to the earth, where they are **disposed** of.（92 學測）

這些袋子一旦用過會被密封、存放直到飛回地球才被處理掉。

語意用法 dispose of，表示處置；此處用被動，物品＋ be disposed of。

dispute
[dɪˋspjut]

爭論、提出質疑、駁斥、抵抗；亦作名詞用
英解 to argue against

例 Under normal circumstances, I should have **disputed** it.（90 學測）

在正常狀況下我會駁斥它。

語意用法 dispute ＋事件或議題，表示論辯某事件或反駁某議題。

disrupt
[dɪsˋrʌpt]

使中斷、使混亂
英解 to interrupt

例 Because of the tragic accident, traffic on the highway was **disrupted** for over two hours.（93 指考補）

由於這件悲慘的事故，快速道路的交通被迫中斷超過 2 小時。

語意用法 事件＋ be disrupted，表示某事件被中斷，為被動用法。

dissolve
[dɪˋzɑlv]

溶解、融化、分解、消失
英解 to melt

例 Unlike hard candies, chocolate **dissolves** quickly in the mouth.（96 學測）

不同於硬糖，巧克力在口中快速融化。

語意用法 物＋ dissolve in ＋物，表示某物在某物中溶解。

distinguish
[dɪ`stɪŋgwɪʃ]

區別、辨別、分類
英解 to discriminate

例 For the most part, these are hard to **distinguish** from the originals.（94 指考）

這些大部分都看不出和正品有何不同。

語意用法 distinguish ＋物＋ from ＋物，表示將兩件物品加以區別。

distort
[dɪs`tɔrt]

扭曲、使變形、曲解
英解 to twist

例 Anger **distorted** her face.

她氣到臉部表情扭曲。

語意用法 人＋ distort ＋物；常用被動 be distorted，例：Her face has been distorted because of anger。

disturb
[dɪs`tɝb]

攪動、擾亂、妨礙、使心神不寧
英解 to interrupt

例 Mr. Smith won't tolerate talking during class; he says it **disturbs** others.
（83 學測）

史密斯老師不容許課堂上聊天，他說那樣會打擾其他人。

語意用法 事件＋ disturb ＋人，表示某事件打擾了某人。

diversify
[daɪ`vɝsəˌfaɪ]

使多樣化、擴展不同業務
英解 to make or become varied

例 In order to expand its foreign market, the company decided to **diversify** its products and provide more varieties to the customer.（97 指考）

為了擴展海外市場，公司決定將產品多樣化以提供更多的種類給顧客。

語意用法 人或公司＋ diversify ＋物品，表示某人或公司讓物品多樣化。

dominate
[ˈdɑməˌnet]

支配、凌駕、佔主要地位、俯視
英解 to have the most important place

例 Our products **dominate** the pet-food market.

我們的產品在寵物食品市場佔有主導地位。

語意用法 人、事、物＋ dominate ＋事物，表示某人、事、物支配某事物。

dwell
[dwɛl]

居住、存在、思索
英解 to reside

例 The King **dwells** in a castle.

國王住在城堡裡。

語意用法 人＋ dwell on/upon ＋事情，表示某人仔細思索某事。

eliminate
[ɪˈlɪməˌnet]

消滅、淘汰
英解 to exclude

例 **Eliminate** illegal music downloads? Impossible!（98 指考）

消除非法下載音樂？不可能！

語意用法 人＋ eliminate ＋事、物，表示某人把某事物刪除。

embrace
[ɪmˈbres]

擁抱、接受、包含、信奉；亦作名詞用
英解 to hug

例 We have completely **embraced** paper technology.（98 學測）

我們全然接受紙張技術。

語意用法 人＋ embrace ＋人／事／物，表示某人接受、擁抱某人事物。

emerge
[ɪˈmɝdʒ]

出現、發生、露出
英解 to appear

例 More distance runners may **emerge** from Bekoji.（99 學測）

更多長跑選手可能會出現在貝科吉。

語意用法 人＋ emerge from/out of ＋地方，表示某人從某處出現。

emphasize
[ˈɛmfəˌsaɪz]

強調、著重
英解 to stress

例 The new study **emphasizes** that pain has both physical and psychological elements. (97 學測)

這項新的研究強調疼痛同時包含生理和心理二種元素。

語意用法 研究或人＋ emphasize ＋事情，表示強調某事情；emphasize ＋ that ＋子句，表示強調……。

encompass
[ɪnˈkʌmpəs]

包含、圍繞
英解 to include

例 My art history course **encompasses** the 19th and 20th centuries.

我的藝術史課程包含 19 到 20 世紀。

語意用法 encompass ＋事、物，表示包含某事物。

encounter
[ɪnˈkaʊntə]

遭遇、邂逅；亦作名詞用
英解 to meet by chance

例 We **encountered** some friends at the concert.

我們在音樂會上巧遇一些朋友。

語意用法 人＋ encounter ＋人，表示巧遇某人。

encourage
[ɪnˈkɜɪdʒ]

鼓勵、慫恿、助長
英解 to urge

例 America **encourages** its young people to drink. (83 學測)

美國鼓勵他們的年輕人喝酒。

語意用法 人、物＋ encourage ＋人＋ to V，表示鼓勵某人去做某事。

endanger
[ɪnˈdendʒə]

危及、使陷於危險
英解 to jeopardize

例 They went fishing on a typhoon day and **endangered** their lives.

他們在颱風天跑去釣魚陷自己的生命於危險中。

語意用法 人＋ endanger ＋ their lives，表示某人冒著生命危險。

enlarge [ɪn`lɑrdʒ]	擴充、放大、詳述 英解 to make larger

例 Their pictures can be **enlarged** as desired.（91 學測補）

這些照片可以放大到他們想要的。

語意用法 enlarge ＋物，表示放大某物；此處為被動 be enlarged。

ensure [ɪn`ʃur]	保證、擔保、使安全 英解 to make sure

例 It **ensures** that the terrorist will proceed to the gate to board his plane.
（92 指考）

這確保恐怖份子會前進到登機門登上他的專機。

語意用法 事件＋ ensure ＋ that ＋子句，表示確認……。

entertain [ˌɛntɚ`ten]	娛樂、款待、懷抱 英解 to amuse

例 They performed magical tricks to **entertain** people.（92 學測補）

他們表演魔術娛樂大眾。

語意用法 人＋ entertain ＋人，表示娛樂某人。

equip [ɪ`kwɪp]	裝備、配備、使有資格 英解 to outfit

例 The robot is **equipped** with a camera that can recognize text.

這機器人配備了可以判讀文字的相機。

語意用法 人＋ be equipped with ＋物品，表示某人配備某物。

escape
[ə`skep]

逃脫、溜出、避免、被遺忘；亦作名詞用
英解 to break out

例 All of them successfully **escaped** the destruction of postwar redevelopment and remained unchanged. （97 學測）

他們全部順利從戰後重建的毀滅中逃脫而沒有改變。

語意用法 escape ＋事件，表示從某事件逃脫、免除。

establish
[ə`stæblɪʃ]

創辦、確立、證實、認可
英解 to found

例 Steve Jobs **established** a new-tech kingdom.

史帝夫賈伯建立一個新的科技王國。

語意用法 人＋ establish ＋機構、組織，表示設立、創立一個組織。

esteem
[ɪs`tim]

尊重、視爲、評估；亦作名詞用
英解 to honor

例 No one can **esteem** my teacher more than I do.

沒有人比我更敬重我的老師了。

語意用法 人＋ esteem ＋人，表示尊重某人。

evaluate
[ɪ`væljʊˌet]

評估、評價
英解 to study and make a judgment about

例 It is very important that he or she be **evaluated** by a professional. （96 指考）

由專家來幫他或她做評估是非常重要的。

語意用法 人＋ be evaluated as，表示某人被評價爲……。

evolve
[ɪ`vɑlv]

發展、進化、放射出、引伸出
英解 to develop

例 They **evolved** separately.（92 學測）

他們各自進化。

語意用法 人或動物＋ evolve from，表示從……進化。

---

exaggerate
[ɪɡˋzædʒəˌret]

誇大、誇張、言過其實
英解 to overstate

例 A tall tale, in other words, is a story in which the truth has been **exaggerated**.（91 學測補）

換言之，一則荒誕不經的故事就是把故事裡頭的事實誇大。

語意用法 exaggerate ＋事物，表示誇張、強調某事物；此處為被動 be exaggerated。

---

exceed
[ɪkˋsid]

超過、勝過
英解 to be more than

例 The elevation gain from the subtropical plains to the glacier-covered Himalayan heights **exceeds** 7,000 m.（96 指考）

從亞熱帶平原到冰帽覆蓋的喜馬拉雅山，海拔高度超過 7,000 公尺。

語意用法 物＋ exceed ＋數量，表示某物超過某個數量。

---

exclude
[ɪkˋsklud]

拒絕、排除、逐出、排斥
英解 to omit

例 The gym **excluded** teenagers from membership.

這家健身房拒絕青少年加入。

語意用法 人、物＋ exclude ＋人，表示將某人排除在外。

---

execute
[ˋɛksɪˌkjut]

處決、表演、生效、製作
英解 to put to death

例 Tuck kills the man and is jailed and sentenced to be **executed**.（93 學測）

塔克因為殺人被監禁且被宣判處以死刑。

語意用法 人＋ be executed，表示某人被執行死刑。

exhaust [ɪg`zɔst]	耗盡、使力竭、抽盡、排出氣體；亦作名詞用 英解 to deplete

例 He would **exhaust** himself just for a performance tour.（94 學測）
他會為了一場巡迴表演耗盡全力。

語意用法 人＋ exhaust ＋ oneself，表示某人耗盡全力。

exist [ɪg`zɪst]	存在、生存、生活 英解 to present physically or emotionally

例 If you don't print it out, the message doesn't physically **exist**.（95 指考）
如果你不把訊息列印出來，實體上它等於不存在。

語意用法 事物＋ exist，表示某事物存在。

expand [ɪk`spænd]	擴充、發展、膨脹、展開 英解 to enlarge

例 Ms. Li's business **expanded** very quickly.（96 學測）
黎小姐的事業迅速拓展。

語意用法 事物＋ expand，表示某事物擴充發展。

expend [ɪk`spɛnd]	使用、花費（時間、金錢） 英解 to spend or use

例 The government **expended** large sums of money in maintaining the national park.
政府花大把經費維護這座國家公園。

語意用法 人或機構＋ expend ＋錢、經費＋ on/upon/in ＋事物，表示花費經費在某事物上。

explain [ɪk`splen]	解釋、辯解、闡釋、說明 英解 to explicate

例 Many factors may **explain** why people are addicted to the Internet.（96 指考）
很多因素或許能解釋人們為什麼會沈溺於網際網路。

語意用法 人＋ explain ＋原因，表示澄清意圖、解釋原因。

| **explode**
[ɪkˋsplod] | 爆炸、爆發、推翻、迅速擴張
英解 to burst |

例 Helen **exploded** with anger when she saw her boyfriend kissing an attractive girl.（92 學測）
看到男友親吻一個很有魅力的女孩時，海倫氣炸了。

語意用法 人＋ explode ＋ with anger，表示憤怒被激發。

| **explore**
[ɪkˋsplor] | 探險、探索、研究
英解 to scout |

例 They are ready and eager to **explore** further.（93 指考）
他們渴望並做好準備去進一步探索。

語意用法 人＋ explore ＋事、物，表示某人探索、研究某事物。

| **expose**
[ɪkˋspoz] | 暴露、揭發、曝光、陳列
英解 to make known |

例 The more one is **exposed** to the English-speaking environment, the better he or she will learn the language.（89 學測）
一個人越能置身於說英語的環境中，就越能將這語言學好。

語意用法 be exposed to ＋環境或事物，表示暴露在某環境或事物之中。

| **express**
[ɪkˋsprɛs] | 表達、快遞、擠出；亦作名詞、形容詞用
英解 to speak about |

例 It is an inability to **express** one's feelings.（97 指考）
這是沒有能力表達一個人的情感。

語意用法 express one's feelings，表示某人表達感情。

falsify [ˋfɔlsəˌfaɪ]	竄改、偽造、曲解 英解 to doctor

例 The student **falsified** his GPA to get into college.

這名學生偽造學業平均成績進大學。

語意用法 人＋ falsity ＋事物，表示某人偽造事物。

familiarize [fəˋmɪljəˌraɪz]	使熟悉、使家喻戶曉、通俗化 英解 to become acquainted with

例 He tried to **familiarize** himself with the new operating systems.

他試著熟悉新的作業系統。

語意用法 人＋ familiarize oneself with ＋人、事、物，表示某人使自己熟悉某人／事／物。

fascinate [ˋfæsn̩ˌet]	使神魂顛倒、強烈地吸引 英解 to engross

例 Throughout history, people have been **fascinated** by the mystery of what lies beyond our planet.（97 指考）

綜觀歷史，長久以來人類一直著迷於外太空的奧秘。

語意用法 人＋ be fascinated by ＋事物，表示被某事物吸引。

fasten [ˋfæsn̩]	繫緊、關緊、釘牢、攫住目光 英解 to affix

例 He **fastened** paintings on the wall with nails.

他將畫緊緊釘在牆上。

語意用法 人＋ fasten ＋物品＋ to/on ＋地點，表示把某物繫牢於某地。

flourish
[ˈflɝɪʃ]

繁榮、茂盛、炫耀；亦作名詞用
英解 to grow strong

例 Folk medicine **flourished** long before the development of scientific medicine and was more successful in ancient times than doctor medicine.（92 學測補）

古代的民間醫學遠在科學醫藥之前就已蓬勃發展，而且比醫生處方更成功。

語意用法 物品、事物＋ flourish，表示某事物繁榮發展。

flow
[flo]

流動、氾濫、飄動、來自、漲（潮）；亦作名詞用
英解 to stream

例 Rivers and streams **flow** slowly through jungles of shaded greens.（88 學測）

小河和小溪慢慢流過綠油油的叢林。

語意用法 物＋ flow，表示某物不斷流動。

fold
[fold]

折疊、籠罩、包圍、擁抱；名詞又作坑窪解
英解 to turn one part of sth. over another part

例 Some umbrellas **fold** up, so it is easy to carry them.（83 學測）

有些傘可以折疊易於攜帶。

語意用法 物品＋ fold up，表示某物可以折疊起來。

forgive
[fɚˈgɪv]

原諒、豁免
英解 to excuse

例 She **forgave** me for what I had said to her.

她原諒我對她說過的那些話。

語意用法 人＋ forgive ＋人＋ for ＋事件，表示原諒某人某事。

foresee
[for`si]

預知、預見
英解 to predict

例 It is hard to **foresee** what will happen in 2012.

很難預見 2012 會發生什麼事。

語意用法 foresee ＋事件，表示預料到某事。

formulate
[`fɔrmjə,let]

制定、公式化、規劃
英解 to create

例 The manager **formulated** a marketing plan for this coming year.

經理為即將來臨的新年度制定行銷計畫。

語意用法 人＋ formulate ＋計畫，表示制定計畫。

freeze
[friz]

結冰、凝固、冷藏
英解 to change into a solid state due to low temperature

例 The water in the lake **freezes** in winter.

這湖水到了冬天會結冰。

語意用法 水＋ freeze，表示水結冰。

frighten
[`fraɪtṇ]

吃驚、驚恐、使害怕
英解 to cause fear

例 The world of fantasy **frightens** us.（91 學測）

這個虛構的世界嚇著我們了。

語意用法 事、物＋ frighten ＋人＋ away，表示某事物嚇走某人。

frustrate
[`frʌs,tret]

受挫、感到灰心、使無效
英解 to thwart

例 Jack felt **frustrated** by repeated failures.

傑克因一再失敗感到挫折。

語意用法 人＋ be frustrated by，表示某人因……感到挫敗。

| **fulfill**
[fʊlˋfɪl] | 履行、滿足、實現
英解 to perform |

例 The delicate vision took decades to be **fulfilled**. (93 指考)

花了幾十年才完成這個精緻的視覺饗宴。

語意用法 人＋ fulfill ＋任務，表示履行責任、義務；此處為被動用法 be fulfilled。

| **gaze**
[gez] | 注視、凝視；亦作名詞用
英解 to look steadily at sb. or sth. for a long time |

例 He turned to **gaze** at his fiancée.

他轉過身凝視他的未婚妻。

語意用法 人＋ gaze at/into/on/upon ＋人，表示驚訝地凝視某人。

| **generate**
[ˋdʒɛnə͵ret] | 產生、引起、生殖
英解 to initiate |

例 An estimated 2.5 million tons of carbon dioxide were **generated** in 2006 by the production of plastic for bottled water. (99 學測)

2006 年生產的裝水保特瓶，估計製造了 250 萬噸的二氧化碳。

語意用法 人、事、物＋ generate ＋事物；此處用被動 be generated by。

| **govern**
[ˋgʌvən] | 統治、管理、影響、控制、支配
英解 to rule a country, city, company, etc. |

例 The city mayor **governs** our city.

市長管理我們的城市。

語意用法 人＋ govern ＋事、物。

grab [græb]	抓取、奪取、把握、吸引住；亦作名詞用 英解 to snatch

例 So, **grab** a copy and start learning how you can reduce stress in your life.（94 學測）

所以，抓一本書並開始學著如何減輕你生活中的壓力。

語意用法 人＋ grab ＋物，表示某人拿取某物。

grant [grænt]	允許、答應、承認、授予；名詞又作獎學金用 英解 to give or allow what is ask for

例 Another spectator said that too many Americans take the achievements of the space program for **granted**.（88 學測）

另一名觀眾認為太多美國人把太空計畫的成就視為理所當然。

語意用法 人＋ grant ＋事＋ to ＋人，表示答應某人某事；此處 take ＋事物＋ for granted，表示把某事物視為理所當然。

greet [grit]	招呼、歡迎、迎接、接受、感知 英解 to meet

例 What he had to say was **greeted** by an uncomfortable silence.（86 學測）

迎接他的話的是一陣讓人不舒服的沈默。

語意用法 人＋ greet ＋人，表示迎接某人；此處用被動 be greeted by。

guard [gɑrd]	守衛、看守、監視、防範；亦作名詞用 英解 to protect property

例 The dog **guards** against entry by strangers.

這條狗在看門阻止陌生人進入。

語意用法 人＋ guard against ＋人、物，表示保護免於某人或某物的傷害。

harass [hə`ræs]	使煩惱、侵擾、不斷騷擾 英解 to badger

例 She **harassed** me for months about the mistake I made.

她為了我犯的錯誤騷擾了我好幾個月。

語意用法 人＋ harass ＋人；表示某人騷擾某人。

harm [hɑrm]	傷害、損害、危害；亦作名詞用 英解 to hurt

例 Many believe that the aliens are here to help us, while others hold that the aliens will **harm** us.（93 學測）

很多人認為外星人是來幫助我們的，而其他的人則認為外星人可能傷害我們。

語意用法 人＋ harm ＋人，表示傷害某人。

hesitate [`hɛzə͵tet]	躊躇、猶豫、支吾其詞 英解 to pause

例 If I can help you with the project, don't **hesitate** to call me.（87 學測）

這項計畫如果有用得著我的地方，請儘管打電話給我。

語意用法 人＋ hesitate ＋ to V，表示猶豫不敢做某事。

hide [haɪd]	躲藏、隱藏、隱瞞、遮蔽；亦作名詞用 英解 to secret

例 Those illegal workers **hide** their real identities.（93 指考）

那些非法勞工隱藏真實身份。

語意用法 人＋ hide ＋事、物，表示隱藏某事物。

highlight [ˈhaɪ͵laɪt]	突顯強調、用強光照射；亦作名詞用 英解 to emphasize

例 In his speech, Dr. Huang presented all the reports about the energy crisis to **highlight** the need for developing new energy resources.（95 指考）

黃教授在他的演說中提出所有關於能源危機的報告以突顯開發新能源的必要性。

語意用法 人＋ highlight ＋事物，表示突顯某項事物

hijack [ˈhaɪ͵dʒæk]	劫機 英解 to control an airplane or vehicle by threatening its pilot, usu. with gun

例 An International criminal **hijacked** a plane from Paris to New York.

一名國際罪犯劫持一架由巴黎飛往紐約的班機。

語意用法 人＋ hijack ＋飛機，表示某人劫機。

howl [haʊl]	嗥叫、狂吼、大哭大笑；亦作名詞用 英解 to wail

例 Female monkeys **howl** to protect their babies.（97 學測）

母猴用嗥叫來保護她們的孩子。

語意用法 人或動物＋ howl ＋ to V，表示某人或某種動物用吼叫來做某動作。

hug [hʌg]	擁抱、緊靠、堅持；亦作名詞用 英解 to encircle sb. with the arms

例 To show his love, he **hugged** his kids.

他擁抱他的孩子們來表示關愛。

語意用法 人＋ hug ＋人，表示擁抱某人。

identify
[aɪ`dɛntəˌfaɪ]

鑑定、識別、認明、視爲同一物、一致
英解 to prove or recognize as being a certain person or thing

例 The moral lesson is "First **identify** your strengths, and then change the playing field to suit them."（98 學測）

寓意就是「先認清你的長處，然後發揮在適合的場所。」

語意用法 人＋ identify ＋事物，表示認清某事物。

ignore
[ɪg`nor]

忽視、不理睬、駁回
英解 to pay no attention to

例 Mr. Chang always tries to answer all questions from his students. He will not **ignore** any of them even if they may sound stupid.（94 學測）

張老師總是盡力回答學生的所有提問，即使有些問題聽起來愚蠢他也不會忽略。

語意用法 人＋ ignore ＋事物或問題。

illustrate
[`ɪləstret]

闡明、舉例說明、圖解
英解 to give examples

例 Mr. Chang **illustrated** the answer by telling a story.

張老師藉由說故事來解答問題。

語意用法 人＋ illustrate ＋事件，表示舉例說明某事件。

imply
[ɪm`plaɪ]

暗指、暗示、意味
英解 to intimate

例 He didn't come out and say that he would quit, but that's what he **implied**.

他沒有跳出來說要辭職，但那正是他所暗示的。

語意用法 人、事、物＋ imply ＋事物或意義，表示某人事物暗示某種意義。

impress [ɪm`prɛs]	使印象深刻、使感動、銘記、印記 英解 to create and give an image of sb. or sth.

例 Many workers want to wear casual clothes to **impress** people.（91 學測）

許多工作者想穿著輕便的服裝讓人留下深刻印象。

語意用法 人＋ impress ＋人＋ with/by ＋事物，表示以某事物打動人心。

improve [ɪm`pruv]	增進、提高、利用 英解 to make better

例 Her handwriting has **improved** a lot after entering the company.（98 學測）

她進到這家公司後，字寫得好多了。

語意用法 事物＋ improve a lot，表示某事物得到大大的改善、進步。

include [ɪn`klud]	包含、包括、計入 英解 to make sth. a part of sth. else

例 These **include** not only external behavior, but also all the organs, the whole skeleton, every single bone and tooth.（90 學測）

不單只有外在行為，所有的器官、骨骼，甚至一塊骨頭一顆牙齒都包含在內。

語意用法 事、物＋ include ＋事、物，表示包括某事物在內。

increase [ɪn`kris]	增加、增值、增大、增強；亦作名詞用 英解 to go up in number

例 As it turns out, such a "swarm moves" model **increases** sales without the need to give people discounts.（97 指考）

結果證明在這種「一窩蜂行動」的模式下，不需要給予顧客折扣一樣能增加銷售量。

語意用法 某事件＋ increase ＋某種結果，表示某事件增強某種結果。

indicate [`ɪndə͵ket]	指示、指出、象徵 英解 to show where or what sth. is

例 In December 1987, a U.S. Government report **indicated** that non-smokers could risk getting lung cancer from breathing in other people's cigarette smoke.（83 學測）

1987 年 12 月，美國官方報告指出，不吸煙者可能因為吸入二手煙而有罹患肺癌的風險。

語意用法 報告或研究＋ indicate ＋ that ＋ S ＋ V，表示某項報告或研究指出……。

---

infect
[ɪnˋfɛkt]

傳染、感染、影響
英解 to give sb. a sickness or disease

例 Avian influenza, or "bird flu," is a contagious disease caused by viruses that normally **infect** only birds and, less commonly, pigs.（93 指考）

禽流感是一種由病毒引起的接觸性傳染疾病，通常只會在鳥類與少數豬隻間相互感染。

語意用法 疾病＋ infect ＋人，表示某項疾病感染某人。

---

infer
[ɪnˋfɝ]

推論、推斷、猜想、意味
英解 to surmise

例 It can be **inferred** that today's language learning laboratories owe their success mainly to the introduction of video materials.（93 指考補）

可以推論今天語言學習實驗室的成功主要歸因於影像素材的引進。

語意用法 It can be inferred that ...，表示可以推論出……。

---

inform
[ɪnˋfɔrm]

告知、告發、報告
英解 to notify

例 With the help of modern technology, some supermarkets are now able to keep customers **informed** about what others are buying.（96 指考）

有了現代科技的幫助，有些超市現在可以讓顧客知道其他人都買些什麼產品。

語意用法 keep ＋人＋ informed about/of ＋事件，表示讓某人知道關於某事。

inherit [ɪn`hɛrɪt]	繼承、遺傳 英解 to receive after one dies

例 Christopher **inherited** his grandfather's castle.

克里斯多夫繼承了他祖父的城堡。

語意用法 人＋ inherit ＋事物，表示某人繼承某物。

insist [ɪn`sɪst]	堅決要求、堅持主張、力言、強調 英解 to demand

例 In the dream the cloakroom attendant at a theater stopped me in the lobby and **insisted** on my leaving my legs behind. (90 學測)

夢中，戲院衣帽間的服務員在大廳中叫住我，並堅持要我把腿留在外面。

語意用法 人＋ insist on/upon ＋ Ving/ 事件，表示極力主張、強調某事。

inspire [ɪn`spaɪr]	鼓舞、激勵、給予靈感、吸氣 英解 to cause to work hard or be creative

例 Jordan's performance **inspired** his teammates and they finally beat their opponents to win the championship. (92 指考)

喬登的表現激勵了隊友們，他們最終擊敗對手贏得冠軍。

語意用法 事件＋ inspire ＋人，表示某事件鼓舞某人。

institute [`ɪnstətjut]	創立、制定、開始、著手、任命；亦作名詞用 英解 to initiate

例 In order to reduce costs, I've decided to **institute** a new work-at-home policy for the entire marketing department.

為了降低成本，我決定為整個行銷部門制定一個在家工作的新政策。

語意用法 人＋ institute ＋物，表示創立某物。

instruct [ɪnˋstrʌktɪ]	指導、指示、命令 英解 to teach

例 She is **instructed** by an engineer standing next to her.（93 指考）

站在她旁邊的工程師在指導她。

語意用法 人＋ instruct ＋人＋ in ＋學科，表示教授某學科；此處用被動，人＋ be instructed。

insult [ɪnˋsʌlt]	侮辱、羞辱；亦作名詞用 英解 do or say bad, unkind things to sb.

例 He participated in three revolutions and fought with people when he was **insulted**.（90 學測）

他參與三次革命，當他覺得遭受侮辱時起身對抗。

語意用法 人＋ insult ＋人，表示侮辱某人；此處用被動，人＋ be insulted。

intend [ɪnˋtɛnd]	意欲、想要、打算 英解 to plan to do sth.

例 In one study, nearly 600 children from kindergarten to sixth grade took part in a nutrition curriculum **intended** to get them to eat more vegetables and whole grains.（98 學測）

將近 600 名從幼稚園到六年級的孩童參與了營養課程，意圖讓他們多吃蔬菜與五穀雜糧。

語意用法 intend ＋ to V，表示打算去做……。

intensify [ɪnˋtɛnsəˌfaɪ]	增強、強化 英解 to increase

例 These two countries are trying to **intensify** trade and cultural exchanges between them.（91 學測補）

這二個國家正試圖加強兩國間的文化和貿易交流。

語意用法 人或機構＋ intensity ＋某種關係，表示人或單位強化某種關係。

interact [͵ɪntə˙ækt]	互動、相互影響 英解 to communicate with sb. through conversation, looks, or action

例 Just observe closely how he **interacts** with customers and do likewise.（93 指考）

只要仔細觀察他如何和客戶互動並照著作。

語意用法 人＋ interact with ＋人，表示人與人互動。

intercept [͵ɪntə˙sɛpt]	中途攔截、截斷、竊聽 英解 to stop or catch sth. while it is in the air or going toward sth.

例 The coast guard last night successfully **intercepted** boats which were trying to smuggle drugs and other illegal items from a neighboring country.（93 指考補）

昨晚，海岸警衛隊成功攔截從鄰國試圖走私毒品和其他違禁品的船隻。

語意用法 人或單位＋ intercept ＋人，表示某人或某單位攔截某人。

interfere [͵ɪntə˙fɪr]	衝突、抵觸、妨礙、干預 英解 to disrupt

例 In Taiwan, using electronic devices is prohibited on domestic flights because it **interferes** with the communication between the pilots and the control tower.（93 指考）

台灣的國內航班禁止使用電子設備，因為會干預機長與塔台的通訊。

語意用法 物＋ interfere with ＋物，表示妨礙、抵觸。

interpret [ɪn˙tɝprɪt]	詮釋、理解、認為、口譯 英解 to translate (usu. orally) from one language into another

例 This poem may be **interpreted** in several different ways and each of them makes sense. （90 學測）

這首詩或許可以用幾種方法來詮釋，而且每一種都成立。

語意用法 人＋ interpret ＋事、物＋ as ＋意義，表示將某事解釋為⋯⋯；此處為被動，事、物＋ be interpreted。

interrupt [ˌɪntəˈrʌpt]	打斷（談話）、中斷、阻礙 英解 to stop sth. from continuing

例 It is impolite to **interrupt** when someone else is speaking. （92 學測補）

打斷別人的話是不禮貌的行為。

語意用法 interrupt ＋人，表示打斷別人說話。

intoxicate [ɪnˈtɑksəˌket]	使喝醉、使陶醉、使中毒 英解 to stupefy or excite by the action of a chemical substance such as alcohol

例 By the end of the 18th century, all of Paris was **intoxicated** with coffee and the city supported some 700 cafés. （97 指考）

到了 18 世紀末，整個巴黎對咖啡上了癮，這座城市足以有大約 700 家的咖啡館。

語意用法 人＋ be intoxicated with ... ，表示人沉醉於⋯⋯。

invade [ɪnˈved]	侵略、入侵、侵襲 英解 to enter by force

例 Some Europeans **invaded** Africa to increase their colonies. （97 指考）

有些歐洲人入侵非洲以擴增他們的殖民地。

語意用法 人＋ invade ＋地方，表示某人入侵某地。

| **invent**
[ɪnˋvɛnt] | 發明、創造、虛構
英解 to create sth. new |

例 Therefore, to make tall buildings more accessible to their users, the elevator was **invented**. (92 指考)

因此，為了讓高樓的出入更便利，於是發明了電梯。

語意用法 人＋ invent ＋物品，表示發明某物，此處用被動，物＋ be invented。

| **invest**
[ɪnˋvɛst] | 投資、投入（時間、金錢）
英解 to put money into a business idea in the hope of making money |

例 They will **invest** US$20 million to promote their tourism. (98 學測)

他們將投資 2 千萬美元推廣觀光。

語意用法 人＋ invest ＋錢＋ to V，表示投資錢做某事。

| **investigate**
[ɪnˋvɛstəˌget] | 研究、調查
英解 to look at sth. carefully |

例 In 1996, the team was asked to **investigate** the feasibility of bag-matching. (92 指考)

1966 年，該小組被要求研究行李比對的可行性。

語意用法 人或單位＋ investigate ＋事件，表示調查某事件。

| **invite**
[ɪnˋvaɪt] | 邀請、請求、招致
英解 to ask sb. to come to an event |

例 But one special sculpture gallery **invites** art lovers to allow their hands to run over the works. (99 指考)

然而有家特殊的雕刻藝廊邀請並容許藝術愛好者用手觸摸作品。

語意用法 人＋ invite ＋人＋ to V，表示邀請某人去做某事。

involve [ɪnˋvɑlv]	包括、牽連、使涉入、專注於 英解 to implicate

例 Being an athlete **involves** more than competing in athletic events.（97 指考）

作為一名運動員不僅僅是運動項目的競爭。

語意用法 事件＋ involve ＋事件、人，表示某事件牽涉到某事或某人。

irritate [ˋɪrəˏtet]	激怒、刺激、使過敏、使煩躁 英解 to annoy

例 And I started to feel **irritated** when Derek licked my cheek at dawn.（92 指考）

當德里克在黎明舔我的臉頰，我開始感到煩躁。

語意用法 人＋ feel irritated，表示某人感到生氣、煩躁。

isolate [ˋaɪsḷˏet]	使孤立、隔離 英解 to separate from others

例 In society, the former player does not look upon himself as a lone wolf who has the right to remain **isolated** from the society and go his own way.（99 學測）

在社會上，前球員不視自己為獨行俠，有權力走自己的路與社會繼續隔離。

語意用法 人＋ be (feel) isolated from，表示某人感覺孤立於……。

justify [ˋdʒʌstəˏfaɪ]	證明正當、合法、開釋 英解 to give acceptable reasons for an action

例 She cannot take any criticism and always finds excuses to **justify** herself.（96 學測）

她無法接受任何批評且總是找理由為自己開釋。

語意用法 人＋ justify oneself，表示證明自己是對的。

knock [nɑk]	敲、擊、批評、撞擊、碰；亦作名詞用 英解 to hit lightly

例 At the end of the fifth week, the boys came back again and **knocked** at the old man's house. （96 學測）

第五週結束，男孩們再次回來敲了老先生的門。

語意用法 人＋ knock at sb.'s door，表示敲某人的門。

lack [læk]	缺乏、缺少、需要；亦作名詞用 英解 to be without

例 A new study by the Department of Health in Taiwan shows that more than half of the adult population **lacks** an understanding of important health problems. （91 學測補）

台灣衛生署一項新的研究顯示，超過半數的成年人欠缺對重要健康問題的瞭解。

語意用法 人＋ lack ＋事、物，表示缺乏某事、物。

lag [læg]	落後、延遲、衰退；亦作名詞用 英解 to straggle

例 The little girl **lagged** behind the line.

這小女孩落在隊伍之後。

語意用法 人＋ lag behind ＋事、物，表示落後於某事物。

launch [lɔntʃ]	下水（船）、升空、開辦；亦作名詞用 英解 to push into the water, to start

例 Why did the French government decide to **launch** the free newspaper program? （99 指考）

為什麼法國政府決定開始施行免費報紙方案？

語意用法 人或機構＋ launch ＋計畫，表示開始進行某項計畫、工作。

| **maintain**
[men`ten] | 保持、維持、維修、保養、贍養
英解 to keep in good condition |

例 Many athletes train year round to **maintain** excellent form and technique and peak physical condition.（97 指考）

許多運動員長年週而復始地訓練以維持絕佳的身形和技巧，以及顛峰的體能狀態。

語意用法 人＋ maintain ＋狀況，表示維持某種狀況。

| **manipulate**
[mə`nɪpjə͵let] | 操作、操縱、竄改、巧妙處理
英解 to handle |

例 Yo-Yo Ma **manipulated** the strings of a cello.

馬友友巧妙地撥弄大提琴的琴弦。

語意用法 人＋ manipulate ＋物品，表示熟悉地操作某項物品。

| **manufacture**
[͵mænjə`fæktʃə] | 製造、捏造；亦作名詞用
英解 to fabricate using machinery |

例 Heidi's company **manufactures** furniture for offices.

海蒂的公司製造辦公室傢俱。

語意用法 公司＋ manufacture ＋產品。

| **measure**
[`mɛʒə] | 測量、計量、權衡；亦作名詞用
英解 to calculate |

例 Different methods have been employed by economists to **measure** the standard of living.（92 學測補）

經濟學家採用不同的方法來衡量生活水平。

語意用法 人＋ measure ＋事、物＋ by ＋方法，表示用某種方法來評價、判斷某事物。

mention [ˈmɛnʃən]	提及、述及；亦作名詞用 英解 to say or write sth. briefly

例 The idea of long hair as a symbol of male strength is even **mentioned** in the Bible.（98 指考）

用長髮來象徵男性力量的這個想法甚至在聖經裡也有提及。

語意用法 人＋ mention ＋事、物＋ to ＋人，表示對某人提及某事；此處用被動 be mentioned。

move [muv]	移動、搬家、調職、使感動；亦作名詞用 英解 to go from one place to another

例 Plants cannot **move** from place to place and do not need to learn to avoid certain things.（94 學測）

植物沒辦法從一個地方移動到另一個地方，不需要學習避免某些事物。

語意用法 人、事、物＋ move from ＋地方＋ to ＋地方，表示移動。

multiply [ˈmʌltəplaɪ]	相乘、倍增、繁殖 英解 to increase a number by a certain number of times

例 Bacteria can **multiply** if the water is kept on the shelves for too long or if it is exposed to heat or direct sunlight.（99 學測）

如果水長時間放在架上或受熱、受陽光直射曝曬，細菌就會倍增繁殖。

語意用法 細菌或生物＋ multiply，表示細菌或生物倍數成長或繁殖。

navigate [ˈnævəˌget]	飛行、航行、導航、駕駛 英解 to figure out the course of a ship or airplane, using maps and mechanical aids

例 Small animals such as mole rats living underground are known for the use of magnetism to **navigate**.（98 學測）

像鼴鼠這類生活在地底的小動物便是以運用磁性導航而聞名。

語意用法 人或動物＋ navigate ＋ by ＋方法或物品，表示某人或動物以某種方法導航。

neglect [nɪgˋlɛkt]	忽視、忽略、忘了做；亦作名詞用 英解 to not give enough care or attention to sb. or sth.

例 Although Jeffery had to keep two part-time jobs to support his family, he never **neglected** his studies.（96 學測）

儘管傑佛瑞必須兼二份差來幫助家計卻從來沒有忽略自己的課業。

語意用法 人＋ neglect ＋工作，表示某人忽略工作。

negotiate [nɪˋgoʃɪͺet]	談判、協商、議價 英解 to reach an agreement through discussion

例 Our government will never **negotiate** with the terrorists.

我們的政府絕不和恐怖份子談判。

語意用法 人或機構＋ negotiate with ＋人或機構，表示與某人或機構協商、談判。

nominate [ˋnɑməͺnet]	提名、任命、命名、指定 英解 to appoint sb. to a position

例 The movie director **nominated** me to attend the Cannes Film Festival.

導演指定我出席坎城影展。

語意用法 人＋ nominate ＋人＋ for ＋職務，表示提名某人擔任某職位；人＋ nominate ＋人＋ to V，表示指定某人去做某事。

notify [ˋnotəͺfaɪ]	告知、通知、公布 英解 to inform

例 The chef **notified** his customers that his restaurant is moving.

主廚告知顧客們餐廳就要搬了。

語意用法 人＋ notify ＋人＋ that ＋ S ＋ V，表示通知某人……。

observe [əb`zɜv]	看到、觀察、注意 英解 to view

例 In order to write a report on stars, we decided to **observe** the stars in the sky every night.（93 學測）

為了寫一份關於星星的報告，我們決定每晚觀察夜空中的星星。

語意用法 人＋ observe ＋事物，表示觀察某事物。

obtain [əb`ten]	獲得、公認、流行 英解 to get

例 I am curious about how John **obtained** such a large sum of money.（85 學測）

我很好奇約翰從哪裡獲得那麼一大筆財富。

語意用法 人＋ obtain ＋財物＋ from/through ...，表示從何而得財物。

occupy [`ɑkjə,paɪ]	佔據、佔用時間、擔任職務 英解 to be in a place or work

例 The reading room is being **occupied**.

閱覽室被佔用了。

語意用法 人＋ occupy ＋地方；此處用被動 be occupied。

offend [ə`fɛnd]	傷害感情、觸怒、使不悅、犯錯、犯罪 英解 to hurt the feelings of people

例 They didn't really feel **offended**.（89 學測）

他們並未覺得被冒犯。

語意用法 人＋ feel offended，表示某人感覺被冒犯。

82

operate [ˈɑpəˌret]	工作、運轉、營運、開刀、起影響 英解 to function

例 It's an admirable project, and it is worth finding out if a similar one **operates** in your hometown.（86 學測）

這是個令人欽佩的計畫，值得探究你的家鄉有沒有類似的計畫在運作。

語意用法 事物＋ operate，表示某樣東西起作用、在運轉。

oppose [əˈpoz]	反對、反抗、使相對、對抗 英解 to be against sth. or sb.

例 U.S. airlines have **opposed** bag-matching for years.（92 指考）

美國航空公司反對行李比對已經好幾年了。

語意用法 人、公司＋ oppose ＋事件，表示反對某事件。

organize [ˈɔrgəˌnaɪz]	組織、安排 英解 to make a group for a specific purpose

例 Since the 1990s, alternative proms have been **organized** in some areas to meet the needs of particular students.（99 學測）

從一九九○年代開始，許多地區開始安排另類舞會以符合特定學生族群的需求。

語意用法 人＋ organize ＋事件，表示組織或安排；此處用被動 have been organized。

originate [əˈrɪdʒəˌnet]	發源、來自、引起、產生、創始 英解 to begin

例 Some say that life on Earth **originated** "out there" and was seeded here.
（93 學測）

有些人說地球上的生命源自「某處」，並在這裡播種。

語意用法 事物＋ originate in ＋地方，表示源於某地。

| **overlook** [ˌovɚˈluk] | 俯瞰、漏看、忽略、寬恕、監督 |
| | 英解 to look upon |

例 So we went to the restaurant and sat by a window **overlooking** the bay.
（88 學測）

於是我們去了餐廳坐在窗邊俯瞰海灣。

語意用法 人＋ overlook ＋地方，表示俯瞰某個地方。

| **overwhelm** [ˌovɚˈhwɛlm] | 擊潰、淹沒、壓倒、征服 |
| | 英解 to upset |

例 I sent out dozens of resumes, but I haven't exactly been **overwhelmed** with job offers yet.

我寄出數十封履歷，不過並沒有接到雪片般飛來的工作邀約。

語意用法 人＋ be overwhelmed with/by ＋事、物，表示被某事物淹沒、佔據。

| **paralyze** [ˈpærəˌlaɪz] | 使麻痺、使癱瘓、使無效 |
| | 英解 to cause a state of parplysis |

例 Thousands of people flooded into the city to join the demonstration; as a result, the city's transportation system was almost **paralyzed**. （94 指考）

成千上萬湧進城裡參加示威的群眾幾乎癱瘓市區的交通系統。

語意用法 事、物＋ be paralyzed，表示某事物被癱瘓了。

| **participate** [pɑrˈtɪsəˌpet] | 參與、參加、分享 |
| | 英解 to take part |

例 The number of athletes **participating** in the Summer Paralympic Games has increased from 400 athletes from 23 countries in 1960 to 3,806 athletes from 136 countries in 2004. （98 學測）

參加夏季殘障奧運會的選手已從 1960 年來自 23 個國家的 400 名選手增加到 2004 年來自 136 國的 3,806 名選手。

語意用法 人＋ participate in ＋事件，表示參與某事件。

pave [pev]	鋪路、鋪設、鋪滿 英解 to cover over a road

例 They **paved** the field with flowers to make a garden.

他們把這區域鋪滿花打造一座花園。

語意用法 人＋ pave ＋地點＋ with ＋物品，表示以某物鋪設、填滿某地方。

penalize [ˈpinḷ‚aɪz]	宣告有罪、處罰、使不利 英解 to punish

例 The government instituted a law to **penalize** those who sell blood diamonds. （86 指考）

政府立法處罰那些販賣血鑽石的人。

語意用法 人或機構＋ penalize ＋人＋ for Ving，表示因為某人做了某事而施以處罰。

perform [pəˈfɔrm]	演出、履行、執行、演奏 英解 to do or complete a task

例 Hseu Fang-yi, a young Taiwanese dancer, recently **performed** at Lincoln Center in New York and won a great deal of praise. （97 學測）

台灣的年輕舞蹈家許芳宜最近在紐約林肯中心演出獲得滿堂彩。

語意用法 人＋ perform at ＋地方，表示在某地表演。

perish [ˈpɛrɪʃ]	死去、枯萎、毀壞 英解 to die

例 A kid fell from the window and **perished** on the street.

一個小孩從窗口跌落死在大街上。

語意用法 人＋ perish at/on ＋地方，表示在某地方死亡。

| **permit**
[pə`mɪt] | 允許、准許、許可、容許；亦作名詞用
英解 to allow |

例 The teacher would not **permit** students to leave the classroom.

老師不准學生離開教室。

語意用法 人＋ permit ＋人＋ to V，表示允許某人做某事。

| **persist**
[pə`sɪst] | 堅持、固執、持續
英解 to continue steadily in the same manner in spite of obstacles |

例 He **persisted** in asking her to marry him until she finally said, "yes".

他持續向她求婚直到她說「願意」為止。

語意用法 persist in/with ＋ Ving，表示堅持、主張做某事。

| **personify**
[pə`sɑnə,faɪ] | 使擬人化、使具體化、象徵
英解 to represent an idea or thing as a person |

例 The priest **personifies** the values of his church.

神父使教會的價值具體化。

語意用法 人＋ personify ＋事物，表示將某物擬人化。

| **persuade**
[pə`swed] | 說服、使信服、使相信
英解 to convince |

例 Shopkeepers know that filling a store with the smell of freshly baked bread makes people feel hungry and **persuades** them to buy more food than they intended.（96 指考）

店主知道充滿剛出爐麵包香氣的店鋪能誘發人們的飢餓感，並說服他們購買超出自己所需的食物。

語意用法 人＋ persuade ＋人＋ to V，表示勸服某人做某事。

pick
[pɪk]

挑選、摘採、挖鑿、找碴；亦作名詞用

英解 to choose or select

例 A person who likes to **pick** on others is definitely not easy to get along with.（89 學測）

一個喜歡找別人碴的人鐵定不好相處。

語意用法 人＋ pick at/on ＋人，表示找某人碴。

plunge
[plʌndʒ]

投入、跳入、陷入；亦作名詞用

英解 to dive

例 A lifesaver **plunged** into the river from a shore.

一名救生員從岸邊跳入河裡。

語意用法 人＋ plunge in/into ＋水（water、river、lake），表示某人投入水中。

polish
[ˈpɑlɪʃ]

磨光、擦亮、使光滑

英解 to rub sth. until it is smooth and shiny

例 The soldier **polished** his gun.

士兵擦亮他的槍。

語意用法 人＋ polish ＋物品，表示磨亮某物。

possess
[pəˈzɛs]

擁有、掌握、支配、迷惑

英解 to own

例 Superman, Peter Pan, and Harry Potter have charmed many people because they **possess** powers that ordinary people don't have.（91 學測）

超人、彼得潘以及哈利波特迷倒許多人，就在於他們擁有平凡人所沒有的力量。

語意用法 人＋ possess ＋能力，表示擁有某種能力。

postpone
[post`pon]

延期、延後、暫緩
英解 to move sth. to a later time

例 The young couple decided to **postpone** their wedding until all the details were well taken care of.（92 學測）

這對年輕情侶決定把婚期延後直到所有的細節都能妥善安排。

語意用法 人＋ postpone ＋事件＋ until ...，表示將事件延後到……。

predict
[prɪ`dɪkt]

預言、預報
英解 to foretell

例 Dogs bark before earthquakes; cattle **predict** rainfall by sitting on the ground.（98 學測）

地震前狗會吠，下雨前牛會坐地上。

語意用法 人、生物＋ predict ＋事件，表示預測某事件。

prefer
[prɪ`fɝ]

寧可選擇、更喜歡
英解 to like one thing better than another

例 Some people might **prefer** easier exercises to more challenging ones.

有些人可能喜歡輕鬆些的運動勝過有挑戰性的運動。

語意用法 人＋ prefer ＋物＋ to ＋物，表示喜歡某物勝過另一物。

preserve
[prɪ`zɝv]

保護、維護、保存、防腐；亦作名詞用
英解 to guard

例 Like Gupo Island, Baisha (White Sand) Island is also uninhabited and has **preserved** the primitive, unspoiled character.（94 指考）

白沙島就像龜浦島一樣，杳無人跡，保有原始未受破壞的風貌。

語意用法 人或地方＋ preserve ＋事物，表示保存某事物。

press [prɛs]	按、壓、強迫；亦作名詞用
	英解 to push against

例 **Press** F1 to bring up the Help menu.

按下 F1 鍵來檢閱「Help」目錄。

語意用法 press ＋物品，表示按壓某物品。

pretend [prɪˋtɛnd]	假裝、佯裝、自命、覬覦
	英解 to make believe

例 He would pick up a broom and **pretend** to be playing guitar for the entertainment of family guests.（94 學測）

他會拿起掃帚假裝在彈吉他娛樂家裡的訪客。

語意用法 人＋ pretend ＋ to V，表示假裝做某事。

prevent [prɪˋvɛnt]	避免、阻止
	英解 to avoid

例 Superman always arrives in the nick of time to **prevent** a disaster from happening.（91 學測）

超人總在千鈞一髮之際趕到阻止災難發生。

語意用法 人＋ prevent ＋事件或災難＋ from happening，表示阻止某事件發生。

produce [prəˋdjus]	產生、生產、創作、生育
	英解 to create, invent from the mind

例 The mind and body work together to **produce** stress.（95 學測）

頭腦與身體共同製造壓力。

語意用法 人或事物＋ produce ＋事物，表示創作或生產某物。

prohibit [prə`hɪbɪt]	法令禁止、防止 英解 to ban by order or law

例 This country's law **prohibits** people from smoking.

這個國家的法令明訂禁止吸煙。

語意用法 法律＋ prohibit ＋人＋ from Ving，表示法律禁止人們做某事。

prolong [prə`lɔŋ]	拖延、延長 英解 to make sth. take longer

例 Such resistance is hurting the effectiveness of the policies, which may thus **prolong** the aging problem.（96 指考）

這樣的抵制是在損害政策的成效，可能因而延長老化問題。

語意用法 事件＋ prolong ＋問題，表示某事件拖延某問題。

promote [prə`mot]	發揚、宣傳、晉升 英解 to advance in rank

例 Nowadays health specialists **promote** the idea of wellness for everybody.（95 學測）

時下的健康專家倡導的是全民健康理念。

語意用法 人＋ promote ＋觀念，表示宣揚某些觀念。

pronounce [prə`naʊns]	聲明、宣稱、宣判、發聲 英解 to speak

例 Early this past summer the three whales were **pronounced** fit enough to be returned to the Atlantic Ocean.（84 學測）

今年剛過的這個初夏即宣稱這三條鯨魚已健康到足以回到大西洋。

語意用法 人或機構＋ pronounce ＋物＋修飾語，表示宣稱某物為何狀態；此處用被動 be pronounced。

propose [prəˋpoz]	提出、建議、求婚、舉杯祝賀 英解 to suggest

例 The school **proposes** alternatives for doing community service.（98 指考）
學校提出做社區服務的替代方案。

語意用法 人或機構＋ propose ＋方案，表示提出某方案或計畫。

protect [prəˋtɛkt]	保護、防護 英解 to shield

例 Plants make antioxidants to **protect** themselves from the sun's ultraviolet (UV) light.（97 指考）
植物會製造抗氧化劑以保護自己不受陽光中的紫外線傷害。

語意用法 人或生物＋ protect oneself from/against ＋傷害，表示保護自己免受某種傷害。

provide [prəˋvaɪd]	提供、供給、扶養、準備、規定、任命 英解 to supply

例 They must **provide** a travel visa and itinerary upon arrival.（93 指考補）
他們抵達後必須提供簽證以及行程。

語意用法 人或機構＋ provide ＋事物，表示提供事物。

provoke [prəˋvok]	煽動、引發、誘導 英解 to incite

例 Michael Jackson **provoked** new concerns for his children's welfare after he took them to the zoo covered in strange, bright-colored veils "to protect them from kidnappers."（92 指考）
麥可傑克森帶他的小孩去動物園時讓他們戴上顏色鮮豔的奇怪面紗，說是為了「保護他們不被綁架」，此舉引發對他小孩福利的關切。

語意用法 人＋ provoke ＋議論或議題，表示某人引發某些議題。

publish
[ˈpʌblɪʃ]

出版、發行、發表、刊載
英解 to print and distribute sth. to the public

例 Recently, Dr. Stuart Campbell of a private health center in London **published** some ultrasound images of unborn babies between 26 and 34 weeks. (95 指考)

最近，倫敦一家私人健康中心的史都華坎培爾醫生發表了一些介於 26 至 34 週胎兒的超音波影像。

語意用法 人＋ publish ＋報告或文件，某人發表某些文件報告。

---

pull
[pʊl]

拖拉、撕破、搬移、引誘、招攬、逮捕；亦作名詞用
英解 to tug

例 My sister pushed him down because he **pulled** her hair.

我姊把他推倒，因為他拉扯她的頭髮。

語意用法 pull ＋物品，表示拉扯某物。

---

punish
[ˈpʌnɪʃ]

處罰、懲罰
英解 to discipline

例 Mayor Abraham Beame announced that the city would not **punish** "The Human Fly." (83 學測)

市長阿布拉罕比姆宣布本市不會懲罰「飛行人」。

語意用法 人或機構＋ punish ＋人＋ for Ving，表示某人因做了某事而受處罰。

---

purchase
[ˈpɝtʃəs]

購買、贏得；亦作名詞用
英解 to buy sth.

例 People tend to **purchase** something they don't need when going shopping.

人們在逛街時常會買些不必要的東西。

語意用法 人＋ purchase ＋物品。

purify
[ˋpjʊrəˌfaɪ]

淨化、洗滌、使純淨
英解 to make sth. clean

例 An air filter **purifies** the air of dust.

空氣清淨機淨化了空氣中的灰塵。

語意用法 物品＋ purify ＋空氣，表示某物淨化了空氣。

pursue
[pəˋsu]

追捕、追求夢想
英解 to chase

例 Pan **pursued** the goal of perfection in her personal art.

潘追尋她個人藝術上的完美。

語意用法 人＋ pursue ＋目標，表示某人追尋某項目標。

qualify
[ˋkwɑləˌfaɪ]

使合格、使具資格
英解 to pass tests to show one's fitness for sth.

例 According to studies, as many as 8.9 percent of the American population **qualify** as compulsive buyers.（98 指考）

根據研究顯示，多達百分之 8.9 的美國人口符合強迫買家的資格。

語意用法 人＋ qualify as ＋某項資格，表示合格擔任某項職務。

quote
[kwot]

引證、引用、引述；亦作名詞用
英解 to repeat sth. that another has said or written

例 He **quoted** extensively from an article in *the Lancet* about genetic research.（94 指考）

他大量引用《刺絡針》期刊中一篇關於基因研究的文章。

語意用法 人＋ quote from ＋文章，表示引用自某文章。

realize
[`rɪəˌlaɪz]

達成；認識、瞭解、贏得
英解 to recognize

例 We work very hard to **realize** this dream.（94 學測）

我們很努力地去實現這個夢想。

語意用法 人＋ realize dreams，表示達成夢想。

recall
[rɪ`kɔl]

回憶、回想、召喚、使甦醒、撤銷；名詞又作罷免權解
英解 to remember sth.

例 The famous film director Ang Lee **recalls** his father's disappointment with him when he was young.（94 學測）

知名導演李安回想起年輕時的自己曾讓父親感到失望。

語意用法 人＋ recall ＋事件，表示某人想起某事件。

recognize
[`rɛkəgˌnaɪz]

認清、認識、想起、承認
英解 to recall

例 They **recognized** that their eating habits might have also contributed to their heart problems.（93 學測）

他們了解到他們的飲食習慣或許導致了他們的心臟問題。

語意用法 人＋ recognize ＋ that ＋ S ＋ V，表示某人認清……。

recommend
[ˌrɛkə`mɛnd]

推薦、介紹、勸告
英解 to tell others about sth. one likes

例 Are there any Italian restaurants near the hotel that you could **recommend**?

飯店附近有什麼義大利餐廳可以推薦的嗎？

語意用法 人＋ recommend ＋人＋ to V，表示推薦某人去做某事。

| **record**
[rɪ`kɔrd] | 記錄、記載、標明、錄下；亦作名詞用
英解 to make a written record of sth. |

例 They take many photographs to **record** their observations.（95 學測）

他們拍攝許多照片來記錄他們的觀察。

語意用法 人＋ record ＋事件。

| **recover**
[rɪ`kʌvə] | 復原、失而復得、彌補、覆蓋
英解 to regain one's health |

例 To find an expert, who would **recover** the lost information for you, is probably the easiest solution.（86 學測）

去找一名可以幫你復原遺失資訊的專家，可能是最簡單的解決方法。

語意用法 人＋ recover ＋事件或物品，表示復原某物品。

| **recycle**
[rɪ`saɪkḷ] | 使循環、再利用
英解 to process and reuse materials |

例 Irene does not throw away used envelopes. She **recycles** them by using them for taking telephone messages.（94 學測）

艾琳沒有丟掉舊信封，她回收它們用來作為電話留言的便條紙。

語意用法 人＋ recycle ＋物品，表示回收某些物品。

| **reduce**
[rɪ`djus] | 減少、降低、使限於、使簡化
英解 to make sth. smaller in size or weight |

例 Studies have proved that watching funny movies can **reduce** pain and promote healing.（94 學測）

研究證明，看喜劇有助於減低痛苦、加快復原。

語意用法 物品＋ reduce ＋痛苦，表示某物品減少痛苦。

reflect [rɪˋflɛkt]	反映、反射、反思、反省 英解 to give off a shine

例 A person's self-concept is **reflected** in the way he or she behaves, and the way a person behaves affects other people's reactions.（83 學測）

一個人的自我概念反映在他或她的行為上，而一個人的行為模式則會影響他人的反應。

語意用法 某事物＋ reflect ＋某事物，表示反映；此處用被動 be reflected。

reform [ˌrɪˋfɔrm]	改革、改良、革除弊端 英解 to change sth.

例 The president wants to appoint someone to **reform** the nation's health care system.

總統想要任命某人來改革國家的健保制度。

語意用法 人或機構＋ reform ＋事件或制度，改革某些制度。

refresh [rɪˋfrɛʃ]	提神、使清新、恢復精神 英解 to revive

例 Ann enjoyed going to the flower market. She believed that the fragrance of flowers **refreshed** her mind.（97 學測）

安喜歡逛花市，她相信花的香氣能幫她提神。

語意用法 物品＋ refresh one's mind，表示提神。

refuse [rɪˋfjuz]	拒絕、不准 英解 to decline

例 Airlines **refuse** to let passengers carry razor blades, scissors, or screwdrivers on flights.（92 指考）

航空公司不准乘客攜帶刮鬍刀、剪刀或螺絲起子登機。

語意用法 人或機構＋ refuse ＋ to V，表示拒絕做某動作。

regain [rɪˋgen]	取回、收回、回復、返回 英解 to recover

例 They **regained** weight after coming back from the summer camp.（94 學測）

他們從夏日營回來後回復體重。

語意用法 人＋ regain ＋事物，表示重新獲得某事物。

regard [rɪˋgɑrd]	考慮、視為、關心、尊敬；亦作名詞用 英解 to value

例 They do not **regard** criticism as personal rejection.（83 學測）

他們不把批評視為個人的拒絕。

語意用法 人＋ regard ＋事物＋ as ＋事物，表示將某事物視為某事物。

regulate [ˋrɛgjəˌlet]	管理、制定規章、調節 英解 to control sth.

例 During warm weather, sweating helps humans **regulate** their body

temperature.（85 學測）

在溫暖的天氣裡，出汗可以幫助人體調節體溫。

語意用法 人或物品＋ regulate ＋物品或事件。

rehabilitate [ˌrihəˋbɪləˌtet]	恢復（地位、名譽）、復興 英解 to help sb. or sth. become better

例 When she finished her studies, she found a job with a small company

that mainly **rehabilitates** old houses in the city.（93 指考補）

當她完成學業，她在一家主要負責修復城市裡的老房子的小公司找到一份工作。

語意用法 人或機構＋ rehabilitate ＋身體／房子，表示修復房子或身體。

rehearse [rɪˋhɜs]	排演、排練 英解 to practice

例 She **rehearsed** the songs in the new show.

她在新節目裡排演新歌。

語意用法 人＋ rehearse ＋事件，表示彩排演練某事件。

reincarnate [ˌriɪnˋkɑrˌnet]	使化身爲、使轉世爲 英解 to cause to be reborn in another body

例 The leaders were always "**reincarnated**" in the households of lowly families rather than noble ones. (93 學測)

領導人總是在卑微的家庭轉世，而非貴族家庭。

語意用法 人＋ be reincarnated，表示某人轉世。

reinforce [ˌriɪnˋfɔrs]	增援、增強、強化 英解 to add strength to sth.

例 "This just **reinforces** the belief that newspapers should be free, which is a very bad idea," Mr. Schwartzenberg said. (99 指考)

Schwartzenberg 說，此舉只會加深報紙是免費的這種信念，是很糟的主意。

語意用法 事件＋ reinforce ＋觀念或印象，表示某事件加深或強化某印象或觀念。

relate [rɪˋlet]	有關、認同、講述 英解 to be connected with

例 His creations are closely **related** to his unique personal history. (99 指考)

他的創作與他獨特的個人歷史息息相關。

語意用法 事物＋ be related to ＋事物，表示有關連。

relax [rɪ`læks]	使鬆弛、休息、放鬆、緩和 英解 to stop work and enjoy oneself

例 Then we could **relax** and have a drink.（89 學測）

然後我們就可以放鬆喝一杯。

語意用法 人＋ relax，表示放鬆。

release [rɪ`lis]	釋放、鬆開、免除、放棄；亦作名詞用 英解 set it free

例 Without the carbon dioxide **released** from the process, all plant life would die out.（88 學測）

少了釋放二氧化碳的過程，所有的植物將會死亡。

語意用法 事、物＋ release from ＋處所或過程，表示事物從……釋放。

relieve [rɪ`liv]	緩和、紓解、減輕、解除、使寬慰 英解 to free from worry

例 Using a heating pad or taking warm baths can sometimes help to **relieve** pain in the lower back.（99 學測）

使用熱敷墊或泡個熱水澡有時有助於緩和下背部疼痛。

語意用法 人、事、物＋ relieve ＋痛苦或病痛，表示紓解病痛。

remain [rɪ`men]	留存、保持、剩下 英解 to stay after others are gone

例 It is better for those objects to **remain** at a certain place than to be moved around.（93 學測）

將那些物品保持在一個地方比到處搬移好。

語意用法 人、事、物＋ remain at ＋地點或層次，表示某人、事、物維持在某個地點。

remark
[rɪ`mɑrk]

談到、評論、察覺;亦作名詞用
英解 to make a comment about sth.

例 Someone else **remarked** that "a merry heart does good, like medicine"— and infectious laughter is often catching.(86 學測)

有人說,「一顆快活的心就像良藥」,而充滿感染力的笑聲總是吸引人。

語意用法 人+ remark on/upon +名詞;人+ remark that ...,表示談論、述說⋯⋯。

remind
[rɪ`maɪnd]

提醒、使記起
英解 to cause sb. to remember

例 The aim of the campaign is to **remind** people of the damage the deadly weed does to their body.(94 學測)

這項活動的目的是要提醒人們這種致命的煙草對他們的身體造成的傷害。

語意用法 人、事、物+ remind +人+ of/about +事,表示提醒某人注意到某事。

remove
[rɪ`muv]

移開、刪除、免職
英解 to move or take sth. away

例 Your desk is crowded with too many unnecessary things. You have to **remove** some of them.(91 學測)

你的書桌塞滿了太多不需要的東西,你必須移走一些。

語意用法 人+ remove +事物,表示移除某事物。

renew
[rɪ`nju]

更新、重建、復原
英解 to remodel

例 Architects design new buildings and oversee work when old buildings are **renewed**.(93 指考補)

當老建築重建時,建築師設計了新建築並親自監工。

語意用法 人+ renew +物品,表示更新事物,此處用被動 be renewed。

repeat
[rɪˋpit]

重複、複誦、重播、重說
英解 to say or do sth. over again

例 Many times the man screamed, "Say 'Catano' or I'll kill you!" But the parrot would not **repeat** the name.（87 學測）

好幾次那男人大聲吼道，「說『卡塔尼奧』，不然我就殺了你！」但那隻鸚鵡如何也不複誦那個名字。

語意用法 人或動物＋ repeat ＋事物。

replace
[rɪˋples]

替代、歸位、歸還
英解 to substitute

例 I can't believe it's cheaper to **replace** my cell phone than it is to repair it.

我不敢相信，換支新的手機比修理還便宜。

語意用法 人＋ replace ＋事物＋ with/by ＋事物，表示以某事物取代、更換另一事物。

represent
[ˌrɛprɪˋzɛnt]

象徵、意味、描繪、扮演、代表
英解 to show

例 In a wedding banquet it is common to see a pair of ice-sculpted swans that **represent** the union of the new couple.（97 學測）

在婚宴上經常可以看到一對冰雕的天鵝象徵這對伴侶的結合。

語意用法 事物＋ represent ＋某項意義，表示某事物象徵某種意義。

reproduce
[ˌriprəˋdjus]

繁殖、複製、再生、重現
英解 to have babies

例 The red ant can **reproduce** young ants very quickly.（94 學測）

紅螞蟻可以迅速繁殖幼蟻。

語意用法 人或動物＋ reproduce ＋年輕的後代，表示繁殖後代。

request [rɪˋkwɛst]	要求、請求；亦作名詞用 英解 to ask for sth.

例 The train conductor **requested** all passengers to show their tickets.

火車車掌要求所有旅客出示車票。

語意用法 人＋ request ＋人＋ to V，表示要求、請求某人做某動作。

require [rɪˋkwaɪr]	需要、要求 英解 to need

例 Hotels and corporate offices now **require** guests to present a photo ID at check-ins and entrances.（92 指考）

現在，登記住宿或進入時，旅館和公司辦公室會要求訪客出示有照片的證件。

語意用法 人＋ require ＋人＋ to V，表示要求某人做某事。

reserve [rɪˋzɝv]	預約、保留；亦作名詞用 英解 to book

例 For the reunion, my father has **reserved** a table at the restaurant.

為了全家團聚，我爸爸在飯店預訂了桌位。

語意用法 人＋ reserve ＋事物，表示預訂某事物。

resign [rɪˋzaɪn]	辭去、放棄 英解 to choose to leave one's job or post

例 The manager **resigned** without hesitation after he had been offered a better job in another company.（96 學測）

在別家公司得到更好的工作之後，經理不帶遲疑地辭職。

語意用法 人＋ resign，表示放棄、辭職。

resist
[rɪˋzɪst]

抵抗、對抗、忍住
英解 to fend off

例 Stradivarius, the undeniable king of violin makers, could not **resist** creating a variety of guitars.（92 學測補）

公認的小提琴製造第一把交椅史特拉第瓦里，忍不住製造各式各樣的吉他。

語意用法 人＋ resist ＋ Ving，抵抗、忍住做某事。

resort
[rɪˋzɔrt]

依賴、訴諸、求助
英解 to do or use sth. extreme

例 When his children left him, he **resorted** to the help of the police.

孩子離開他後，他借助警方的協助。

語意用法 人＋ resort to ＋協助或手段。

respond
[rɪˋspɑnd]

回答、做出反應
英解 to answer

例 The "patient" **responds** verbally or with gestures to indicate emotions such as pain, stress or anxiety.（98 指考）

「病人」用言詞或手勢做出情緒上的回應，如疼痛、壓力或焦慮。

語意用法 人＋ respond to ＋物，表示對某物做出回應。

restore
[rɪˋstor]

歸還、修復、使恢復
英解 give back

例 The police **restored** the stolen car to its owner.

警察將失車歸還給車主。

語意用法 人＋ restore ＋物，表示歸還、修復某物。

restrict [rɪˋstrɪkt]	限制、約束、侷限 英解 restrain

例 The drug problem is universal. It is not **restricted** to one country.（90 學測）

毒品問題是全球性的，不侷限於一個國家。

語意用法 人或機構＋ restrict ＋事物＋ to ＋事物，表示侷限某事物於某事物；此處用被動 be restricted to。

retain [rɪˋten]	保持、保留 英解 to keep sth.

例 If we want to **retain** our most talented employees, we'll have to offer significant pay increases.（97 學測）

如果我們想留住最優秀的員工，我們必須給予大幅加薪。

語意用法 人＋ retain ＋物，表示保留、留住某物。

retreat [rɪˋtrit]	撤退、退縮；亦作名詞用 英解 to move away from sth.

例 The enemy was hitting heavily, so the army had to **retreat** to safety.

敵軍猛烈攻擊，所以軍隊退回安全地帶。

語意用法 人或團隊＋ retreat to ＋地點，表示撤退、後退至某地點。

retrieve [rɪˋtriv]	尋回、恢復、補救 英解 to fetch

例 Skilled professionals can sometimes **retrieve** a file from a computer's hard disc even after it has been deleted.

優秀的專業人員有時候可以從電腦硬碟救回檔案，即使是它已經被刪除。

語意用法 人＋ retrieve ＋事物＋ from/out of ＋事物，表示從某事物取回、拯救某事物。

reuse
[ˌriˋjuz]

重複使用；亦作名詞用
英解 to use sth. again

例 If we **reuse** our papers, bottles, and cans, there will be less garbage in the world.

如果我們重複使用紙張、瓶子和罐子，這個世界就會少一些垃圾。

語意用法 人＋ reuse ＋物品，重複使用某物。

reveal
[rɪˋvil]

展露、顯露
英解 to disclose

例 His talents are **revealed** in a variety of disciplines.（99 指考）

他的才華展露在各種領域上。

語意用法 人＋ reveal ＋才能，表示某人展露才能；此處用被動 be revealed。

review
[rɪˋvju]

復習、復審、檢查、評論
英解 to peruse

例 My tutor **reviewed** the last lesson before starting a new one.

我的家教在教新課前，先幫我溫習了上次的課程。

語意用法 人＋ review ＋事物，表示復習、檢查某事物。

revise
[rɪˋvaɪz]

修正、校訂
英解 to read carefully to change and correct sth.

例 Students were asked to **revise** or rewrite their compositions based on the teacher's comments.（98 學測）

學生們被要求依照老師的建議修改或重寫他們的作品。

語意用法 人＋ revise ＋事物，表示某人修訂某事物。

rid [rɪd]	免除、解除、擺脫 英解 to free

例 It's impossible to completely **rid** your home of insects, but you can discourage them from moving in.

要讓住家完全免於蚊蟲是不可能的事，但是你可以阻撓牠們進入。

語意用法 rid ＋事物＋ of ＋事物，表示讓某事物擺脫某事物。

ridicule [ˋrɪdɪkjul]	譏笑、嘲弄、奚落；亦作名詞用 英解 to deride

例 A critic on TV **ridiculed** the mayor's speech.

有個評論家在電視上揶揄市長的演說。

語意用法 人＋ ridicule ＋事物。

scatter [ˋskætɚ]	分佈、分散、驅散、散佈 英解 to go in all directions

例 The mirror slipped out of the little girl's hand, and the broken pieces **scattered** all over the floor.（98 指考）

鏡子從小女孩手上滑落，碎片到處散佈在地板上。

語意用法 物品＋ scatter on/over ＋地方，表示物品散放於某處。

scratch [skrætʃ]	搔癢、抓破 英解 to stop an itch by rubbing it with the fingernails

例 It is not easy for old people to **scratch** their backs, so they need help when their backs itch.（97 學測）

老年人要抓到自己的背很不容易，所以背癢時需要別人幫忙。

語意用法 人＋ scratch one's back，表示某人搔自己的背。

scream
[skrim]

尖聲喊叫、高聲說話；亦作名詞用
英解 to cry out with a high, loud voice in pain or fear

例 When he was about to cut its throat, the little pig suddenly **screamed**, "Stop!"（97 學測）

當他正要往牠的喉嚨割下去時，小豬突然大叫，「住手！」

語意用法 人＋ scream ＋事情，表示因某種情緒而放聲大叫某事。

sculpt
[skʌlpt]

雕刻、造型
英解 to shape

例 Its latest exhibit is a collection of **sculpted** lions, snakes, horses and eagles.（99 指考）

它最新的展覽集合了獅子、蛇、馬以及老鷹的雕刻。

語意用法 此處 sculpted 來修飾名詞，sculpted lions, snakes 等。

search
[sɜtʃ]

搜查、搜尋、探查
英解 to look for sth.

例 They are often more active and tend to **search** for food during the night.（99 指考）

在夜間，牠們往往會更積極地尋找食物。

語意用法 人＋ search for ＋事物，表示尋找某事物。

seek
[sik]

尋找、探索、追求
英解 to look for sth.

例 Habitual drinkers may find alcohol not stimulating enough after a while and want to **seek** other more stimulating substances.（97 指考）

習慣喝酒的人過了一段時間之後會發現酒精對他們來說已不夠刺激，進而尋求其他更刺激的物質。

語意用法 人＋ seek ＋事物，表示尋找搜索某事物。

seize [siz]	抓住、攻佔、擄獲 英解 to take sth. and hold it with force

例 This was to ensure that no single and powerful noble family could **seize** the title and pass it to the next generation.（93 學測）

這是為了確保沒有單一且強而有力的貴族家庭可以掠奪這個稱號，並傳給下一代。

語意用法 人＋ seize ＋事物，表示抓住某事物。

select [sə`lɛkt]	選擇、挑選；亦作形容詞用 英解 to choose

例 First, ice must be carefully **selected** so that it is suitable for sculpting.
（97 學測）

首先，必須仔細挑選適合用來雕刻的冰。

語意用法 人＋ select ＋事物＋ for ＋目的或理由，表示為某理由挑選某物，此處用被動 be selected。

separate [`sɛpə͵ret]	分開、分隔、脫離、分手；亦作形容詞用 英解 to move sth. apart from sth. else

例 Brought up in town, the girl finds it difficult to **separate** rice from barley.

在城裡長大，這女孩很難區分米和大麥。

語意用法 人＋ separate ＋物＋ from ＋物，表示分開兩事物。

shave [ʃev]	剃、刮鬍子、削、切成薄片；亦作名詞用 英解 to cut off thin layers

例 They **shaved** their heads.（98 指考）

他們剃光頭。

語意用法 人＋ shave one's head，表示剃頭。

| **shiver**
[ˈʃɪvə] | 發抖、打顫；亦作名詞用
英解 to tremble |

例 The little girl is **shivering** as she sells the match in the snow.

小女孩在雪中賣火柴時不停地發抖。

語意用法 人＋ shiver，表示人顫抖。

| **shrink**
[ʃrɪŋk] | 收縮、退縮、縮小
英解 to make or become smaller |

例 India is **shrinking**. （96 學測）

印度正在縮小。

語意用法 人或事物＋ shrink，表示人或事物退縮或縮小。

| **shuffle**
[ˈʃʌfl] | 拖著腳步而行、洗牌、蒙混、擺脫
英解 to walk without lifting the feet |

例 The old lady **shuffled** down the stairs.

老太太拖著腳步走下樓梯。

語意用法 人＋ shuffle，表示人拖著腳步移動。

| **signify**
[ˈsɪgnəˌfaɪ] | 表示、表明、意味
英解 to show |

例 Our company's new logo is a rocket, which is supposed to **signify** "technology, growth, and progress."

我們公司的新標誌是火箭，應該是意味著「科技、成長與進步」。

語意用法 事物＋ signify ＋事情，表示某事物表達著某件事。

simplify [`sɪmpləˌfaɪ]	簡化、單純化 英解 to make less complex

例 Let's **simplify** the work by dividing it into smaller tasks.

讓我們把它分成一小件一小件的任務來簡化這份工作。

語意用法 人＋ simplify ＋工作，表示簡化工作。

slant [slænt]	傾斜、曲解、歪曲；亦作名詞用 英解 to make diagonal

例 Don't **slant** your letters like that—it makes your handwriting really hard to read.

不要把你的字歪曲成那樣──那讓你的字跡很難辨識。

語意用法 slant ＋物品，表示把某物傾斜、歪曲。

slide [slaɪd]	滑動、滑行、悄悄走掉 英解 to move sth. across a surface

例 She **slid** out of the concert.

她悄悄從演唱會溜走。

語意用法 人＋ slide out of ＋地方，表示某人從某處悄悄溜走。

slip [slɪp]	失足、滑倒、鬆脫、溜走、犯錯；亦作名詞用，如 a slip of tongue 表示脫口而出 英解 to fall or almost fall because of sth. slippery

例 He **slipped** on the ice.

他在冰上滑倒。

語意用法 人＋ slip on ＋地方，表示在某處滑倒。

smuggle [ˈsmʌgl]	走私、偷運 英解 to bring things into or out of another country illegally

例 Diamonds mined in some rebel-held areas, such as Liberia, are being **smuggled** into neighboring countries and exported as conflict-free diamonds.（96 指考）

在一些叛亂地區例如利比亞開採的鑽石，被走私到鄰國並以無爭議鑽石的名目輸出。

語意用法 人＋ smuggle ＋物品，表示把物品偷偷運入或運出，此處用被動 be smuggled。

soak [sok]	浸泡、使濕透；亦作名詞用 英解 to put or be in water for a long time

例 The baby **soaked** in the tub with bubble bath.

小嬰兒浸泡在浴缸的泡泡浴中。

語意用法 人＋ soak in ＋地點，表示某人浸泡於某處。

solve [sɑlv]	解決、解答、溶解、償還債務 英解 to find a solution for sth.

例 I could not help you **solve** the problem.（92 學測補）

我無法幫你解決這個問題。

語意用法 人＋ solve the problem，表示某人解決問題。

spare [spɛr]	使免於、騰出、分出、節約、省略、饒恕 英解 to save or prevent sb. from harm

例 They wrote letters to the tuna companies and supermarkets asking them to find a way to **spare** dolphins.（91 學測補）

他們寫信給鮪魚公司和超市，要求他們放海豚一條生路。

語意用法 人＋ spare ＋物，表示使某物免於受傷害。

speculate [ˈspɛkjəˌlet]	思索、推測、投機 英解 to guess about

例 Although stories about aliens have never been officially confirmed, their existence has been widely **speculated** upon. (93 學測)

儘管關於外星人的故事從未經官方證實，但他們的存在已廣泛地被猜測。

語意用法 人＋ speculate upon ＋事物，表示思索、推測某事。

split [splɪt]	劈開、分配、劃分、分裂、離開；亦作名詞用 英解 to divide sth. by cutting or breaking

例 We **split** the profits equally with our distributors.

我們與經銷商平分利潤。

語意用法 人＋ split ＋物，表示把某物分開。

spread [sprɛd]	塗敷、展開、覆蓋、延續；亦作名詞用 英解 to cover a surface by pushing sth. toward the edges of the surface

例 Though convenient, international air travel is the main reason that many diseases can now quickly **spread** around the world.

雖然方便，但國際航空旅遊是許多疾病快迅在世界散佈的主因。

語意用法 事物＋ spread，表示某物散佈、延展開來。

sprinkle [ˈsprɪŋkl̩]	灑、撒、散佈、微雨、如星般遍佈 英解 to rain lightly

例 I bet that pasta would taste even better if you **sprinkled** a little cheese on top.

我敢打賭，如果你在上面灑一些起司，這義大利麵會更好吃。

語意用法 sprinkle ＋物品，表示灑某物品。

squeeze
[skwiz]

壓、擠、搾、擰、壓榨、勒索；亦作名詞用
英解 to press from two or more sides

例 After the water is **squeezed** out, the ball-shaped pieces are put under the sun to dry before they can be used as a firewood or charcoal substitute.
（93 指考）

水被擠壓出來後，一片片的球型體放在陽光下曬乾以作為柴火或木炭的替代品。

語意用法 人＋ squeeze ＋物品，表示擠壓、擠出；此處用被動 be squeezed out。

startle
[ˋstɑrtl]

使吃驚、驚動、驚嚇
英解 to surprise

例 Every time we watch apes in their cages we are **startled** by their manlike behavior.（90 學測）

我們每次看著籠子裡的黑猩猩，都會因為牠們做出跟人類一樣的舉動而吃驚。

語意用法 人＋ be startled by ＋事物，表示為某事物所驚嚇。

stimulate
[ˋstɪmjəˌlet]

激勵、刺激、鼓舞、促使
英解 to increase energy or activity

例 Simple objects can **stimulate** our imagination.（90 學測）
簡單的物件可以激發我們的想像力。

語意用法 事物＋ stimulate ＋事物（或想像力），表示刺激、鼓舞（想像力）。

strengthen
[ˋstrɛŋθən]

加強、增強、鞏固
英解 to make or become stronger

例 We are more than willing to **strengthen** our ties with those countries that are friendly to us.（84 學測）

我們很願意加強與這些對我們很友善的國家的聯繫。

語意用法 人或機構＋ strengthen ＋關係，表示強化某項關係。

stretch
[strɛtʃ]

伸直、伸展、延續、舒展肢體；亦作名詞用
英解 to make wider

例 Now, however, men have developed huge fishing nets that form underwater "walls" that **stretch** for miles. (91 學測補)

然而，現今人類開發出巨型魚網，在水底形成一道延展好幾哩的牆。

語意用法 事物＋ stretch，表示某事物延伸或展開。

strike
[straɪk]

打擊、攻擊
英解 to hit hard

例 No one can possibly know in advance when an earthquake will **strike**.
(90 學測)

沒有人可能預先知道地震何時來襲。

語意用法 事物＋ strike，表示某事物來襲。

strive
[straɪv]

努力、奮鬥、鬥爭
英解 to work hard for sth.

例 But I cannot **strive** solely for others. (97 指考)

但我不能僅為別人奮鬥。

語意用法 人＋ strive for ＋目標，表示為追求某目標而努力。

struggle
[ˋstrʌgl]

掙扎、奮鬥、競爭、對抗；亦作名詞用
英解 to use much physical or mental effort and energy to do sth.

例 The group saw the worm go down into the water and soon begin to **struggle** for survival. (93 指考補)

這個小組看到蠕蟲沈到水裡，並很快地開始為生存而掙扎。

語意用法 人＋ struggle for ＋目標，表示為某項目標奮鬥。

stumble
[ˋstʌmbl̩]

絆倒、蹣跚而行、結巴、犯錯、偶遇；亦作名詞用
英解 to trip or have trouble walking

例 Be careful not to **stumble** as you walk across the stage to receive your diploma.

你走過講臺領取學位證書時小心別絆倒了。

語意用法 人＋ stumble，表示絆倒。

submit
[səbˋmɪt]

屈從、忍受、遞交
英解 to surrender

例 Over a period of thirty-five years, more than eighty thousand wolf carcasses were **submitted** for bounty payments in Montana.（95 指考）

在 35 年間，超過 8 萬具狼屍被提交給蒙大拿政府以求賞金。

語意用法 人＋ submit ＋事物＋ to ＋人，表示遞交某事物給某人；此處用被動 be submitted。

succeed
[səkˋsid]

成功、繼任、接連發生
英解 to accomplish a task or reach a goal

例 The man did everything he could to teach the parrot to say "Catano," but he never **succeeded**.（83 學測）

這男人試了一切的方法還是無法成功教鸚鵡說出「卡塔尼奧」。

語意用法 人＋ succeed，表示順利完成或成功。

supply
[səˋplaɪ]

供給、提供、補充；名詞亦作替代品解
英解 to give or provide sth. needed

例 If we used more of this source of heat and light, it could **supply** all the power needed throughout the world.（99 指考）

如果我們使用更多的光和熱源，就可以供給全球所需的能源。

語意用法 人、事、物＋ supply ＋事物，表示供給、提供某項事物。

support [səˋport]	支持、扶持、資助、鼓勵、維持；亦作名詞用 英解 to hold up

例 We **support** the President.

我們支持總統。

語意用法 support ＋人，表示支持某人。

surpass [səˋpæs]	超越、優於、大於 英解 to exceed or go beyond

例 The Internet has **surpassed** newspapers as a medium of mass communication. (98 指考)

網際網路已經超越報紙成為大眾傳播媒介。

語意用法 人、事、物＋ surpass ＋人、事、物，表示勝過、超越。

surround [səˋraʊnd]	包圍、圍繞、圈住 英解 to encircle

例 It would take 10 people holding hands to **surround** the base of its trunk. (91 學測)

需要 10 個人手牽著手才有辦法圈住樹幹的底部。

語意用法 人、物＋ surround ＋物或地方，表示包圍某物或某地。

survey [səˋve]	調查、測量、環視；亦作名詞用 英解 to take a wide view of sth.

例 Of all the students **surveyed**, 27 percent said they had never used the Net. (91 學測)

所有接受調查的學生中百分之二十七表示他們從沒有使用過網路。

語意用法 survey ＋人，表示調查某人；此處用被動 (be) surveyed。

survive [sə`vaɪv]	倖存、存活、死裡逃生 英解 to continue to live or exist

例 Rwanda has **survived** the mass killing.（96 學測）

盧旺達在大屠殺中倖存下來。

語意用法 人＋ survive ＋事件，表示從某事件存活下來。

suspend [sə`spɛnd]	懸掛、靜止、停權、停辦、暫時歇業 英解 to hang from a point so as to allow free movement

例 The two security guards will be **suspended** from all their duties until further investigation is completed.（89 學測）

兩名警衛將暫停所有職務直到完成進一步的調查。

語意用法 機構＋ suspend ＋人＋ from ＋工作或職位，表示暫停某人的工作或職位。

sustain [sə`sten]	支撐、維持 英解 to keep in existence by providing support

例 Rap's rise and **sustained** global popularity is a good illustration of how influential youth culture is on youth attitudes and behavior.（92 學測補）

饒舌歌的崛起與持續地受到全球歡迎，是青少年的態度和行為受到青少年文化影響的一個好例子。

語意用法 此處 sustained 當修飾語，sustained global popularity 持續的全球歡迎度。

sway [swe]	搖擺、傾斜、動搖、支配 英解 to rock

例 Farther north, the aurora frequently looks like fiery draperies which hang from the sky and **sway** to and fro while flames of red, orange, green, and blue play up and down the moving folds.（96 指考）

再往北，極光常常看起來像是掛在天空中如火般的帷幔，來回搖擺，而紅色、橘色、綠色以及藍色的火焰則在流動的皺摺上下跳動。

語意用法 物＋ sway to and fro，表示某物來回擺動。

tempt [tɛmpt]	勸誘、引誘、吸引、勾引 英解 to entice

例 The ancient Greek word for curls and locks is related to intriguing and **tempting** someone.（98 指考）

捲髮和鎖二個字在古希臘文裡有勾引和引誘某人的相關意思。

語意用法 tempt ＋受＋ to V，表示誘使某人去做某事。

tend [tɛnd]	走向、趨向、傾向 英解 to lean

例 Boys **tend** to pay less attention in class than girls.（96 學測）

相較於女生，男生在課堂上通常較不專心。

語意用法 人＋ tend ＋ to V，表示傾向於做某事。

thrust [θrʌst]	用力推、插入、衝刺、戳、突擊；亦作名詞用 英解 to move one's arm or foot forward quickly

例 Laura was at the door, **thrusting** a bracelet into Amy's pocket.

蘿拉站在門口將手鐲塞入艾咪的口袋裡。

語意用法 人＋ thrust ＋物品＋ into ＋地方，表示將某物品塞進一個地方。

tolerate [ˋtɑləˌret]	忍受、容忍、寬恕 英解 to suffer

例 Since our classroom is not air-conditioned, we have to **tolerate** the heat during the hot summer days.（97 學測）

因為我們的教室沒有冷氣，我們必須忍受夏日的酷暑。

語意用法 人＋ tolerate ＋事件，表示容忍某件事。

transfer
[træns`fɚ]

搬移、轉換、調動；亦作名詞用
英解 to move from one place

例 We **transferred** our bags from the ferry to the taxi.

我們將行李從渡輪搬到計程車上。

語意用法 人＋ transfer ＋物＋ from ＋地方＋ to ＋地方，表示把物品由某處轉到某處。

transform
[træns`fɔrm]

改觀、轉變為、改革
英解 to change from one shape to another

例 These days, even a walk in the woods can be **transformed** into an "extreme" sport.（93 指考）

在這時日即使是在樹林中散步也可以被轉化為一種「極限」運動。

語意用法 事物＋ transform into/to ＋事物，表示轉變成另一種事物，此處使用被動 be transformed into。

translate
[træns`let]

翻譯、轉移、轉變、調動
英解 to convert

例 His works were all written originally in French and were later **translated** into English.（94 指考）

他所有的作品原先皆以法文創作，之後被翻譯為英文。

語意用法 人＋ translate ＋作品＋ into ＋語言，表示把作品翻譯成某種語言；此處使用被動 be translated into。

transplant
[træns`plænt]

移植、移居
英解 to move an organ

例 In order to successfully **transplant** an organ, the donor and recipient must share certain genetic characteristics.

為了成功移植器官，捐贈者和接受者必須有共同的基因特徵。

語意用法 transplant ＋器官，表示移植器官。

transport
[træns`pɔrt]

運輸、搬運、放逐；亦作名詞用
英解 to convey

例 The new law would require that no checked bag be **transported** on a plane if its owner doesn't board the flight.（92 指考）

新法律要求，如果持有者沒有登機，已通關拖運的行李不得運上飛機。

語意用法 人＋ transport ＋物品＋ to ＋地點，表示將物品運送至某處；此處用被動 be transported。

tremble
[`trɛmbl]

戰慄、發抖、顫抖；亦作名詞用
英解 to shake as with fear

例 My girl **trembled** in fear when she watched *The Exorcist*.

我女朋友邊看大法師邊怕得發抖。

語意用法 tremble in fear，表示因害怕而發抖。

undertake
[ˌʌndə`tek]

著手進行、承擔、保證
英解 to accept and begin work on sth.

例 Therefore, government authorities usually **undertake** aggressive emergency control measures as soon as an outbreak is detected.（93 指考）

因此，政府當局一旦偵測疫情通常會採取緊急的控制措施。

語意用法 人＋ undertake ＋措施，表示採取措施。

unfold
[ʌn`fold]

打開、呈現、發生
英解 to open up

例 He **unfolded** the letter and read it.

他打開信封讀信。

語意用法 unfold ＋物品，表示打開某物品。

update
[ʌpˋdet]

更新、使現代化；亦作名詞用

英解 to make sth. current

例 The TV **updated** a news story on the typhoon coming to Taiwan.

電視上更新了一則颱風即將侵襲台灣的新聞。

語意用法 update ＋事物，表示更新某事物。

upload
[ʌpˋlod]

上載

英解 to transfer (data or programs)

例 My stupid computer crashed again before I could **upload** my report to the server.

我的笨電腦又再次掛了，我還未能把我的報告上傳到伺服器。

語意用法 upload ＋物，表示上傳某物。

upset
[ʌpˋsɛt]

顛覆、弄亂、擊敗、使心煩意亂；亦作形容詞用

英解 to distress or trouble sb.

例 I'm so sorry. I didn't mean to **upset** you.

抱歉，我無意讓你心煩。

語意用法 upset ＋人，表示使某人心煩意亂。

urbanize
[ˋɝbənˏaɪz]

城市化

英解 to make urban in nature or character

例 The city is incredibly **urbanized**, but beneath its modern appearance lies an unmistakable Thai-ness.（92 指考）

這座城市的都市化令人難以置信，然而在它現代化的外表下有著顯著的泰國特質。

語意用法 urbanized 在此處為修飾語，形容城市的都市化。

urge
[ɝdʒ]
驅策、力勸、激勵、慫恿；亦作名詞用
英解 to pressure

例 The project manager **urged** us to work overtime on Saturday, but he didn't require that we come in.

專案經理強烈建議我們週六加班，但他沒有要求我們一定要進辦公室。

語意用法 urge ＋人＋ to V，表示力勸某人去做某事。

vanish
[`vænɪʃ]
消失、絕跡
英解 to disappear

例 I was back at the car in less than five minutes but the girls had **vanished**!

（89 學測）

我不到五分鐘內就回到車上，但女孩們都消失了！

語意用法 人物事＋ vanish，表示某人事物消失了。

violate
[`vaɪəˌlet]
違反、侵犯、褻瀆
英解 to breach

例 They **violated** the law.

他們違反法律。

語意用法 人＋ violate ＋法律，表示某人犯法。

visualize
[`vɪʒuəˌlaɪz]
想像、顯現、形象化
英解 to picture sth. in the mind

例 When it snows, I like to **visualize** a vacation on a sunny beach.

下雪時，我喜歡想像自己身在陽光海灘度假。

語意用法 visualize ＋人＋ doing，表示想像某人做某事。

wake [wek]	喚醒、覺醒、警覺、覺悟 英解 to stop sleeping

例 It won't magically transport a student to school on time every day, but it just might make **waking** up a little easier.（90 學測）

它沒有神奇到可以每天將學生準時送達學校，只能讓起床變得比較容易。

語意用法 wake up 表示起床、醒來。

wander [ˋwɑndɚ]	流浪、徘徊、閒逛、漫遊 英解 to roam

例 If you have time after the conference, let's just **wander** around the city a little bit.

如果你在會後有時間，我們就在這城市閒晃一下吧。

語意用法 wander around，表示到處晃。

warn [wɔrn]	警告、告誡、提醒 英解 to caution

例 Doctors have repeatedly **warned** people of the serious effect of noise on their hearing.（85 學測）

醫生一直警告人們有關噪音影響聽力的嚴重性。

語意用法 warn ＋人＋ of ＋事情，表示警告某人某事。

wrap [ræp]	包裝、隱藏、纏繞、覆蓋；亦作名詞用 英解 to cover

例 The butcher **wrapped** the meat in waxed paper.

屠夫用蠟紙包肉。

語意用法 wrap ＋物＋ in ＋物，表示把某物包裹在某物裡。

yield
[jild]

產生、放棄、讓渡；亦作名詞用
英解 to produce sth. of value

例 It has consistently **yielded** many of the world's best distance runners.
（99 學測）

它持續造就出很多世上一流的長跑運動員。

語意用法 yield ＋人、物，表示產生出某人或某物。

名詞篇

▶ ▶ ▶ **Nouns**

agreement

abuse

ability

accident

advocate

admission

| **ability**
[əˋbɪlətɪ] | 能力、技能
英解 competence |

例 They respected the animals' endurance and hunting **ability**, and warriors prayed to hunt like them.（95 指考）

他們敬重動物的耐力與狩獵技能，戰士們都祈求擁有那樣的狩獵能力。

語意用法 ability + to V，表示有做某事的能力；ability + in/at/for ...，表示具有……的能力。

| **aborigine**
[æbəˋrɪdʒəni] | 原住民
英解 a native |

例 The **aborigines** of Australia have lived there for thousands of years.

澳洲原住民已經在那邊住了幾千年。

語意用法 the aborigines of + 地方，表示某地方的原住民。

| **abuse**
[əˋbjus] | 辱罵、濫用、虐待；亦作名詞用
英解 mistreatment |

例 The writer's purpose of writing this passage is to report a case of child **abuse**.（97 指考）

作者寫這篇文章主要是為了虐待兒童的案例報告。

語意用法 drug abuse 藥物濫用。

| **access**
[ˋæksɛs] | 接近、進入、使用、門路、存取
英解 the right to get into sth. |

例 **Access** to the laboratory is limited to researchers and safety inspectors.

（99 學測）

只有研究員和安檢人員可以進入研究室。

語意用法 access to + 地方或事物，表示可接近或使用該處所或事物。

accident
[ˈæksədənt]

事故、意外、偶然

英解 mishap

例 There is increasing scientific evidence that large cars cause more highway **accidents** than small cars.（84 學測）

愈來愈多的科學證據顯示，大型車造成的快速道路交通意外比小型車多。

語意用法 by accident，表示偶然發生；by accident of ...，表示因……而偶然發生。

accommodation
[əˌkɑməˈdeʃən]

住宿、適應、調節

英解 lodgings

例 **Accommodation** near the conference center is limited, so please book early.

會議中心附近的住宿有限，所以儘早預訂。

語意用法 reach an accommodation 取得和解，此處做住宿解。

account
[əˈkaʊnt]

解釋、說明

英解 a report about an event

例 The driver was seriously injured in the accident, and is not yet able to provide an **account** of what happened.

駕駛在意外中嚴重受傷，目前還未能描述事發經過。

語意用法 an account of ＋事件，表示描述某件事的經過。

acknowledgment
[əkˈnɑlɪdʒmənt]

確認、承認、感謝

英解 response

例 I received an **acknowledgment** of my order in the mail.

我收到確認訂單的郵件。

語意用法 in acknowledgment of ...，表示藉以感謝……。

activity
[æk`tɪvətɪ]

活動、行動、敏捷、消遣活動
英解 movement

例 Magic was the major daily **activity** for the pharaohs. （92 學測補）
魔術是法老每天主要的消遣活動。

語意用法 school activities 學校活動。

addict
[ə`dɪkt]

成癮成痴之人
英解 a devotee

例 David Smith refers to himself as having been "a clothes **addict**." （91 學測）
大衛史密斯提到自己曾是個「愛衣成痴」的人。

語意用法 drug addict 毒癮者；coffee addict 喝咖啡成癮的人。

admission
[əd`mɪʃən]

進入許可、門票、坦白、承認
英解 the right to enter a place

例 When she applied for **admission** to a local music school in 1917, she was turned down because she was black. （91 學測）
1917 年，當她申請進入一所當地的音樂學校時，因為身為黑人被拒絕入學。

語意用法 admission to/into ...，表示允許進入……。

adolescence
[ˌædḷ`ɛsṇs]

青少年時期、青春期
英解 the teenage years between puberty and adulthood

例 The NFW developed the project more than a decade ago to address the self-esteem problems that many girls experience when they enter **adolescence**. （98 指考）
NEF 早在十年多前已發展這項計畫，處理許多女孩進入青春期時都會經歷的自尊問題。

語意用法 adolescence 指青春期，puberty 指少年發育期，adult 指成年。

advance
[əd`væns]

進步、上進
英解 progress

例 The **advance** in medicine is quite impressive.

醫學上的進展令人印象深刻。

語意用法 the advance in (of) ＋領域或學科，表示某領域或學科的進步。

advantage
[əd`væntɪdʒ]

優勢、利益、好處
英解 superiority

例 One major **advantage** of the soybean as a food source is that it is cheap to produce.（92 學測補）

大豆作為食物來源的主要好處是生產成本低。

語意用法 advantage ＋ to，表示對某事有利；advantage ＋ of，表示某方面之優勢。

advocate
[`ædvəkɪt]

提倡者、擁護者；亦作動詞用
英解 a supporter

例 He has been a strong **advocate** of peace and justice.（99 指考）

他一直大力倡導和平與正義。

語意用法 advocate of ＋人或事，表示倡導擁護某人／事。

affection
[ə`fɛkʃən]

愛慕、感情、情愛
英解 warmth for sb.

例 During adulthood, the purchase, instead of the toy, is substituted for **affection**.（91 指考）

在成人期，購物取代了玩具，成為情感的替代品。

語意用法 affection for/toward ＋人，表示對某人的情愛。

agreement [əˋgrimənt]	同意、協議、一致 英解 a decision between two or more people

例 They may fill out an **agreement** spelling out who shoulders which responsibilities if a problem arises.（99 學測）

他們會填寫一份協議，說明清楚如果出現問題後的責任歸屬。

語意用法 in agreement with，表示一致同意；fill out an agreement 填寫同意書。

alarm [əˋlɑrm]	警報、警報器、鬧鐘；亦作動詞用 英解 a warning device

例 This is the new Projection **Alarm** Clock.（90 學測）

這就是新發明的投影鬧鐘。

語意用法 alarm clock 鬧鐘；take the alarm，表示對某事驚恐、警戒。

alliance [əˋlaɪəns]	聯盟、同盟國 英解 the act of allying or state of being allied

例 There is an **alliance** of labor unions opposing the bill.

有個工會聯盟反對該法案。

語意用法 in/an alliance with ...，表示與……結盟、合作。

amateur [ˋæməˌtʃʊr]	業餘從事者、外行人 英解 one engaging in a pursuit but lacking professional skill

例 They sent an **amateur** to negotiate the contract, so we got a really good deal.

他們派一個外行人來協商合約，所以我們談得一個好交易。

語意用法 an amateur at/in ＋方面，表示對某方面有業餘的研究興趣。

amount [ə`maʊnt]	總額、數量；亦作名詞用 英解 a total

例 Sales of rap music and videos each exceed that **amount**. （92 學測補）

饒舌音樂和錄影帶每種的銷量都超過那數量。

語意用法 the amount，表示數量；amount of，表示多少量。

analysis [ə`næləsɪs]	分析、解析 英解 a study

例 A new **analysis** of satellite-based data has given precisely the rate at which the country is losing size as it pushes northward against the Himalayas. （96 學測）

一項新的衛星數據分析已得出精確的比例，當這國家向北推向喜馬拉雅山，它的面積也逐漸縮小。

語意用法 an analysis of ＋事件或資料，表示分析某項資料或事件。

angle [`æŋgl]	角度、觀點、立場 英解 the figure formed by two lines diverging from a common point

例 When you take photos, you can move around to shoot the target object from different **angles**. （98 學測）

拍照時，你可以移動從各個不同的角度拍攝目標。

語意用法 an angle of 30 degrees 三十度的角。

anniversary [ˌænə`vɝsərɪ]	週年紀念、週年紀念日；亦作形容詞用 英解 the date on which an event occurred in some previous year

例 This year Lego fans all over the world are celebrating the 50th **anniversary** of the tiny building blocks. （97 指考）

今年全球的樂高迷共同慶祝這個小積木的 50 週年。

語意用法 the 50th anniversary of ＋事件，表示某事件的 50 週年紀念。

anxiety [æŋˋzaɪətɪ]	焦慮、掛念 英解 a state of uneasiness and apprehension

例 Depression, **anxiety**, and learning disabilities may co-exist with AD/
HD. (98 指考)

沮喪、焦慮以及學習障礙有可能與注意力不足 / 過動症並存。

語意用法 anxiety for ＋人事物，表示對人 / 事 / 物的渴望。

appeal [əˋpil]	感染力、吸引力、請求、呼籲；亦作動詞用 英解 attracting

例 If not eaten in a day or two, leftovers quickly lose their **appeal**.

如果沒在一、二天內吃掉，剩菜很快就會失去美味。

語意用法 appeal ＋ for，表示懇求某事 / 物；appeal ＋ to，表示訴之於某物。

appetite [ˋæpəˌtaɪt]	食慾、胃口 英解 desire and capacity for food

例 Eating dessert before meals may kill your **appetite**. (91 學測補)

飯前吃甜食可能會讓你失去食慾。

語意用法 appetite for ＋事物，表示對某事物的渴求或有胃口。

applause [əˋplɔz]	鼓掌、喝采 英解 hand clapping in approval of a performance

例 As the **applause** died down, the curtain on the stage dropped slowly.

(90 學測)

隨著掌聲漸漸平息，舞台上的幕緩緩落下。

語意用法 enthusiastic applause 熱烈的掌聲；win applause 博得掌聲。

appliance
[ə`plaɪəns]

器材、裝備、用具
英解 a machine or device

例 We decided to buy some **appliances** for our new apartment, including a refrigerator, a vacuum cleaner, and a dishwasher.（98 指考）
我們決定為我們的公寓添購一些冰箱、吸塵器和洗碗機之類的用具。

語意用法 household appliances，表示家庭用品；medical appliances，表示醫療用品。

approval
[ə`pruvl]

批准、許可
英解 permission

例 Building codes are still waiting **approval**.（93 指考補）
建築法規在等待批准中。

語意用法 for sb.'s approval，表示求得某人的同意。

architect
[`ɑrkə,tɛkt]

建築師
英解 a person qualified to design buildings and to superintend their erection

例 Fifty years ago, teams of **architects** began restoring the historic treasures of the city.（94 學測）
五十年前，建築團隊開始修復這座城市的歷史珍寶。

語意用法 the architect of ＋建築物，表示某個建築物的建築師或設計師。

artist
[`ɑrtɪst]

藝術家、畫家、大師
英解 a person who creates art

例 He was trained to be an **artist** though he wanted to be a poet.（98 指考）
他被栽培成一位藝術家，但他想成為的卻是詩人。

語意用法 an artist at/in ＋方面，表示為某方面的專家、藝術家。

award
[əˋwɔrd]

獎項、獎品

例 The many **awards** that Professor Wang has won over the years are clear evidence that he is a distinguished scholar.（92 學測補）
王教授歷年來獲頒無數的獎項，證明了他是一名卓越的學者。

語意用法 win the award 獲得獎項。

associate
[əˋsoʃɪˌet]

合夥人、同事、伙伴；亦作動詞用
英解 a companion

例 My **associate** and I work for the city government.
我和我的同事幫市政府工作。

語意用法 management associate 儲備幹部。

astronaut
[ˋæstrəˌnɔt]

太空人
英解 a person who flies into outer space

例 **Astronauts** often work 16 hours a day on the space shuttle in order to complete all the projects set out for the mission.（95 學測）
太空人為了完成所有的任務在太空艙內經常一天工作 16 個小時。

語意用法 Chinese astronauts 中國太空人

athlete
[ˋæθlit]

運動員、運動家
英解 a person trained to compete in sports

例 The Paralympics are Olympic-style games for **athletes** with a disability.
（98 學測）
殘障奧運是專為殘障人士所設的仿奧林匹克運動會。

語意用法 amateur athlete 業餘運動員；professional athlete 專業運動員。

atmosphere [ˈætməsˌfɪr]	大氣層、空氣、氛圍 英解 the air space above the earth

例 The space shuttle glides through the **atmosphere**. (95 學測)

太空梭穿過大氣層滑行。

> 語意用法 the atmosphere，表示大氣層；atmosphere of ...，表示某種環境。

attitude [ˈætətjud]	態度、姿勢、意見、看法 英解 a position of the body or manner of carrying oneself

例 Mr. Johnson was disappointed at his students for having a passive learning **attitude**. (95 學測)

詹森老師對他的學生們被動的學習態度感到失望。

> 語意用法 attitude to/toward ＋人或事，表示對某人的態度、對某事的看法。

auction [ˈɔkʃən]	拍賣、競叫橋牌；亦作動詞用 英解 a public sale of goods or property

例 When a lot of dead mail has piled up, the dead mail offices hold public **auctions**. (89 學測)

當大量過期郵件堆積成山，過期郵件辦公室就會舉辦公開拍賣會。

> 語意用法 public auction 公開拍賣。

audience [ˈɔdɪəns]	聽眾、觀眾、讀者群 英解 a group of spectators or listeners

例 This talk show, on the whole, is quite popular with the **audience**. (91 學測補)

整體而言，這個脫口秀節目相當受到觀眾的歡迎。

> 語意用法 be received in audience 召見；have an audience with 拜見。

author [`ɔθɚ]	作家、作者 英解 a person who writes books as a profession

例 Sometimes **authors** write about these things to entertain readers. （88 學測）

有時作家會寫這類的題材來娛樂讀者。

語意用法 best-selling author 暢銷作家；prolific author 多產作家。

authority [ə`θɔrətɪ]	權力、職權、官方、權威人士、依據、判例、授權書 英解 the power or right to control, judge, or prohibit the actions of others

例 Deputies were given **authority** to make arrests.

代理人被賦予拘捕權。

語意用法 with authority 憑藉某人的威信；authority ＋ to V，表示做某事的權限。

aviation [ˌevɪ`eʃən]	航空、航空業、飛行 英解 the operation of aircraft

例 The **aviation** industry is extremely sensitive to oil prices.

航空業對於油價相當敏感。

語意用法 aviation safety 航空安全；aviation experts 航空專家。

background [`bæk,graʊnd]	背景、遠因 英解 a backdrop

例 They often concern very strong or clever people who come from humble **backgrounds**. （91 學測補）

他們往往關注非常強壯或很聰明卻出身卑微的人。

語意用法 keep ＋人＋ stay in the background，表示隱身幕後活動。

| **bacteria**
[bæk`tɪrɪə] | 細菌（複數）
英解 a very large group of microorganisms comprising one of the three domains of living organisms |

例 Colds are caused by viruses, not **bacteria**, so taking medicine is absolutely no use at all.（91 學測補）

感冒是由病毒而非細菌引起，吃藥一點用也沒有。

語意用法 harmful bacteria 害菌；beneficial bacteria 益菌。

| **baggage**
[`bægɪdʒ] | 行李、裝備
英解 luggage |

例 The flight attendants are supposed to help passengers move their **baggage**.

空服員應該幫乘客搬行李。

語意用法 carry-on baggage 隨身行李；baggage claim 提領行李。

| **balance**
[`bæləns] | 平衡、協調、結餘；亦作動詞用
英解 the ability to stand |

例 The mind and body work together to produce stress, which is a bodily response to a stimulus, a response that disturbs the body's normal physiological **balance**.（94 學測）

腦和身體共同運作產生壓力，一種肉體對某種刺激的回應，藉以擾亂人體生理的正常平衡。

語意用法 strike a balance 尋求兩者間的公平解決辦法、妥協。

| **bankruptcy**
[`bæŋkrʌptsɪ] | 破產者；亦作動詞與形容詞用
英解 a person without money or credit |

例 The number of business **bankruptcies** in the US is expected to exceed 50,000 again this year.

美國今年破產的企業預計會再次超過五萬。

語意用法 go into bankruptcy 破產。

bargain
[`bɑrgɪn]

協議、議價、交易、特價品；亦作動詞用
英解 a deal

例 I got a **bargain** when I bought that suit for half price.

我用半價買到那套衣服，很划算。

語意用法 at a bargain 以特價地。

barrier
[`bærɪə]

障礙物、路障、柵欄
英解 an obstacle

例 A tree fell across the road and made a **barrier** to traffic.

有棵倒下的樹橫亙在路上造成交通阻塞。

語意用法 cross the barrier of ... 跨越……的障礙；put a barrier between 挑撥離間。

behalf
[bɪ`hæf]

代表、利益
英解 as the representative of

例 I'd like to thank you for your hospitality on **behalf** of our group.（89 學測）

我僅代表我們集團感謝你的熱情招待。

語意用法 on behalf of ... 代表……。

behavior
[bɪ`hevjə]

行為、舉止、態度
英解 a way of acting

例 John's reckless **behavior** gave rise to endless trouble for his parents.

（86 學測）

約翰魯莽的行為替他父母帶來無止盡的麻煩。

語意用法 good behavior 好的行為；unusual behavior 不尋常的行為。

belief [brˋlif]	相信、信念、信仰 英解 a conviction

例 The war challenged his naive **belief** that people are essentially good.

戰爭挑戰了他人性本善的天真信仰。

語意用法 strong belief 強烈的信仰。

benefit [ˋbɛnəfɪt]	利益、好處、津貼；亦作動詞用 英解 gain

例 The **benefits** include an easier visibility of the time, and an alarm that gets increasingly louder until turned off.（90 學測）

好處包括可以更清楚看見時間，還有鬧鐘會越來越大聲直到關掉。

語意用法 for the benefit of ... 為了……的利益。

billion [ˋbɪljən]	十億（美、法）、萬億（英、德） 英解 one thousand million

例 It is reported that hip-hop fashion alone generates $750 million to $1 **billion** annually.（92 學測補）

根據報導，光嘻哈時尚每年即可產生 7.5 億到 10 億的收益。

語意用法 billions of ... 數目龐大的……。

biology [barˋɑlədʒɪ]	生物學 英解 the science and study of life

例 Later in the afternoon, Nelson came to Adam's office with Peter for their **biology** project.（88 學測）

下午稍後，尼爾森和彼得為了他們的生物學計畫案去到亞當的辦公室。

語意用法 human biology 人類生物學；biology class 生物課。

blessing [ˋblɛsɪŋ]	賜福、祈福、祝福、禱告 英解 an act of making sth. holy

例 It is a **blessing** to have good health.

健康就是福。

語意用法 a blessing in disguise 塞翁失馬。

blog [blɔg]	部落格 英解 a shared on-line journal where people can post diary entries

例 If you have a small business **blog**, you should be aware of the ways you can use your blog to drive traffic to your Website.

如果你有一個小型商務部落格，你應該知道如何利用你的部落格增加網站的流覽率。

語意用法 blog post 網誌貼文；personal blog 個人的網誌。

board [bord]	木板、甲板、黑板、委員會；亦作動詞用 英解 a thin, flat piece of wood

例 Tim felt it would be safer to stay on **board** the boat. (91 學測)

提姆認為留在甲板上比較安全。

語意用法 across the board 全面地、一律地。

boarding [ˋbordɪŋ]	寄膳、登機、上船 英解 the act of embarking on an aircraft, train, ship, etc

例 **Boarding** was delayed because of a mechanical problem with the plane.

由於飛機的機械問題延遲登機。

語意用法 delay boarding 延遲登機；boarding pass 登機證。

border [`bɔrdə]	邊界、國界、邊緣;亦作動詞用 英解 a boundary

例 Thanks to gloablization and the Internet, national **borders** are less important than ever before.

由於全球化與網路,國界已不若以往重要。

語意用法 on the border of ... 在……的邊緣。

borderline [`bɔrdə͵laɪn]	邊緣、邊界;形容詞作邊境上的、不明確的解 英解 a line that establishes or marks a border

例 When the colonies became independent nations, these same **borderlines** were often maintained.（97 指考）

當殖民地變成獨立國家,所有的邊界通常會依原樣保留。

語意用法 (right) on the borderline（就在）邊緣上。

breakdown [`brek͵daʊn]	故障、病倒、衰退、崩潰 英解 a malfunction

例 The truck had a **breakdown** on the highway.

卡車在快速道路上故障了。

語意用法 a nervous breakdown 神經衰弱。

breakthrough [`brek͵θru]	突破性發展、突圍 英解 an advance

例 The discovery of the new vaccine is an important **breakthrough** in the fight against avian flu.（95 指考）

新發現的疫苗用來對抗禽流感是一項很重大的突破。

語意用法 breakthrough in ... 在……有突破的發展。

breath [brɛθ]	呼吸、氣息、微風、氣音 英解 an inhalation

例 She opened her mouth and took a deep **breath**.

她張開嘴深深吸了口氣。

語意用法 take a deep breath 深呼吸；out of breath 上氣不接下氣；at/in a breath 一口氣地。

breeze [briz]	微風、謠傳、輕而易舉之事；亦作動詞用 英解 a light wind

例 The **breeze** felt good on a hot day.

熾熱天氣裡的微風令人感到舒爽。

語意用法 a gentle breeze 柔風；a strong breeze 勁風。

brochure [bro`ʃʊr]	小冊子 英解 a pamphlet or booklet

例 Students interested in such matters should read the **brochure** of Arnold Bentham soon to be published.

對這類主題有興趣的學生應該讀阿諾德邊沁即將出版的小冊子。

語意用法 the brochure of ＋事物或人，表示某事物或人的小冊子。

brush [brʌʃ]	刷子、毛筆、刷狀物 英解 a tool made of bristles on a hard back

例 Besides historical figures, landscape painting was also common in Chinese **brush** painting.（93 指考）

除了歷史人物，風景畫也常見於中國水墨畫中。

語意用法 brush painting 水墨畫；tooth brush 牙刷。

| **budget** [ˋbʌdʒɪt] | 經費、預算；亦作動詞用 英解 a plan of expected income and expenses over time |

例 After all, you must live within a limited **budget**.（95 學測）

畢竟你必須依靠有限的經費過活。

語意用法 budget for ＋事件，表示為某事件編列的預算。

| **bulletin** [ˋbʊlətɪn] | 公報、公告、新聞快報 英解 a newsletter |

例 A TV news **bulletin** said there is a big earthquake in Nantou.

電視上的新聞快報說南投發生大地震。

語意用法 news bulletin 新聞公告；bulletin board 佈告欄。

| **business** [ˋbɪznɪs] | 職業、商業、交易、行業、本分 英解 the occupation, work, or trade in which a person is engaged |

例 In the early 1600s, tea was introduced to Europe due to **business**.（95 學測）

十七世紀初，茶葉因為商業因素被引進歐洲。

語意用法 go out of business 停業；get down to business 專心從事工作；business is brisk 生意興隆。

| **calendar** [ˋkæləndə] | 日曆、月曆、日程表 英解 a chart of the days and months of a year or years |

例 Maybe the lines were to carry water for farming, or were used as a **calendar**.（95 指考）

也許這些線條是用來引水灌溉或是作為日曆。

語意用法 the solar calendar 陽曆；the lunar calendar 陰曆。

campaign
[kæm`pen]

活動、戰役；亦作動詞與形容詞用
英解 an organized effort by people to reach a goal

例 The French government plans to promote the program with an advertising **campaign** aimed at young readers and their parents. (99 指考)
法國政府計畫針對青少年讀者以及他們的父母推出廣告活動促進該方案。

語意用法 campaign ＋ to V，表示做某事的活動；campaign against/for ＋事物，表示反對 / 支持某事物的活動。

candidate
[`kændədet]

候選人、應試者
英解 a person running for a political office

例 The successful **candidate**, usually aged two or three, was then removed from his family to Lhasa to begin spiritual training for his future role. (93 學測)
勝出的候選人通常介於二、三歲，之後被帶離開家前往拉薩，開始為他將來的角色進行精神訓練。

語意用法 a candidate for ＋職位，表示某職位之候選人；a candidate for fame，表示未來可能成為名人。

capacity
[kə`pæsətɪ]

能力、能量、才能、資格、容積
英解 the ability to contain

例 No doubt his ability to listen contributed to his **capacity** to write. (88 學測)
無庸置疑，他善於傾聽的能力對他的寫作能力有所貢獻。

語意用法 a capacity ＋ to V，表示有做某事的能力。

capital
[`kæpətl]

首都、首府
英解 the official place where a government located

例 The world's largest collection of Khmer sculpture resides at Angkor, the former royal **capital** of Cambodia. (94 指考)
世上最大的高棉雕塑聚集地在吳哥，柬埔寨的前皇朝首府。

語意用法 the capital of ＋國家，表示某國家的首都。

carbon
[ˋkɑrbən]

碳
英解 the chemical element found in coal

例 **Carbon** dioxide is produced during the process of decomposition.（88 學測）
二氧化碳是在分解的過程中產生的。

語意用法 carbon dioxide 二氧化碳；carbon monoxide 一氧化碳。

career
[kəˋrɪr]

職業、職業生涯
英解 a life's work

例 He began his **career** as a zoologist, studying mollusks and their adaptations to the environment.（94 指考）
他開始了他的動物學家職業生涯，研究軟體動物以及它們對環境的適應力。

語意用法 make a career of ＋行業，表示以某行為職業；begin one's career 開始某人的生涯。

castle
[ˋkæsl̩]

城堡、城堡式建築
英解 a large building with thick walls and other defenses against attack

例 Bam was a city of mud-brick houses, old monuments, and an ancient **castle**.（94 學測）
巴姆是一座泥磚造的城市，有老舊的紀念碑以及古老的城堡。

語意用法 an ancient castle 古老城堡。

category
[ˋkætəˏgorɪ]

種類、部門、範疇
英解 a group or type of thing

例 Tablet computers are expected to be the fastest growing **category** of consumer electronics next year.
平板電腦預計是下一年度成長最快的電子消費產品類別。

語意用法 a category of ＋物，表示某物品的種類，如：a category of musical instrument 樂器的種類。

145

caution
[ˋkɔʃən]

小心、謹慎、告誡

英解 concern about not making a mistake

例 Foreign stocks can offer huge returns, but investors should proceed with **caution**.

海外股票可以提供很大的收益,但投資者要小心進行。

語意用法 caution in +方面,表示在某方面謹慎;caution of/about +事物,表示對於某事物多加小心、留意。

cell
[sɛl]

細胞

英解 the basic unit of living things

例 Researchers at Purdue University recently concluded that a compound in green tea slows down the growth of cancer **cells**. (97 學測)

普渡大學的研究人員最近推斷出綠茶裡的化合物可以減緩癌細胞的成長。

語意用法 cancer cells 癌症細胞。

center
[ˋsɛntə]

中央、中樞、中心、核心

英解 the middle

例 The language **center** in the brain that is believed to control speech production is called Broca's area. (95 學測)

被視為掌管說話的大腦語言中心稱為布洛卡氏區。

語意用法 the center,表示場所中央;center of ...,表示……的核心、焦點。

ceremony
[ˋsɛrəˏmonɪ]

典禮、儀式

英解 a formal event usu. with rituals

例 At City Hall, Mayor Abraham Beame hosted a news conference that turned into a **ceremony** in George Willig's honor. (83 學測)

市長亞伯拉罕比姆在市政廳舉辦的記者會變成表揚喬治威利格的典禮。

語意用法 a ceremony in one's honor 表揚某人的典禮。

146

certainty
[ˋsɝtəntɪ]

確實、必然
英解 a certitude

例 With the bad weather, it is a **certainty** that the planes will not fly.

遇到壞天候飛機必然無法起飛。

語意用法 certainty of ...，表示對……有把握。

certificate
[səˋtɪfəkɪt]

證書、執照、結業證書
英解 a formal document that offers proof of sth.

例 Nowadays people have to pass various tests for professional **certificates** so that they can be qualified for a well-paid job.

現在的人必須通過各種專業認證考試來使自己有資格勝任高薪的工作。

語意用法 professional certificates 專業證照。

channel
[ˋtʃænl]

頻道、水道、海峽、途徑、溝渠
英解 a TV station's place on the dial and its broadcasts of news, sports, etc.

例 In Taiwan, some cable TV companies have up to 70 or 80 **channels**.

台灣有些有線電視的頻道已經高達七、八十台了。

語意用法 TV channels 電視頻道。

chaos
[ˋkeɑs]

混亂、雜亂一團
英解 mass confusion

例 It's difficult for most of us to imagine what life is like in countries where diamonds are the source of so much **chaos** and suffering.（96 指考）

對於我們大部分的人來說，難以想像在那些鑽石帶來混亂與痛苦的國家的生活。

語意用法 in utter chaos 處於一團混亂中。

character
[ˋkærɪktə]

角色、性格、人物
英解 a person in a novel, play, or film

例 Paintings of historical **characters** and stories of everyday life became extremely popular.（93 指考）

歷史人物的畫作以及日常生活的故事變得極受歡迎。

語意用法 fictional characters 小說虛構的人物；historical characters 歷史人物。

charity
[ˋtʃærətɪ]

慈善團體、慈悲、施捨、善舉
英解 an organization that helps poor people

例 They give all the money they earn to **charity**.

他們將賺得的錢全給了慈善機構。

語意用法 charity work 慈善工作；charity organization 慈善機構。

charlatan
[ˋʃɑrlətn̩]

庸醫、吹噓之人
英解 a quack

例 Most witch doctors are guaranteed to be **charlatans**, not real doctors, who go after some quick money from tourists.（95 指考）

那些想在遊客身上打撈一筆的巫醫，絕大部分都是江湖術士，不是真正的醫生。

語意用法 call sb. a charlatan 指稱某人為密醫

charm
[tʃɑrm]

魅力、魔力、可愛；亦作動詞用
英解 the ability to please, attractiveness

例 Chester was not a handsome man, but he won her over with his **charm**.

契斯特不是個帥氣的人，但他用他的魅力贏得她的芳心。

語意用法 natural charm 自然的魅力；resist sb.'s charms 抗拒某人的魅力

chisel [ˋtʃɪzl̩]	鑿子;亦作動詞用
	英解 a metal tool with V-shaped point for cutting wood or stone

例 Ice sculptors use razor-sharp **chisels** that are specifically designed for cutting ice. （97 學測）

冰雕家使用專門特製用來冰雕的剃刀狀鑿子。

語意用法 ice chisel 冰雕鑿子。

cholesterol [kəˋlɛstəˌrol]	膽固醇
	英解 a slippery white crystal-like substance found in the body

例 Research shows that consuming a minimum of 25 grams of soy protein a day can lower blood **cholesterol** levels in people with high cholesterol problems. （92 學測補）

研究指出,每天食用最少 25 公克的大豆蛋白,有高膽固醇問題的人可以降低血液裡的膽固醇濃度。

語意用法 high cholesterol 高膽固醇。

chore [tʃor]	家事、例行工作
	英解 a boring but necessary act

例 How did you talk your sister into doing the **chores** for you? （91 學測補）

妳怎麼說服妳姊妹幫妳做家事?

語意用法 do the chores 做家事雜務。

circle [ˋsɝkl̩]	圓圈、環狀物、循環;亦作動詞用
	英解 a closed curved line whose every point is equally far from the center

例 The building is a symphony of triangles, ovals, arcs, **circles**, and squares. （93 指考）

這棟建築是由三角形、橢圓形、弧形、圓形以及方形和諧地組成。

語意用法 circle 圓圈;in a circle 成圓形地。

circumstance
[ˋsɝkəmˌstæns]

情勢、情況、境遇

英解 a condition that affects sth. else

例 Firstborns, under normal **circumstances**, are usually the most strongly motivated toward achievement. （92 學測補）

正常情況下，長子長女們通常具有最強烈的成就動機取向。

語意用法 under ... circumstance 在……狀況之下；from unavoidable circumstances 在無可避免的狀況下。

citizen
[ˋsɪtəzn̩]

市民、公民

英解 a legal member of a country, state, or city

例 Only R.O.C. **citizens** are allowed to vote in elections in Taiwan.

在台灣只有中華民國國民可以在選舉時投票。

語意用法 citizens of the world 世界公民。

civilization
[ˌsɪvl̩əˋzeʃən]

文明、文明國家、文明化

英解 a high level of government, laws, written language, art, music, etc., within a society or culture

例 The Maya, Aztec, and Inca **civilizations** all built amazing temples and pyramids.

瑪雅、阿茲特克、印加文明全都建造了讓人歎為觀止的寺廟和金字塔。

語意用法 ancient civilization 古老文明；Chinese civilization 中國文明。

client
[ˋklaɪənt]

客戶、顧客、委託人

英解 a customer of sb. who provides a professional service

例 They were trying to settle details of an important new plant site for a major **client**. （86 學測）

他們試著替一名主要客戶重要的新廠區安排細節。

語意用法 a client of our bank 我們銀行的客戶。

clue
[klu]

線索、跡象、提示、情節；亦作動詞用
英解 evidence

例 These experiments provide some **clues** about the interactions between body rhythms, learning and memory. (99 指考)

這些實驗為肢體節奏與學習、記憶間的交互影響提供了一些線索。

語意用法 clues to/about ＋事件，表示某事件的線索。

code
[kod]

密碼、代碼、法規、規範
英解 a system of signals used to represent letters or numbers in transmitting messages

例 Recognizing the flashing **code** of her own species, a female signals back to the male, and he lands beside her. (93 學測)

識別出她同類的閃爍訊號，雌性回應訊號給雄性，雄性於是降落在雌性旁。

語意用法 international code 國際電碼；code book 密碼簿；civil code 民法。

commitment
[kə`mɪtmənt]

承諾、決定
英解 a promise

例 An honest person is faithful to his promise. Once he makes a **commitment**, he will not go back on his own word. (96 指考)

一個誠實的人會信守自己的諾言。他一旦許下承諾就不會食言。

語意用法 commitment ＋ to V，表示約定做某事；make a commitment 承諾。

committee
[kə`mɪtɪ]

委員會
英解 a group of people organized for a purpose

例 To have a full discussion of the issue, the **committee** spent a whole hour exchanging their ideas at the meeting. (98 學測)

為了讓議題得到充分討論，委員會花了整整一小時的會議時間交流想法。

語意用法 audit committee 審計委員會。

communication
[kə‚mjunə`keʃən]

溝通、交流、傳達、傳染
英解 an act of passing on information, feelings, etc.

例 Email, instant messaging, and other forms of electronic **communication** have almost completely replaced the handwritten letter.
電子郵件、即時通和其他形式的電子溝通幾乎完全取代了手寫信件。
語意用法 mass communication 大眾傳播。

community
[kə`mjunətɪ]

社區、公眾、聚落、社群
英解 the people as a group in a town, city, or other area

例 The term "standard of living" usually refers to the economic well-being enjoyed by a person, family, **community**, or nation.（92 學測補）
所謂「生活水準」通常是指個人、家庭、社區或國家所享受的經濟福利。
語意用法 community center 社區中心；community college 社區大學。

companion
[kəm`pænjən]

同伴、伴侶
英解 a person who goes with another person

例 John was her **companion** on the trip to Europe.
約翰是她這趟歐洲行的旅伴。
語意用法 companion 指的是同伴、夥伴，與 friend 不同。

company
[`kʌmpənɪ]

公司、同伴、陪伴
英解 a business

例 Jack and a few of his friends set up a **company** called "Jack's Disk Doctor Service" in 1984.（86 學測）
1984 年，傑克和幾個朋友創立了一家名為「傑克磁碟維修醫師」的公司。
語意用法 limited company 有限公司，常簡寫成 Co., Ltd.；keep sb. company 陪伴某人。

compass
[ˋkʌmpəs]

羅盤、指南針
英解 a device to determine direction

例 The closer you get to the North Pole, the less reliable **compasses** become.

你越接近北極，羅盤會變得越不可靠。

語意用法 compass bearing 羅盤方位；moral compass 道德準則。

compassion
[kəmˋpæʃən]

憐憫、同情、關懷
英解 sympathy for sb.

例 Fashion can go hand in hand with **compassion** for life.（96 學測）

時尚和對生命的關懷可以息息相關。

語意用法 have compassion on/upon/for ...，表示對……寄予同情或關懷。

competitor
[kəmˋpɛtətə]

競爭者、對手、敵手
英解 a person or team that participates in sports

例 He set out to beat all the other **competitors**.（96 指考）

他開始大展身手擊敗所有敵手。

語意用法 compete 競爭；competition 競爭。

completion
[kəmˋpliʃən]

完成、結束
英解 the act of completing or the state of being completed

例 Both Guggenheim and Wright would die before the building's 1995 **completion**.（93 指考）

古根漢與萊特二人於 1995 年建築完工前過世。

語意用法 bring completion to ...，表示做完某事。

compliment
[ˋkɑmpləmənt]

稱讚、恭維、致意;亦作動詞用
英解 a useful, appropriate addition to sth.

例 He's always paying her **compliments**.

他總是給予她讚美。

語意用法 pay one's compliment 對某人讚美。

concept
[ˋkɑnsɛpt]

概念、觀念、想法
英解 a general idea that usu. includes other related ideas

例 First quarter sales were terrible, so we asked an advertising agency to come up with some **concepts** for a new commercial.

第一季的銷售很慘,所以我們請廣告商提出幾個新廣告的概念。

語意用法 concept of ＋物,表示某物的概念。

condition
[kənˋdɪʃən]

狀況、情況、條件、形勢;亦作動詞用
英解 the state of sth.

例 Climbing the most difficult mountains requires a very special mental **condition**. (86 學測)

攀登最難爬的山需要具備非常特殊的精神狀況。

語意用法 condition ＋ to V,表示做某事的狀態。

conference
[ˋkɑnfərəns]

會議、討論會、協商會
英解 a professional meeting

例 Many scholars and experts from all over the world will be invited to attend this yearly **conference** on drug control. (93 學測)

許多學者和專家將從世界各地應邀來參加這場藥品管制的年度大會。

語意用法 in conference 在會議中;a peace conference 和平會議。

confidence
[ˋkɑnfədəns]

自信、信心、信賴、把握
英解 belief in one's abilities, self-esteem

例 She has had great **confidence** in herself since childhood.（97 指考）

她從孩童時代起就很有自信。

語意用法 have confidence in ＋事情或人，表示對某事或某人很有信心。

conflict
[ˋkɑnflɪkt]

衝突、抵制、爭執、分歧
英解 an argument

例 **Conflicts** have arisen over the way in which ethnic groups were split apart and thrown together.（97 指考）

各種族分化又融合，衝突因而產生。

語意用法 in conflict with ＋人，表示與某人產生衝突。

congestion
[kənˋdʒɛstʃən]

擁擠、壅塞
英解 a condition of overcrowding

例 As close to nature as one gets in New York, the park offered relief from the noise and **congestion** of the city.（93 指考）

在紐約沒有比這座公園更接近自然的地方，它遠離了城市的擁擠與喧囂。

語意用法 traffic congestion 交通壅塞。

conjunction
[kənˋdʒʌŋkʃən]

結合、連接、連接詞
英解 together with

例 In **conjunction** with the Health Ministry and the Malaria Center, The National Daily News will distribute the news to the most affected areas of the country.

結合衛生部與瘧疾中心，國家日報將消息傳給這個國家感染最嚴重的區域。

語意用法 in conjunction with ... 與……有關連或結合。

consciousness
[ˈkɑnʃəsnɪs]

知覺、意識、意念、感覺
英解 the state of being awake

例 It seems not unlike any afternoon in the village, but all of a sudden, people and animals lose **consciousness**. (91 學測)

與這個村莊平日的下午沒有任何不同，但突然地，所有的人和動物全都失去了意識。

語意用法 lose consciousness 喪失意識與知覺。

consequence
[ˈkɑnsəˌkwɛns]

結果、重要、推論、必然
英解 the result of doing sth.

例 Unfortunately, without the threat of **consequences**, students are just not changing their behavior. (98 指考)

遺憾的是，沒有嚴重的威脅，學生就是不會改變行為。

語意用法 ... of consequence 有嚴重後果的……；give consequence to ... 重視……；in consequence of ＋原因，表示由於某原因造成的結果。

contempt
[kənˈtɛmpt]

輕視、藐視
英解 scorn

例 She has **contempt** for anyone who is not as intelligent as she is.

她輕視每一個不像她那般聰明的人。

語意用法 with contempt 輕蔑地；show contempt for ... 對……表示輕視。

contest
[ˈkɑntɛst]

競賽、比賽；亦作動詞用
英解 a competition

例 Michael Phelps, an American swimmer, broke seven world records and won eight gold medals in men's swimming **contests** in the 2008 Olympics. (99 學測)

美國泳將邁克菲爾普斯在 2008 年的奧運會中破了七項世界記錄，並贏得八枚男子游泳競賽項目的金牌。

語意用法 swimming contest 游泳比賽；win a contest 贏得比賽。

context
[ˋkɑntɛkst]

上下文、文章脈絡、來龍去脈

英解 that precede and follow a word or passage and contribute to its full meaning

例 A good reader can often figure out what new words mean by using **context**.（83 學測）

一個善於閱讀的人往往能夠藉由上下文來理解新單字的意思。

語意用法 in the context 在此文章脈絡之中，就此而論；out of context 斷章取義。

control
[kənˋtrol]

控制、統治、管理

英解 in charge

例 They were the last animals killed in the park's wolf **control** programs.

（95 指考）

他們是公園內狼群控管計畫中最後被殺的動物。

語意用法 control of/over ... 管制、監督……。

convenience
[kənˋvinjəns]

便利、方便、合宜

英解 a situation suitable to one's time or needs

例 Many Internet users sacrifice their privacy for the **convenience** of using online tools that collect and sell personal information.

許多網路使用者為了線上工具的便利而犧牲了隱私，這些線上工具可能收集和販賣個人資料。

語意用法 convenience store 便利商店，如 7-11；as a matter of convenience 為了方便。

conversation
[ˌkɑnvəˋseʃən]

會話、談話

英解 a talk

例 With friendly smiles, he could easily get into **conversation** with strangers.

帶著友善的微笑，他很容易與陌生人攀談。

語意用法 be in conversation with sb.，表示與某人交談中。

copyright
[ˋkɑpɪˌraɪt]

著作權、版權

英解 ownership of written or visual material

例 Mike Lewinski paid US$4,000 to settle a lawsuit against him for **copyright** violation.（98 指考）

邁克李文斯基付了 4 千美元解決他的侵害版權官司。

語意用法 a book copyright 書的版權。

courtesy
[ˋkɝtəsɪ]

禮貌、殷勤

英解 good manners

例 When you enter a building, be sure to look behind you and hold the door open for someone coming through the same door. It is a common **courtesy** in many cultures.（96 指考）

當你進入一棟建築，記得看看後面並幫要進同扇門的人把門開著。在眾多文化中，這是一種很普遍的禮節。

語意用法 by courtesy 禮貌上。

craft
[kræft]

工藝；亦作動詞用

英解 a skilled trade

例 The industrial revolution destroyed the weavers' **craft**, and the family had to leave for new possibilities in America.（96 指考）

工業革命摧毀了編織工藝，家族必須前往美國尋找新的發展性。

語意用法 with great craft 以卓越的技術。

crash
[kræʃ]

墜毀、對撞、當機；亦作動詞用

英解 a smashup

例 A lot of passengers were killed in the plane **crash**.

許多乘客在飛機墜毀中喪生。

語意用法 plane crash 飛機墜毀。

credit
[ˈkrɛdɪt]

信用、學分
英解 a cause for admiration

例 The editor worked on the book for a year, but the writer, who spent less than a month writing it, got all the **credit**.

編輯在這本書花了一年時間，但作者只花了不到一個月的時間並得到所有好處。

語意用法 credit card 信用卡。

crisis
[ˈkraɪsɪs]

危機、轉折、伏筆
英解 an emergency

例 If all the manufacturers can hang on during this financial **crisis**, the economy may get better next quarter. (98 學測)

假使所有的製造業者能夠撐過這次的金融危機，下一季的經濟可能會轉好。

語意用法 pass the crisis 或 survive the crisis，表示度過危機。

critique
[krɪˈtik]

評論
英解 a formal evaluation of sth.

例 I wrote a **critique** of a novel for my English class.

我為了英文課寫了一篇小說評論文。

語意用法 offer a critique of sth. 提供某物的評論；a devastating critique 激烈的評論；a thorough critique 詳細的評論。

cruelty
[ˈkruəltɪ]

殘忍、殘酷
英解 an act of causing others mental or physical pain

例 Many people want to protect animals and live their lives without causing unnecessary **cruelty**. (96 學測)

很多人想要保護動物並避免造成不必要的殘酷行徑地過自己的生活。

語意用法 an act of cruelty 殘酷的行為；cruelties 暴行。

名詞篇

cultivation
[ˌkʌltəˈveʃən]

耕作、栽培
英解 preparation of land

例 Java developed tea **cultivation** earlier than India. (94 學測)

爪哇比印度更早發展茶葉培植。

語意用法 land under cultivation 開墾地。

---

culture
[ˈkʌltʃɚ]

文化
英解 the total of the inherited ideas, beliefs and values which become the shared bases of social action

例 Fashion designer Tommy Hilfiger was fully aware of the power of youth **culture**. (92 學測補)

時裝設計師湯米‧希爾費格充分察覺青少年文化的力量。

語意用法 popular culture 通俗文化；a man of culture 有教養的人。

---

custody
[ˈkʌstədɪ]

監護、拘禁
英解 safekeeping

例 With one out of every two American marriages ending in divorce, **custody** of children has become an issue in the American society. (95 指考)

每二對美國夫妻便有一對以離婚收場，小孩的監護權已經成為美國社會的問題。

語意用法 be in the custody of ... 受……監督。

---

damage
[ˈdæmɪdʒ]

破壞、損害；亦作動詞用
英解 harm

例 A variety of preventive measures are now in place in order to minimize the potential **damage** caused by the deadly disease. (93 指考)

眼前各種預防措施已到位，以求將致命疾病帶來的危害降到最低。

語意用法 potential damage 潛在的損害；cause damage to ... 造成……的損失。

darkness
[`dɑrknɪs]

黑暗、陰暗、陰鬱
英解 nighttime

例 After **darkness** falls in some parts of North America, female fireflies gather on the ground. （93 學測）

夜幕在北美某些地區降臨後，雌螢火蟲聚集在地面上。

語意用法 in darkness 在黑暗之中；在無知、愚昧之中。

deception
[dɪˋsɛpʃən]

詭計、欺騙、詐欺
英解 trickery

例 Investment advisors who engage in any type of **deception** will lose their license and may be charged with a crime.

投資顧問若從事任何詐欺行為將會失去他們的執照，或許還會吃上官司。

語意用法 engage in deception 從事詐欺；self-deception 自欺。

decision
[dɪˋsɪʒən]

決定、果斷、決心
英解 a choice made

例 Later children are often less ambitious and may be uncomfortable making **decisions** for others. （92 學測補）

晚生的小孩往往少了企圖心，甚至無法為別人下決定。

語意用法 make decisions 下決定。

decoration
[ˌdɛkəˋreʃən]

裝飾、點綴、裝潢
英解 sth. added to create a beautiful effect

例 Ice sculptures are used as **decorations** in some cuisines, especially in Asia. （97 學測）

冰雕也被用來裝飾一些菜餚，尤其是在亞洲。

語意用法 interior decoration 室內設計。

| **deficit**
[ˋdɛfəsɪt] | 赤字、虧損
英解 the amount by which an amount (of money etc.) is less than the amount required |

例 It often makes sense for national governments to run a **deficit** during a recession.

一國政府在經濟衰退時期出現赤字是合理的。

語意用法 a budget deficit 預算赤字；a deficit in/of ＋方面，表示某方面的不足。

| **degree**
[dɪˋgri] | 度數、等級、學位
英解 a unit of measurement |

例 A human body usually has a steady temperature of about 37 **degrees** C.

（91 學測補）

人體恆溫通常維持在攝氏 37 度上下。

語意用法 27 degrees Celsius 攝氏 27 度；a man of high degree 地位高的人。

| **delegate**
[ˋdɛləgɪt] | 代表、會議代表、代表團團員
英解 a representative with the power to speak |

例 Marian Anderson was a U.S. **delegate** to the United Nations in 1958 and won the UN peace prize in 1977.（91 學測）

瑪麗安安德森是美國 1958 年的聯合國代表，榮獲 1977 年的聯合國和平獎。

語意用法 a delegate to ＋國際或國家，表示派到一個國際或國家的代表。

| **delinquency**
[dɪˋlɪŋkwənsɪ] | 少年犯罪、懈怠
英解 lawbreaking, esp. by young people |

例 Community service can help prevent juvenile **delinquency**.（98 指考）

社區服務有助於預防青少年犯罪。

語意用法 juvenile delinquency 青少年犯罪。

delivery
[dɪˋlɪvərɪ]

遞送、交付、送走、引渡
英解 transmittal

例 The postal special **delivery** service is very efficient.（91 學測）

郵政快遞服務非常有效率。

語意用法 special delivery 特別郵遞；have a good delivery 能言善道。

desert
[ˋdɛzət]

沙漠、荒野
英解 a region that is devoid or almost devoid of vegetation, esp. because of low rainfall

例 In the **desert** of southwest Peru, enormous shapes, complex patterns, and thousands of perfectly straight lines are cut into the desert's surface.
（95 指考）

在秘魯沙漠西南部，巨大的形體、複雜的圖案、以及數以千計的完美直線，刻畫在沙漠表面上。

語意用法 Mongolian Desert 蒙古沙漠。

design
[dɪˋzaɪn]

設計、設計圖、計畫
英解 motif

例 In 1958, the modern interlocking brick **design** was finally developed and patented.（97 指考）

1958 年，現代連結磚的設計終於得以拓展並取得專利。

語意用法 interior design 室內設計。

destination
[ˌdɛstəˋneʃən]

終點站、目的地、目標
英解 the place where sb. is going

例 The great photographer Henri Cartier-Bresson would often grab his camera and wander through the city with no particular **destination** in mind.

偉大的攝影師亨利卡迪爾布列松常抓著相機沒特定目標地在城裡遊蕩。

語意用法 reach a destination 抵達終點。

destiny
[ˋdɛstənɪ]

命運、宿命
英解 the future destined for a person or thing

例 **Destiny** ought to have brought you to this place.

命運注定將你帶到這個地方。

語意用法 a man of destiny 支配命運的人。

destruction
[dɪˋstrʌkʃən]

破壞、毀滅
英解 the act of destroying

例 The **destruction** caused by the tsunami was greater than that caused by the earthquake.

海嘯造成的毀壞比地震來得強大。

語意用法 bring ... to destruction 使⋯⋯毀滅。

detour
[ˋditʊr]

繞路、繞道、迂迴
英解 a deviation from a direct, usually shorter route or course of action

例 I awaited the coming of daylight and then went down to the front of the chateau, and made a **detour**, examining every trace of footsteps coming towards it or going from it.

我等候黎明的降臨，下樓走到莊園前方，並繞道，細查追蹤每一個走近或走離的腳印。

語意用法 make a detour 繞路。

device
[dɪˋvaɪs]

儀器、設備、裝置
英解 an electrical or mechanical machine

例 Loaded with some **devices**, Cindy is the first doll that can see, think, and do as she's told.（93 指考）

裝備了一些設備，辛蒂成為第一具能看、能思考並按照指示行動的娃娃。

語意用法 device for ＋目的，表示為某目的而設的裝置。

diagnosis
[ˌdaɪəgˈnosɪs]

診斷報告、判斷結論
英解 a finding, conclusion

例 When the material has been recovered, the disk is returned to the sender with a **diagnosis** and a prescription for avoiding the problem in the future.（86 學測）

當資料被恢復，磁碟被送回寄送者，附上一診斷報告及未來如何避免問題的處方。

語意用法 make/undertake a diagnosis of ＋事，表示診斷或調查某事。

diet
[ˈdaɪət]

飲食、節食；亦作動詞用
英解 a weight loss program

例 Some simple strategies can help even the pickiest eater learn to like a more varied **diet**.（98 學測）

一些簡單的策略有助挑食者學著喜歡更多樣化的飲食。

語意用法 go on a diet 節食；put a person on a diet 使某人節食。

dignity
[ˈdɪgnətɪ]

自尊、尊貴、高尚
英解 self-respect, a calm and formal manner

例 My dentist is a woman of great **dignity**.

我的牙醫是一名很高貴的女士。

語意用法 a man of dignity 有尊嚴、高貴的人士。

disadvantage
[ˌdɪsədˈvæntɪdʒ]

缺點、不利、損失
英解 a drawback

例 Besides these safety issues, bottled water has other **disadvantages**.
（99 學測）

撇開這些安全問題，瓶裝水仍有其它缺點。

語意用法 to sb.'s disadvantage，表示對某人不利。

disapproval
[͵dɪsə`pruvl̩]

不贊成、非難
英解 bad opinion, objection

例 The punk protest movement today uses hair as a symbol of **disapproval** of the "middle-class, conventional lifestyle" by wearing provocative haircuts and shockingly colored hair.（98 指考）

今天龐克族用頭髮來作為抗議運動的象徵，藉由挑釁的髮型與嚇人的髮色表達對「中產階級、傳統生活方式」的不滿。

語意用法 frown in disapproval 以皺眉表示不贊同；a symbol of disapproval 不滿的象徵；approval 贊成。

disaster
[dɪ`zæstə]

災難、不幸
英解 a catastrophe

例 With some six hundred years of architecture nearly untouched by natural **disaster** or war, the city retains much of its medieval appearance.（97 學測）

一些六百年的建築幾乎未遭天災與戰爭的損傷，這座城市保有了大部分中世紀時期的外觀。

語意用法 natural disasters 天災。

disbelief
[͵dɪsbə`lif]

懷疑、不相信
英解 a refusal or unwillingness to believe

例 When the nuclear disaster was first announced, the public received the news with shock and **disbelief**.

當核能事故首次公開，得知新聞的大眾除了震驚外更難以置信。

語意用法 with disbelief 不相信地；belief 相信；disbelief/belief in ... 對……不相信／相信。

discipline
[ˋdɪsəplɪn]

紀律、訓練、懲罰
英解 obedience to rules of good behavior and order

例 They have good **discipline**.

他們紀律良好

語意用法 keep sb.'s passions under discipline 抑制情慾。

discomfort
[dɪsˋkʌmfət]

不適、不安、不舒服；亦作動詞用
英解 pain that is not serious

例 The chemicals can be absorbed into the body and cause physical **discomfort**, such as stomach cramps and diarrhea. （99 學測）

這些化學物質可以被身體吸收造成肉體上的不適，像是胃痙攣和腹瀉。

語意用法 physical discomfort 身體不舒服；comfort 舒適。

discovery
[dɪsˋkʌvərɪ]

發現
英解 the finding of sth. new

例 The **discovery** did not surprise me any more than the original findings.
（90 學測）

相較於原來的發現，我對於這項發現一點也不驚訝。

語意用法 the discovery of ＋事物，表示發現某事物。

discrimination
[dɪˌskrɪməˋneʃən]

歧視、辨別
英解 unfair treatment

例 Unlike the U.S., Japan has no law against **discrimination** based on age.
（96 指考）

不同於美國，日本沒有法律禁止年齡方面的歧視。

語意用法 race discrimination 種族歧視；without discrimination 沒有歧視、一視同仁。

discussion
[dɪˋskʌʃən]

討論、商討
英解 serious conversation

例 None of the students had read the book, so it was impossible to have a **discussion** about it.

沒有學生讀過這本書，所以不可能針對它進行討論。

語意用法 discussion about/on/of ＋某事，表示商討某事。

disease
[dɪsˋziz]

疾病、弊病
英解 a bodily condition that causes discomfort or dysfunction

例 Most **diseases** affect the elderly much more severely than the young.

大部分疾病對老年人的影響都大過於年輕人。

語意用法 catch a disease 患病。

disorder
[dɪsˋɔrdə]

混亂無序、失調；亦作動詞用
英解 a state of rebellion and confusion

例 AD/HD is a neurological **disorder** which stems not from the home environment, but from biological and genetic causes. (96 指考)

注意力不足／過動症是一種神經失調，非源於家庭環境因素，而是由生物基因造成。

語意用法 be in disorder 在混亂中；fall into disorder 陷入混亂。

distribution
[ˌdɪstrəˋbjuʃən]

分發、配給
英解 a giving or dealing out of sth.

例 The Red Cross was responsible for the **distribution** of medical supplies.

紅十字會負責分發醫療補給物品。

語意用法 distribution of ＋物品，表示散佈、分配某物品。

distrust
[dɪsˋtrʌst]

懷疑、不信任；亦作動詞用
英解 lack of trust

例 Children normally have a **distrust** of new foods.（98 學測）

孩童通常對新食物抱有懷疑。

語意用法 have a distrust of ＋事物，表示不相信某事物。

disturbance
[dɪsˋtɝbəns]

干擾、打擾、不安、憂慮、騷動
英解 an interruption

例 My little sister caused quite a **disturbance** in the supermarket because my dad wouldn't buy us any ice cream.

我的小妹在超市引起一陣大騷動，因為爸爸不肯買冰淇淋給我們。

語意用法 cause/make a disturbance 引起騷動。

division
[dəˋvɪʒən]

分割、分裂、分界、除法
英解 a separation

例 The little girl can tell time and do simple math, including multiplication and **division**.（93 指考）

這小女孩會看時間、作些簡單的算數，包括乘法和除法。

語意用法 addition 加法；subtraction 減法；multiplication 乘法；division 除法。

divorce
[dəˋvors]

離婚、分開
英解 a legal ending of a marriage

例 The reality is that most women still win custody of their children in a **divorce**.（95 指考）

現實是大部分的婦女仍在離婚中贏得子女的監護權。

語意用法 a divorce lawsuit 離婚官司。

document [ˋdɑkjəmənt]	重要文件、公文 英解 a paper, such as contract

例 Many important legal **documents** concerning the tragic incident have now been preserved in the museum.（96 學測）

許多與這件悲慘事故有關的重要法律文件，現在全保存在博物館裡。

語意用法 legal documents 法律文件。

dominance [ˋdɑmənəns]	優勢、優越、支配地位、統治地位 英解 the condition or fact of being dominant

例 Many types of animals—from geese to orcas—establish **dominance** in their groups through aggressive posturing.

從鵝到虎鯨，許多種類的動物都藉由侵略性的姿態在族群中建立支配地位。

語意用法 gain dominance over ＋事情，表示取得某事的優勢。

donation [doˋneʃən]	捐獻、捐款、捐贈 英解 a contribution

例 He and five other boys took turns jumping rope for two and half hours and collected more than US$1,200 in **donations** for the American Heart Association.（98 指考）

他以及另外五個男孩輪流跳了 2 個半小時的繩，並為美國心臟協會募集了超過 1,200 美元的捐款。

語意用法 make donations to ＋機構，表示捐獻給某機構。

dress [drɛs]	衣服、穿衣打扮；亦作動詞用 英解 a style of clothes

例 One reason is that it's easier for a company to attract new employees if it has a casual **dress** code.（91 學測）

其中一個理由是，如果公司規定穿著輕鬆，比較容易吸引新員工。

語意用法 dress code 穿衣服的規定。

| **drop**
[drɑp] | 點滴、水珠、落下
英解 a very small amount of liquid |

例 The rain was leaking in large **drops** through the roof.

雨從屋頂大滴地漏下來。

語意用法 rain drop 雨滴。

| **drowsiness**
[ˈdrauzɪnɪs] | 嗜睡、困倦、假寐
英解 a very sleepy state |

例 The medicine you take for a cold may cause **drowsiness**; try not to drive after you take it.（94 學測）

你吃的這種感冒藥可能會導致嗜睡，盡量不要在食用後開車。

語意用法 cause drowsiness 造成嗜睡。

| **economy**
[ɪˈkɑnəmɪ] | 節約、經濟
英解 careful, thrifty management of resources, such as money, materials |

例 Packaging has, therefore, attained an important place in Japan's **economy**.（95 指考）

包裝因此在日本經濟上取得重要的一席之位。

語意用法 practice economy 力行節儉。

| **effect**
[ɪˈfɛkt] | 結果、影響、效力；亦作動詞用
英解 a consequence |

例 They concluded that birth order **effects** did not exist.（94 指考）

他們得出的結論是出生順序的影響並不存在。

語意用法 effect on/upon ＋方面，表示在某方面的影響。

element
[`ɛləmənt]

元素、成分

英解 a part, aspect

例 Marketers often use **elements** of youth culture to promote their products.
（92 學測補）

行銷者往往利用青少年文化元素去推銷他們的產品。

語意用法 elements of a good life 好生活的要素。

eloquence
[`ɛləkwəns]

口才流利、雄辯

英解 ease in using language to best effect

例 I admired the mayor's **eloquence**, but at the end of his speech I was still unpersuaded by his arguments.

我欣佩市長的口才，但直到他演說的最後我仍然未被他的論點說服。

語意用法 形容一個人口才很好，可用形容詞 eloquent。

embarrassment
[ɪm`bærəsmənt]

尷尬、困窘、難堪

英解 the state of being embarrassed

例 The arrest of the police chief's son was a major **embarrassment** to the entire department.

警長的兒子被拘捕讓整個部門大感丟臉。

語意用法 financial embarrassment 財政困窘。

emotion
[ɪ`moʃən]

情緒、感情

英解 a feeling

例 Many of my subconscious **emotions** were related to my relationship with my father.（97 指考）

我的許多潛意識情感都與我和父親間的關係有關。

語意用法 suppress one's emotions 抑制感情。

employment
[ɪmˋplɔɪmənt]

雇用、就業
英解 a job paying a salary

例 Many African Americans were not given equal opportunities in education or **employment**.（91 學測）

許多非裔美國人在受教育以及就業上沒有得到平等的機會。

語意用法 out of employment 失業的。

endurance
[ɪnˋdjʊrəns]

耐力、持久力、忍讓
英解 the capacity, state, or an instance of enduring

例 "You underrate their powers of **endurance**," the official replied.

「你低估了他們的耐力」官員回應。

語意用法 beyond endurance 忍無可忍的。

enthusiasm
[ɪnˋθjuzɪˌæzəm]

熱忱、熱情
英解 zeal

例 After ten years with the company, he had completely lost the **enthusiasm** he had once had for his job.

在公司待了十年之後，他對於工作上的曾經作為已完全喪失熱情。

語意用法 enthusiasm for/about ＋事物，表示熱衷於某事物。

entry
[ˋɛntrɪ]

進入、入場、加入
英解 an act of entering

例 He should obtain a visa for **entry** into the Republic of China before getting on board the flight to Taiwan.（85 學測）

登機飛往台灣前，他應該先取得獲准進入中華民國的簽證。

語意用法 entry into ＋國家，表示進入某國家。

environment [ɪnˋvaɪrənmənt]	環境、氛圍 英解 external conditions or surroundings

例 The salary is good, and I really like the work **environment**, but it's just too far to commute every day.

薪水很棒，我也很喜歡這個工作環境，但每天通車到這裡實在太遠了。

語意用法 the natural environment 自然環境。

epidemic [ˌɛpɪˋdɛmɪk]	流行性傳染病、流行；亦作形容詞用 英解 a disease that spreads quickly among many people

例 While all bird species are thought to be susceptible to infection, domestic poultry flocks are especially vulnerable to infections that can rapidly reach **epidemic** proportions.（93 指考）

雖然所有的鳥類都被認為易受感染，成群養殖的家禽尤其容易傳染，迅速就能達到流行性傳染病的程度。

語意用法 epidemic of ＋事物，表示某事物的盛行。

equality [ɪˋkwɑlətɪ]	相等、平等 英解 a condition of being equal

例 In many countries women have attained legal **equality** but have yet to achieve economic equality.

在很多國家，女性已獲得法律上的平等，但在經濟上尚未如此。

語意用法 on an equality with ＋人，表示和某人平等相處。

error [ˋɛrə]	錯誤、過失 英解 a mistake

例 The teacher has corrected every student's speech **errors**.（93 指考補）

任課老師糾正每位學生言語上的錯誤。

語意用法 make an error 犯錯；correct an error 改正錯誤。

| **evidence**
[ˋɛvədəns] | 證據、跡象；亦作動詞用
英解 a thing or things helpful in forming a conclusion or judgment |

例 Joy Hirsch, a neuroscientist in New York, has recently found **evidence** that children and adults don't use the same parts of the brain when learning a second language.（95 學測）

紐約神經科學家喬依赫喜最近發現一項證據指出，孩童與成人在學習第二語言時，使用的大腦部位不一樣。

語意用法 evidence of/for ＋事件，表示作為某事件的證據。

| **excellence**
[ˋɛksləns] | 優秀、傑出、卓越
英解 extreme merit |

例 The university professor has won a grant for teaching **excellence**.

此大學教授已經贏得教學卓越的補助。

語意用法 excellence in design 設計上的卓越。

| **exhibition**
[ˌɛksəˋbɪʃən] | 展覽、展示會、展覽品
英解 a public display of art, products, skills, activities, etc. |

例 Students went to an **exhibition** of Impressionism paintings at Arts museum.

學生去美術館參觀印象派畫展。

語意用法 an exhibition of ＋物品，表示某物品的公開展示。

| **expectation**
[ˌɛkspɛkˋteʃən] | 期待、預期
英解 hope, desire |

例 The more educated a man is, the higher is the **expectation** for dowry at the time of marriage.（98 指考）

教育程度越高的男性，對結婚時的嫁妝期待也越高。

語意用法 in expectation of ＋事物，表示對某事物的預期、期待。

exposition
[ˌɛkspəˈzɪʃən]

解說、說明
英解 a systematic interpretation or explanation

例 He was in the midst of his **exposition** when the door from the corridor opened slowly and without noise.

當走廊那道門緩緩無聲地開啟時,他正在解說之中。

語意用法 an exposition of +事件,表示解釋說明某事。

exposure
[ɪkˈspoʒɚ]

暴露、揭露、曝光
英解 the act of exposing

例 **Exposure** of one's inner thoughts is essential for enduring relationships.
(86 學測)

為了關係能持久,表達自己內在的想法是必要的。

語意用法 exposure to +事物,表示置身於某事物的攻擊或影響。

extension
[ɪkˈstɛnʃən]

伸展、延伸、延期、分機
英解 the act of extending or the condition of being extended

例 The cafés are like an **extension** of the French living room, a place to start and end the day, to gossip and debate. (97 指考)

這咖啡館彷彿是法國客廳的延伸,一個開始與結束一天、談論八卦與討論意見的地方。

語意用法 by extension 擴大來看。

extent
[ɪkˈstɛnt]

程度、範圍、寬廣度、淵博
英解 the range over which sth. extends

例 The **extent** of the damage caused by the typhoon won't be known for several days.

颱風造成的損害程度無法在幾天內估知。

語意用法 to the extent that ... 到……的程度。

extravaganza
[ɪkˌstrævəˈgænzə]

狂歡、狂想
英解 a spectacular

例 Stretch limousines were hired to drive the prom-goers to expensive restaurants or discos for an all-night **extravaganza**. (99 學測)

雇用加長型禮車載送舞會賓客去昂貴的餐廳或舞廳,狂歡一整夜。

語意用法 an all-night extravaganza 整晚狂歡。

facility
[fəˈsɪlətɪ]

設備、能力、技術
英解 sth. designed to serve a specific function

例 For the past two years, the doctor has used the medical **facility** in the center and has offered state-of-the-art 3-D/4-D scanning services for expectant parents. (95 指考)

過去二年裡,醫生在醫療中心使用醫療設備,並提供先進的 3D 和 4D 掃瞄為準父母們服務。

語意用法 medical facility 醫療設備;cooking facilities 烹調設備。

factor
[ˈfæktə]

因素、要素、代理商;亦作動詞用
英解 a fact to be considered

例 One key **factor** to success is to have a definite goal first and then do your best to attain the goal. (87 學測)

成功的要素首先要有明確的目標,然後盡全力去達成目標。

語意用法 a key factor to ＋事件,某事件的重要因素。

faith
[feθ]

信仰、信念、信賴
英解 of therapy conviction

例 I have every **faith** that the new management team will return the company to profitability by the end of the year.

我全心相信新的管理團隊可在今年年底前幫公司轉虧為盈。

語意用法 put one's faith in ... 相信、信任……。

fake [fek]	偽造品、贗品、假裝、騙子；亦作動詞用 英解 a copy, imitation

例 The experts discovered several **fakes** in the art museum.

專家在美術館中發現幾件贗品。

語意用法 fake 可以指人，如：冒充者、騙子，也可以指物，如：假冒品。

fame [fem]	聲譽、名譽、聲望 英解 renown

例 Marian Anderson (1897-1993) was an African American woman who gained **fame** as a concert singer in this climate of racism. （91 學測）

瑪莉安安得森（1897-1993）是在種族主義氛圍下，贏得演唱會歌手聲望的美國非裔女性。

語意用法 come to fame 成名；gain fame 獲得名聲。

fantasy [ˋfæntəsɪ]	幻想、幻想曲、幻想出的作品 英解 daydream, illusion

例 That is why, every once in a while, we like to escape into the world of **fantasy**—a place where things always go our way and there is always a happy ending. （91 學測）

這就是為什麼，我們偶爾喜歡逃進幻想世界裡；一個事情都按著我們的希望發展、總是有美好結局的地方。

語意用法 a world of fantasy 幻想的世界。

fashion [ˋfæʃən]	時尚、流行、風氣、服裝 英解 any style of dress popular for a period of time

例 In the classical Greek period, curly hair was not only the **fashion**, but it also represented an attitude towards life. （98 指考）

古典希臘時代，捲髮不僅是時尚，還代表了一種生活態度。

語意用法 in similar fashion，表示作風相同；fashion magazine，表示時尚雜誌。

fatigue
[fə`tig]

疲倦、疲乏；亦作動詞用
英解 exhaustion

例 If they stay in a museum too long, a feeling of boredom and monotony will build up, leading eventually to impatience and **fatigue**. （95 指考）

如果他們在博物館待太久，無聊、單調的感覺會油然而生，最終導致焦躁與疲勞。

語意用法 fatigue 表示極度勞累，very tired。

fault
[fɔlt]

錯誤、責任、缺點、毛病
英解 a flaw, defect

例 "Sorry, sir. It's not really your **fault**. Today is my first day as a cab driver. I've been driving a funeral van for the last 25 years." （94 指考）

「抱歉，先生。這真的不是你的錯。今天是我第一天當計程車司機，過去的 25 年，我都在開送葬禮車。」

語意用法 It's my fault. 表示這是我的錯，口語中常用。

feature
[`fitʃə]

容貌、特徵、相貌、特色；亦作動詞用
英解 the overall appearance of the face or its parts

例 This is a key **feature** of our school.

這是我們學校的主要特點。

語意用法 a feature of ＋事物，表示某事物的特點。

female
[`fimel]

雌性動植物、女性；亦作形容詞用
英解 a member of the sex that produces ova or bears young

例 The odds that someone in this class will become an astronaut are very low, and if you are a **female** they are, unfortunately, even lower.

在這班上有人成為太空人的機率很低，如果你是女性，不幸地這個機率更低。

語意用法 female 女性；male 男性。

fertility
[fɝˋtɪlətɪ]

肥沃、繁殖力

英解 the ability to produce offspring or new plants

例 The high cost of raising and educating children has had an adverse impact on **fertility** in Taiwan.

養育和教育小孩的高成本對台灣的生育率有不利影響。

語意用法 fertility drug 受孕藥。

festival
[ˋfɛstəvl]

節慶、節日、慶祝活動

英解 a public celebration or feast

例 The evening concerts are held at different locations during the 10-day **Festival**.（93 指考補）

為期 10 天的節慶裡，夜間音樂會在不同地點舉辦。

語意用法 Lantern Festival 燈節；Dragon Boat Festival 端午節

fetus
[ˋfitəs]

哺乳類的胚胎、滿三個月的胎兒

英解 the developed embryo in humans and other mammals

例 A writer for the liberal *American Prospect* said that the new technology "blurred the distinction between a **fetus** and a newborn infant."（95 指考）

一名《美國展望》的自由主義作家說，新技術「模糊了胎兒與新生兒的界線」。

語意用法 fetus 指的是三個月後成型的胎兒。

fever
[ˋfivɚ]

發燒、狂熱

英解 higher than normal body temperature

例 Over 100,000 people with "gold **fever**" made this trip hoping to become millionaires.（90 學測）

超過 10 萬人帶著「淘金熱」走這趟旅程，希望成為百萬富翁。

語意用法 fever heat 病態的狂熱；fever of ＋事物，表示對某事物的狂熱、激昂。

finance [ˈfaɪnæns]	財政、金融、財政學；亦作動詞用 英解 the system of money, credit, etc.

例 He is an expert in **finance**.

他是一名財政專家。

語意用法 a country's finance 國家的財政。

flight [flaɪt]	飛行、航班 英解 the act of traveling through the air

例 They fear the snow might delay **flights** and persuade short-haul travelers to take a train or drive instead.（92 指考）

他們擔心大雪可能延誤航班，說服短程乘客改搭火車或開車替代。

語意用法 a domestic flight，表示國內班機。

flood [flʌd]	洪水、水災；動詞作淹沒、氾濫解 英解 an overflow

例 There is a lot to see and do in Bangkok if you can tolerate the traffic, noise, heat (in the hot season), **floods** (in the rainy season), and somewhat polluted air.（92 指考）

如果你能忍受交通、噪音、夏季的熾熱、雨季的洪災，還有些微污染的空氣，在曼谷有很多值得去看去做的事。

語意用法 the floods in this area，表示在此地區的洪水。

folk [fok]	人們；民俗 英解 a certain group of people

例 These **folk** healers use observation and logic, but they are not so aware of it.（92 學測補）

民俗治療師運用觀察力與邏輯力，但他們自己並不知道

語意用法 folk songs 民俗歌；folklore 民俗傳統。

名詞篇

footprint
[ˋfʊtˏprɪnt]

足跡、腳印
英解 an indentation or outline of the foot of a person or animal on a surface

例 The police discovered two pairs of **footprints** leading away from the broken window.

警方發現兩對走離破裂窗戶的足印。

語意用法 footprints in the snow/sand 雪地／沙地的腳印。

formality
[fɔrˋmælətɪ]

正式、拘謹、禮俗
英解 a requirement of rule, custom, etiquette, etc.

例 I think that even then I had an instinctive doubt whether formlessness was really better than **formality**.

即便那時，我認為我有種本能的懷疑是否不拘形式真的比拘泥形式來得好。

語意用法 formality 指的是俗套、禮節、正式的程序；without formality 不拘形式或不拘禮節。

fortune
[ˋfɔrtʃən]

財富、好運
英解 wealth, fate

例 Jack and his company have made a **fortune** from their service.（86 學測）

傑克和他的公司藉由他們的服務賺進大筆財富。

語意用法 make a fortune 賺大錢。

foundation
[faʊnˋdeʃən]

創立、基金會、基礎
英解 the basis on which sth. is grounded

例 This is especially noteworthy when one considers that public television stations must often survive on very limited budgets, on viewers' donations, and on private **foundations** and some governmental funding.（96 學測）

當考慮到公共電視台常常必須在極少的預算、觀眾的捐款以及私人基金會及一些政府的基金下生存時，這點特別值得注意。

語意用法 foundation 原意指基礎，此處指的是基金會，如：a foundation for child adoption 領養小孩的基金會。

fragrance [ˈfreɡrəns]	芬芳、香味、香氣
	英解 a pleasant or sweet odor; scent; perfume

例 They are as a rose whose **fragrance** has been exhausted by greedy and indiscriminate smelling.

他們就像一朵玫瑰，其香味被貪婪、濫聞而消耗殆盡。

語意用法 fragrance 指的是花香，或香水的味道。

freak [frik]	畸形、怪誕的行為、怪念頭、怪胎；亦作形容詞用
	英解 a person or animal with an abnormal shape

例 Magicians were thought of as **freaks** and were only allowed to perform in a circus.（92 學測）

魔術師被認為是怪胎，且只能在馬戲團表演。

語意用法 a freak 怪胎、反常，有時用來罵人。

frequency [ˈfrikwənsɪ]	頻率、頻繁、周率
	英解 the rate at which sth. happens

例 Bag-matching caused domestic flights to change their schedules and to reduce their **frequency** of service.（92 指考）

行李比對造成國內航班的班次改變，並降低他們的服務頻率。

語意用法 frequency of ＋事件，表示某事發生的頻率。

名詞篇

friendliness
[ˈfrɛndlɪnɪs]

友善、親切
英解 a feeling of liking for another person

例 It's impossible to know whether the **friendliness** of salespeople is genuine.

無法知道銷售人員的親切是否真心。

語意用法 user-friendliness 符合使用者需求的；child-friendliness 符合兒童需求的。

frustration
[ˌfrʌsˋtreʃən]

挫折、失敗
英解 the feeling that accompanies an experience of being thwarted in attaining your goals

例 The taped materials were often poorly designed, leading to student's **frustration** and boredom. (93 指考補)

錄影素材往往缺乏設計，導致學生的挫折與厭倦。

語意用法 frustration on ＋人或事，表示對某人或某事感到挫折。

function
[ˈfʌŋkʃən]

功能、作用；亦作動詞用
英解 purpose, use

例 What's the key **function** of this machine?

這機器的主要功能為何？

語意用法 function of ＋物，表示某物的功能。

fund
[fʌnd]

資金、專款；亦作動詞用
英解 a sum of money for a specific purpose

例 In 1914, ranchers persuaded the United States Congress to provide **funds** to exterminate wolves on public lands. (95 指考)

在 1914 年，農場經營者說服美國議會提供經費來消滅公共土地上的狼群。

語意用法 raise funds 募款。

furniture
[ˈfɝnɪtʃə]

傢俱
英解 the movable, generally functional, articles that equip a room, house, etc.

例 Some students make products that range in size from earrings to quite elaborate **furniture** for the home.（93 指考）

一些學生製造產品，尺寸範圍從耳環到家中的精巧傢俱。

語意用法 a piece of furniture，表示一件傢俱。

future
[ˈfjutʃə]

未來、將來；亦作形容詞用
英解 the time yet to come

例 He felt confident in the **future**.

他對未來充滿信心。

語意用法 a great future 光明的前途。

gate
[get]

大門、柵欄門、閘門、登機口
英解 an opening in a wall or fence for entrance or exit

例 It wasn't until our pigs dug up the neighbor's vegetable garden that Dad finally decided to fix the **gate** of the pigpen.

一直到我們家的豬翻挖鄰居的菜圃，爸爸才終於決定修理豬舍大門。

語意用法 at the gate 在大門口。

gender
[ˈdʒɛndə]

性別
英解 sexual identity, especially in relation to society or culture

例 Research about learning styles has identified **gender** differences.（93 學測）

研究顯示，學習的方式因性別差異而不同。

語意用法 gender differences 性別差異；gender issues 性別議題。

generation
[ˌdʒɛnəˋreʃən]

世代、同時代的人事物
英解 all of the offspring that are at the same stage

例 Folk tales are stories passed down by word of mouth **generation** after generation. (91 學測補)

民間傳說就是代代口耳相傳的故事。

語意用法 for generations 接連著幾代；generation gap 代溝。

genetics
[dʒəˋnɛtɪks]

遺傳學
英解 the branch of biology that studies heredity and variation in organisms

例 While the twins knew that **genetics** might have played a role in their condition, they recognized that their eating habits might have also contributed to their heart problems. (93 學測)

雖然雙胞胎知道以他們的狀況遺傳學可能扮演了重要的角色，他們認為他們的飲食習慣或許也造成他們的心臟問題。

語意用法 a genetic disorder 遺傳疾病。

geography
[dʒiˋɑgrəfɪ]

地形
英解 the earth's surface

例 With e-mail, **geography** is no obstacle and time is not important. (95 指考)

隨著電子郵件的出現，地形不再是障礙，時間也變得不重要。

語意用法 human geography 人文地理學。

glacier
[ˋgleʃə]

冰河
英解 a large mass of ice that moves slowly

例 After the creation of the **Glacier** National Park in Montana, the growing number of park visitors increased the need for roads. (97 學測)

蒙大拿冰河國家公園創立後，與日遽增的公園訪客需要更多的道路。

語意用法 continental glaciers 大陸冰川。

graduation
[ˌɡrædʒʊˈeʃən]

畢業
英解 the awarding of an academic degree

例 She hoped to get a good job after **graduation**.

她希望畢業後能找到一份好工作。

語意用法 upon graduation 在畢業時。

gratitude
[ˈɡrætəˌtjud]

感謝、感激、感恩
英解 appreciation

例 The temple stages performances of Taiwanese opera every year as an expression of **gratitude** to the Goddess of Mercy.（93 指考）

廟宇每年策畫演出台灣歌仔戲，以表達對觀音菩薩的感謝。

語意用法 gratitude to ＋人，表示對某人的感謝；gratitude for ＋行為，表示對某行為的謝意。

growth
[ɡroθ]

生長、發育、成長、栽培
英解 maturation

例 The **growth** of public television in the past two decades has been dramatic.（96 學測）

公共電視在過去二十年的成長很驚人。

語意用法 the growth of ＋物，表示某物的成長。

guidance
[ˈɡaɪdn̩s]

指引、指導
英解 counsel

例 The events in which they compete include both **guidance** sports, such as baseball, basketball, and soccer, and individual sports, such as golf, tennis, and bowling.（91 指考）

在他們的競賽項目中同時包括輔導運動，像是棒球、籃球、足球，以及個別運動，如高爾夫球、網球和保齡球。

語意用法 under sb.'s guidance，表示在某人的引導下。

harmony
[ˈharmənɪ]

和諧、融洽、和睦、一致
英解 agreement in opinion

例 We hope that there will be no war in the world and that all people live in peace and **harmony** with each other. (98 學測)

我們希望這個世上將不再有戰爭，所有的人彼此都能在和平中融洽共存。

語意用法 in harmony with ... 與……調和。

harvest
[ˈharvɪst]

收成、收割、收穫；亦作動詞用
英解 the gathering of crops

例 Since the orange trees suffered severe damage from a storm in the summer, the farmers are expecting a sharp decline in **harvests** this winter. (99 學測)

自從柳橙樹遭受夏季風暴嚴重的損壞後，果農們預期這個冬天的收成會大幅下跌。

語意用法 gather a harvest 收割、採收。

healthcare
[ˈhɛlθˌkɛr]

健康保健、保健事業
英解 the preservation of mental and physical health

例 More than 2,000 adults took part in the survey to find out about their knowledge of diet, **healthcare**, disease control, and medication. (91 學測補)

超過二千個成年人參與問卷調查，以瞭解他們對飲食、健康保健、疾病控制以及藥物方面的知識。

語意用法 healthcare center 健康中心。

hemisphere
[ˈhɛməsˌfɪr]

半球、半球體
英解 half of a sphere

例 The left **hemisphere** of our brain deals with rules, lists of information, and short-term memory. (85 學測)

我們大腦的左半球體負責控制、條列資訊，以及短期記憶。

語意用法 in the Northern hemisphere 在北半球。

heritage
[ˋhɛrətɪdʒ]

遺產、繼承物
英解 property that is or can be inherited

例 The Waterton-Glacier International Peace Park was named as a World **Heritage** Site in 1995.（97 學測）

瓦特頓冰河國際和平公園在 1995 年被指定為世界遺產。

語意用法 a culture heritage 文化遺產。

honor
[ˋɑnɚ]

榮譽、光榮、尊敬、勳章；亦作動詞用
英解 high respect, as that shown for special merit

例 She is an **honor** to our country.

她是我們國家之光。

語意用法 show honor to ＋人，表示對某人表示尊敬；in honor of ＋人，表示對某人的敬意。

hospitality
[ˌhɑspɪˋtælətɪ]

好客、熱情款待
英解 kindness in welcoming strangers or guests

例 Wherever you travel in Central America, you're sure to be welcomed with wonderful, heartfelt **hospitality**.

不論你在美國中部的何處旅行，你一定會受到美好、貼心的熱情歡迎。

語意用法 hospitality suite 飯店的貴賓接待室。

hotel
[hoˋtɛl]

飯店、旅館
英解 a building where travelers stay

例 These large ice blocks are used for large ice sculpting events and for building ice **hotels**.（97 學測）

這些大冰磚是用於大型冰雕以及建造冰旅館。

語意用法 run a hotel 經營旅館；stay at a hotel 在旅館住宿。

household
[ˋhaʊsˌhold]

家庭成員、家族、一家人
英解 the person or people living together in one home

例 According to a recent marketing study, young adults influence 88% of **household** clothing purchases.（99 學測）

根據最近的市場調查，年輕成年人影響了家中的 88% 衣物購買。

語意用法 a large household 大家族。

humor
[ˋhjumɚ]

幽默、幽默感
英解 the quality that makes sth. amusing

例 A good sense of **humor** can help relieve the anxiety of our life.

一點幽默感可以減輕生活中的焦慮。

語意用法 a good sense of humor 有幽默感。

hunger
[ˋhʌŋgɚ]

飢餓
英解 a strong desire for food

例 There was nothing to awaken for until danger threatened, or the pangs of **hunger** assailed.

沒有任何覺醒，直到遭受危險的威脅或是飢餓之苦來襲。

語意用法 hunger strike 節食抗議；a hunger for/after knowledge 強烈的求知慾。

illness
[ˋɪlnɪs]

生病、疾病
英解 sickness, disease

例 It is an **illness** that makes one want to stop eating.（97 指考）

那是一種疾病，讓人不想進食。

語意用法 a slight illness，表示輕微的疾病、微恙。

imagination
[ɪˌmædʒə`neʃən]

想像力、創造力、想像
英解 ability to think creatively

例 Through the power of **imagination**, folktales can turn humble people into heroes.（91 學測補）

透過想像的力量，民間傳說將出生卑微的人變成英雄。

語意用法 beyond all imagination 難以想像的。

imitation
[ˌɪmə`teʃən]

模仿、偽造、仿造
英解 a copy, a duplication

例 Although babies imitate the facial expressions they see, smiling isn't just learned by **imitation**.（92 學測補）

雖然嬰兒會模仿他們見到的表情，微笑卻非純粹藉著模仿學習而來。

語意用法 in imitation of ＋人或物，表示模仿、仿效某人或某物。

immigrant
[`ɪməgrənt]

移民、僑民
英解 a person who leaves one country to live in another

例 Like most **immigrants**, he was looking for a better life.（85 學測）

與大多數的移民一樣，他在尋求更好的生活。

語意用法 immigrants from other countries 來自其他國家的移民。

impact
[`ɪmpækt]

影響、衝擊（力）、撞擊（力）
英解 the act of one body, object, etc.

例 Problems of this kind can make an **impact** on the properties of a product.
（94 指考）

這類問題會對產品性能造成影響。

語意用法 have an impact on/upon ＋事物，表示對某事物產生影響。

importance
[ɪmˋpɔrtn̩s]

重要、重大
英解 the state of being important

例 A strong foundation in math and science education is essential, but at the same time we must not discount the **importance** of the arts and humanities.

數學和科學教育的札實基礎是重要的，但同時我們也不能忽略藝術和人文的重要性。

語意用法 be of importance 重要的；be of no importance 微不足道的。

impulse
[ˋɪmpʌls]

衝動、刺激
英解 a sudden urge

例 Jane usually buys things on **impulse**. (93 學測)

珍買東西通常都是憑藉一股衝動。

語意用法 on impulse 憑著一股衝動。

inability
[͵ɪnəˋbɪlətɪ]

無能、無力
英解 lack of power or capacity to do sth.

例 I have come to realize that I cannot alter my father's **inability** to express his feelings. (97 指考)

我認清我無法改變父親無能表達自己情感的事實。

語意用法 inability + to V，表示沒有做某事的能力。

independence
[͵ɪndɪˋpɛndəns]

獨立、自主
英解 self-sufficiency

例 The **independence** of each separate state had never been declared.

每個州的自主性從沒有被公開承認。

語意用法 independence of +物，表示某物之獨立性、自主性。

individual
[ˌɪndəˈvɪdʒuəl]

個人、個體；亦作形容詞用
英解 one person

例 Cloning is the genetic process of producing copies of an **individual**.
（91 學測）

無性繁殖是複製個體的基因過程。

語意用法 a private individual 個人。

inferiority
[ɪnˌfɪrɪˈɑrətɪ]

劣勢、次等、自卑感
英解 a person lower in rank, status, or accomplishment than another

例 Shyness is only the effect of a sense of **inferiority** in some way or other.
羞怯不過是自卑感以某種方式產生作用。

語意用法 a sense of inferiority 自卑感；a sense of superiority 優越感。

inflation
[ɪnˈfleʃən]

通貨膨脹
英解 a rise in prices and lowering of currency's value

例 Due to **inflation**, prices for daily necessities have gone up and we have to pay more for the same items now.（99 學測）
由於通貨膨脹，日常民生用品的價格上漲，我們必須付更多的錢買相同的東西。

語意用法 inflation rate 通膨率。

influence
[ˈɪnfluəns]

影響、作用；亦作動詞用
英解 the power to change or persuade others

例 The **influence** of one upon the other can be either positive or negative.
（95 學測）

此項對另一項的影響可能是正面，也可能是負面的。

語意用法 influence of ＋人事物＋ on/upon/over ＋人事物，表示某人事物對某人事物的影響。

名詞篇

information
[ˌɪnfəˈmeʃən]
情資、消息、詢問處
英解 knowledge, news, facts

例 Many people ask me questions, and I give them the necessary **information**.（92 學測）
許多人問我問題，而我給予他們所需的資訊。

語意用法 information on/about ＋事物，表示關於某事物的資訊。

infrastructure
[ˈɪnfrəˌstrʌktʃə]
公共建設、基礎建設
英解 the basic structure or features of a system

例 Much of the tax money in the government pays for its **infrastructure**.
政府大部分的稅收都用在公共建設上。

語意用法 infrastructure of ＋組織，表示某組織的基礎。

ingenuity
[ˌɪndʒəˈnuətɪ]
巧妙、精巧、匠心獨具、足智多謀
英解 inventive skill or imagination

例 I am sure he has **ingenuity** enough.
我確信他有足夠的聰明才智。

語意用法 exercise ingenuity 動腦筋；show ingenuity in ＋方面，表示展現某方面的才智。

innovation
[ˌɪnəˈveʃən]
改革、革新、創新
英解 sth. new made or improved with creativity

例 The group singles out twenty-five non-medically related technological **innovations** that have become widely used since 1980.（94 指考）
小組挑選出 25 項自 1980 年起即被廣泛運用的非醫療相關創新技術。

語意用法 technological innovation 技術創新。

input
[ˈɪnˌpʊt]

投入、輸入、鍵入；亦作動詞用
英解 the act of putting in

例 The city council was criticized for its sudden decision to close the library without having sought any **input** from local residents.
市議會因突然決定關掉圖書館卻未詢問當地居民意見，而遭到批評。

語意用法 input to ＋物，表示輸入資料至某物。

insomnia
[ɪnˈsɑmnɪə]

失眠症
英解 not able to sleep

例 The only reported negative effect of drinking green tea is a possible allergic reaction and **insomnia** due to the caffeine it contains.（97 學測）
報告中指出，喝綠茶唯一負面的影響是可能的過敏反應和所含咖啡因造成的失眠。

語意用法 suffer insomnia 受失眠所苦。

inspection
[ɪnˈspɛkʃən]

檢驗、審視、檢查
英解 a formal or official examination

例 He began its **inspection** without delay, scouring it from cellar to garret.
他毫不遲疑地開始檢視，從地窖搜尋到閣樓。

語意用法 on first inspection 經過初步調查。

inspiration
[ˌɪnspəˈreʃən]

靈感、鼓舞人心的事物
英解 stimulation or arousal of the mind and feelings

例 It is a great privilege to have the **inspiration** and the opportunity.
能擁有靈感與機緣是莫大的恩典。

語意用法 have an inspiration 想到好主意。

installment
[ɪnˋstɔlmənt]

分期付款、期刊的一回
英解 a payment of part of a debt

例 He settled down with his young wife and began buying a house on the **installment** plan.

他與他年輕的妻子定居下來並開始分期付款買房子的計畫。

語意用法 by monthly installments 按月分期付款。

instance
[ˋɪnstəns]

例子、場合
英解 a case or particular example

例 For **instance**, people who have a positive sense of self-esteem usually act with confidence.（83 學測）

例如，有自尊的人通常舉止都帶著自信。

語意用法 for instance、for example 例如。

instrument
[ˋɪnstrəmənt]

儀器、機械、樂器
英解 a tool that helps sb. do work

例 He used an **instrument** called an MRI (magnetic resonance imaging) to study the brains of two groups of bilingual people.（95 學測）

他使用一種名為 MRI（核磁共振成像）的儀器研究二組雙語人士的大腦。

語意用法 musical instruments 樂器。

insurance
[ɪnˋʃʊrəns]

保險、保險契約、保險業、保費、保險理賠金
英解 promise of reimbursement in the case of loss

例 Bangkok offers attractive travel **insurance** to visitors.（92 指考）

曼谷提供遊客極具吸引力的旅遊保險。

語意用法 travel insurance 旅行保險；life insurance 人壽保險。

integrity
[ɪnˋtɛgrətɪ]

清高、正直、誠實、完善
英解 adherence to moral principles

例 Once known for his **integrity**, the judge suddenly resigned and disappeared after being accused of corruption.

先前以清廉聞名的法官，在被控貪污後突然辭職並消失。

語意用法 relics in their integrity 保持完整狀態的遺物。

intellectual
[ˌɪntlˋɛktʃʊəl]

知識份子、高智商者
英解 a thinker

例 In the 19th century, European **intellectuals** tried hard to explain the complexities involving science and religion.

在 19 世紀，歐洲的知識份子努力想解釋有關科學與宗教間的複雜問題。

語意用法 the intellectual class 知識階層。

intention
[ɪnˋtɛnʃən]

意圖、目的、含意
英解 a purpose or goal

例 My **intention** in writing "this poem" was not to shock anybody.

我寫《這首詩》的意圖不是要震驚任何人。

語意用法 show one's intention 表達意願。

interpretation
[ɪnˌtɝprɪˋteʃən]

闡釋、口譯、詮釋
英解 the act or process of interpreting or explaining

例 I asked him the **interpretation** of his movements.

我請他解釋他的動向。

語意用法 interpretation of ＋事，表示對某事的解釋、解析。

intimacy [ˋɪntəməsɪ]	熟悉、親密、親近、私下、性行為 英解 emotional closeness

例 While **intimacy** is often limited to the sexual bond, we can be intimate with many people without sexuality. （86 學測）

雖然親密行為往往被侷限於性的結合，我們還是可以在沒有性行為的情況下與很多人保持親密。

語意用法 be on terms of intimacy 關係親密。

intrigue [ɪnˋtrig]	陰謀、詭計、私通、複雜的情節 英解 a secret or underhand scheme

例 He became involved in a palace **intrigue**, and only saved himself by betraying his accomplices.

他涉及一樁宮廷陰謀，藉由背叛他的同伙來保全他自己。

語意用法 political intrigue 政治陰謀。

investment [ɪnˋvɛstmənt]	投資、投資額、投資標的 英解 the act of investing

例 He did not hesitate in making **investments** in his hometown. （96 指考）

他對於投資家鄉毫不遲疑。

語意用法 make an investment in ＋事物，表示投資於某事物。

isolation [ˌaɪslˋeʃən]	隔離、獨立 英解 separating from others

例 Because of the **isolation** of his house, no one came to tell him.

因為他的住所與世隔絕，沒有人前往通知他。

語意用法 keep ... in isolation 使……保持分離、孤立。

itinerary
[aɪˋtɪnəˏrɛrɪ]

旅遊行程
英解 proposed route of a journey

例 That's my **itinerary**, Bunny, but I really can't see why you should come with me.

這是我的行程，邦妮。不過我真的看不出來妳有什麼理由非跟我去不可。

語意用法 on one's itinerary 在某人的旅程中。

journey
[ˋdʒɝnɪ]

旅行、旅程
英解 a trip

例 No one would ever know why she planned a wedding **journey** to Rome.

沒有人會知道她為何要計畫去羅馬旅行結婚。

語意用法 a journey to ＋地方，表示去某地旅行。

judgment
[ˋdʒʌdʒmənt]

審判、判決、判斷
英解 an opinion formed by judging sth.

例 Her **judgment** was as young as she, but her instincts were as old as the race and older.

她作出的判斷跟她一樣稚嫩，但她的本能與這種族一樣甚至更老。

語意用法 make a judgment 下判斷；show judgment in Ving 做某事時展現見識。

knowledge
[ˋnɑlɪdʒ]

知識、熟悉、認知
英解 an area of learning

例 I feel secure now that I can live with that **knowledge** safely locked in my mind.（97 指考）

我感到安全，因為我能與那些安全鎖在我腦海裡的知識共存。

語意用法 knowledge of ＋方面，表示對某方面知識的精通。

名詞篇

laboratory [ˋlæbrəˌtorɪ]	實驗室、研究室、化工廠 英解 a workplace for scientific research

例 In a **laboratory**, make sure your measure meets your needs.（95 指考）

在實驗室裡，確認你使用的方法配合需求。

語意用法 a chemical laboratory 化學實驗室。

landmark [ˋlændˌmɑrk]	地標、界標、里程碑 英解 a well-known object in a particular landscape

例 Taipei 101 is a well-known **landmark**.

台北 101 是個眾所皆知的地標。

語意用法 a well-known landmark 著名的地標。

landscape [ˋlændˌskep]	景觀、風景 英解 an expanse of scenery

例 Before he had gone far he observed that the **landscape** was growing more distinct.

在他走遠之前，他觀察到景色越來越清晰。

語意用法 a peaceful/good landscape 寧靜／美麗的景色。

landslide [ˋlændˌslaɪd]	土石流、坍方 英解 a slide of a large mass of dirt and rock down a mountain

例 The week-long rainfall has brought about **landslides** and flooding in the mountain areas.（93 學測）

為期一週的降雨為山區帶來土石流和山洪。

語意用法 a landslide victory 壓倒性的勝利。

lawsuit
[ˈlɔˌsut]

訴訟案件
英解 a proceeding in a court of law

例 It was a land speculation as usual, and it had gotten complicated with a **lawsuit**.

這是一件普通的土地投機買賣，由於法律訴訟變得很複雜。

語意用法 enter a lawsuit against ＋人，表示對某人提出訴訟。

layer
[ˈleə]

層、階層；亦作動詞用
英解 a coating, covering

例 Unlike fresh onions, they have multiple **layers** of thick, dark, papery skin.
（99 學測）

不像新鮮的洋蔥，它們擁有多層次、又厚又黑如紙般的皮層。

語意用法 a layer of ... 一層……。

layoff
[ˈleˌɔf]

臨時解雇、停工
英解 the act of laying off an employee

例 Mass **layoff** events were down by 77 from October 2008.

自 2008 年 10 月起，大量裁員事件數下降 77 件。

語意用法 lay off 解雇員工，當動詞用。

leadership
[ˈlidəˌʃɪp]

領導、領導階層、領導能力
英解 the position or function of a leader

例 It was inevitable that the clash for **leadership** should come.

領導階層的衝突是無可避免的。

語意用法 under the leadership of ＋人，表示在某人領導下。

leap
[lip]

跳躍、躍進、激增、驟變、跳躍的距離
英解 a jump into the air

例 His salary went up with a **leap**.

他的薪水驟增。

語意用法 take a leap 跳躍。

leather
[ˈlɛðə]

皮革、皮革製品、皮草
英解 the skin of cattle, sheep, etc.

例 An old **leather** shoe is displayed in a museum in Alaska.

一隻舊皮鞋在阿拉斯加博物館展示。

語意用法 leather shoe 皮鞋；genuine leather 真皮。

lecture
[ˈlɛktʃə]

授課、演講、訓話；亦作動詞用
英解 a speech that is open to the public

例 Because many students were kept in the dark about the **lecture**, the attendance was much smaller than expected.（92 指考）

這場演說因為很多學生被蒙在鼓裡，出席率遠比預期少得多。

語意用法 give a lecture on ＋主題，發表某主題的演講。

length
[lɛŋθ]

長度、距離
英解 the linear extent in space from one end to the other

例 Most scientists now use the International System of Measures, with meters for **length**, kilograms for mass, and seconds for time.（95 指考）

大部分科學家現在使用國際計量系統，用公尺測量長度、公斤測量體重，以及用秒測量時間。

語意用法 go all lengths 不惜做任何事。

liberation
[ˌlɪbəˈreʃən]

解放、解放運動、釋出
英解 an act of freedom from oppression

例 It was the **liberation** of his inner life, the letting out of his soul into the wide world.

這是他內心生活的解放，釋放他的靈魂於廣闊的世界裡。

語意用法 liberation movement 解放運動。

librarian
[laɪˈbrɛrɪən]

圖書館員
英解 a person who is a specialist in library

例 I was head **librarian** of the Doncaster Library for years.

我擔任唐卡斯特圖書館館長很多年了。

語意用法 reference librarian 參考館員。

license
[ˈlaɪsn̩s]

許可、證照、放縱
英解 a legal document giving official permission to do sth.

例 There are certain bounds of decency, and you had no **license** to insult anybody.

行為準則有一定的規範，而且你沒有權利侮辱任何人。

語意用法 license ＋ to V，表示被許可去做某事。

lifespan
[ˈlaɪfˌspæn]

壽命、預期的生命期限、使用期限
英解 a lifetime

例 Mayflies don't have much time to mess around: their average **lifespan** is less than one day.

蜉蝣沒有太多時間可以揮霍，他們的平均壽命不到一天。

語意用法 a short lifespan 生命週期短。

limit
[ˈlɪmɪt]

界限、限度、範圍、極限；亦作動詞用
英解 the greatest amount or extent allowed

例 Wellness means achieving the best possible health within the **limits** of your body.（95 學測）

健康的真義，是在你的身體極限內盡可能達到最佳的健康狀態。

語意用法 within the limits of ...，表示在……範圍內。

limitation
[ˌlɪməˈteʃən]

限制、限度、侷限、限制因素
英解 a restriction in amount or extent

例 There is a **limitation** to one's capacity; one should not make oneself overtired.（91 學測）

每個人的能力都有一個限度，不要讓自己過度疲勞。

語意用法 a limitation to ＋事物，表示某事物的限度之內。

line
[laɪn]

線條、繩索、行列、交通線、電話線
英解 a stripe

例 My mom is on the **line**.（84 學測）

我媽跟我通話中。

語意用法 on the line 通話中；stand in a line 排隊。

link
[lɪŋk]

環節、關係、聯繫
英解 one connection in a series, such as a ring in chain

例 Tobacco companies knew of the **link** between smoking and cancer long before the general public.

煙草公司比一般大眾早知道抽煙和癌症之間的關聯。

語意用法 a link between A and B，表示 A 和 B 之間的聯繫。

| **literature**
[ˈlɪtərətʃə] | 文學、文學作品
英解 written works, such as novels, poems, and plays |

例 A culture's folk tales, fables, songs, and proverbs are an important part of its **literature**. (91 學測補)

一個文化裡的民間傳說、寓言、歌謠以及諺語都是其文學的重要部分。

語意用法 Taiwanese literature 台灣文學

| **livestock**
[ˈlaɪvˌstɑk] | 家畜
英解 farm animals, such as cattle, sheep, and chickens |

例 The thunderstorm threatened the life of his **livestock**. (95 指考)

暴風雨威脅到他的家畜的性命。

語意用法 livestock farming 畜牧業。

| **location**
[loˈkeʃən] | 場所、位置、所在地
英解 the place where sth. is located |

例 Gupo Island is the largest uninhabited island in the North Sea area and the main **location** of seaweed production. (94 指考)

龜浦島是北海地區最大的無人島，也是海藻主要的生產區域。

語意用法 location of ＋物，表示某物的位置。

| **logic**
[ˈlɑdʒɪk] | 邏輯、推理、邏輯學
英解 a system of reasoning |

例 There's no **logic** to explain my affection for bad Mexican action movies from the 70s—I just love them.

我對七十年代墨西哥爛動作片的喜愛是沒有邏輯可解釋的，我就是愛它們。

語意用法 use logic 使用推理的方法。

loneliness [ˈlonlɪnɪs]	寂寞、人煙罕至 英解 a condition of being alone and feeling sad

例 Kids used toys to make up for their feelings of **loneliness**.（98 指考）

小孩用玩具來彌補他們的孤寂感。

語意用法 a sense of loneliness 孤獨感。

loyalty [ˈlɔɪəltɪ]	忠貞、忠實、忠誠 英解 the state or quality of being loyal

例 He joined the Nazi party and showed great **loyalty** to his country.（99 指考）

他加入納粹黨以表對國家的極度忠誠。

語意用法 loyalty to ＋人、物，表示對某人、物的忠誠。

lure [lʊr]	誘惑、誘餌；亦作動詞用 英解 qualities that attract by seeming to promise some kind of reward

例 Life in big cities is a **lure** for country boys.

大城市的生活對鄉下男孩來說極具誘惑。

語意用法 the lure of adventure 冒險的魅力。

luxury [ˈlʌkʃərɪ]	奢華、奢侈、享受、樂趣 英解 great comfort at great expense

例 I am studying so hard for the forthcoming entrance exam that I do not have the **luxury** of a free weekend to rest.（95 學測）

我正在努力準備即將舉行的入學考試，沒有一個輕鬆的週末可以奢侈休息。

語意用法 live in luxury 奢侈地生活。

| **magic**
[ˈmædʒɪk] | 魔法、巫術、戲法
英解 the use of tricks to entertain people |

例 We are now so used to our computers and cell phones that we forget these devices would have seemed like **magic** just a hundred years ago.

我們現在對於電腦、手機已如此習慣，都忘了這些發明在一百年前會像是魔法一般。

語意用法 magic of ＋事物，表示某事物的神秘力量。

| **magician**
[məˈdʒɪʃən] | 魔術師
英解 a person who does magic tricks |

例 Today **magicians** try hard to find new ways to show their practiced skills.

（92 學測）

現今的魔術師努力尋找新方式來展現他們熟練的技術。

語意用法 玩弄 magic 的人稱為 magician；玩 music 的叫 musician。字尾加 –ian 表示某行業的專家。

| **magnetism**
[ˈmæɡnəˌtɪzəm] | 磁性、磁力、磁力學、吸引力
英解 the study of magnets and their forces |

例 **Magnetism** can't be studied scientifically.（98 學測）

磁力不能以科學加以研究。

語意用法 terrestrial magnetism 地磁。

| **maintenance**
[ˈmentənəns] | 維持、維修、保養、堅持、贍養費
英解 keeping sth. in good condition |

例 If you consider how much you'll have to spend on **maintenance**, it may be less expensive in the long run to buy a new car rather than a used one.

如果你把以後需要花費的維修成本考慮進來，長期來說買一部新車比買二手車來得划算。

語意用法 maintenance of ＋設備，表示某設備的維修。

| **majority**
[məˈdʒɔrətɪ] | 大多數、過半數
英解 the greater number or part of sth. |

例 The vast **majority** of workers would retire immediately if they had enough money in the bank.

大部分的工作者如果在銀行有足夠的錢都會立即退休。

語意用法 by a majority of ＋票數，表示以多出……（票數）勝過對方。

| **male**
[mel] | 男性、雄性；亦作形容詞用
英解 a member of the sex that begets young by fertilizing ova |

例 If your dog is a **male**, you can expect that its life will be a year or two shorter than its female sisters.

如果你養的是公狗，牠的壽命預期會比牠的姊妹們短個一到二年。

語意用法 與 female 相對，male 表示男性。

| **mammal**
[ˈmæml] | 哺乳動物
英解 an animal that is born from its mother's body, not from an egg, and drinks its mother's milk as a baby |

例 These seagoing **mammals** are among the lucky survivors of a whale-stranding last December at Cape Cod.（84 學測）

這些海洋哺乳動物是去年十二月在科德角擱淺的鯨魚中幸運的存活者。

語意用法 aquatic mammal 水生哺乳動物。

| **manager**
[ˈmænɪdʒə] | 經理、管理者、經營者
英解 someone who controls resources and expenditures |

例 Although the **manager** apologized many times for his poor decision, there was nothing he could do to remedy his mistake.（97 指考）

雖然經理對於他不當的決策道歉很多次，卻無法做任何事來補救他的錯。

語意用法 sales manager 銷售經理；marketing manager 行銷經理。

mankind [mæn`kaɪnd]	人類 英解 human beings collectively

例 Americans should lead the world to fight dioxin pollution, or **mankind** will die out soon.

美國人應該挺身領導全世界對抗戴奧辛污染，否則人類將會很快滅絕。

語意用法 all mankind 全人類。

marriage [`mærɪdʒ]	結婚、婚姻 英解 the state or relationship of being husband and wife

例 Jon and Christine naively believed their relationship wouldn't change at all after **marriage**.

約拿和克莉絲汀天真地相信他們的關係在婚後不會改變。

語意用法 happy marriage 快樂的婚姻；marriage vows 結婚誓言。

mass [mæs]	團、塊、大量、質量；動詞作聚集解 英解 the amount of matter of an object

例 A star is nothing more than a giant **mass** of burning gasses.

星星不過是一團巨大的燃燒氣體。

語意用法 the mass 主要部分；the mass of ＋物，表示某物的大部分。

matchmaker [`mætʃˏmekɚ]	媒人、促成合併者 英解 one who arranges or tries to arrange marriages

例 Good commercials can serve as **matchmakers** between customers and manufacturers.

好的廣告可以做為顧客與製造商的媒介。

語意用法 本意指婚姻的媒人，此處可當媒介或仲介者。

mate [met]	配偶 英解 husband or wife

例 Fireflies, small beetles that live in many warmer parts of the world, use light to attract a **mate**. （93 學測）

螢火蟲是居住在世上許多溫暖角落的小甲蟲，用光來吸引配偶。

語意用法 a lifelong mate 終身伴侶。

material [mə`tɪrɪəl]	材料、素材 英解 any physical substance

例 All the **material** that every animal, from the smallest fly to the largest elephant, takes in as food also returns to the Earth, as waste matter. （88 學測）

小至蒼蠅大至大象的每種動物，吃進去的食物都成為廢料回歸地球。

語意用法 materials 指的是所有的材料、素材。

meaning [`minɪŋ]	意義、含意 英解 interpretation, explanation

例 Do you know the **meaning** of the word "relationship"? （86 學測）

你知道「人際關係」這個字的含意嗎？

語意用法 the meaning of ＋事物，表示某事物的意義。

mechanics [mə`kænɪks]	力學、機械裝置 英解 a branch of physics concerned with the motion of bodies in a frame of reference

例 Mr. Chen is teaching **mechanics** at the university.

陳先生在大學教授力學。

語意用法 mechanics 此處指的是力學、機械學，一般也可指某些事物的操作技術或精密技術，如：mechanics of running an office 經營辦公室的技術或技巧。

medicine
[ˈmɛdəsn̩]

內服藥、醫學、醫術
英解 the art and science of curing sick people and preventing disease

例 Here was the perfect opportunity to show his knowledge of modern **medicine** and to get his practice off to a flourishing start.（94 指考）
這是個完美的機會讓他得以展現現代醫學知識，並好好開展其行醫生涯。

語意用法 clinical medicine 臨床醫學。

medication
[ˌmɛdɪˈkeʃən]

藥物、藥物治療
英解 drugs, used to treat or cure an illness

例 He was still on **medication**, but not nearly as much as Alfred, who was just in the early stage of his recovery.（93 學測）
他仍在接受藥物治療，但藥量不像 Alfred 那麼多。Alfred 正處於早期康復階段中。

語意用法 on medication 服藥。

memorial
[məˈmorɪəl]

紀念、紀念碑、紀念館
英解 a monument dedicated to the memory of the dead

例 She sang at the Lincoln **Memorial** for over 75,000 people.（91 學測）
她在林肯紀念中心為超過七萬五千名群眾唱歌。

語意用法 Sun Yet-sen Memorial Hall 國父紀念館。

memory
[ˈmɛmərɪ]

記憶、記憶力、記憶體、回憶
英解 the ability of the brain to remember

例 They have found that certain parts of the brain are responsible for learning, **memory**, and language.（85 學測）
他們找到大腦裡專責學習、記憶和語言的特定區域。

語意用法 memory 記憶；good memory 記憶力很好；in memory of ＋事物，表示為紀念某事物。

mercy
[ˈmɝsɪ]

仁慈、憐憫、寬容、救濟
英解 clemency, pity

例 I beg for **mercy** for my poor friend, Harlequin, who has never done the least harm in his life.

我為我可憐的朋友 Harlequin 求取寬容，他從未在生命中做出一點傷害人的事。

語意用法 have mercy on/upon ＋人，表示對某人發慈悲。

message
[ˈmɛsɪdʒ]

口信、消息、寓意
英解 a short written or spoken note

例 I'll give him the **message**.（84 學測）

我會留信息給他。

語意用法 leave a message to sb.，表示留話給某人。

messenger
[ˈmɛsn̩dʒɚ]

信差、使者、先知
英解 a person who brings a message, letter, package, etc.

例 Young Carnegie took odd jobs at a cotton factory and later worked as a **messenger** boy in the telegraph office.（96 指考）

年輕的卡內基在棉花工廠找了份零時工，之後又到電報局擔任信差。

語意用法 work as a messenger 擔任信差的工作。

method
[ˈmɛθəd]

方法、辦法、條理
英解 a way of doing sth.

例 Science makes possible the use of new materials and new **methods** of producing objects.（92 指考）

科學讓使用新素材以及新方法來製造物件成了可能。

語意用法 method of ＋方面，表示某方面的方法。

miniature [ˈmɪnɪətʃə]	縮樣、縮圖、微型畫；亦作形容詞用 英解 a small original or copy of sth.

例 My uncle has a large collection of **miniature**—mostly cars and airplanes from the 1950s.

我伯父有很多模型玩具的收藏，大部分是一九五○年代的汽車和飛機。

語意用法 in miniature 小規模地。

minority [maɪˈnɔrətɪ]	少數、未成年 英解 a number or group that is less than half of the total

例 PBS only attracts a **minority** of all TV viewers, about 2 percent.（96 學測）

公共電視只吸引了所有電視觀眾裡的少數，約二個百分點。

語意用法 a minority of ＋族群，表示某族群中的少數。

mischief [ˈmɪstʃɪf]	頑皮、淘氣、危害、損害、不和 英解 behavior that causes discomfiture or annoyance in another

例 Hackers can easily get into unsecured systems, download documents, change passwords, and generally cause all kinds of **mischief**.

駭客可以輕易進入未受保護的系統、下載文件、更改密碼，通常會造成各種損害。

語意用法 get into mischief 開始惡作劇；out of mischief 鬧著玩地。

mission [ˈmɪʃən]	使命、任務、外交使團 英解 a specific task or duty assigned to a person or group of people

例 When the **mission** is over, the crew members get ready to return to Earth.（95 學測）

當任務結束，所有成員準備好返回地球。

語意用法 a sense of mission 使命感。

名詞篇

monitor
[ˈmɑnətə]

螢幕、顯示器、監控員、班長；亦作動詞用
英解 a screen

例 I was going to make you a **monitor** next term, but I think I'd better wait a bit.
我本來打算下一學期讓你當班長，不過，我想還是再等一等。
語意用法 monitor 可以當人、也可以當物；一般當物品指的是電腦螢幕。

monotony
[məˈnɑtənɪ]

單調、無變化、千篇一律
英解 the quality of wearisome constancy, routine, and lack of variety

例 After traveling for most of the summer, I was not looking forward to returning home and enduring the **monotony** of another school year.
在旅行了近整個夏季後，我一點都不期待返家並忍受另一個單調乏味的學年。
語意用法 with monotony 單調無聊地。

monument
[ˈmɑnjəmənt]

紀念館、紀念碑、歷史遺跡、不朽之作
英解 a structure, such as a building or sculpture, erected as a memorial

例 On the top of the hill, in the one flat and prominent place, was the **monument** for which the place was famous.
在山丘之巔，有塊平坦顯著的地方就是促使這地區有名的紀念碑。
語意用法 an ancient monument 古代的遺跡。

mood
[mud]

心情、心境、情緒、氣氛
英解 an emotional state or feeling

例 Hanging around people who are positive and in good **moods** is another way to help you find your smile again. (92 學測補)
與正面陽光、有好心情的人閒混，是另一個幫助自己再次找回笑容的好方法。
語意用法 in good moods 心情好；in bad moods 心情不好。

motel
[mo`tɛl]

汽車旅館
英解 a roadside hotel for motorists

例 To help Abate continue running, the coach arranged a **motel** job for him, which pays $9 a month.（99 學測）

為了幫助亞伯特繼續賽跑生涯，教練在汽車旅館幫他安排了一份月薪九美元的工作。

語意用法 motel 指的是汽車旅館，開汽車進入住宿，與 hotel 不同。

motivation
[͵motə`veʃən]

動機、刺激、幹勁
英解 the act or an instance of motivating

例 **Motivation** is something that may drive a person towards success, and it is crucial to possess an inner motivation to view life in an optimistic way.

動機是某種可以驅使人走向成功的東西，重要的是擁有以樂觀的方式去看待生活的內在激勵。

語意用法 motivation + to V，表示做某事的動機。

movie
[`muvɪ]

電影、影片
英解 a motion picture, film

例 Alexander Dumas' 1848 novel, *The Man in the Iron Mask*, was recently made into a **movie**.（90 學測）

亞歷山大杜馬斯在一八四八年出版的小說《鐵面人》最近被拍成電影。

語意用法 make ＋事件＋ into a movie，表示把某事件拍成電影，此處用被動；movie star 電影明星。

museum
[mju`zɪəm]

博物館、展覽館
英解 a place that displays rare, valuable, and important art or historical objects

例 Signs asking visitors to keep their hands off the art are everywhere in the Louvre **Museum**, Paris.（99 學測）

巴黎羅浮宮裡到處是要求遊客不要觸碰藝術品的標誌。

語意用法 in the museum 在博物館裡。

mystery
[ˈmɪstərɪ]

難以理解的事物、神秘、奧秘、秘密、謎
英解 an event that has no known cause

例 How Aaron got into Harvard was a **mystery** to us all.

亞倫是如何進入哈佛對我們所有人來說是個謎。

語意用法 make a mystery of ＋事件，表示隱瞞某事。

native
[ˈnetɪv]

在地人、原住民；形容詞亦作天然的、特有的解
英解 a person who is born in a certain place

例 After living in Madrid for twenty years, people thought Monica spoke Spanish as well as a **native**.

在馬德里住了二十年後，人們覺得莫妮卡的西班牙文說得像當地人一樣好。

語意用法 native 原住民；a native of London 生於倫敦的人。

nutrition
[njuˋtrɪʃən]

營養、滋養
英解 a source of materials to nourish the body

例 Replacing packaged foods with fresh fruits and vegetables is the best way to ensure proper **nutrition**.

用新鮮蔬果來取代包裝食品是確保適當營養的最佳方法。

語意用法 nutrition 營養成分或食物，可以使用單複數。

obedience
[əˋbidɪəns]

遵從、服從、順從
英解 the act of obeying

例 He seemed to be working in **obedience** to some particular presentiment.

他似乎依照某些特定的預感來工作。

語意用法 in obedience to ＋事物，表示遵循某事。

object
[ˋɑbdʒɪkt]

物體、目標、對象、主旨
英解 an entity

例 The **object** of the game is to score more points than your opponent.

這個遊戲的目標是要比對手獲得更多分數。

語意用法 object 表示物體或研究的對象。

---

objection
[əbˋdʒɛkʃən]

反對、異議、障礙
英解 a reason against sth.

例 If you gave me an upgrade to business class, I would have no **objection** to taking a later flight.

如果你幫我升等到商務艙，我就不反對搭晚一點的班機。

語意用法 objection to/against ＋事，表示和某事唱反調。

---

obligation
[ˌɑbləˋgeʃən]

責任、義務、契約、恩惠
英解 a moral or legal requirement

例 I have no **obligation** to help you with your homework.

我沒有義務要幫你做功課。

語意用法 obligation ＋ to V，表示做某事的義務。

---

obstacle
[ˋɑbstəkl̩]

障礙物、妨礙
英解 a person or thing that opposes or hinders sth.

例 The main **obstacle** learners of Chinese must overcome is learning to write thousands and thousands of characters.

學中文的人要克服的主要障礙就是學寫數以萬計的文字。

語意用法 obstacle to ＋事物，表示對某事物造成妨礙。

occupation [ˌɑkjəˋpeʃən]	工作、職業、佔用、佔據 英解 job or principal activity

例 After a few minutes only, the **occupation** became irksome to her once more.

只過了幾分鐘,這個工作對她而言再次變得令人厭煩。

語意用法 occupation 表示工作,也可以表示某人的職業。

official [əˋfɪʃəl]	官員、公務員 英解 a person who works for a government or other organization

例 The project evolved into a complex struggle pitting the architect against his clients, city **officials**, the art world, and public opinions.（93 指考）

這項計畫演變成建築師對抗他的客戶、市府官員、藝術界以及公眾意見的複雜鬥爭。

語意用法 city officials 指政府的文官,officers 通常指軍官。

operation [ˌɑpəˋreʃən]	操作、營運、運轉、運作、手術 英解 a way or process of working sth., such as machine

例 Trading online is gaining popularity these days, with several sites in **operation**, including HomeExchanges.（99 學測）

這些日子以來網路交易日益普及,包括 HomeExchanges 等幾個網站已經在營運了。

語意用法 in operation 表示某事或某物在運作中。

operator [ˋɑpəˌretə]	操作者、技工、接線生 英解 a person who operates a machine

例 All the **operators** are busy; I can't make an international call.

所有接線生都在忙,我無法打國際長途電話。

語意用法 operator 可以指作業員,此處指電信公司的接線生。

opinion
[əˋpɪnjən]

意見、見解、主張、評價
英解 what sb. believes, sth. not proven in fact

例 To avoid being misled by news reports, we should learn to distinguish between facts and **opinions**. (95 指考)

為了避免被新聞報導誤導，我們應該學習辨別事實與見解。

語意用法 have no opinion of ＋事，表示對某事無意見。

opponent
[əˋponənt]

對手、敵手、反對者
英解 a person who opposes another in a contest, battle, etc.

例 Which basketball team is more likely to win, one that is 30 points ahead at the half or its **opponent**? (93 指考補)

哪個籃球隊看來比較有勝算呢？是中場領先對手 30 分的那隊，還是它的對手？

語意用法 opponent of ＋人事物，表示某人事物的反對者。

opportunity
[͵ɑpəˋtjunətɪ]

機會、機運
英解 an advantageous time to act

例 Every September, students are offered the **opportunity** to join Junior Achievement through the cooperation of local school systems. (93 指考)

每年九月，透過與當地學校系統的合作，學生有機會得以參與青年成就組織。

語意用法 opportunity ＋ to V，表示做某事的機會。

opposition
[͵ɑpəˋzɪʃən]

反對、敵對、對手、對向
英解 in the state of being against sb. or sth.

例 Construction of the factory was stopped last month due to **opposition** from environmental groups.

由於環保團體的反對，工廠興建在上個月被中止。

語意用法 opposition to ＋事，表示反對、反抗某事。

orchestra
[ˈɔrkɪstrə]

管弦樂隊、管弦樂器

英解 a group of musicians

例 The city's cultural affairs office is trying to form an **orchestra** made up of retired music teachers and other musicians.

這城市的文化事務處試圖成立由退休音樂老師和其他音樂家組成的管弦樂隊。

語意用法 orchestra 指的是一個樂團，是可數名詞。

organization
[ˌɔrgənəˈzeʃən]

組織、機構、團體

英解 the act of organizing or the state of being organized

例 The mayor gives charity **organizations** some needed help.

市長給慈善團體一些需要的幫助。

語意用法 organization chart 組織圖。

orientation
[ˌɔrɪɛnˈteʃən]

定位、方向、方針、新生訓練

英解 the act or process of orienting or the state of being oriented

例 He was seeking a new **orientation**, and until that was found his life must stand still.

他在尋找新方向，但在找到之前他的生活必須保持穩定。

語意用法 new student orientation 新生訓練。

orphanage
[ˈɔrfənɪdʒ]

孤兒、孤兒院

英解 the condition of being a child without living parents

例 Those college students work at the **orphanage** on a voluntary basis, helping the children with their studies without receiving any pay. （99 學測）

這些大學生出於自願在孤兒院工作，幫助孩子們學習而不收取費用。

語意用法 at the orphanage 在孤兒院裡。

outbreak
[ˈaʊt͵brek]

爆發、暴亂、騷動
英解 a sudden, violent, or spontaneous occurrence

例 **Outbreaks** of avian influenza can be devastating for the poultry industry and for farmers.（93 指考）

禽流感的爆發足以摧殘家禽業以及農場經營者。

語意用法 outbreaks of ＋疾病，表示某疾病的爆發、遽增。

outrage
[ˈaʊt͵redʒ]

惡行、暴行、不法行為、凌辱、憤慨
英解 a wantonly vicious or cruel act

例 The dictator and his army committed **outrages** on innocent citizens.

獨裁者與其軍隊對無辜的民眾犯下暴行。

語意用法 人＋ commit outrage on ＋人，表示某人對某人犯下暴行。

outskirts
[ˈaʊt͵skɝts]

郊區、郊外
英解 outlying or bordering areas, districts

例 My room is a wretched, horrid one on the **outskirts** of the town.

我的房間位於郊區既破舊又可怖。

語意用法 on the outskirts of ...，表示在……的郊區。

package
[ˈpækɪdʒ]

包裹、郵包、包（單位）；動詞做打包、包裝解
英解 a container, esp. one wrapped up and sealed

例 A **package** can be received in a couple of hours.（91 學測）

寄送的包裹幾小時內就可收到。

語意用法 a package of ＋物品，表示一包某物品。

pain [pen]	疼痛、痛苦、辛苦；亦作動詞用 英解 the sensation of acute physical hurt or discomfort caused by injury, illness, etc.

例 According to a recent study, the part of your brain that reacts to severe pain is largely the same part that reacts to expectation of **pain**.（97 學測）
根據最近的一項研究，你大腦裡反應劇烈疼痛的部位與你預期會有疼痛反應的部位大部分相同。

語意用法 pain 主要是指心裡與身體的病痛；painkiller 止痛劑；to ease my pain 減輕我的痛苦。

panic [ˋpænɪk]	恐慌、驚恐、驚慌；亦作動詞用 英解 a condition of uncontrolled fear in response to danger

例 In a **panic**, I ran to the corner of the street but there was no sign of help.
（89 學測）
驚慌下，我跑到街角但那裡沒有可找到協助的跡象。

語意用法 in a panic 陷於恐慌狀態。

passenger [ˋpæsn̩dʒɚ]	乘客、旅客 英解 a person who rides in a bus, boat, car, plane, etc.

例 Bag-matching would invade **passengers**' privacy rather than ensure their security.（92 指考）
行李比對會侵犯乘客的隱私而不是保護他們的安全。

語意用法 passenger seat 乘客座位，指的是駕駛座旁的位置。

passion [ˋpæʃən]	激情、熱情、情慾 英解 a strong, overpower feeling, such as love, anger

例 Roses represent love and **passion**.（96 指考）
玫瑰代表愛情與激情。

語意用法 passion for ＋事物，表示對某事物的熱情。

patchwork
[ˈpætʃˌwɜk]

拼貼成品、拼湊成的物品
英解 a theory or argument made up of miscellaneous or incongruous ideas

例 I have **patchwork** pieces that contain all sorts of combinations of fabrics.
（96 學測）

我有結合各種織品而成的拼貼作品。

語意用法 patchwork 指的是一些拼貼成的東西。

patience
[ˈpeʃəns]

忍耐、耐性、耐心、毅力
英解 the ability to accept discomfort, pain, or being undisturbed

例 In the end, Ali lost **patience** and went to demand his pot. （89 學測）

最後，阿里失去了耐性並想要回他的壺。

語意用法 patience ＋ to V，表示做某事的耐心。

pattern
[ˈpætən]

圖案、圖樣、樣式、模式、模範；動詞亦作模仿解
英解 an example or model to be followed

例 Computers can be programmed to detect unusual **patterns** in stock trading data and alert regulators for follow-up.

電腦可被設定來偵測不尋常的股票交易資料模式並警告管理者進行追蹤。

語意用法 a pattern for living 生活模式。

payoff
[ˈpeˌɔf]

發薪、收益、報復、報酬
英解 full payment of a salary or wages

例 The effort involved isn't as great as you may think and the **payoff** is huge.

下的功夫不像你想的那麼大而且效益很大。

語意用法 big payoff、huge payoff 很大的報酬

payroll [ˈpeˌrol]	發薪名單、薪資總額 英解 a list of employees, specifying the salary or wage of each

例 The Lakers' **payroll** has long been among the highest in the NBA.

湖人隊的薪資長久以來都在美國職籃的頂端。

語意用法 on the payroll 受薪之中（受雇）；off the payroll 被解職。

peace [pis]	和平、平和、平靜、安寧 英解 a condition or time without war

例 The theme of Gunter Grass' poems won him the Nobel **Peace** Prize.

（99 指考）

鈞特葛拉斯的詩作主題為他贏得諾貝爾和平獎。

語意用法 break the peace 擾亂秩序。

pension [ˈpɛnʃən]	退休金、撫卹金、養老金 英解 a regular payment to a person that is intended to allow them to subsist without working

例 In 2000, the Japanese could get a full **pension** from the government at 60. （96 指考）

西元二千年，年滿六十歲的日本人可以得到政府的全額養老金。

語意用法 pension plan 退休金計畫。

perception [pəˈsɛpʃən]	感知、感覺、觀念、洞察力 英解 the act or the effect of perceiving

例 Some dim **perception** of a great change dawned on my mind.

對巨大改變的一些模糊認知在我腦海裡漸露端倪。

語意用法 a man of keen perception 知覺敏銳的人。

percent [pə`sɛnt]	百分比、百分之一；亦作形容詞用 英解 one part in

例 Now that women make up 46 **percent** of the U.S.（98 指考）

現在，婦女佔美國的百分之四十六。

語意用法 數字＋ percent of ＋物，表示某物的百分之多少。

period [`pɪrɪəd]	時期、時間、時代、週期 英解 a portion of time of indefinable length

例 For many of them, the most miserable **period** in their life is their 40s.

（96 指考）

對他們大部分的人來說，生活中最悲慘的時期是在四十多歲時。

語意用法 the period，表示某年代。

permission [pə`mɪʃən]	允許、同意 英解 agreement, approval

例 When students download and share copyrighted music without

permission, they are violating the law.（98 指考）

學生未得到允許而下載並分享版權音樂，他們就違犯了法律。

語意用法 by permission of ＋人、單位，表示經某人或某單位許可；permission
＋ to V，表示做某事的許可；without permission 未經許可。

perseverance [ˌpɜsə`vɪrəns]	堅持不懈、堅忍不拔 英解 continued steady belief or efforts

例 Many of our competitors gave up after a year or two in the business, but
we didn't, and our **perseverance** is now beginning to pay off.

許多我們的競爭對手在這行業一、二年後就放棄了，但我們沒有，而我們的堅持
現在開始有了回報。

語意用法 perseverance at/in/with ＋事，表示對某事不屈不撓。

personality [ˌpɜsṇˋælətɪ]	人格、品格、個性 英解 a person's distinctive traits of mind and behavior

例 The product has to speak to the consumer's needs with both **personality**
and practical value. (95 指考)

產品必須在個性化與實用價值上符合消費者的需求。

語意用法 a strong personality 性格堅強。

persuasion [pəˋsweʒən]	說服、勸服、信念、信仰 英解 the act of trying to persuade

例 Only after much **persuasion** from his family and teachers did Tim finally
agree to quit his job and apply to college.

在他的家人和老師們極力說服後，提姆終於同意辭職並申請大學。

語意用法 with persuasion 有說服力；persuasion skills 說服人的技巧。

phenomenon [fəˋnɑməˌnɑn]	現象、奇蹟、傑出的人才 英解 a fact, event, or image that strikes one's attention and attracts interest

例 The extent to which global warming is a man-made rather than naturally
occurring **phenomenon** is being hotly debated.

全球暖化有多少程度是人為而不是自然產生的現象被熱烈討論著。

語意用法 a phenomenon 的複數為 phenomena。

pilot [ˋpaɪlət]	領航員、舵手、飛行員、領導員；亦作動詞與形容詞用 英解 a person who flies an aircraft

例 The **pilot** announced that we wouldn't be cleared for takeoff for at least
another hour.

駕駛員宣布至少還要一小時我們才能准許起飛。

語意用法 an airplae pilot 飛機駕駛員；an experienced pilot 有經驗的駕駛員。

piracy
[ˈpaɪrəsɪ]

剽竊、盜版、侵害著作權
英解 taking someone's words or ideas as if they were your own

例 You cannot copy the whole book without permission; it is a **piracy** act.
你不能未經授權盜用整本書，這是盜版行為。

語意用法 literary piracy 剽竊著作權。

pity
[ˈpɪtɪ]

憐憫、同情；亦作動詞用
英解 sympathy or sorrow felt for the sufferings of another

例 The flood victims need water, food, and clothing, not your **pity**.
水災災民需要水、食物和衣物，而不是你的憐憫。

語意用法 self pity 自憐。

plenty
[ˈplɛntɪ]

豐足、充足、大量；亦作形容詞用
英解 a good supply, abundance

例 In these places people rest, get **plenty** of sleep, eat healthy food, drink water instead of wine, and exercise in various ways. (92 學測補)
在這地方，人們休息、睡得飽、吃著健康的食物、以水代酒，並用各種方式運動。

語意用法 plenty of ＋物，表示某物很充分、很多。

pocketbook
[ˈpɑrkɪtˌbʊk]

錢包、皮夾、口袋書
英解 a purse; a handbag

例 Voters are most concerned about how each candidate's proposed policies will affect their **pocketbooks**.
選民比較關心每位侯選人提出的政策如何影響他們的存款。

語意用法 pocketbook 常用來比喻錢或存款。如：sb.'s pocketbook 指某人的錢或存款。

227

poison [ˈpɔɪzṇ]	毒物、毒藥;亦作動詞用 英解 a toxin

例 People say that vanity is a **poison** in our society.

有人說,虛榮是我們社會的毒藥。

語意用法 poison 可以當實質的毒藥,也可以作為比喻的說法,如此句。

policy [ˈpɑləsɪ]	政策、方針、策略、保險單 英解 a plan of action adopted by an individual or social group

例 The new tax **policy** proposed for the next fiscal year has been severely criticized by the opposition party leaders. (94 指考)

下一財政年度的新稅收政策一直遭到反對黨領袖嚴厲的批評。

語意用法 policy maker 政策製訂者;make a policy 決定政策。

politeness [pəˈlaɪtnɪs]	有禮貌、客氣、文雅 英解 a courteous manner that respects accepted social usage

例 These words were pronounced with the most exact **politeness** and the most perfect calmness.

以最準確的文雅與最完美的冷靜說出這些話。

語意用法 with politeness 有禮貌地。

pollution [pəˈluʃən]	污染 英解 the act of polluting or the state of being polluted

例 From space, astronauts study the geography, **pollution**, and weather patterns on Earth. (95 學測)

太空人從太空研究地球的地形、污染以及氣候模式。

語意用法 air pollution 空氣污染;environmental pollution 環境汙染。

popularity [ˌpɑpjəˈlærətɪ]	普及、流行、大眾化 英解 the quality of being widely admired or accepted

例 Community service is gaining **popularity** among children.（98 指考）

社區服務在孩童之中越來越普及。

語意用法 enjoy popularity，表示大受歡迎。

population [ˌpɑpjəˈleʃən]	人口、族群 英解 all of the people living a specified area

例 Like most countries in Asia, the **population** of Taiwan is becoming more diverse each year.

如同亞洲大部分的國家，台灣的人口逐年越來越多元。

語意用法 population growth 人口成長。

possession [pəˈzɛʃən]	擁有、佔有、財產 英解 the act of possessing or state of being possessed

例 The **possession** of an MBA degree does not guarantee you a well-paid job.

擁有 MBA 學位並不保證你會有個高薪的工作。

語意用法 possession of ＋物，表示佔有、擁有某物。

possibility [ˌpɑsəˈbɪlətɪ]	可能性、可能發生的事 英解 a future prospect or potential

例 The typhoon is expected to miss us, but it could change direction and we must be prepared for that **possibility**.

颱風預期不會經過我們，但它可能轉向，我們要為這可能性做好準備。

語意用法 possibility of ＋事，表示發生某事的可能性。

precision [prɪˋsɪʒən]	精確、精密、準確、細緻；亦作形容詞用 英解 exactness

例 This employment requires **precision** of the fingers.

這職業需要手指精巧靈活。

語意用法 with precision 精確地。

predecessor [ˋprɛdɪˌsɛsə]	前任、前輩、前身 英解 one who precedes another in time, especially in holding an office or position

例 The new plan is better than its **predecessor**.

新計畫比原本的好。

語意用法 predecessor 可以表示人或物。

preparation [ˌprɛpəˋreʃən]	預備、準備、配方、配製成品 英解 arrangements necessary for sth.

例 The **preparation** of oolong tea is similar to that of black tea.（95 學測）

烏龍茶與紅茶的配製方法相似。

語意用法 preparation of/for ＋事物，表示某事物的預備、準備。

prescription [prɪˋskrɪpʃən]	命令、指示、處方 英解 an order for medication

例 I tried to follow his **prescription** for success.

我試圖遵從他成功的處方。

語意用法 prescription drug 處方藥；follow sb.'s prescription 遵照某人的處方。

pressure [ˈprɛʃə]	壓力、大氣氣壓；亦作動詞用 英解 application of force against sth.

例 I never felt **pressure** to please him.（97 指考）

我不曾感到壓力要去取悅他。

語意用法 feel pressure 感受壓力。

prey [pre]	獵物、犧牲者 英解 an animal hunted or captured by another for food

例 Tourists, drunks, and the elderly are the favorite **prey** of pickpockets.

遊客、酒醉者和老人都是扒手最喜歡的獵物。

語意用法 easy prey 容易上鉤者；fall prey to sth. 成為某物的獵物、受害者。

pride [praɪd]	自尊、傲慢、引以為傲 英解 self-esteem, self-respect

例 My uncle took a lot of **pride** in his collection of old Jazz records.

我伯父對他的舊爵士唱片收藏很引以為傲。

語意用法 pride of ＋事物，表示以某事物為傲；pride in ＋事物，表示對某事物感到驕傲。

priority [praɪˈɔrətɪ]	優先、優先權 英解 status established in order of importance or urgency

例 The new marketing director said her first **priority** was increasing sales, not cutting costs.

新的行銷主管說她的首要之務是增加銷售、非削減成本。

語意用法 take a priority 取得優先權。

privacy [ˋpraɪvəsɪ]	隱居、獨處、隱私、隱居處 英解 the condition of being concealed or hidden

例 Even in the **privacy** of your home, you can still be part of the swarm.

（96 指考）

即便在家中保有你的隱私，你仍然可以成為群體的一部份。

語意用法 in privacy 私下、秘密。

privilege [ˋprɪvḷɪdʒ]	特權、優待、殊榮 英解 a special advantage

例 Jack was given the rare **privilege** of using the president's office, which made others quite jealous. （97 學測）

傑克被給予使用會長辦公室的稀有特權，讓很多人相當嫉妒。

語意用法 have a privilege of ...，表示擁有……的特權。

prize [praɪz]	獎賞、獎品、獎金；亦作動詞與形容詞用 英解 a reward or honor for victory or for having won a contest, competition, etc.

例 Gunter Grass was the winner of the 1999 Nobel **Prize** in Literature. （99 指考）

鈞特葛拉斯是 1999 年的諾貝爾文學獎得主。

語意用法 the first prize 第一名。

procedure [prəˋsidʒɚ]	程序、手續、步驟 英解 a particular course of action intended to achieve a result

例 In the orderly **procedure** of social evolution there was no place for violence.

在社會井然有序的進化過程中，沒有暴力的容身之地。

語意用法 in the procedure of ＋事，表示在某事的進行程序中。

proceeding
[prəˋsidɪŋ]

行為、事項、會議紀錄
英解 an act or course of action

例 The **proceedings** of the meeting were sent to all the committee members.

會議紀錄寄給所有委員會成員。

語意用法 the proceedings of ＋會議，表示某會議的紀錄。

process
[ˋprɑsɛs]

程序、步驟、過程；動詞亦作加工解
英解 general methods of doing sth.

例 Students keep regular checks on the learning **process** by themselves.
（93 指考補）

學生自己對學習過程做定期檢驗。

語意用法 learning process 學習過程；in process 在進行中。

prodigy
[ˋprɑdədʒɪ]

奇才、天才、奇事、奇觀
英解 a genius

例 Before turning her attention to painting in high school, Janice was a bit of a chess **prodigy**.

在她在中學注意到繪畫之前，潔妮絲可說是個西洋棋天才。

語意用法 a child prodigy 神童；a math prodigy 數學天才。

profession
[prəˋfɛʃən]

專業人員、專家
英解 an occupation requiring an advanced degree

例 Used to caring for others, they are more likely to move toward such leadership **professions** as teaching and politics.（92 學測補）

他們習慣關愛他人的特質，較有可能走向如教學與政治方面的專業領導。

語意用法 by profession 就專業而言。

profit [`prɑfɪt]	利潤、營收、紅利、利益 英解 the monetary gain derived from a transaction

例 Many teenagers make a lot of **profits** in the fashion market today.
（92 學測補）

現今有許多青少年在時裝市場獲得很大的收益。

語意用法 make profit 獲得利益。

program [`progræm]	程序表、節目、方案、課程；亦作動詞用 英解 any organized plan to accomplish a goal

例 Contrary to what you think, our TV **program** has been enjoyed by a large audience.（91 學測）

與你想的正好相反，我們的電視節目已經擁有廣大的觀眾了。

語意用法 TV program 電視節目。

progress [`prɑgrɛs]	前進、行進、進步、發展；亦作動詞用 英解 advancement, movement toward a goal

例 Although scientists have not been able to solve all the mysteries of this amazing organ, they have made some **progress**.（85 學測）

雖然科學家們尚未能解答這個驚人器官帶來的所有謎團，他們已經有一些進展。

語意用法 in progress 進行中；make some progress 有所進展。

project [`prɑdʒɛkt]	計畫、企畫、專案 英解 a specific task

例 Everyone considers the government **project** creative.（99 指考）

每個人都認為政府的企畫有創意。

語意用法 do a project 進行研究；project manager 專案經理人；science project 科學研究計畫。

prom [prɑm]	高中畢業舞會 英解 a dance usu. in formal dress at a high school

例 The high school **prom** is the first formal social event for most American teenagers. (99 學測)

對大部分的美國青少年來說，高中畢業舞會是他們的第一個正式社交活動。

語意用法 go to the prom 去參加舞會。

prominence [ˋprɑmənəns]	突出、引人注目的事物、聲望 英解 renown

例 During the 1st century A.D., the art of painting religious murals gradually gained in **prominence**. (93 指考)

西元一世紀期間，繪製宗教壁畫的藝術逐漸被注目。

語意用法 come into prominence 出名。

promise [ˋprɑmɪs]	承諾、諾言、前途、希望；亦作動詞用 英解 a pledge

例 The company did lose money this year, but I still think it shows a lot of **promise**.

今年公司虧錢，但我仍然認為它很有可為。

語意用法 make a promise 承諾。

promotion [prəˋmoʃən]	提升、增進、促銷、創建 英解 movement to a new and better job

例 In order for a new product to sell well, manufacturers often invest a large sum of money on its **promotion**. (89 學測)

為了讓新產品暢銷，製造商通常投入大量金錢做促銷。

語意用法 product promotion 產品促銷。

proof
[pruf]

證據、物證、證明；動詞亦作檢驗解
英解 evidence that sth. is true

例 They asked if I had any **proof** of my husband's death.

他們問我是否有任何證據證明我丈夫的死。

語意用法 proof of ＋事，表示某事的證明。

proposal
[prə`pozl]

提出、建議、提案、求婚
英解 an offer

例 Although most economists don't support the president's **proposal** to
lower taxes, it has received a lot of popular support.

雖然大部分經濟學家不支持總統的減稅提案，它仍然獲得很多大眾的支持。

語意用法 proposal ＋ to V，表示做某事的提案。

prosecutor
[`prɑsɪ͵kjutə]

檢察官、公訴人
英解 a lawyer for the plaintiff

例 The special **prosecutor** for the government tried to find solid evidence
for his case.

政府的特別檢察官試圖為案子找到可靠的證據。

語意用法 federal prosecutor 聯邦檢察官；special prosecutor 特別檢察官。

prospect
[`prɑspɛkt]

預期、希望、前景、視野
英解 an expectation

例 Mr. Wang rejoiced at the **prospect** of the London trip.

王先生對即將成行的倫敦之旅感到喜悅。

語意用法 prospect of ＋事，表示對某事的預期、期望。

prosperity
[prɑs`pɛrətɪ]

興旺、繁榮、昌盛
英解 a good economic period

例 Many countries have been in recession for a long time; therefore, a lot of people look forward to economic **prosperity** in the coming year.（93 指考補）
許多國家處於經濟衰退好一段時間了，因此，很多人期待著新的一年經濟能繁榮。

語意用法 economic prosperity 經濟繁榮。

protection
[prə`tɛkʃən]

保護、防護
英解 action taken against harm or less

例 He is the head of an animal **protection** organization.（96 學測）
他是某個動物保護組織的領導人。

語意用法 protection against ＋事物，表示防止某項事物。

protein
[`protiɪn]

蛋白質
英解 a substance

例 The soybean is an almost perfect source of **protein**.（92 學測補）
大豆可說是蛋白質的最佳來源。

語意用法 protein 為人類生命必要之元素。

protest
[`protɛst]

抗議、反對
英解 public, often organized, opposition

例 The demonstration has a **protest** against the inflation.
此次示威是抗議通貨膨脹。

語意用法 protest against ＋事物，表示抗議某事物。

proverb [ˈprɑvɝb]	俗語、諺語、箴言 英解 a well-known saying that gives good advice or expresses a supposed truth

例 He used so many **proverbs** when he spoke that it was impossible to know if the man ever had an original thought.

他在談到不可能知道人是否有原創概念時用了很多諺語。

語意用法 proverb 表示社會上經常使用到的諺語。

publication [ˌpʌblɪˈkeʃən]	出版品、出版、發行 英解 the act or process of publishing a printed work

例 The book was discredited in advance of **publication**.

這本書在出版前被抹黑。

語意用法 publication of ＋事，表示公布某事。

publicity [pʌbˈlɪsətɪ]	公開、出名、宣傳、廣告文案、公開場合 英解 a message issued in behalf of some product or cause

例 To gain more **publicity**, some legislators would get into violent physical fights so that they may appear in TV news reports. (94 學測)

為了獲得更多知名度，有些立委會參與暴力肢體衝突好讓他們能在電視新聞曝光。

語意用法 give publicity to ＋事，表示公開某事。

pulse [pʌls]	脈搏、意向、活力、脈衝波 英解 the rhythm of blood pumped through the blood vessels

例 Each volunteer wore a device that gave out 20-second-long **pulses** of heat to the right leg. (97 學測)

每個志願者的右腳各配戴了一個裝置，可以發散二十秒長的脈衝熱能。

語意用法 feel sb.'s pulse 診脈。

qualification [ˌkwɑləfəˋkeʃən]	賦予資格、資格、能力、證照、限定條件 英解 the act of qualifying or the condition of being qualified

例 She passed her **qualification** for the high-ranking position.

她通過取得高階職位的資格。

語意用法 qualification for ＋事物，表示針對某事物的資格。

quality [ˋkwɑlətɪ]	品質、特質；亦作形容詞用 英解 the overall nature or general character of sth.

例 The blood diamonds are of exceptionally high **quality**. (96 指考)

血鑽石的品質特別地高。

語意用法 of high quality 高品質的；of low quality 低品質的。

quantity [ˋkwɑntətɪ]	量、數量、大量 英解 a general amount

例 There is a large **quantity** of wine left in the bottle.

瓶子裡還剩大量的酒。

語意用法 in quantity 大量地。

racism [ˋresɪzəm]	種族主義、種族歧視 英解 discrimination or prejudice based on race

例 Some people believe **racism** is a problem of the past, when in fact many groups are still suffering from discrimination every day.

有些人相信種族歧視是過去的問題，事實上很多族群每天仍為歧視所苦。

語意用法 racism 表示對種族的歧視。

range [rendʒ]	範圍、區域、行列、山脈；亦作動詞用 英解 an amount or extent of variation

例 In addition to being an excellent athlete, she had a wide **range** of artistic interests, which included painting, photography, and the piano.

除了是一名優秀的運動員，她在藝術方面有很廣泛的興趣，像是繪畫、攝影和鋼琴。

語意用法 a wide range of ＋物，表示某物有很廣泛的範圍。

rank [ræŋk]	等級、身份、地位；亦作動詞用 英解 a relative position in a society

例 At first I appointed men of no **rank** to act as umpires, but I had to discontinue that.

起初我任命沒有身份的人作為仲裁者，但我不得不中斷。

語意用法 take rank with ＋人事物，表示與某人事物並列、並肩。

rate [ret]	比例、比率；亦作動詞用 英解 a quantity measured with respect to another measured quantity

例 New packaging is introduced to Japanese store shelves at a **rate** of 20 percent per year, the highest rate in the world.（95 指考）

日本商店貨架上每年引進的新包裝佔百分之二十的比例，為全球最高的比率。

語意用法 rate of ＋物，表示某物的比率。

rebel [ˋrɛbl]	造反者、反叛者；亦作動詞用 英解 a person who opposes or fights against people in authority

例 Considered a **rebel** by his teachers, Jasper dropped out of school at the age of 17 and started his own fashion label.

被他老師認為造反，賈斯伯在十七歲輟學並開始了自己的時尚品牌。

語意用法 rebel against/at ＋事物，表示對某事物感到反感、厭惡。

receipt
[rɪ`sit]

收到、接到、收據；亦作動詞用
英解 the act of receiving

例 You'll need the store **receipt** to show proof of purchase if you want to return any items you bought.（98 指考）

如果你要退還任何你購買的商品，你需要出示店家的購買收據證明。

語意用法 in receipt of ＋物，表示收到某物。

recession
[rɪ`sɛʃən]

後退、退回、經濟衰退期
英解 the act of withdrawing or going back

例 Community service is particularly important in this **recession** time.（98 指考）

社區服務在這個經濟衰退期特別重要。

語意用法 recover from the recession 景氣復甦。

recipe
[`rɛsəpɪ]

食譜、處方、訣竅
英解 a list of ingredients and directions for making sth.

例 The Moon Lake Restaurant's menu included French-fried potatoes, a popular food **recipe** brought back from France by Thomas Jefferson.
（90 學測）

月湖餐廳的菜單包括法式炸洋芋，由湯瑪士傑弗遜從法國帶回來的熱門食譜。

語意用法 recipe for ＋菜餚，表示某菜餚的烹調方法。

recognition
[ˌrɛkəg`nɪʃən]

認出、確認、賞識
英解 the act of recognizing or fact of being recognized

例 Guffman's paintings didn't receive widespread **recognition** until long after her death.

古夫曼的畫作一直到她死後許久才獲得諸多賞識。

語意用法 give recognition to ＋事，表示承認某事。

reference
[ˋrɛfərəns]

提及、出處、參照、關於、查詢
英解 a source of information

例 The **references** listed in the paper show that the author's information came entirely from the Internet.

列在論文中的參考書目可看出，作者的資訊全都來自網路。

語意用法 for reference 供參考的；make reference to ＋人事物，表示向某人打聽、或參考某事物。

refinement
[rɪˋfaɪnmənt]

優雅、有教養、精細、精鍊的產品
英解 elegance

例 He invested his money in developing new technology in steel **refinement**. (96 指考)

他把錢投資在發展鋼製品精緻化的新技術。

語意用法 refinement of ＋物，表示某物的精細之處。

region
[ˋridʒən]

地區、領域、部位
英解 a geographical area of a country

例 Children in this **region** often start running at an early age. (99 學測)

這地區的孩童通常在很小的年紀就開始跑步。

語意用法 in the region of ＋物，表示在某物附近。

regularity
[ˌrɛgjəˋlærətɪ]

規律性、整齊、定期
英解 repetition of a happening or behavior

例 Droughts have occurred in the area with **regularity** over the last 400 years.

過去四百年來，這地區規律性地出現乾旱。

語意用法 with regularity 有規律地。

relation [rɪˋleʃən]	關係、關連、親戚、親屬 英解 a connection

例 **Relations** among the smaller nations in South East Asia have improved in recent years.

東南亞小國間的關係近年來已轉好。

語意用法 have relation to ＋人事物，表示與某人事物有關。

relationship [rɪˋleʃənˏʃɪp]	人際關係、親屬關係、戀愛關係 英解 the state of being connected or related

例 Researchers have yet to discover a definitive **relationship** between cell phone use and cancer rates.

研究員還未發現使用手機和癌症之間的明確關係。

語意用法 have a good relationship with ＋人，和某人有良好關係。

relative [ˋrɛlətɪv]	親屬；形容詞作相對的、相關的、相應的解 英解 a person who is related by blood or marriage

例 There never seemed to be enough time to go to church, which disturbed some friends and **relatives**.（87 學測）

似乎從沒有足夠的時間上教堂，這造成一些朋友和親戚的困擾。

語意用法 relative 也可做為形容詞，當相對的、相關的解，relative to ＋事物，表示與某事物有相關。

relaxation [ˏrilæksˋeʃən]	放鬆、緩和、消遣 英解 rest or refreshment

例 Golf has been my only **relaxation** for many years.

好些年來，高爾夫球一直是我唯一的消遣。

語意用法 the relaxation of international tension 國際緊張情勢的緩和。

relic
[ˈrɛlɪk]

遺物、遺風、遺俗、廢墟
英解 sth. that has survived from the past

例 He showed up to the party wearing a tie that looked like a **relic** left over from the previous century.

他戴著一條像是上世紀遺物的領帶出現在派對。

語意用法 ancient relic 古代遺跡；discover a relic 發現遺跡；relic of the past 過去的遺跡。

relief
[rɪˈlif]

減輕、寬心、解救、解圍、換班者
英解 the taking away of or lessening of pain

例 It was such a **relief** to learn that you were out of the country when the earthquake struck.

地震時你不在國內真是讓人鬆了一口氣。

語意用法 What a relief!，表示總算放心了。

religion
[rɪˈlɪdʒən]

宗教、宗教團體、信仰
英解 a personal or institutionalized system grounded in such belief and worship

例 Airlines are required to prepare special meals for believers of several different **religions**.

航空公司必須為一些不同宗教信仰者準備特殊餐點。

語意用法 world religions 世界宗教；organized religion 有組織的宗教；monotheistic religion 一神信仰。

reluctance
[rɪˈlʌktəns]

不情願、勉強
英解 lack of eagerness or willingness

例 None of us could understand his **reluctance** to accept the promotion.

我們沒有人能理解他為何不接受升遷。

語意用法 reluctance ＋ to V，表示不願去做某事。

remedy [`rɛmədɪ]	治療、補救、賠償；亦作動詞用 英解 a cure

例 For me, the best **remedy** for a cold is just a day resting in front of the TV.

對我來說，在電視前休息一整天對感冒有最好的療效。

語意用法 remedy for ＋病，表示針對某病症的治療法。

repression [rɪ`prɛʃən]	抑制、壓抑、制止、鎮壓 英解 oppression

例 My grandparents had to leave the country because they were targets of political **repression**.

我祖父母必須離開這個國家因為他們是政治迫害的目標。

語意用法 brutal repression 冷酷的迫害；political repression 政治迫害；a target of repression 迫害的目標

reputation [͵rɛpju`teʃən]	名譽、聲望、信譽 英解 the estimation in which a person or thing is generally held

例 He gradually built up a **reputation** as a successful lawyer. （93 指考補）

他逐步建立起身為一名成功律師的聲譽。

語意用法 make a reputation for oneself，表示為自己贏得名聲。

research [`risɝtʃ]	研究、調查、探究；亦作動詞用 英解 an inquiry

例 According to one **research**, 90% of the bottles used are not recycled and lie for ages in landfills. （99 學測）

根據一項調查，百分之九十使用過的瓶子沒被回收，長年躺在垃圾掩埋場底下。

語意用法 research into/on ＋領域，表示針對某領域的研究。

reservation
[ˌrɛzəˈveʃən]

保留、保護區、預約
英解 a booking

例 These islands are designated as natural **reservations**. （94 指考）
這些島嶼被指定為自然保留區。

語意用法 with reservations 有保留地。

residence
[ˈrɛzədəns]

居住、合法居留資格、住所
英解 the place in which one resides

例 He spent the summers writing in a cabin in the mountains, but his main **residence** was in the city.
他夏季在山上小屋寫作，但他主要的住所是在城裡。

語意用法 have one's residence in ＋地方，表示居住於某地。

resolution
[ˌrɛzəˈluʃən]

決意、決心、解答、分析
英解 a solution to a problem

例 If the company and the union do not reach a **resolution** today, the workers will strike tomorrow.
如果公司和工會今天沒有達成決議，工人明天就會罷工。

語意用法 resolution ＋ to V，表示做某事的決心。

resource
[rɪˈsors]

資源、對策、物力、財力
英解 a new or reserve supply that can be drawn upon when needed

例 Laboratories can be used as **resource** centers, or libraries, giving learners extra opportunities to practice at their chosen level. （93 指考補）
實驗室可以作為資源中心或圖書館，給予學習者額外的機會依他們選擇的程度做練習。

語意用法 natural resources 天然資源；human resources 人力資源。

respect
[rɪˋspɛkt]

尊敬、敬重；亦作動詞用
英解 admiration

例 Teachers who want to earn their students' **respect** should start by respecting their students.
想要贏得學生尊敬的老師得先尊重他們的學生。

語意用法 in respect of ＋事，表示就某事而言；with respect to ＋事，表示關於某事。

responsibility
[rɪˌspɑnsəˋbɪlətɪ]

責任、責任感、職責、義務
英解 a duty

例 Keeping yourself healthy has to be your own **responsibility**.（95 學測）
維持自己的健康是你自己的責任。

語意用法 responsibility for/of/to ＋事，表示對某事的責任。

result
[rɪˋzʌlt]

結果、成果；動詞亦作發生、產生解
英解 an effect

例 Most of us understand the **results** of not controlling our reactions to stress.（92 學測）
我們大部分都瞭解，不控制我們對壓力的反應會有什麼結果。

語意用法 as a result 結果。

revenge
[rɪˋvɛndʒ]

復仇、報仇；亦作動詞用
英解 the act of retaliating for wrongs or injury received

例 Harry Potter has his magic power to take **revenge** on his uncle.（91 學測）
哈利波特有神奇的魔法力量對他姨丈進行報復。

語意用法 revenge on/upon 用於人；revenge for 用於事或行為。

| **revenue** [ˋrɛvəˌnu] | 稅收、收益、總收入
 英解 amounts of income of a person, a state, etc. |

例 Obviously, an increase in **revenue** does not guarantee an increase in profits.

很明顯地，營業額的成長並不保證獲利的增加。

語意用法 defraud the revenue 逃稅。

| **revolution** [ˌrɛvəˋluʃən] | 革命、改革、公轉、循環
 英解 a big change, sometimes caused by force or war |

例 The company claims its new microchip will cause a **revolution** in the computer gaming industry.

公司宣稱它的新微芯片將會造成電腦遊戲產業的改革。

語意用法 revolution in ＋方面，表示在某方面的改革。

| **reward** [rɪˋwɔrd] | 獎賞、獎金、報酬；動詞亦作報應解
 英解 an award |

例 My boss always says the respect of one's colleagues is the best **reward**, but personally, I'd prefer a large cash bonus.

我老闆總是說同事的尊敬是最好的報酬，但我個人偏愛一筆巨額的現金紅利。

語意用法 in reward for ＋事物，表示做為某事物的獎賞。

| **risk** [rɪsk] | 風險、危險；亦作動詞用
 英解 a chance, danger of losing sth. important |

例 Many athletes push their bodies to the limit during both practice and play, so career-ending injury always is a **risk**. （97 指考）

許多運動員在練習與比賽的過程中將自己的身體逼到極限，所以總是冒著因傷結束職業生涯的風險。

語意用法 a risk of ＋事，表示某事的風險。

| **rite**
[raɪt] | 儀式、慣例
英解 ceremony |

例 Watching the World Series on television has been a **rite** of passage for young Americans since the 1940s.

從一九四〇年代開始，觀看電視的世界錦標巡迴大賽已成為美國年輕人的成年禮。

語意用法 funeral rites 葬禮；rite of passage 成年禮、人生大事及其慶祝儀式。

| **ritual**
[ˋrɪtʃʊəl] | 宗教儀式、典禮
英解 the prescribed order of a religious ceremony |

例 Dooley attempts to save the old man by a **ritual** learned from comic books.（93 學測）

杜力試圖藉由在漫畫書中學習到的宗教儀式挽救這名老人。

語意用法 ancient ritual 古代宗教儀式；perform a ritual 執行宗教儀式。

| **routine**
[ruˋtin] | 例行公事、慣例、例行程序；形容詞亦作一般的解
英解 a usual or regular method of procedure |

例 Derek became part of our life and seemed to fit into our family **routine**.

（92 指考）

德瑞克成為我們生活的一部分，似乎融入了我們的日常家庭生活中。

語意用法 daily routine 日常事務。

| **ruin**
[ˋruɪn] | 崩毀、毀壞、崩潰、遺跡；亦作動詞用
英解 a state of destruction |

例 Today, the **ruins** of the old castle are the area's primary tourist attraction.

舊城堡遺跡是這地區現在的主要觀光景點。

語意用法 come to ruin，表示毀滅、荒廢。

sacrifice
[ˋsækrəˏfaɪs]

犧牲、獻祭；亦作動詞用
英解 loss, or giving up of sth. valuable, for a specific purpose

例 The glory lies not in the achievement but in the **sacrifice**. （95 學測）

榮耀不在於成就而在於犧牲。

語意用法 make a sacrifice 做出犧牲。

sake
[sek]

目的、理由、緣故、利益
英解 prupose

例 Study for your own **sake**, not to please your parents.

為了你自己學習，不是為了取悅你的父母。

語意用法 for the sake of ＋人／ for sb.'s sake，表示為了某人的緣故。

salary
[ˋsælərɪ]

薪資、薪水
英解 paid to a person on a regular basis

例 I really cannot venture to name her **salary** to you.

我真的不能冒險把她名下的薪資給你。

語意用法 a high salary 高薪；a low salary 低薪；monthly salary 月薪。

salesman
[ˋselzmən]

推銷員、業務員、店員
英解 a man salesperson

例 **Salesmen** expect digital cameras to be popular gifts this holiday season.

（91 學測補）

銷售員期待數位相機會成為這假期季節的流行商品。

語意用法 a car salesman 汽車銷售員。

sanctuary
[ˈsæŋktʃʊˌɛrɪ]

庇護所、聖殿、保護區
英解 a safe, protected place

例 He informs Oedipus that a stranger who has taken **sanctuary** at the altar of Poseidon wishes to see him.

他通知歐迪普斯有個在海神祭壇避難的陌生人希望能跟他見面。

語意用法 give sanctuary to ＋人，表示提供某人庇護。

sanitation
[ˌsænəˈteʃən]

公共衛生、下水道設備
英解 the state of being clean and conducive to health

例 On December 28ᵗʰ last year, the New York City **sanitation** department offered people a new way to bid farewell to 2007. (97 指考)

去年十二月二十八日，紐約市公共衛生部門提供市民一種新方式向 2007 道別。

語意用法 sanitation department 公共衛生部門。

satellite
[ˈsætlˌaɪt]

衛星、追隨者、衛星城、衛星國
英解 a celestial body orbiting around a planet or star

例 They couldn't tell a cow's head from its tail in the **satellite** pictures. (98 學測)

從衛星照片上，他們無法區分母牛的頭和牠的尾巴。

語意用法 an artificial satellite 人造衛星。

satisfaction
[ˌsætɪsˈfækʃən]

滿意、滿足、稱心
英解 the act of satisfying or state of being satisfied

例 After doubling the number of sales clerks, customer **satisfaction** increased by over twenty percent.

增加兩倍的銷售員之後，客戶滿意度成長超過二成。

語意用法 with great satisfaction 非常滿意地。

scandal
[ˋskændl̩]

醜事、醜聞、流言蜚語
英解 a disgraceful action or event

例 As the rumor of his **scandal** spread quickly during the election campaign, more and more people began to question the honesty of the candidate. (92 學測補)

他的醜聞流言在選舉期間迅速傳播，愈來愈多人開始質疑候選人的誠信度。

語意用法 hush up a scandal 掩蓋醜聞。

scenery
[ˋsinərɪ]

風景、景色、舞台布景
英解 the natural features of a landscape

例 Kauai, the oldest of the main Hawaiian Islands, has some of the state's most stunning **scenery**. (88 學測)

考艾島是夏威夷群島中最古老的主要島嶼，擁有一些國內最讓人驚歎的景色。

語意用法 stunning scenery 讓人驚歎的景色。

schedule
[ˋskɛdʒul]

日程表、時刻表；亦作動詞用
英解 a list of timed, planned activities or events

例 Wendy doesn't like to work according to a fixed **schedule**. (88 學測)

溫蒂不喜歡按照排定的時間表工作。

語意用法 ahead of schedule 進度超前；behind schedule 進度落後。

scheme
[skim]

計畫、方案、體制、結構、詭計；亦作動詞用
英解 a systematic plan for a course of action

例 My brother came up with a **scheme** to make money by offering free boat rides to the island, but then charging them $100 dollars to come back.

我兄弟想出一個賺錢的詭計，用船免費載客到島上，然後回程索價 100 美元。

語意用法 a scheme + to V，表示做某事的圖謀。

scorn
[skɔrn]

輕蔑、藐視、奚落、不屑；亦作動詞用

英解 open contempt or disdain for a person or thing

例 He suggested everyone agree to a ten percent pay cut, but unsurprisingly the idea was met with **scorn**.

他建議大家減薪一成，沒有意外地，他的意見遭到奚落。

語意用法 with scorn 輕蔑地。

sculpture
[ˈskʌlptʃə]

雕塑品、雕像

英解 a three-dimensional work of plastic or wood art

例 Some **sculptures** can be completed in as little as ten minutes if power tools are used. (97 學測)

如果使用電動工具，有些雕塑可以在短短十分鐘內完成。

語意用法 wood sculpture 木雕。

seal
[sil]

印章、圖章、封印、封條、標誌；亦作動詞用

英解 a device impressed on a piece of wax, moist clay, etc.

例 The contract is not valid until each party affixes its **seal**.

合約要等到每一方都蓋章後才生效。

語意用法 affix sb.'s seal 某人蓋章；an official seal 官印；break a seal 拆封。

section
[ˈsɛkʃən]

部分、片、塊、節、截

英解 a piece or part of sth.

例 After 11 years of work, the final **section** of the road was completed in 1932. (97 學測)

經過十一年的工程，最後這段路於一九三二年完成了。

語意用法 a section of sth. 某東西的一部分；a large/small section 一大／小部分。

security [sɪˋkjʊrətɪ]	安全、安全感、保安 英解 protection from danger

例 After the computers were stolen, we considered several ways to increase **security** at the company.

電腦被偷後，我們考量了幾個提高公司安全性的方法。

語意用法 public security 公共安全。

sensibility [ˌsɛnsəˋbɪlətɪ]	感覺能力、善感、多感、鑑賞力 英解 the ability to feel things physically

例 Even though they were a technology company, they tried to recruit engineers who had an artistic **sensibility**.

雖然他們是一家科技公司，他們設法招募對美感有敏銳度的工程人員。

語意用法 sensibility to ＋物，表示對某物的敏感，如：sensibility to pain。

sensitivity [ˌsɛnsəˋtɪvətɪ]	敏感性、感受性、感光性 英解 the state or quality of being sensitive

例 Like many brilliant surgeons, he showed a complete lack of **sensitivity** toward his patients.

就像許多優秀的外科醫生，他完全無法感受病人的感覺。

語意用法 show sensitivity 表現出在乎；lack of sensitivity 不敏感。

sex [sɛks]	性別、性行為、性交、性 英解 gender

例 The professor said that it's quite risky for parents not to educate their children about **sex**.

教授說父母不教導小孩關於性的知識是很危險的。

語意用法 a sex crime 性犯罪；sex education 性教育。

| **share**
[ʃɛr] | 部分、分攤、股票;亦作動詞用
英解 one's own part or portion of sth. |

例 He realizes that only by cooperating can he do his **share** in making society what it should be. (99 學測)

他體會到唯有透過合作他才能盡他的本分維持社會秩序。

語意用法 go shares 為口語用法,表示平分、均攤。

| **shipment**
[ˈʃɪpmənt] | 裝運、裝載的貨物
英解 the act of shipping sth. |

例 Many of the Lego Group's **shipments** were returned, following poor sales. (97 指考)

樂高集團許多出貨的貨物被退還,造成銷售不佳。

語意用法 shipment date 運送日期;shipment term 運送條件。

| **shock**
[ʃɑk] | 衝擊、震動、電擊、休克;亦作動詞用
英解 a sudden psychological blow |

例 Before the disciple could recover from the **shock** of hearing the little pig speak in a human voice, the pig continued, "Don't kill me." (97 學測)

在信徒從聽到小豬說人話的震驚中回復前,小豬繼續說著「別殺我」。

語意用法 give sb. a shock 讓某人大吃一驚。

| **shortage**
[ˈʃɔrtɪdʒ] | 缺少、不足、匱乏
英解 a state of not having enough |

例 This year's East Asia Summit meetings will focus on critical issues such as energy conservation, food **shortages**, and global warming. (99 指考)

今年的東亞高峰會將著重在關鍵問題上,如節約能源、糧食短缺以及全球暖化。

語意用法 the shortage of energy 能源短缺。

shuttle [ˈʃʌtl]	定期往返之運輸工具、來回穿梭之物、梭子、太空梭；亦作動詞用 英解 sth. that weaves or hold thread

例 On paper, the Dubai Tower looks something like a giant space **shuttle** about to be launched into the clouds.（94 指考）

在紙上，杜拜塔看起來就像是即將發射進入雲端的巨大太空梭。

語意用法 a space shuttle 太空梭。

sibling [ˈsɪblɪŋ]	兄弟姊妹 英解 a person's brother or sister

例 I have two **siblings**: my brother and my sister.

我有二個兄弟姊妹，一個哥哥和一個姊姊。

語意用法 have a sibling 有一個兄弟姊妹；elder/older/younger sibling 最長的 / 較長的 / 較年輕的兄弟姊妹

sign [saɪn]	符號、招牌、手勢、徵兆、症狀；亦作動詞用 英解 a perceptible indication of sth. not immediately apparent

例 A movement of even a few millimeters (mm) of the earth's crust is a **sign** of possible earthquakes.（96 學測）

即使地表只有移動幾釐米，這也是地震的可能徵兆。

語意用法 a roan sign 交通標誌。

signal [ˈsɪgnl]	信號、暗號、交通指示燈號；亦作動詞用 英解 any nonverbal action or gesture that encodes a message

例 Give us a **signal** so we know when to turn on the lights and shout "Surprise!"

給我們一個信號，我們才知道何時開燈並大叫「Surprise ！」

語意用法 a signal for ＋人＋ to V，表示要某人做某事的信號。

significance
[sɪgˋnɪfəkəns]

重要性、重要、含意、意義
英解 the importance of sth.

例 In all cultures and throughout history hair has had a special **significance**.
（98 指考）

在所有文化中，髮型從過往歷史看來都有一個特殊重要性。

語意用法 a person of no significance 不重要的人。

silence
[ˋsaɪləns]

寂靜、沈默、無聲、無音訊；亦作動詞用
英解 quiet, no noise

例 Jeremy likes to listen to jazz all day, but I prefer to work in **silence**.
傑瑞米喜歡整天聽爵士音樂，但我比較喜歡安靜工作。

語意用法 in silence 沈默地。

situation
[ˌsɪtʃuˋeʃən]

情況、處境、局勢、場面、崗位、位置
英解 state of affairs

例 By the next day, city officials had reevaluated the **situation**.（83 學測）
到了第二天，市府官員已經重新評估狀況。

語意用法 the political situation 政治局勢；save the situation 挽回局勢。

solution
[səˋluʃən]

溶解、解決方法、消散
英解 a homogeneous mixture of two or more substances

例 I can stop the leak with a little glue right now, but that is not a long-term **solution**.
我現在可以用膠來止漏，但這不是一個長期的解決之道。

語意用法 solution of/to/for ＋問題，表示某問題的解決方法。

sorrow [ˋsɑro]	悲痛、悲傷、遺憾、懊悔之事 英解 an emotion of great sadness associated with loss or bereavement

例 The **sorrow** in her face was so profound, I didn't dare ask her what had happened.

她臉上的哀傷如此凝重，我不敢問她發生什麼事。

語意用法 feel sorrow at sb.'s misfortunes 為某人的不幸感到悲傷。

souvenir [ˌsuvəˋnɪr]	紀念品、紀念物 英解 a mememto

例 Bangkok is a place where visitors can buy many **souvenirs**. （92 指考）
觀光客在曼谷可以買到很多紀念品。

語意用法 souvenir shop 紀念品商店。

species [ˋspiʃɪz]	物種、種類 英解 a grouping of living things

例 On the island of New Zealand, there is a grasshopper-like **species** of insect that is found nowhere else on earth. （99 學測）
在紐西蘭的島上，有一種像蚱蜢的昆蟲物種在地球上其他地方都找不到。

語意用法 birds of many species 許多種類的鳥。

spirit [ˋspɪrɪt]	心靈、靈魂、精神、潮流；亦作動詞用 英解 the vital principle or animating force within living beings

例 Rwanda is a symbol of the triumph of the human **spirit** over evil. （96 學測）
盧旺達是人類精神戰勝邪惡的象徵。

語意用法 the spirit of the age 這時代的精神；the spirit of the law 法律的精神。

| **spite**
[spaɪt] | 惡意、居心不良、怨恨
英解 feeling a need to see others suffer |

例 His resignation letter was so filled with **spite** for his former supervisor that he asked him to leave the office immediately.

他的辭呈充滿了對前主管的怨恨，以致於他要他立即離開公司。

語意用法 in spite of，表示雖然、儘管。

| **sponsor**
[ˋspɑnsɚ] | 發起者、倡導者、贊助者；亦作動詞用
英解 a person or group that provides funds for an activity |

例 My son's baseball team is looking for a **sponsor** to pay for new uniforms and equipment.

我兒子的棒球隊正在尋找新制服和設備的贊助商。

語意用法 sponsor of/for ＋物，表示某物的贊助者。

| **stability**
[stəˋbɪlətɪ] | 穩定、穩定性、堅定、安定
英解 the quality or attribute of being firm and steadfast |

例 The government offered the bank a large loan to ease concerns about its **stability**.

政府提供銀行大筆貸款來消除不安定的疑慮。

語意用法 emotional stability 情緒穩定。

| **staff**
[stæf] | 全體人員、職員
英解 a group of workers |

例 Few modern languages **staff** had received training in materials design or laboratory use.（93 指考補）

很少現代語言的職員接受了培訓教材設計或實驗室使用的訓練。

語意用法 to be on the staff 在職；a staff of 25 二十五名的職員。

standard
[`stændəd]

標準、規範、直立支柱；亦作形容詞用
英解 sth. against which other things or ideas are measured

例 Because we weren't told by what **standards** our essays would be evaluated, we felt the test was unfair.

因為我們未被告知論文會以何標準來評分，我們覺得考試不公。

語意用法 the living standard 生活水平。

starvation
[star`veʃən]

飢餓、挨餓、餓死
英解 the act or process of starving

例 I have witnessed the deaths of old and young, and even infants, from sheer **starvation**.

我親眼目睹了老老少少甚至嬰兒因為過於飢餓而死亡。

語意用法 die of starvation 死於飢餓。

statement
[`stetmənt]

陳述、聲明、表達方式
英解 a declaration

例 Usually, when an actor is caught doing something illegal, he releases a **statement** to his fans apologizing for his actions.

通常當一個演員被逮到從事不法行為，他會發表一份聲明給粉絲為他的行為道歉。

語意用法 make a statement 陳述、聲明。

statistics
[stə`tɪstɪks]

統計、統計資料、統計學
英解 quantitative data on any subject

例 His claims were quite surprising, but he had the **statistics** to back them up.

他的主張讓人跌破眼鏡，但他有統計數字來支持論點。

語意用法 Statistics show that ＋子句，表示統計資料顯示……。

statue
[ˋstætʃʊ]

雕像、塑像
英解 a sculpture representing a human or animal

例 These devices made it possible for doors to open by themselves and wine to flow magically out of **statues**' mouths. （92 學測）

這些裝置讓這些門可以自動開啓，酒則神奇地從雕像口中流出來。

語意用法 the Statue of Liberty 自由女神像。

status
[ˋstetəs]

地位、身份、狀況
英解 position relative to that of others

例 His **status** as a financial expert was called into question after he lost his savings in the stock market crash.

他在股市大跌把積蓄賠光後，財務專家的地位遭到質疑。

語意用法 social status 社會地位。

steel
[stil]

鋼、鋼鐵製品、堅硬、冷酷；亦作動詞用
英解 any of various alloys based on iron containing carbon

例 Some 20th-century chairs are made of **steel** and plastic. （92 指考）

二十世紀的一些椅子就是用鋼和塑料製成。

語意用法 be made of steel 用鋼製成。

stereotype
[ˋstɛrɪəˌtaɪp]

刻板印象、老套、鉛版製版
英解 a person who is typical of a group

例 Before I was mugged, I used to believe in the romantic **stereotype** of gangsters as protectors of the poor and powerless.

在被襲擊之前，我對流氓有浪漫的刻板印象，他們會保護窮人和弱勢族群

語意用法 gender stereotype 性別刻板印象。

stimulus [ˈstɪmjələs]	刺激、刺激品、興奮劑 英解 any stimulating information or event

例 The government lowered interest rates, hoping the move would act as a **stimulus** to the sluggish economy.

政府調降利率，期望此舉能激勵衰退的經濟。

語意用法 under the stimulus of ＋物，表示在某物的刺激下。

strategy [ˈstrætədʒɪ]	戰略、策略、對策 英解 an elaborate and systematic plan of action

例 These indicators can provide vital information to the company regarding its marketing **strategy**.（94 指考）

這些指標可以提供公司關於市場策略的重要資訊。

語意用法 strategy for/of ＋事，表示為達成某事的策略。

strength [strɛŋθ]	力量、實力、強度、長處 英解 the quality or state of being strong

例 Because of its **strength**, steel soon became a useful building material.

（92 指考）

由於它的強度，鋼很快成為有用的建築材料。

語意用法 strength ＋ to V，表示做某事的體力。

stress [strɛs]	壓力、強調、重音；亦作動詞用 英解 special emphasis or significance attached to sth.

例 If you don't handle **stress** well, don't study medicine.

如果你不能妥善應付壓力，別學醫。

語意用法 under a lot of stress 處於很大的壓力之下。

structure
[ˈstrʌktʃə]

結構、建築物、構造、組織；亦作動詞用
英解 a building of any kind

例 The brain of a chimpanzee has the same internal **structure** and on its surface the same pattern of folds as the human brain.（90 學測）
黑猩猩的大腦內部結構以及表面皺摺模式與人類相同。

語意用法 the structure of ＋物，表示某物之結構、構造。

studio
[ˈstjudɪˌo]

工作室、電影攝影棚、錄音室、套房
英解 a place where an artist works

例 After we purchased the painting, the artist invited us to tour his **studio**.
在我們買了這幅畫之後，畫家邀請我們參觀他的工作室。

語意用法 artist's studio 藝術家工作室；movie studio 電影工作室；recording studio 錄音室。

subscription
[səbˈskrɪpʃən]

訂購；訂閱費、捐款、認捐
英解 payment for consecutive issues of a newspaper or magazine for a given period of time

例 Now is a good time to get your **subscription** to the Widows' and Orphans' Society.
現在是你捐款給遺孀孤兒協會的好機會。

語意用法 raise a subscription 募捐。

substitute
[ˈsʌbstəˌtut]

替代品、替身；亦作動詞用
英解 a replacement

例 The school canceled the class because they couldn't find a suitable **substitute** in time.
學校取消這堂課，因為他們無法及時找到合適的代課老師。

語意用法 a substitute for ＋人物，表示某人或某物的替代者。

suicide
[ˋsuəˏsaɪd]

自殺、自殺者、自毀；亦作動詞用
英解 the taking of one's own life

例 Stress is linked to the six leading causes of death—heart disease, cancer, lung disease, accidents, liver disease, and **suicide**. (92 學測)

壓力與六種造成死亡的主要成因相關連：心臟病、癌症、肺病、意外、肝病以及自殺。

語意用法 commit suicide 自殺。

suitcase
[ˋsutˏkes]

手提箱、行李箱
英解 a portable rectangular container for carrying clothes

例 They could take only what they could carry, and her two **suitcases** were already full. (92 學測補)

他們只能攜帶他們能夠提拿的，而她的二個手提箱都已經滿了。

語意用法 suitcase belt 行李箱束帶。

suppression
[səˋprɛʃən]

壓制、抑制、鎮壓
英解 the act of suppressing

例 After the development of the Internet, the **suppression** of subversive ideas has become increasingly difficult.

網路發展之後，破壞性思想的抑制變得更困難。

語意用法 self-suppression 自我壓抑。

surface
[ˋsɝfɪs]

表面、外觀；亦作動詞用
英解 the outside layer of an object

例 The acid destroys the **surface** of the teeth. (96 學測)

酸會破壞牙齒表面。

語意用法 come to the surface 浮上（水面）。

surgery [ˋsɝdʒərɪ]	外科、手術、開刀房 英解 the branch of medicine concerned with treating disease, injuries, etc.

例 His heart transplant **surgery** was more successful than Anthony's.（93 學測）

他的心臟移植手術遠比安東尼的成功。

語意用法 plastic surgery 整型手術。

survival [səˋvaɪvl]	倖存、殘存、倖存者 英解 remaining alive

例 Stealing food isn't wrong if it's necessary to ensure a person's **survival**.

如果偷食物才能確保生存那麼就不是錯的。

語意用法 survival kit 急救箱。

switch [swɪtʃ]	開關、轉轍器、細枝、轉換、變更；亦作動詞用 英解 a device that turns sth. on or off

例 I want to turn on the light, but I can't find the **switch**.

我想要開燈但找不到開關。

語意用法 turn off a switch 關掉開關；turn on a switch 打開開關。

sympathy [ˋsɪmpəθɪ]	同情、同情心、同感、慰問 英解 the sharing of another's emotions

例 Most people probably don't feel **sympathy** for these endangered creatures, but they do need protecting.（99 學測）

大多數人無法對這些瀕臨絕種的生物感同身受，但他們真的需要保護。

語意用法 sympathy for/with ＋人，表示為某人感到憐憫或同情。

symphony [ˋsɪmfənɪ]	交響樂、交響樂團、和諧、和聲 英解 a long and complex sonata for symphony orchestra

例 It will be generally admitted that Beethoven's Fifth **Symphony** is the most sublime noise that has ever penetrated into the ear of man.

普遍公認貝多芬的第五號交響曲是歷來進入人類耳裡最崇高的聲響。

語意用法 symphony orchestra 交響樂團。

symptom [ˋsɪmptəm]	症狀、徵候、表徵 英解 a characteristic sign or indication of the existence of sth. else

例 If you experience a sore throat, runny nose, cough or similar **symptoms** for more than two days, please see a doctor.

如果你有喉嚨痛、流鼻水、咳嗽或其他類似症狀超過兩天,請看醫生。

語意用法 symptom of ＋事物、疾病,表示某事物或某疾病的徵兆。

system [ˋsɪstəm]	系統、制度、秩序 英解 an assembly of things arranged in a series that conforms to a plan

例 Our hotel is putting in a new **system** that will allow guests to choose their room when making a reservation online.

我們的飯店正在採用新系統,可以讓客人在線上訂房時選擇自己的房間。

語意用法 an educational system 教育制度;the nervous system 神經系統。

talent [ˋtælənt]	天資、天才、有才能的人 英解 a marked innate ability

例 Most people have no **talent** for languages.

大部分的人沒有語言的天份。

語意用法 talent for ＋方面,表示某方面的才能。

| **target**
[ˋtɑrgɪt] | 靶、目標、攻擊目標；又作動詞用
英解 a goal |

例 If the sales team doesn't meet its **target** this month, they won't get a bonus.
如果銷售團隊這個月不能達成目標，他們無法得到紅利。

語意用法 target of/for ＋事物，表示某事物的目標，如：a target of criticism 受批評的目標。

| **taste**
[test] | 味覺、味道、一口、嗜好；亦作動詞用
英解 quantity eaten or tasted |

例 With its delicate **taste**, the fresh onion is an ideal choice for salads and other lightly-cooked dishes.（99 學測）
憑藉著它的美味，新鮮洋蔥是做為沙拉或其他近生食菜餚的理想選擇。

語意用法 a taste of banana 吃起來有香蕉的味道。

| **teamwork**
[ˋtim͵wɜk] | 團隊合作、協力、配合
英解 the cooperative work done by a team |

例 The man who has played football knows that **teamwork** is essential in modern living.（99 學測）
有玩足球的人便知道團隊合作是現代生活中不可或缺的。

語意用法 good/excellent teamwork 優秀的團隊合作；encourage teamwork 鼓勵團隊合作。

| **technique**
[tɛkˋnik] | 技巧、技術、技法
英解 a practical method, skill, or art applied to a particular task |

例 Laser eye surgery has become common, but the **technique** carries some significant risks.
眼睛雷射手術變得普遍，但技術上還是帶有很大的風險。

語意用法 traditional technique 傳統技術；new technique 新技術；effective technique 有效的技術。

technology [tɛkˋnɑlədʒɪ]	科技、工藝、技術、術語 英解 the application of practical sciences to industry or commerce

例 Charles has a strong interest in **technology**.（88 學測）

查爾斯對工藝有強烈的興趣。

語意用法 industrial technology 生產技術。

teenager [ˋtinˏedʒɚ]	十幾歲的青少年 英解 a person between the ages of 13 and 19

例 Recent studies have shown that alcohol is the leading gateway drug for **teenagers**.（97 指考）

最近的研究顯示，酒是帶領青少年進入毒品的門戶。

語意用法 rebellious teenager 反叛的青少年；difficult teenager 麻煩的青少年。

term [tɜm]	期限、任期、學期、條款；亦作動詞用 英解 a limited period of time

例 Cleveland is the only U.S. president to have served two nonconsecutive **terms**.（99 指考）

克里夫蘭是美國唯一擔任不連任的二期總統。

語意用法 in the long term 長期；in terms of ＋物，表示從某物的觀點、與某物有關聯的。

territory [ˋtɛrəˏtorɪ]	領土、版圖、地區、領域 英解 a region

例 If a slaver runs slaves through British **territory** he ought to pretend that they're his servants.

如果一個奴隸販子要偷運奴隸經過英國境內，他應該要他們裝成他的僕人。

語意用法 the territory of science 科學領域。

terrorist [ˈtɛrərɪst]	恐怖主義者、恐怖份子 英解 a person who employs terror or terrorism

例 It wasn't immediately clear whether the person who started the fire was a **terrorist** or just an average criminal.

縱火犯是恐怖份子或是一般罪犯並未立即明朗。

語意用法 terrorist attack 恐怖攻擊。

textbook [ˈtɛkstˌbʊk]	教科書、課本 英解 a book prepared for use in schools or colleges

例 This **textbook** is considerably more difficult to read than the other one.
（90 學測）

與另一本教科書比較起來，這本讀起來要難得多。

語意用法 an English textbook 英文教科書。

texture [ˈtɛkstʃə]	質地、構造、紋理、結構、組織 英解 a structure of interwoven fibers or other elements

例 The **texture** of this piece of cloth is too coarse.（90 學測）

這塊布的料子質地太粗糙。

語意用法 texture of skin 皮膚的質地。

theater [ˈθiətə]	劇場、戲院、劇團、戲劇界 英解 a building where theatrical performances or films can be presented

例 We fully support the city's plan to build an 800-seat **theater** for dramatic, musical, dance, and opera performances.

我們完全支持建造一座可容納八百個座位的戲院的城市計畫，可供戲劇、音樂、舞蹈和歌劇演出。

語意用法 a movie theater 電影院。

theme [θim]	論題、主題、題材 英解 a topic of discourse or discussion

例 The right **theme** for ice sculpting is not easy to find.（97 學測）

適合冰雕的主題不容易找到。

語意用法 theme song 主題曲。

theory [ˈθiərɪ]	學說、理論、推測 英解 a well-substantiated explanation of some aspect of the natural world

例 In physics, there are numerous **theories** that make perfect mathematical sense but have yet to be supported by experimental evidence.

在物理學，有許多理論在數學上完全合理，然而卻缺乏實證支持。

語意用法 economic theory 經濟理論。

thirst [θɜst]	口渴、渴望；亦作動詞用 英解 a physiological need to drink

例 My **thirst** is gone.

我不渴了。

語意用法 thirst for/after ＋物，表示對某物的渴望。

threat [θrɛt]	威脅、恐嚇、恐嚇者 英解 sth. that is a source of danger

例 I always thought the **threat** was just a scare tactic.（98 指考）

我總認為威脅不過是一種嚇人的伎倆。

語意用法 make threats 恐嚇；threat to ＋人，表示對某人構成威脅。

tolerance
[ˈtɑlərəns]

寬容、寬大、忍耐、忍耐力
英解 the state or quality of being tolerant

例 The teacher showed **tolerance** for the noise in the classroom and continued with his lecture as if he had not heard anything.（92 學測補）

這個老師展現他在課堂上對於吵鬧聲的容忍力,繼續講課就像他什麼也沒聽見一樣。

語意用法 tolerance of/to ＋事物,表示對某事物的忍受力。

torture
[ˈtɔrtʃə]

拷打、折磨、歪曲;亦作動詞用
英解 physical or mental anguish

例 It's a **torture** to me to see him.

去探望他對我來說是一種折磨。

語意用法 be in torture,表示處境痛苦。

tourism
[ˈturɪzəm]

旅遊、觀光、觀光業
英解 the business of providing services to tourists

例 Anticipating a large increase in **tourism**, several international chains are building hotels in the region.

預期觀光會有大幅成長,幾個國際連鎖企業正在這地區建造飯店。

語意用法 domestic / international tourism 國內 / 國際觀光;an increase / a drop in tourism 觀光成長 / 下跌。

track
[træk]

行蹤、軌跡、小徑、思路;亦作動詞用
英解 the mark or trail left by sth. that has passed by

例 An enormous three-toed **track** was imprinted in the soft mud before us.

一個巨大的三趾足跡印在我們眼前的軟泥上。

語意用法 keep track of 掌握……的行蹤;cover (up) sb.'s track 隱匿某人的行跡。

trade
[tred]

貿易、交易、職業、交換；亦作動詞用
英解 the business of buying and selling commodities

例 Healers and witch doctors converge on this beautiful lakeside town in March to make their yearly **trade**. (95 指考)

三月，治療者與女巫醫在美麗的湖畔小鎮會合進行他們的年度交易。

語意用法 free trade 自由貿易。

tradition
[trə`dɪʃən]

傳統、傳統思想、常規
英解 an inherited pattern of thought or action

例 Experts say that creativity by definition means going against the **tradition** and breaking the rules. (94 學測)

專家說，創造力的定義就是違背傳統並打破規則。

語意用法 true to tradition 名不虛傳。

traffic
[`træfɪk]

交通、交流、運輸
英解 the vehicles coming and going in a street, town, etc.

例 If there's too much **traffic** on the highway we'll get off and take surface streets.

如果高速公路上交通擁塞，我們會下來改走市區道路。

語意用法 control traffic 交通管制。

tragedy
[`trædʒədɪ]

悲劇、災難、慘案
英解 an event resulting in great loss and misfortune

例 In the face of this **tragedy**, food and other supplies from around the world landed in the provincial capital of Kerman on Sunday. (94 學測)

面對這場悲劇，食物以及其他補給品在星期天從世界各地運至克爾曼的省會。

語意用法 terrible tragedy 恐怖的悲劇；end in tragedy 以悲劇收場；prevent a tragedy 避免悲劇。

tranquility
[træŋˋkwɪlətɪ]

平靜、平穩、安寧
英解 a disposition free from stress or emotion

例 This silence intensified the **tranquility** of everything.
這種沈默讓周遭一切的寧靜益加明顯。

語意用法 disturb sb.'s tranquility 打擾某人的安寧；domestic tranquility 國內的安寧；inner tranquility 內在的平靜。

transaction
[trænzˋækʃən]

辦理、處置、執行、買賣
英解 the act of transacting within or between groups

例 Forty thousand pounds was a trifling **transaction** to Bulpit Brothers.
四萬磅的買賣對 Bulpit 兄弟來說微不足道。

語意用法 transactions in real estate 不動產買賣。

transcript
[ˋtrænˌskrɪpt]

副本、謄本、抄本、成績單
英解 sth. that has been transcribed

例 Lawyers got **transcripts** of the witness's testimony.
律師拿到證人證詞的副本。

語意用法 official transcript 正式成績單；university transcript 大學成績單。

trap
[træp]

陷阱、圈套、牢籠、陰謀；亦作動詞用
英解 a device in which sth. can be caught and penned

例 If you start answering the salesperson's questions, then you've already fallen into their **trap**.
如果你開始回答推銷員的問題，那你就掉進他們的陷阱了。

語意用法 fall into a trap 落入圈套。

名詞篇

treasure
[ˋtrɛʒɚ]

金銀財寶、寶藏；動詞作珍愛、儲藏解
英解 accumulated wealth in the form of money or jewels etc.

例 Another **treasure** to be found at the museum is a piece of jadeite that looks remarkably like a cabbage.

另一個在這博物館可找到的寶物是一塊看起來很像白菜的玉。

語意用法 in search of treasure 尋寶。

treatment
[ˋtritmənt]

對待、療法、論述
英解 the act, manner, or method of handling or dealing with someone or sth.

例 If you don't get **treatment** for that burn it could get infected.

如果你的燒傷不治療，它會受到感染。

語意用法 medical treatment 醫療。

trend
[trɛnd]

走向、趨勢、傾向；亦作動詞用
英解 a fashion, current style

例 There isn't a brand or a **trend** that these young people are not aware of.（99 學測）

沒有一個品牌或趨勢是這些年輕人不知道的。

語意用法 economic trends 經濟趨勢。

trick
[trɪk]

詭計、花招、把戲、訣竅；亦作動詞用
英解 a ruse

例 The **trick** to making really good coffee at home is to use only freshly roasted beans.

在家裡煮出好咖啡的訣竅就是只能使用現烤的咖啡豆。

語意用法 a trick ＋ to V，表示為了做某事而設的計謀。

trigger
[ˈtrɪgɚ]

扳機、啓動裝置；亦作動詞用
英解 a small projecting lever that activates the firing mechanism of a firearm

例 He pulled the **trigger** with his big toe.

他用他的大腳趾扣動扳機。

語意用法 pull the trigger 扣扳機。

tunnel
[ˈtʌnḷ]

隧道、地道、坑道；亦作動詞用
英解 an underground or underwater passage

例 The **tunnel** through which I crawled was low and dark.

我爬經又低又暗的地道。

語意用法 tunnel vision 短淺的眼光。

twin
[twɪn]

孿生子、雙胞胎之一、極相似的二個人事物；
亦作形容詞用
英解 one of two offspring born at the same birth

例 If one **twin** has the disease, it's ten times more likely that the other twin will have it too.

如果雙胞胎之一得了疾病，另一位得病的機率是一般的十倍。

語意用法 三胞胎為 triplet；四胞胎為 quadruplet。

ultrasound
[ˈʌltrəˌsaʊnd]

超音波
英解 very high frequency sound

例 The doctor did an **ultrasound** to see if the woman's heart was okay.

醫生做了超音波看這名女士的心臟是否沒問題。

語意用法 abdominal ultrasound 腹部超音波。

underwear
[ˈʌndəˌwɛr]

內衣
英解 underclothes

例 Madonna led the fashion of wearing **underwear** outside clothes.(92 學測補)
瑪丹娜引領內衣外穿的風潮。

語意用法 clean/dirty underwear 乾淨／髒的內衣；long underwear 長內衣；
skimpy underwear 太小的內衣。

upside
[ˈʌpˋsaɪd]

上面、上方、有利的一方
英解 the upper surface or part

例 They almost turned the whole house **upside** down. （97 學測）
他們幾乎將整間屋子倒過來了。

語意用法 upside down 顛倒地、傾覆地。

usefulness
[ˈjusfəlnɪs]

有用、有益、有效
英解 the quality of being of practical use

例 That seemed to be my only chance of **usefulness** in life.
這似乎是我生命中唯一有用處的時機。

語意用法 the usefulness of an invention 一項發明的有用性。

utensil
[juˋtɛnsḷ]

器皿、用具
英解 an implement for practical use

例 It's best to use wooden **utensils** with non-stick pots and pans.
不沾鍋具最好搭配木製用具來使用。

語意用法 household utensils 家庭、廚房用具。

vacancy
[ˈvekənsɪ]

空、空間、空房、空缺、空虛
英解 emptiness

例 Had a **vacancy** occurred in the post office at that time, I should have jumped at it.

如果那時郵局有空缺，我應該會積極把握它。

語意用法 job vacancy 工作職缺。

| **vacation**
[veˋkeʃən] | 休假、假期；亦作動詞用 |
| | 英解 leisure time away from work devoted to rest or pleasure |

例 If we can afford to, we will take a **vacation** abroad in the summer.（95 學測）

如果我們負擔得起，這個夏天我們會出國度假。

語意用法 take a vacation 度假；on vacation 休假中。

| **vacuum**
[ˋvækjuəm] | 眞空、空虛、空處、空白、吸塵器；亦作動詞用 |
| | 英解 the absence of matter |

例 There are few qualified doctors in the area, and the **vacuum** is being filled by nurses and medical students.

這地區僅有少數合格醫師，空缺被護士和醫學院學生佔滿。

語意用法 vacuum cleaner 真空吸塵器。

| **value**
[ˋvælju] | 益處、價值、價格；亦作動詞用 |
| | 英解 worth |

例 They believe nice packaging adds **value** because it's a strong signal of quality.（95 指考）

他們相信漂亮的包裝增加了價值，因為那是一種強烈的品質標記。

語意用法 the value of ＋物，表示某物的價值。

| **vandalism**
[ˋvændlɪzəm] | 故意破壞公物或文化藝術的行徑；暴力行爲 |
| | 英解 willful wanton and malicious destruction of the property of others |

例 I wish this **vandalism** could be stopped.

我希望這種破壞行為可以停止。

語意用法 acts of vandalism 野蠻行為。

variation
[ˌvɛrɪˋeʃən]
變化、差異、變形、變種、變奏曲
英解 an instance of change

例 Because our scarves are dyed by hand, there will be some slight **variation** in the color.
因為我們的圍巾是手染，所以顏色上會有些許差異。
語意用法 considerable variation 相當大的變化。

variety
[vəˋraɪətɪ]
多樣化、變化
英解 different types of experiences

例 There are a **variety** of restaurants and social events in Bangkok. (92 指考)
在曼谷有各式各樣的餐館及社交場合。
語意用法 a variety of ＋物，表示各式各樣的某物。

vegetarian
[ˌvɛdʒəˋtɛrɪən]
素食主義者、食草動物；亦作形容詞用
英解 someone who eats no meat or fish

例 I'm not a **vegetarian**, but I try not to eat very much meat.
我不是素食主義者，但我試著不要吃過多肉類。
語意用法 a strict vegetarian 嚴格的素食主義者。

vehicle
[ˋviɪkl]
運輸工具、車輛
英解 a conveyance that transports people or objects

例 There, time almost stands still, and horse-drawn carts outnumber motor **vehicles**. (99 學測)
在那裡，時間幾乎靜止不動，而且馬車比機械汽車來得多。
語意用法 electric vehicle 電動汽車。

venture
[ˋvɛntʃɚ]

冒險的事業、有風險的企業、投機；亦作動詞用
英解 an undertaking that is risky or of uncertain outcome

例 Don't discount the importance of luck to the success or failure of any new **venture**.

不要低估運氣對於新事業成敗的重要性。

語意用法 a joint venture 合資企業；at a venture 冒險地。

version
[ˋvɝʒən]

譯文、譯本、版本
英解 a translation or edition

例 The death and violence present in many traditional children's stories is nowhere to be found in the modern **versions**.

在許多傳統童話中的死亡與暴力在現代新版中已不復見。

語意用法 the film version 電影版；the original version 原著版本。

vice
[vaɪs]

邪惡、罪行、賣淫、惡習、不道德的行為
英解 sin or crime

例 He doesn't gamble, drink, or smoke—in fact, I think his only **vice** is coffee.

他不賭博、喝酒、或抽煙，事實上，我覺得他唯一的惡習是咖啡。

語意用法 virtue and vice 善與惡。

victim
[ˋvɪktɪm]

犧牲者、受害者、遇難者、祭品
英解 one who is harmed or killed by another

例 The Red Cross is accepting donations to aid **victims** of the typhoon.

紅十字會接受捐款來協助颱風災民。

語意用法 victim of ＋物，表示某物的犧牲者。

victory
[ˈvɪktərɪ]

勝利、戰勝

英解 a successful ending of a struggle or contest

例 The judge's decision was a **victory** for the environmental groups that oppose construction of the facility.

法官的判決是環保團體反對設施建造的勝利。

語意用法 victory over ＋對象，表示戰勝、贏過某對象。

view
[vju]

視野、視力、風景、展望；亦作動詞用

英解 a scene

例 Remember when Madonna hit the charts with her bra in full **view** while singing about "virginity"?（92 學測補）

記得當時瑪丹娜在衆目睽睽下穿著胸罩高唱〈貞操〉打進排行榜嗎？

語意用法 be in view，表示在視線之内。

violence
[ˈvaɪələns]

暴力、暴力行爲、激烈、破壞、竄改

英解 the exercise or an instance of physical force

例 The government restricts the sale of DVDs and video games that depict extreme **violence** to those over the age of 18.

政府限定含有極度暴力的 DVD 和遊戲光碟只能販賣給 18 歲以上的人。

語意用法 use violence 使用暴力；acts of violence 暴力行為。

violet
[ˈvaɪəlɪt]

紫羅蘭、紫色、害羞的人

英解 any of numerous low-growing violas with small flowers

例 He showed up at her doorstep with a bouquet of **violets**, saying that their color perfectly complemented her eyes.

他帶著一束紫羅蘭出現在她的門前，說它們的顏色和她的眼睛很相襯。

語意用法 a shrinking violet 不引人注意的人、羞怯的人。

| **volume**
[ˋvɑljəm] | 卷、冊、音量、容積
英解 a collection of written or printed sheets bound together |

例 The only secret contained in this book is revealed midway in the first **volume**.

這本書裡唯一的秘密在第一冊中途被揭露。

語意用法 speak volume (for) 有重大的意義、充分證明。

| **volunteer**
[ˌvɑlənˋtɪr] | 義工、志願者；亦作動詞用
英解 a person who performs or offers to perform voluntary service |

例 Before they begin, **volunteers** at the hospital are required to participate in comprehensive training programs.

醫院裡的志工在開始前必須參與全面性的訓練課程。

語意用法 volunteer for ＋工作，表示某工作的志願者。

| **waterfall**
[ˋwɔtɚˌfɔl] | 瀑布
英解 a cascade |

例 We weren't able to visit the Rainbow **Waterfalls** as we planned. （86 學測）

我們無法如計畫前往彩虹瀑布參觀。

語意用法 a waterfall of ＋物，表示大量湧入的某物。

| **wave**
[wev] | 波、波浪、揮手、浪潮、捲髮；亦作動詞用
英解 one of a series of ridges that moves across the surface of a liquid |

例 The storm is expected to bring strong winds and high **waves** to the entire east coast.

暴風預計會為東海岸帶來強風和巨浪。

語意用法 make waves 興風作浪、把事情鬧大。

| **weight**
[wet] | 重量、體重、重擔、價值；亦作動詞用
英解 a measure of the heaviness of an object |

例 Many of the whales died on the beach—crushed by their own **weight**.

（84 學測）

許多鯨魚被自己的重量壓垮死在海灘。

語意用法 lose weight 減重；gain weight 體重增加。

| **wilderness**
[ˋwɪldənɪs] | 荒野、無人煙處
英解 a state of disfavor |

例 Few of them understood that on their way they would have to cross a harsh **wilderness**.（90 學測）

他們很少人瞭解到他們在路上必須穿越險峻的荒野。

語意用法 a wilderness of ＋物，表示一堆雜亂的某物。

| **wire**
[waɪr] | 金屬線、電話線、電纜、電報：亦作動詞用
英解 a slender flexible strand or rod of metal |

例 The outside of my apartment building is covered with all kinds of **wires**—for the telephone, Internet, cable TV, electricity, and who knows what else.

我住所的外圍佈滿了各種纜線，電話線、網路線、有線電視、電線、誰知道還有些什麼。

語意用法 telephone wire 電話線。

| **wisdom**
[ˋwɪzdəm] | 智慧、知識、看法
英解 accumulated knowledge or erudition or enlightenment |

例 The conventional **wisdom** is that it's dangerous to swim immediately after eating.

傳統觀念認為飯後立即游泳是危險的。

語意用法 the wisdom ＋ to V，表示做某事的明智之舉。

witness [ˈwɪtnɪs]	目擊者、證人、證詞、證物；亦作動詞用 英解 an observe

例 Officer Brown is asking **witnesses** to the accident on Highway 8 this morning to contact her at (206) 555-5011.

布朗警官要今天早上八號公路意外的目擊者與她聯絡，電話是 (206) 555-5011。

語意用法 a witness against sb. 不利某人的證人。

wizard [ˈwɪzəd]	男巫、術士、奇才 英解 a sorcerer

例 Six out of ten British children are likely to have seen a Harry Potter film and then read the first two books about the young **wizard**. (93 指考補)

英國小孩十個裡頭有六個可能看過《哈利波特》電影、讀過前二本關於年輕巫師的書。

語意用法 wizard 在口語中有天才、高手、專家之意。

wonder [ˈwʌndə]	驚異、奇觀、奇才；動詞作疑惑、想知道解 英解 a spectacular thing

例 His films are both critically acclaimed and immensely popular, so it's a **wonder** that he has yet to receive a major award.

他的電影大受好評也十分賣座，所以他還沒得到重大獎項真讓人不解。

語意用法 in wonder 驚異地。

workaholic [ˌwɜkəˈhɔlɪk]	工作狂 英解 a person obsessively addicted to work

例 **Workaholics** tend to suffer more chronic illnesses and have higher rates of anxiety.

工作狂容易受慢性病所苦，焦躁的機率也較高。

語意用法 其他還有許多字尾同是 –holic 的字，如：alcoholic 嗜酒的人、chocoholic 嗜吃巧克力的人、shopaholic 購物狂。

workforce
[`wɜk͵fors]

勞動力、受雇用之人
英解 the force of workers available

例 The least valuable degree for young people now entering the **workforce** is business management.

年青人投入職場價值最低的學位是企業管理。

語意用法 workforce diversity 人力資源多樣化。

worship
[`wɜʃɪp]

崇敬、敬仰、敬神、禮拜儀式；亦作動詞用
英解 the reverent love and devotion accorded a deity, an idol, or a sacred object

例 Since the 18th century, the **worship** of God has been gradually replaced by the worship of money.

從十八世紀以來，對上帝的崇拜逐漸被金錢崇拜所取代。

語意用法 hero worship 英雄崇拜。

zone
[zon]

地帶、地區、時區、區域、範圍、區段；亦作動詞用
英解 a region, area, or section characterized by some distinctive feature or quality

例 Jet lag, caused by traveling between time **zones**, is becoming a common problem for frequent travelers.（94 學測）

在二個時區之間旅行造成的時差，已經是經常旅行者的共通問題。

語意用法 a safety zone 安全地帶。

形容詞篇

▶ ▶ ▶ Adjectives

ambitious

allergic

ancient

apparent

academic

additional

abundant [ə`bʌndənt]	大量的、充足的 英解 plentiful

例 We have had plenty of rain so far this year, so there should be an **abundant** supply of fresh water this summer.（94 指考）
今年到目前為止我們有充足的雨水，所以今年夏季應該有足夠的淡水可以供應。

語意用法 abundant in ＋物，表示有豐富的某物。

academic [͵ækə`dɛmɪk]	大學的、學院的、學術的 英解 pertaining to a college, academy, school or other educational institutions

例 I've always preferred working with my hands to **academic** pursuits.
比起追求學問，我更愛手工藝方面的工作。

語意用法 an academic degree 學位；academic subjects 人文學科。

accurate [`ækjərɪt]	準確的、精準的 英解 conforming exactly to fact

例 **Accurate** measurements are particularly important for scientific experiments.（95 指考）
精準的測量對科學實驗特別重要。

語意用法 to be accurate 正確地說、精準地說。

additional [ə`dɪʃən!]	添加的、額外的、附加的 英解 added or supplementary

例 The user has to spend **additional** money for it.（91 學測補）
使用者必須付額外的費用在這上頭。

語意用法 an additional charge 額外的費用。

admirable
[ˈædmərəb|]

絕妙的、令人欽佩的、值得讚揚的
英解 excellent

例 It's great that she won the award, but it's especially **admirable** that she donated the prize money to charity.

她得獎太棒了,更讓人讚揚的是她把獎金捐給慈善機構。

語意用法 admirable friendship 令人欽羨的友情。

形容詞篇

adventurous
[ədˈvɛntʃərəs]

愛冒險的、大膽的、有危險的
英解 willing to undertake or seeking out new and daring enterprises

例 Preferring rice and lightly steamed vegetables, grandma is not exactly an **adventurous** eater.

喜歡米飯和微蒸過的蔬菜,奶奶在吃的方面不算是個勇於嚐鮮的人。

語意用法 an adventurous explorer 愛冒險的探險家。

aggressive
[əˈgrɛsɪv]

侵略的、挑釁的、有幹勁的
英解 quarrelsome or belligerent

例 His negotiating style was so **aggressive** that we decided not to do business with him again.

他的激進談判風格讓我們決定不要再和他做生意。

語意用法 an aggressive salesman 積極的推銷員。

agricultural
[ˌægrɪˈkʌltʃərəl]

農業的、農藝的
英解 relating to or used in or promoting agriculture or farming

例 Due to the overuse of pesticides, **agricultural** areas are often more polluted than industrial areas.

由於過度使用農藥,農業區的污染通常比工業區嚴重。

語意用法 agricultural products 農產品。

allergic
[ə`lɜdʒɪk]

過敏的
英解 characterized by, or caused by an allergy

例 Are there peanuts in the cookies? I think he may be having an **allergic** reaction!

餅乾裡有花生嗎？我想他可能過敏了。

語意用法 be allergic to ＋物，表示對某物過敏。

alternative
[ɔl`tɜnətɪv]

二選一的、非主流的、替代的；亦作名詞用
英解 serving or used in place of another

例 I understand your concerns, but unless you can offer an **alternative** solution, we'll go with the original plan.

我理解你的顧慮，但除非你可以提供替代解決方案，不然我們還是會採用原來的計畫。

語意用法 an alternative plan 替代方案。

ambitious
[æm`bɪʃəs]

有野心的、炫耀的
英解 having a strong desire for success or achievement

例 He's talented enough to manage the whole company, but he's just not that **ambitious**.

他有管理整個公司的才能，但他沒那個野心。

語意用法 be ambitious for/of ＋物，表示對某物有野心。

analytical
[ˌænḷ`ɪtɪkḷ]

分析的、解析的
英解 using or skilled in using analysis

例 If we want to take a more **analytical** approach in our marketing, we're going to need a lot more data about our customers.

如果我們在行銷要採用分析方法，我們需要更多關於客戶的資料。

語意用法 an analytical approach 分析方法；analytical skills 分析技術。

ancient
[ˈenʃənt]

古代的、古老的、過時的；亦作名詞用
英解 dating from very long ago

例 Have you ever wondered how the **ancient** Egyptians created such marvelous feats of engineering as the pyramids?（95 學測）
你有沒有想過古代埃及人是如何建造像金字塔這樣了不起的工程？

語意用法 an ancient civilization 古代文明。

anonymous
[əˈnɑnəməs]

匿名的、來路不明的、無特色的
英解 having no known name or identity or known source

例 The money for the new library came from an **anonymous** donor.
新圖書館的經費來自一位匿名的捐贈者。

語意用法 an anonymous letter 匿名的信。

anxious
[ˈæŋkʃəs]

焦慮的、掛念的、渴望的
英解 eagerly desirous

例 Anne dreaded giving a speech before three hundred people; even thinking about it made her **anxious**.（95 學測）
安妮對於在三百人面前演講感到害怕，甚至只要想到就讓她焦慮不已。

語意用法 anxious about/for ＋物，表示對某物感到擔憂、不安。

apparent
[əˈpærənt]

顯而易見的、表面的
英解 obvious

例 It became **apparent** that there would be no breakthrough.（93 指考補）
顯而易見的不會有所突破。

語意用法 apparent to ＋人，表示對某人而言是顯而易見的。

形容詞篇

289

appropriate
[əˋproprɪˌet]

適當的、恰當的；亦作動詞用
英解 fitting

例 I can't believe Janis thought it would be **appropriate** to wear a miniskirt to a funeral.

我不敢相信潔妮絲會覺得穿迷你裙到葬禮是一件合宜的事。

語意用法 appropriate to the occasion 適合該場合；appropriate words 適當的言詞。

approximate
[əˋprɑksəmɪt]

近似的、接近的；亦作動詞用
英解 almost accurate or exact

例 I know you can't determine the exact price until next week, but I'll need an **approximate** estimate by Friday.

我知道下星期前你無法決定價格，但我在星期五前需要一個大概的數字。

語意用法 an approximate estimate 大概的估計。

arrogant
[ˋærəgənt]

傲慢的、自大的、自負的
英解 having or showing feelings of unwarranted importance out of overbearing pride

例 I hope he doesn't win the award—he's **arrogant** enough now.

我希望他不會得獎，他現在夠自大了。

語意用法 arrogant people 傲慢的人們。

artificial
[ˌɑrtəˋfɪʃəl]

人造的、矯揉做作的、人為的
英解 contrived by art rather than nature

例 When the prices of natural spices rise, food manufacturers start using more **artificial** flavorings.

當天然香料的價格上漲，食品製造商開始使用更多的人工調味料。

語意用法 artificial flavoring 人工調味料；artificial insemination 人工授精。

ashamed
[əˈʃemd]

羞愧的、感到難為情的

英解 overcome with shame, guilt, or remorse

例 Why didn't you introduce me to your friend? Are you **ashamed** to be seen with me?

你為何不介紹我給你朋友？被撞見我們在一起你會難為情嗎？

語意用法 ashamed of ＋事，表示為某事感到羞愧。

automatic
[ˌɔtəˈmætɪk]

自動的、習慣性的、必然的；亦作動詞用

英解 operating with minimal human intervention

例 I don't have to turn my paper in yet—our professor gave us an **automatic** two-week extension because of the earthquake.

我還不須交報告，教授因為地震的關係給我們自動延長兩星期。

語意用法 automatic updates 自動更新；automatic control systems 自動控制系統。

available
[əˈveləbl]

可用的、可得到的、有效的

英解 obtainable or accessible

例 If there aren't any rooms **available** at the hotel, you could stay at the bed-and-breakfast down the street.

如果飯店沒有空房，你可以住在街尾的民宿。

語意用法 available to ＋人，表示只有某人可取用。

awkward
[ˈɔkwəd]

笨拙的、不靈巧的、不熟練的

英解 lacking dexterity, proficiency, or skill

例 Jane felt **awkward** speaking in front of the class but was quite relaxed talking with her good friends. (92 學測補)

珍在全班面前說話時感到笨拙，但在好朋友面前卻能輕鬆自在聊天。

語意用法 an awkward expression 生硬的語句。

形容詞篇

bilingual
[baɪˋlɪŋgwəl]

雙語的；亦作名詞用
英解 using or knowing two languages

例 Mr. Chen is **bilingual** in English and Chinese.

陳先生英文和中文都可以通。

語意用法 a bilingual speaker 能說兩種語言的人。

bitter
[ˋbɪtə]

苦的、難堪的、嚴厲的
英解 marked by strong resentment or cynicism

例 Hearing the art critic's **bitter** and outrageous comments on her new painting, Molly started a heated argument with him.（95 指考）

聽到藝術評論家對她的新畫作尖刻又荒謬的評論，莫莉與他展開一場激烈的爭論。

語意用法 bitter criticism 嚴厲的批評；bitter tears 悲痛的眼淚。

breathtaking
[ˋbrɛθˌtekɪŋ]

驚人的、令人摒息的
英解 tending to cause suspension of regular breathing

例 The **breathtaking** 4,000-foot cliffs of Na Pali Coast rise grandly from the sea.（88 學測）

納帕里海岸高四千英尺的懸崖宏偉地聳立在海上。

語意用法 a breathtaking beauty 令人摒息的美人。

brilliant
[ˋbrɪljənt]

色彩豔麗的、傑出的、才華洋溢的
英解 sparkling

例 Of two writers one was **brilliant** but indolent; the other though dull, industrious.

兩名作家中，一個才華洋溢但懶惰，另一個資質愚昧卻勤奮。

語意用法 a brilliant idea 絕妙的點子。

brutal [ˈbrutl]	殘忍的、冷酷的、野蠻的 英解 able or disposed to inflict pain or suffering

例 All the bystanders were horrified, and asked him what he could mean by such **brutal** and inhuman conduct.

所有的旁觀者都嚇壞了，並問他如此野蠻和非人道的行為對他意味著什麼。

語意用法 brutal truth 殘酷的事實。

capable [ˈkepəbl]	有能力的、有才幹的 英解 having ability

例 The machines don't look too revolutionary, but you'd be surprised how much they are **capable** of.（90 學測）

這些機器看起來不是很創新，但你會對它們的能力感到驚訝。

語意用法 capable of + Ving，表示有能力做某事。

careless [ˈkɛrlɪs]	粗心的、隨便的、漫不經心的 英解 negligent

例 Tim and Dom were too **careless**.（91 學測）

提姆和唐太粗心了。

語意用法 careless work 草率的工作。

casual [ˈkæʒʊəl]	碰巧的、隨便的、非正式的、臨時的 英解 marked by blithe unconcern

例 Today David wears **casual** clothes.（91 學測）

大衛今天穿便服。

語意用法 casual labor 臨時工。

cheap [tʃip]	便宜的、廉價的 英解 costing relatively little

例 It is **cheap** to produce.（92 學測補）

它的生產成本很便宜。

語意用法 cheap labor 廉價的勞工。

classical [ˋklæsɪkḷ]	古典的、傳統的、經典的、標準的 英解 of or relating to the traditional standard for sth.

例 She encouraged teachers to abandon computers and get back to the basic elements of **classical** education: grammar, logic, rhetoric, and mathematics.

她鼓勵老師們放棄電腦、回歸傳統教育的基本元素：文法、邏輯、修辭和數學。

語意用法 classical literature 古典文學。

clockwise [ˋklɑk͵waɪz]	順時針方向的 英解 in the same direction as the rotating hands of a clock

例 Make three **clockwise** circles, then three anticlockwise circles with your left thumb.

用左手拇指畫三個順時針的圈圈，然後畫三個逆時針的圈圈。

語意用法 clockwise 在美式、英式英語都通用；但逆時針的英式用法為 anticlockwise、美式用法為 counterclockwise。

clumsy [ˋklʌmzɪ]	笨拙的、手腳不靈活的 英解 lacking in skill or physical coordination

例 The slow and **clumsy** wetas have been around on the island since the time of the dinosaurs.（99 學測）

這種緩慢而笨拙的蝗蟲類生物自恐龍時代開始就遍佈在島上。

語意用法 a clumsy dancer 拙於跳舞的人。

coherent
[ko`hɪrənt]

協調的、一致的、條理清晰的、連貫的
英解 capable of logical and consistent speech, thought

例 This paper makes some interesting observations, but the argument isn't very **coherent**.

這篇論文提出一些有趣觀點,但是論述不連貫。

語意用法 a coherent explanation 有條理的解說。

comfortable
[ˋkʌmfətəbl̩]

舒適的、自在的、安逸的
英解 giving comfort or physical relief

例 If it is too cold in this room, you can adjust the air conditioner to make yourself feel **comfortable**.（96 學測）

如果這房間太冷,你可以調整空調讓自己感到舒適。

語意用法 a comfortable sofa 舒適的沙發;a comfortable income 寬裕的收入。

comic
[ˋkɑmɪk]

喜劇的、滑稽的、漫畫的;亦作名詞用
英解 characteristic of or having to do with comedy

例 The **comic** mask is ugly and distorted, but does not imply pain.

這個漫畫面具既醜陋又扭曲,但並不意味著痛苦。

語意用法 a comic book 漫畫書;comic effect 喜劇效果。

compulsive
[kəmˋpʌlsɪv]

強迫的、強制的
英解 relating to or involving compulsion

例 **Compulsive** shopping often begins at an early age.（98 指考）

強迫性購物往往始於很小的年紀。

語意用法 obsessive-compulsive disorder 強迫症。

considerate
[kən`sɪdərɪt]

體貼的、考慮周到的
英解 thoughtful towards other people

例 I agree with his criticisms, but he could have been a lot more **considerate** in the way he expressed them.

我同意他的評論，但他在表達方式上可以更體貼一些。

語意用法 It is considerate of ＋人＋ to V，表示某人做某事是很體貼的。

consistent
[kən`sɪstənt]

前後一致的、始終如一的
英解 in agreement or consistent or reliable

例 It was not **consistent** with David's humor to travel long in silence.

一路沈默的旅行與大衛的幽默個性不符合。

語意用法 consistent with ＋事物，表示與某事物一致的、和諧的。

contagious
[kən`tedʒəs]

接觸性傳染的、會蔓延的
英解 easily diffused or spread as from one person to another

例 Mary's enthusiasm was **contagious**, and before long we were pitching in to help.

瑪麗的熱心是會感染的，不用很久我們全都很起勁地幫起忙來。

語意用法 contagious diseases 傳染性疾病。

contrary
[`kɑntrɛrɪ]

相反的、對立的、逆向的、不利的
英解 opposed in nature, position

例 She suggested selling the company, but we took the **contrary** position.

她建議賣掉公司，但我們持反對立場。

語意用法 contrary to ＋物，表示與某物相反；on the contrary 相反地。

conventional
[kən`vɛnʃənl]

習慣的、傳統的、陳腐的、因襲的
英解 following accepted customs and proprieties

例 She looked like any other girl, but hiding behind that **conventional** exterior was a wonderfully eccentric personality.

她看起來和一般女孩沒兩樣，但在那傳統的外表之下藏著古怪的性情。

語意用法 conventional wisdom 傳統觀念。

costly
[`kɔstlɪ]

寶貴的、昂貴的、代價高的
英解 of great price or value

例 They wanted more **costly** dresses.

他們想要更多昂貴的衣服。

語意用法 costly jewels 昂貴的寶石。

courageous
[kə`redʒəs]

英勇的、勇敢的
英解 possessing or expressing courage

例 The artist must possess the **courageous** soul.

藝術家必須具備勇敢的靈魂。

語意用法 courageous of ＋人＋ to V，表示某人做某事是很勇敢的。

crucial
[`kruʃəl]

決定性的、重要的、嚴酷的
英解 of extreme importance

例 The success of this product is **crucial** to the success of the company.

這項產品的成功對於公司的成敗有決定性影響。

語意用法 crucial to/for ＋事物，表示對某事物具有決定性的影響。the crucial moment 關鍵時刻。

cultural [ˋkʌltʃərəl]	修養的、文化的、人文的 英解 of or relating to culture or cultivation

例 As globalization accelerates, **cultural** differences are becoming less important.

全球化加劇，文化上的差異變得較不重要。

語意用法 cultural conflict 文化上的衝突。

curly [ˋkɜlɪ]	捲曲的、有捲髮的、波紋的 英解 having curls or waves

例 Long **curly** hair has always been popular since ancient times.（98 指考）

長捲髮自古以來一直就很流行。

語意用法 curly hair 捲髮。

dangerous [ˋdendʒərəs]	危險的、不安全的 英解 involving or causing danger or risk

例 Most insurance policies don't cover accidents involving **dangerous** activities like rock climbing or sky diving.

大部分的保險政策不涵蓋諸如攀岩、高空跳傘等危險活動。

語意用法 dangerous road 危險道路；dangerous person 危險的人。

defensive [dɪˋfɛnsɪv]	防禦的、保護的、自衛的；亦作名詞用 英解 good for defense

例 Ruth is a very **defensive** person. She cannot take any criticism and always finds excuses to justify herself.（96 學測）

露絲是一個防禦性很重的人，她不能接受任何批評並總是找理由為自己辯護。

語意用法 take defensive measures 採取防禦措施。

| **definite**
[ˈdɛfənɪt] | 明確的、肯定的
英解 clearly defined |

例 I'd love to attend the conference in Seattle, but I'll have to talk to my wife about it before I can give you a **definite** answer.

我想參加西雅圖的會議，但在給你明確答覆前我得先和老婆談談。

語意用法 a definite answer 明確的答覆。

| **deliberate**
[dɪˈlɪbərɪt] | 深思熟慮的、蓄意的、從容的
英解 carefully thought out in advance |

例 The kids claimed it was an accident, but the store's security video showed that their breaking of the window had been **deliberate**.

這群小孩聲稱它是意外，但商店的監視錄影顯示他們的破窗行為是蓄意的。

語意用法 a deliberate lie 蓄意的謊言。

| **dense**
[dɛns] | 密集的、稠密的、濃厚的
英解 thickly crowded or closely set |

例 Their howls can be heard three miles away through **dense** forests.（97 學測）

他們的吼聲可以穿透稠密森林在三哩外被聽到。

語意用法 a dense population 密集的人口；a dense fog 濃霧。

| **desperate**
[ˈdɛspərɪt] | 絕望的、極度渴望的、極端的、孤注一擲的
英解 arising from or marked by despair or loss of hope |

例 He made a **desperate** effort to extricate himself.

他做出孤注一擲的努力解救他自己。

語意用法 desperate for ＋物，表示非常渴望某物。

| **diligent**
[`dɪləʤnɛt] | 勤奮的、費盡心血的
英解 careful and persevering in carrying out tasks or duties |

例 Brian was a **diligent** and esteemed correspondent of that journal.

布萊恩是那家期刊一名勤奮又受敬重的特派員。

語意用法 diligent in ＋方面，表示在某方面很勤奮。

| **dishonest**
[dɪs`ɑnɪst] | 不誠實的、詐欺的
英解 deceptive or fraudulent |

例 If he was **dishonest** with his ex-wife, why do you think he would be honest with you?

如果他對前妻不忠，你為什麼認為他會對你誠實？

語意用法 dishonest of ＋人＋ to V，表示某人做某事是不誠實的。

| **disposable**
[dɪ`sopzəbḷ] | 可任意處理的、用完即丟的
英解 designed for disposal after use |

例 Paper napkins are **disposable**.

餐巾紙用過就可丟棄。

語意用法 disposable diapers 可棄式尿布。

| **diverse**
[də`vɝs] | 不同的、多樣化的
英解 many and different |

例 Bhutan's **diverse** landscapes include snowcapped peaks, bamboo jungles, meadows, and grasslands.（93 指考補）

不丹多樣化的景觀包括了白雪皚皚的山峰、竹子叢林、草原及綠地。

語意用法 diverse interests 多樣化的興趣。

domestic [də`mɛstɪk]	國內的、家庭的、馴養的;亦作名詞用 英解 of or involving the home or family

例 To reduce the environmental impact of shipping goods long distances, we use only **domestic** raw materials.

為減少運送長程貨物造成的環境影響,我們只用國內原物料。

語意用法 a domestic airline 國內航空公司。

doubtful [`daʊtfəl]	疑惑的、可疑的、難以預測的 英解 open to doubt or suspicion

例 She lay so still that we were **doubtful** if she breathed.

她躺在那兒一動也不動,我們不免懷疑她是否還在呼吸。

語意用法 doubtful about/of +事物,表示對某事物感到懷疑。

dramatic [drə`mætɪk]	戲劇性的、引人注目的 英解 suitable to or characteristic of drama

例 Nobody at the university admissions office could explain the recent **dramatic** increase in the number of applications.

大學入學許可辦公室裡沒有人能夠解釋為何最近的申請人數大幅增加。

語意用法 dramatic increase 大幅增加;dramatic drop 大幅下跌;dramatic development 戲劇性發展。

due [dju]	應支付的、應有的、到期的、由於 英解 owed and payable immediately or on demand

例 They need to cope with health problems **due** to climate change.（96 指考）

因為氣候的變化,他們需要應付健康問題。

語意用法 due to +原因,表示由於、歸因於、歸功於某原因。

| **eccentric**
[ɪkˋsɛntrɪk] | 古怪的、反常的；亦作名詞用
英解 deviating from the customary character |

例 The novel is about an **eccentric** old man who travels around the country on a tiny pink tricycle.

這小說是關於一位古怪的老人，騎著粉紅小三輪車環遊國家。

語意用法 eccentric behavior 古怪的行為。

| **ecological**
[ˌɛkəˋlɑdʒɪkəl] | 生態的
英解 characterized by the interdependence of living organisms in an environment |

例 The **ecological** damage caused by the oil spill will undoubtedly last for decades.

漏油造成的生態破壞無疑會持續數十年。

語意用法 ecological destruction 生態破壞。

| **economic**
[ˌikəˋnɑmɪk] | 經濟上的、經濟學的、有利可圖的
英解 of or relating to an economy, economics, or finance |

例 The proposal offers some short-term benefits, but at the expense of long-term **economic** growth.

這提案帶來一些短期利益，但卻是以長期的經濟成長為代價。

語意用法 economic growth 經濟成長；an economic polocy 經濟政策。

| **effective**
[ɪˋfɛktɪv] | 有效的、起作用的、印象深刻的、有力的
英解 productive of or capable of producing a result |

例 The doctor changed the patient's medication three times before she found a combination that was **effective**.

在找出一個有效的組合前，醫生更換了三次病人的藥。

語意用法 effective in ＋方面，表示對某方面有效的。

efficient [ɪˋfɪʃənt]	效率高的、有能力的、有效的
	英解 being effective without wasting time or effort or expense

例 Cars in the future will be characterized by their **efficient** use of gasoline.

（88 學測）

未來汽車的特色將在於它們使用汽油的高效能。

語意用法 efficient at/in ＋方面，表示在某方面很有能力。

elaborate [ɪˋlæbərɪt]	詳細的、精細的、複雜的
	英解 detailed

例 He began with an **elaborate** discussion of Creutzfeldt-Jakob disease.

（94 指考）

他一開始就很詳細地討論了狂牛症。

語意用法 an elaborate scheme 密謀、詳細策畫的計謀。

elegant [ˋɛləgənt]	優雅的、精緻的、漂亮的
	英解 refined and tasteful in appearance or behavior or style

例 Dressed in an **elegant** silk dress and pearl necklace with matching earrings, Mrs. Baron looked quite out of place at the baseball game.

身著一件優雅的絲質禮服，戴著珍珠項鍊和相配的耳環，巴朗女士在棒球比賽中看起來格格不入。

語意用法 elegant dress 優雅的衣服。

enormous [ɪˋnɔrməs]	巨大的、龐大的
	英解 immense, vast

例 If it weren't for that **enormous** mole on your nose you'd probably be a big movie star.

要不是你鼻上那顆巨大的痣，你應該會是一個電影大明星。

語意用法 enormous 表示很巨大，超過 big 的程度。enormous room 很大的房間；enormous wealth 龐大的財富。

enthusiastic
[ɪn͵θjuzɪˋæstɪk]

熱烈的、熱情的
英解 having or showing great excitement and interest

例 Dr. Thompson had expected to be surrounded by **enthusiastic** people.
（94 指考）

湯普森博士預料會被熱烈的群眾包圍。

語意用法 an enthusiastic fan 狂熱的粉絲。

entire
[ɪnˋtaɪr]

全部的、整個的、全然的；亦作名詞用
英解 whole, complete

例 The **entire** country is mountainous.（96 指考）

整個國家都是山。

語意用法 the entire afternoon 一整個下午。

envious
[ˋɛnvɪəs]

嫉妒的、羨慕的
英解 showing extreme cupidity

例 Victor's classmates are very **envious** of him because he has just received a new cell phone for his birthday.（92 指考）

維多的同學都很羨慕他，因為他剛收到一支新手機作為生日禮物。

語意用法 envious of ＋物，表示因某物而感到嫉妒、羨慕的。

essential
[ɪˋsɛnʃəl]

必要的、不可缺的、本質的、基本的；亦作名詞用
英解 absolutely necessary

例 We human beings may live without clothes, but food and air are **essential** to our life.（96 學測）

人類或許可以不靠衣物生存，但食物與空氣卻是生活中不可或缺的。

語意用法 essential to/for ＋事物，表示對某事物而言是必要的。

ethnic [ˈɛθnɪk]	種族上的、人類學的 英解 denoting or deriving from or distinctive of the ways of living built up by a group of people

例 Africa is a land of many **ethnic** groups. (97 指考)

非洲是一塊多種族族群的土地。

語意用法 ethnic music 民族音樂。

eventual [ɪˈvɛntʃʊəl]	最後的、結果的 英解 happening in due course of time

例 We provide inmates with extensive job training to prepare them for their **eventual** release from prison.

我們提供囚犯廣泛的工作訓練，幫他們做好最後出獄的準備。

語意用法 eventual return 最後的回歸；eventual winner 最後的贏家；eventual death 最後的死亡。

everlasting [ˌɛvɚˈlæstɪŋ]	永久的、不朽的、永遠的；亦作名詞用 英解 eternal

例 Thousands have died while searching for the secret to **everlasting** life.

數千人在尋求永生秘密時死去。

語意用法 everlasting love 永誌不渝的愛。

exceptional [ɪkˈsɛpʃənl]	例外的、特殊的、異常的、卓越的 英解 forming an exception

例 Her talent and skills are **exceptional** for her age. (99 指考)

以她的年紀來說，她的才華與技能是卓越的。

語意用法 exceptional beauty 出眾的美貌。

形容詞篇

excessive
[ɪkˋsɛsɪv]

過度的、過分的、極度的
英解 beyond normal limits

例 Administrators are looking for new ways to curb **excessive** drinking among university students.

管理者在尋求約束大學生飲酒過度的新方法。

語意用法 excessive charge 過高的費用。

exclusive
[ɪkˋsklusɪv]

除外的、獨有的、全部的；亦作名詞用
英解 not divided or shared with others

例 The contract clearly states that we hold the **exclusive** right to distribute the product in Taiwan.

合約明訂我們擁有在台灣獨家經銷該產品的權利。

語意用法 exclusive rights 獨佔權。

expert
[ˋɛkspət]

熟練的、內行的、專門的；亦作名詞用
英解 skillful or knowledgeable

例 Before investing in the stock market, it's best to get **expert** advice from real professionals.

在投資股市前，最好向真正的專家尋求專業建議。

語意用法 expert at/in/with ＋事物，表示對某事物很熟練。

explicit
[ɪkˋsplɪsɪt]

詳盡的、明確的、直率的
英解 precisely and clearly expressed or readily observable

例 He made his instruction **explicit** and direct so that everyone could follow easily.（89 學測）

他做出明確且直接的指示，讓每個人都容易遵循。

語意用法 make sth. explicit 讓某物變得明確。

external
[ɪkˋstɜnəl]

外面的、外來的、外觀的；亦作名詞用
英解 outer

例 In addition to money from the university, the computer science department also receives **external** funding from several local technology companies.

除了從大學來的錢，電腦科技系也從一些當地的科技公司取得外部經費。

語意用法 external trade 對外的貿易。

extinct
[ɪkˋstɪŋkt]

熄滅的、滅亡的、絕種的、過時的
英解 no longer existing or living

例 If the rainforests disappear, many of these species will become **extinct**.
（96 指考）

如果雨林消失，許多物種將會滅亡。

語意用法 an extinct volcano 死火山。

extracurricular
[ˌɛkstrəkəˋrɪkjələ]

課外的、業餘的
英解 outside the regular academic curriculum

例 His **extracurricular** activities include playing football and singing in the choir.

他的課外活動包括踢足球以及在合唱團唱歌。

語意用法 extracurricular activities 課外活動。

extreme
[ɪkˋstrim]

極端的、末端的、盡頭的；亦作名詞用
英解 being of a high or of the highest degree or intensity

例 Some Americans enjoy great wealth, while others suffer in **extreme** poverty.（92 學測補）

有些美國人享有極大的財富，另一些則過著極度貧窮的苦日子。

語意用法 take extreme action 採取極端的手段。

factual [ˋfæktʃʊəl]	根據事實的、眞實的 [英解] existing in act or fact

例 Although very readable, the biography is marred by several **factual** errors.

雖然讀起來有趣，但這傳記由於一些事實上的謬誤而失其價值。

語意用法 a factual story 以事實為依的故事。

false [fɔls]	不正確的、假的、謬誤的 [英解] not in accordance with the truth or facts

例 Male fireflies may deceive females with **false** signals. (93 學測)

雄螢火蟲可能會用假訊號欺矇雌螢火蟲。

語意用法 false ＋名詞，表示錯誤的事物。a false alarm 假警報、一場虛驚。

famous [ˋfeməs]	出名的、著名的 [英解] renowned

例 Mr. Wan is not only a novelist, poet and playwright, but also a **famous** painter and sculptor. (99 指考)

萬先生不僅是一位小說家、詩人以及劇作家，也是知名的畫家與雕刻家。

語意用法 famous for/as ＋事物，表示因某事物而聞名。

fatal [ˋfetl]	致命的、命中注定的、無可挽回的 [英解] bringing death

例 The stings of some types of ants can be **fatal** to livestock and humans. (94 學測)

某種螞蟻的刺可以使牲畜和人類喪命。

語意用法 fatal to ＋人，表示對某人是致命的或有重大危害的。

favorable [ˋfevərəbl]	贊同的、稱讚的、有利的 [英解] encouraging or approving or pleasing

例 The weather lately has not been at all **favorable** for hiking.

最近的天氣一點都不適合出遊。

語意用法 favorable to/for ＋事物，表示對某事物有利的、方便的。

favorite	特別喜歡的；亦作名詞用
[ˋfevərɪt]	英解 a special loved one

形容詞篇

例 Stress has become a **favorite** subject of everyday conversation. （92 學測）

壓力已經成為日常生活對話中最受歡迎的主題。

語意用法 sb.'s favorite song 某人最喜愛的歌曲。

flexible	有韌性的、可彎曲的、可適應的、靈活的
[ˋflɛksəbl̩]	英解 capable of being changed

例 The singer has a marvelously **flexible** voice.

這位歌手的聲音彈性讓人驚嘆。

語意用法 a flexible pipe 容易彎曲的管子。

fluent	流利的、順暢的
[ˋfluənt]	英解 smooth and unconstrained in movement

例 Children become **fluent** in their native language within a few years.

（91 學測）

小孩子們在幾年內就能流暢說母語。

語意用法 fluent in/at ＋語言，表示精通於某種語言。

fond	喜歡的、溺愛的、多情的
[fɑnd]	英解 having or displaying warmth or affection

例 I'm very **fond** of you.

我很喜歡你。

語意用法 fond of ＋人事物，表示喜好某人事物。

| **formal**
[ˋfɔrml] | 正式的、正規的、刻板的、形式上的；亦作名詞用
英解 relating to or involving outward form or structure |

例 People who practice folk medicine need lots of **formal** education on herbs.（92 學測補）

民俗醫學的執業者需要受過很多草藥的正規教育。

語意用法 formal dress 正式的服裝。

| **forthcoming**
[ˌforθˋkʌmɪŋ] | 即將到來的、現有的
英解 about to appear |

例 He wasn't very **forthcoming** about his reasons for wanting to leave the company.

他對於他想離開公司的理由沒有完全坦白。

語意用法 the forthcoming week 下週、即將到來的一週。

| **fortunate**
[ˋfɔrtʃənɪt] | 幸運的、僥倖的
英解 having unexpected good fortune |

例 She devoted countless hours to helping the less **fortunate** members of our community.

他投入無數時間來幫助社區裡較不幸的人們。

語意用法 fortunate in ＋方面，表示在某方面很幸運。

| **frank**
[fræŋk] | 坦白的、直率的、真誠的
英解 candid |

例 The rock star was **frank** about his drug problem.

這個搖滾巨星坦承他有毒品問題。

語意用法 to be frank with you 坦白對你說。

frequent
[ˈfrikwənt]

時常發生的、屢次的、頻繁的；動詞作時常出入解
英解 coming at short intervals or habitually

例 Car theft is a **frequent** occurrence in this area.

汽車竊盜案在這地區時常發生。

語意用法 a frequent guest 常客。

fruitful
[ˈfrutfəl]

成果豐碩的、肥沃的、多產的
英解 bearing fruit in abundance

例 After three days of less than **fruitful** negotiations, both sides gave up.

在三天不怎麼有收穫的協商後，雙方都放棄了。

語意用法 a fruitful meeting 收穫很多的會議。

fundamental
[ˌfʌndəˈmɛntl̩]

基本的、根本的、主要的、原始的
英解 serving as an essential component

例 The **fundamental** question each of us must answer is what to do with the limited amount of time we have.

我們每個人都需要回答的基本問題是，要怎麼利用我們有限的時間。

語意用法 fundamental human rights 基本人權。

furious
[ˈfjʊrɪəs]

狂怒的、強烈的、喧鬧的
英解 marked by extreme and violent energy

例 Instead of being **furious** about her supervisor's ridiculous demands, Stella just laughed in his face and quit.

沒對主管的無理要求發怒，史黛拉只是當著他的面笑了笑並辭職。

語意用法 furious with ＋人，表示對某人大發雷霆；furious at ＋事物，表示對事物發怒。

generous
[ˋdʒɛnərəs]

慷慨的、大方的、寬厚的
英解 willing to give and share unstintingly

例 Professor Suzuki was always so **generous** with her time that I wondered when she did her research.

鈴木教授總是很大方把時間留給學生，我懷疑她是何時做她的研究。

語意用法 generous with ＋方面，表示在某方面很大方。

genetic
[dʒəˋnɛtɪk]

起源的、發生的、基因的
英解 occurring among members of a family usually by heredity

例 Cloning is the **genetic** process of producing copies of an individual.
（91 學測）

無性繁殖是複製個體的基因過程。

語意用法 a genetic disorder 遺傳病。

glamorous
[ˋglæmərəs]

迷人的、富有魅力的
英解 possessing glamour

例 The prom has changed from a modest event to a **glamorous** party over the years.（99 學測）

經過這些年，畢業舞會已經從一個普通事件變成一個富有魅力的派對。

語意用法 a glamorous job 有吸引力的工作。

global
[ˋglobl̩]

全球的、球狀的
英解 involving the entire earth

例 Average **global** temperature has increased by almost 1° F over the past century.（96 指考）

過去一世紀，全球平均氣溫幾乎增加了華氏 1 度。

語意用法 global inflation 全球性通膨。

glorious
[ˋglorɪəs]

光榮的、輝煌的、壯麗的、極好的
英解 having or deserving or conferring glory

例 For some reason, Jay was always telling us that he came from an ancient country with a **glorious** history.

為了某些理由，杰總是告訴我們他來自一個有光榮歷史的古老國家。

語意用法 a glorious victory 光榮的勝利。

gradual
[ˋgrædʒʊəl]

逐漸的、逐步的
英解 advancing or progressing by regular or continuous degrees

例 In the United States, the change from formal to casual office wear has been **gradual**.（91 學測）

在美國，從正式到休閒辦公室穿著的變化是循序漸進的。

語意用法 a gradual change 逐漸的變化。

grateful
[ˋgretfəl]

感謝的、感激的、可喜的
英解 feeling or showing gratitude

例 I will always be **grateful** to Mr. Baldwin, my very first tuba teacher and the man who really inspired my love of music.

我總是對鮑德溫先生心懷感激，他是我的第一位低音號老師，也啓發了我對音樂的喜愛。

語意用法 grateful to ＋人，表示對某人表示感激；grateful for ＋物，表示對某物表示感激。

greedy
[ˋgridɪ]

貪吃的、貪婪的、渴望的
英解 immoderately desirous of acquiring

例 I'm not **greedy**, but I do expect to be paid fairly for my work.

我不貪心，但我希望工作能有合理報酬。

語意用法 greedy for ＋物，表示對某物的渴望、熱望。

guilty [`gɪltɪ]	有罪的、有過失的、內疚的 英解 responsible for an offence or misdeed

例 I feel **guilty** about cheating on my exams.

我對考試作弊感到罪惡。

語意用法 plead guilty to the crime 承認罪行。

handsome [`hænsəm]	英俊的 英解 good-looking

例 He looks **handsome** in casual clothes.（91 學測）

穿便服的他看起來挺英俊的。

語意用法 a handsome income 可觀的收入。

harsh [hɑrʃ]	粗糙的、惡劣的、殘酷的 英解 rough or grating to the senses

例 Her attitude toward the captive was most **harsh** and brutal.

她對待俘虜的態度最為殘酷與粗暴。

語意用法 harsh to sb.，表示對某人嚴苛。

hateful [`hetfəl]	可恨的、可憎的、討厭的 英解 evoking or deserving hatred

例 He decided to close his blog rather than deal with all of the **hateful** comments people were leaving on it.

他決定關掉他的布落格，而不去應付留在版上的惡意評論。

語意用法 a hateful crime 可憎的罪行。

healthful [`hɛlθfəl]	有益健康的 英解 conducive to good health

例 The soybean is **healthful** and has become popular in the western world.

（92 學測補）

大豆有益健康，在西方世界變得很受歡迎。

語意用法 healthful exercise 有益健康的運動。

helpful
[ˋhɛlpfəl]
有幫助的、有利的、有益的
英解 providing assistance or serving a useful function

例 I hope the above advice is **helpful** to you in selecting the right college.

（91 學測補）

我希望上述的建議有助於你選擇適合的大學。

語意用法 helpful advice 有用的建議。

homesick
[ˋhom,sɪk]
想家的、思鄉病的
英解 longing to return home

例 Whenever I walk by a bakery I get a little **homesick** for my mom's home-baked cookies.

每當我經過麵包店，就會懷念起媽媽親烤的餅乾。

語意用法 homesick for ＋物，表示對某物感到懷念。

hostile
[ˋhɑstɪl]
敵方的、不懷好意的、不適合的
英解 antagonistic

例 This team loves to go on the road and play in front of **hostile** crowds.

這球隊喜歡到馬路上在敵對的隊伍前打球。

語意用法 hostile to ＋物，表示與某物敵對的、對某物不適合的。

humane
[hjuˋmen]
有人情味的、高尚的、仁慈的
英解 characterized by kindness, mercy, sympathy, etc.

例 He was a fairly **humane** man toward slaves and other animals.

他是一個對待奴隸以及其他動物相當仁慈的人。

語意用法 humane society 人道的社會。

humble [ˈhʌmbl̩]	謙遜的、卑微的、簡陋的 英解 low or inferior in station or quality

例 I'm just a **humble** farmer from a small town you've never heard of, but I have rights and you had better respect them.

我只是來自一個你從未聽過的小鎮的卑微農夫，但我有權利，你最好尊重這一點。

語意用法 humble about ＋方面，表示在某方面謙虛的。

identical [aɪˈdɛntɪkl̩]	同一個、完全相同、同源的、同卵的 英解 exactly alike

例 **Identical** twins have almost all of their genes in common.（95 指考）

同卵雙胞胎具有幾乎完全相同的基因。

語意用法 identical with/to ＋物，表示與某物完全一致的。

idiotic [ˌɪdɪˈɑtɪk]	白癡的 英解 insanely irresponsible

例 I was sternly criticized for having such an **idiotic** job.（89 學測）

我被嚴苛批評做這麼白癡的工作。

語意用法 It is idiotic of ＋人＋ to V，表示某人做了某事是很愚蠢的。

illegal [ɪˈligl̩]	非法的、違反規則的；亦作名詞用 英解 unlawful

例 Education alone is not enough to stop the extraordinary growth of the **illegal** downloading practice.（98 指考）

光是教育不足以遏止成長迅速的非法下載。

語意用法 illegal drugs 非法藥品。

illegible [ɪˈlɛdʒəbl̩]	難讀的、難認的 英解 not legible

例 Perhaps there is an inadequate or **illegible** address and there is no return address.（89 學測）

或許是有一個不完整或難以便認的地址，而且沒有可退信的地址。

語意用法 illegible fax 難以辨識的傳真。

immediate
[ɪˋmidɪɪt]

立即的、當前的、緊接的
英解 of the present time and place

例 I am in need of **immediate** help.

我需要立即的協助。

語意用法 take immediate action 採取立即的行動。

immortal
[ɪˋmɔrtl]

不朽的、不死的、永生的
英解 not subject to death or decay

例 You have placed his **immortal** soul in jeopardy.

你將他不朽的靈魂置於危險中。

語意用法 immortal glory 永恆的光榮。

immune
[ɪˋmjun]

免疫的、免除的
英解 unresponsive

例 Green tea is helpful for infection and damaged **immune** function.（97 學測）

綠茶對於感染和遭破壞的免疫系統有助益。

語意用法 immune to ＋疾病，表示對某疾病有免疫。

impatient
[ɪmˋpeʃənt]

不耐煩的、著急的、無法忍受的
英解 lacking patience

例 I am **impatient** to be rid of him.

我迫不及待要擺脫他。

語意用法 impatient ＋ to V，表示急著要做某事。

impersonal
[ɪmˋpɝsn̩l]

非個人的、客觀的、冷淡的
英解 not relating to or responsive to individual persons

例 When you call most large companies, you're not greeted by a person, but with a cold, **impersonal** recording.

當你打電話給大部分的大公司，接應你的不是人，而且冰冷、沒有人味的錄音。

語意用法 impersonal remarks 指非特定個人、客觀的評論。

impossible
[ɪmˋpɑsəbl̩]

不可能的、辦不到的
英解 incapable of being done

例 Sometimes it is **impossible** to deliver all the mail that arrives at the post office. (89 學測)

將所有到達郵局的信件送完有時候是不可能的。

語意用法 an impossible task 一項不可能的任務。

inappropriate
[ˌɪnəˋproprɪɪt]

不適當的
英解 not fitting or appropriate

例 They often blurt out **inappropriate** comments or have difficulty taking turns in conversation. (96 指考)

他們常常脫口說出不當的言論，不然就是無法依序進行對話。

語意用法 inappropriate behavior 不當的行為。

inconvenient
[ˌɪnkənˋvinjənt]

不方便的、打擾的、令人爲難的
英解 troublesome, awkward, or difficult

例 It is **inconvenient** to have meetings on holidays.

在假日開會很不方便。

語意用法 at an inconvenient time 在不方便的時間。

incredible
[ɪnˋkrɛdəbl]

難以置信的、不可信的
英解 unbelievable

例 Bottled water produces an **incredible** amount of solid waste.（99 學測）

瓶裝水製造出難以置信的大量固體廢料。

語意用法 an incredible memory 驚人的記憶力。

indifferent
[ɪnˋdɪfərənt]

不感興趣的、冷淡的、無關緊要的、中庸的
英解 marked by a lack of interest

例 They are **indifferent** to the regained weight.（94 學測）

他們對於胖回來的體重漠不關心。

語意用法 indifferent to ＋人事物，表示對某人事物漠不關心的。

inevitable
[ɪnˋɛvətəbl]

不可避免的、必然發生的
英解 unavoidable

例 The will is plain, and the result is **inevitable**.

這意念是清楚的，而結果是不可避免的。

語意用法 an inevitable result 不可避免的結果。

inferior
[ɪnˋfɪrɪə]

次等的、低下的、下方的
英解 lower in value or quality

例 Many consumers can not tell the difference between name-brand handbags and supposedly **inferior** knockoffs.

許多消費者不能分辨名牌手提包和比較劣等的仿冒品。

語意用法 inferior to ＋人，表示不如某人。

influential
[ˌɪnfluˈɛnʃəl]

有影響力的、有權勢的
英解 having or exercising influence or power

例 The magazine did not have a large circulation, but it was read by leading politicians, businesspeople, and cultural critics, and was therefore incredibly **influential**.

這雜誌的流通量不大,但讀者都是頂尖的政治人物、商人和文化評論家,所以它非常有影響力。

語意用法 an influential man 有影響力的人。

informal
[ɪnˈfɔrml]

非正式的、非正規的
英解 not formal

例 By the way, it's an **informal** dinner.（87 學測）

順帶一提,那是非正式的晚宴。

語意用法 an informal visit 非正式的拜訪。

innocent
[ˈɪnəsn̩t]

無罪的、清白的、天真的、單純的
英解 free from evil or guilt

例 Because he spent so much of his youth studying, as an adult he was still quite **innocent** and easily taken advantage of.

因為他年輕時大部分時間都在讀書,所以以成人來說,他仍然很天真、容易被佔便宜。

語意用法 an innocent victim 無辜的受害者。

inquisitive
[ɪnˈkwɪzətɪv]

好奇的、愛打聽的
英解 showing curiosity

例 The little boy is very **inquisitive**: he is interested in a lot of different things and always wants to find out more about them.（93 指考）

這個小男孩很好奇,對於許多不同的事物感到興趣而且總是想要對它們瞭解更多。

語意用法 inquisitive about ＋方面,表示想知道某方面的事。

insane [ɪnˋsen]	瘋狂的、精神錯亂的、極愚蠢的 英解 crazy

例 I just cannot figure out why John did such a stupid thing! He must have gone totally **insane**.（93 指考補）

我就是想不透約翰為什麼會做出那種蠢事！他肯定是精神錯亂了。

語意用法 go insane 發瘋。

形容詞篇

insecure [ˌɪnsɪˋkjʊr]	不安全的、不牢靠的、無把握的、局促不安的 英解 anxious or afraid

例 It describes a situation of feeling **insecure**.（97 指考）

它描述一種感到不安全的狀況。

語意用法 insecure internet activity 不安全的網路活動。

intact [ɪnˋtækt]	完整無缺的、原封不動的 英解 constituting the undiminished entirety

例 The uninhabited islands of Penghu have been kept **intact** without human intervention.（94 指考）

澎湖杳無人跡的島嶼沒有人類的介入一直保持著完整狀態。

語意用法 remain/stay intact 依然完整；leave sth. intact 保持某物的完整。

intelligent [ɪnˋtɛlədʒənt]	有才智的、聰明的、熟悉的 英解 having or indicating intelligence

例 Her forehead was high, and her eyes both **intelligent** and beautiful.

她的額頭有些高，她的眼睛充滿智慧又漂亮。

語意用法 an intelligent reply 機靈的回答。

| **international**
[͵ɪntɚˋnæʃənḷ] | 國際性的、國際間的；亦作名詞用
英解 concerning or belonging to all or at least two or more nations |

例 Jazz is not only an American art form but also an **international** phenomenon.（93 指考補）

爵士不只是美國藝術的一種形式，也是一種國際性的現象。

語意用法 an international airport 國際機場。

| **intimate**
[ˋɪntəmɪt] | 熟悉的、親密的、私人的、怡人的
英解 marked by close acquaintance, association, or familiarity |

例 Today, television, movies, and books have taken over the once personal and **intimate** activity of storytelling.（87 學測）

現今的電視、電影以及書籍已經取代昔日說故事這種既個人又親密的活動。

語意用法 intimate friends 密友。

| **invisible**
[ɪnˋvɪzəbḷ] | 看不見的、無形的、不顯眼的
英解 not able to be perceived by the eye |

例 The wires that held the actor as he soared across the stage were completely **invisible** to the audience.

觀眾完全看不見支撐演員飛過舞台的纜線。

語意用法 an invisible man 隱形人。

| **ironic**
[aɪˋrɑnɪk] | 諷刺的、挖苦的、冷嘲熱諷的
英解 humorously sarcastic or mocking |

例 It's pretty **ironic** that the gun-safety expert shot himself in the foot while teaching a class on gun safety.

一名槍枝安全專家在教授槍枝安全課時射中自己的腳，真是諷刺啊。

語意用法 an ironic twist 諷刺性的轉折。

jealous
[ˋdʒɛləs]

嫉妒的、吃醋的
英解 feeling or showing envy

例 Don't worry—the only reason he's talking to her is to make you **jealous**.

別擔心，他和她講話的唯一理由是要讓你嫉妒。

語意用法 jealous of ＋物，表示因某物而感到嫉妒的、羨慕的。

juvenile
[ˋdʒuvən!]

少年的、孩子氣的
英解 young, youthful, or immature

例 Community service can help prevent **juvenile** delinquency. （98 指考）

社區服務能幫助遏止青少年犯罪。

語意用法 a juvenile court 少年法庭；juvenile literature 少年文學。

legendary
[ˋlɛdʒəndˌɛrɪ]

傳說的、傳奇的；亦作名詞用
英解 so celebrated as to having taken on the nature of a legend

例 Though not a large man, Kobayashi's ability to eat hot dogs is **legendary**.

雖然不是高大的人，小林吃熱狗的能力是一項傳奇。

語意用法 legendary assassin 傳奇的刺客。

legitimate
[lɪˋdʒɪtəmɪt]

合法的、正統的、合理的、婚生的
英解 according to law

例 You can sue, but if the judge rules your claims are not **legitimate**, you may be responsible for court costs.

你可以告，但如果法官判定你的控訴不成立，你可能得負擔開庭成本。

語意用法 a legitimate claim 正當的要求。

lengthy [ˈlɛŋθɪ]	冗長的、囉唆的 英解 relatively long in duration

例 The explanation was so **lengthy** that we could not see the point clearly.

（94 指考）

這個解說太冗長了，我們無法清楚看到重點。

語意用法 lengthy explanation 冗長的解釋。

liberal [ˈlɪbərəl]	慷慨的、大方的、充分的、開明的、自由的、不拘泥字 面意思的；亦作名詞用 英解 showing or characterized by broad-mindedness

例 If we take a **liberal** interpretation of the contract, we wouldn't have to pay anything until after receiving shipment.

如果我們不拘泥字面意思來看合約，我們在收到送貨前是不須支付費用的。

語意用法 liberal with/of ＋方面，表示在某方面不吝嗇的。

logical [ˈlɑdʒɪkḷ]	合邏輯的、合理的、必然的、邏輯學的 英解 capable of or reflecting the capability for correct and valid reasoning

例 It's just not **logical** to put in the new floor before the roof is fixed.

在屋頂修好前安裝新地板是不合理的。

語意用法 logical argument 合理的論證。

lonesome [ˈlonsəm]	寂寞的、孤單的、寂涼的 英解 being the only one

例 The image of the **lonesome** cowboy riding off into the sunset has been used at the end of so many movies that it's now a cliché.

孤單牛仔騎馬走向落日的景象被用來做為許多電影的結尾，現在這已經變成陳腔濫調了。

語意用法 feel lonesome 感到寂寞。

loose [lus]	鬆散的、寬鬆的、未受拘束的、散漫的、放蕩的 英解 not compact or dense in structure or arrangement

例 My socks are so damn **loose** they keep sliding down into my shoes.

我的襪子也太鬆了，一直下滑到鞋子裡。

語意用法 a loose coat 寬大的外套；come loose（螺絲等）變鬆。

magnetic [mæg`nɛtɪk]	磁鐵的、有磁性的、有吸引力的、地磁的 英解 of or relating to or caused by magnetism

例 Dr. Begall and her colleagues wanted to know whether larger mammals also have the ability to perceive **magnetic** fields.（98 學測）

畢高博士和她的同事想知道大型哺乳動物是否也有感知磁場的能力。

語意用法 a magnetic field 磁場。

magnificent [mæg`nɪfəsn̩t]	壯麗的、豪華的、極好的 英解 characterized by grandeur

例 If you visit in the fall when the leaves change color, you'll be treated to one of the most **magnificent** sights in all of nature.

如果你在秋天葉子變色時來參觀，迎接你的是大自然中最壯麗的景象之一。

語意用法 a magnificent palace 壯麗的宮殿。

manageable [ˋmænɪdʒəbl̩]	可管理的、可控制的 英解 able to be managed or controlled

例 This company, with its serious financial problems, is no longer **manageable**.（91 學測）

這間公司有嚴重的財務問題，再也無法控制。

語意用法 a manageable problem 可處理的問題。

manual
[`mænjuəl]
手工的、用手操作的、實際佔有的
英解 of or relating to the hands

例 If the computer goes offline, you can still operate the machine with these **manual** controls here.

如果電腦離線，你還是可以用這邊的手動控制來操作機器。

語意用法 a manual worker 體力勞動者。

marvelous
[`mɑrvḷəs]
令人驚嘆的、非凡的、了不起的
英解 extraordinarily good or great

例 It has become a **marvelous** experience for people to ride horses on this road.（97 學測）

對在這條路上騎過馬的人來說成了一個不可思議的經驗。

語意用法 a marvelous experience 不可思議的經驗。

mature
[mə`tur]
成熟的、成人的、熟慮的
英解 characteristic of maturity

例 I don't know whether you are **mature** or not.

我不知道你到底成不成熟。

語意用法 a mature age 成熟的年紀；a mature plan 深思熟慮的計畫。

meaningful
[`minɪŋfəl]
有意義的、意味深長的
英解 having a meaning or purpose

例 The key to a successful speech is to make it **meaningful** and relevant to the audience.（94 指考）

一場成功演說的關鍵在於讓它有意義且與聽眾息息相關。

語意用法 a meaningful life 有意義的生活。

medical
[`mɛdɪkḷ]
醫學的、醫療的；亦作名詞用
英解 relating to the study or practice of medicine

例 **Medical** waste is a major source of dioxin pollution in the country.（92 學測補）

醫療廢棄物是這個國家戴奧辛污染的主要來源。

語意用法 medical care 醫療；medical science 醫學。

| **memorable**
[ˈmɛmərəbl̩] | 值得懷念的、難忘的
英解 worth remembering |

例 A very **memorable** event took place in 1643.

在一六四三年發生一個非常值得紀念的事件。

語意用法 a memorable event 值得紀念的事件。

| **mental**
[ˈmɛntl̩] | 精神的、心理的
英解 involving the mind or an intellectual process |

例 Only by entering this quiet **mental** state can a climber really do his or her best.（86 學測）

唯有進入這種安定的精神狀態才能讓登山者做到他（她）最好的程度。

語意用法 mental disorder 精神錯亂；mental health 精神上的健康。

| **middle**
[ˈmɪdl̩] | 中間的、中部的、中等的、中古的
英解 central |

例 I'm from Alice Springs, a small town right in the **middle** of Australia.

我來自愛麗絲泉，澳洲中部的一個小鎮。

語意用法 the middle class 中產階級。

| **minor**
[ˈmaɪnɚ] | 較小的、較少的、次等的、副修的、無生命危險的
英解 of lesser importance or stature or rank |

例 Even **minor** injuries may put a player at risk of replacement.（97 指考）

即便是輕微的傷害也可能讓運動員處於被替換的風險。

語意用法 a minor subject 副修科目；a minor party 少數黨。

| **miserable**
[ˈmɪzərəbl] | 痛苦的、悲慘的、不幸的
英解 very unhappy |

例 I don't know if I have a cold or the flu or what—I just feel **miserable**.

我不知道我是傷寒、得流感還是怎麼了，我就是很不舒服。

語意用法 a miserable life 悲慘的生活；miserable people 悲慘的人們。

| **mobile**
[ˈmobil] | 移動式的、機動的、易變的
英解 movable |

例 The army is developing a new **mobile** medical station that can be
delivered anywhere in the world in under 24 hours.

軍隊在發展一種移動式的醫療站，可以在 24 小時內運送到世界各地。

語意用法 a mobile shop 流動商店。

| **moderate**
[ˈmɑdərɪt] | 中等的、平庸的、有節制的、溫和的
英解 not extreme or excessive |

例 There were three levels of heat, producing mild, **moderate**, or strong
pain. (97 學測)

有三種程度的熱度，造成輕度、中度或強烈的疼痛。

語意用法 a moderate winter 溫和的冬天；a moderate request 不過分的要求。

| **modern**
[ˈmɑdən] | 現代的、近代的、時髦的
英解 of or relating to recent times or the present |

例 E-mail plays a vital role in **modern** communication. (90 學測)

電子郵件在現代的溝通中扮演舉足輕重的角色。

語意用法 modern times 現代；modern dance 現代舞。

| **modest**
[ˈmɑdɪst] | 謙虛的、審慎的、端莊的、有節制的
英解 marked by simplicity |

例 The prom was a **modest**, home-grown affair in the school gymnasium.
（99 學測）

高中畢業舞會是學校體育館裡一項相當節制的本地活動。

語意用法 a modest attitude 謙虛的態度。

multiple [ˋmʌtəpl]	複合的、多樣的、由許多部分組成的 英解 individual

例 Each nest used to have but one queen, but now many mounds are often found with **multiple** queens.（94 學測）

以往每個巢中只有一隻蟻后，然而現在很多土堆裡經常發現有多隻蟻后。

語意用法 multiple personality 多重人格。

mutual [ˋmjutʃuəl]	相互的、彼此的、共有的 英解 common to or shared by two or more parties

例 He said he loved me, but I had to tell him the feeling wasn't **mutual**.

他說他愛我，但我必須告訴他這種感覺不是互相的。

語意用法 mutual interest 共同的利益；mutual understanding 相互理解。

naive [nɑˋiv]	天真的、幼稚的、輕信的 英解 ingenuous

例 You think he's just going to loan you all that money and ask for nothing in return? Don't be **naive**!

你以為他會借你那筆錢而不求任何回報？別天真了。

語意用法 a naive girl 天真的女孩。

neat [nit]	整齊的、乾淨的、勻稱的、整潔的 英解 clean, tidy

例 He wanted his clothes to look **neat** all the time.（91 學測）

他希望他的衣服隨時看起來都很乾淨。

語意用法 a neat room 整齊的房間；neat handwriting 工整的字跡。

necessary
[`nɛsəsɛrɪ]

必須的、必要的、必然的
英解 required

例 Many people ask me questions, and I give them the **necessary** information.（92 學測）

很多人問我問題，我則提供他們所需的資訊。

語意用法 necessary measures 必要的手段、方法。

negative
[`nɛgətɪv]

否定的、負面的、消極的
英解 expressing or meaning a refusal or denial

例 Only 4 percent of employers said that casual dress has a **negative** impact on productivity.（91 學測）

只有百分之四的雇主表示休閒的穿著對生產力有負面影響。

語意用法 a negative impact 負面影響；a negative vote 反對票。

nervous
[`nɝvəs]

緊張不安的、神經質的
英解 very excitable or sensitive

例 When it was time to go to college, Whitney was quite **nervous**.（98 指考）

到了該上大學的時候，惠妮相當緊張。

語意用法 a nervous person 緊張的人；the nervous system 神經系統。

neutral
[`nutrəl]

中立的、模糊的、略帶灰色的
英解 having no personal preference

例 When two siblings fight, it's essential for the parents to remain **neutral**.

當兩小孩在打架，父母保持中立是很重要的。

語意用法 take a neutral stand 持中立立場。

normal [ˋnɔrml]	正常的、正規的 英解 typical

例 Under **normal** circumstances, the chef on duty would prepare the meals, but because it was the president, I did it myself.

在平常狀況下，值勤的主廚會準備餐點，但由於是總統，所以我親自準備。

語意用法 sth. seems normal 某物似乎很正常；perfecly normal 十分正常。

noticeable [ˋnotɪsəbl]	顯而易見的、顯著的、重要的 英解 easily seen or detected

例 There was a **noticeable** change in the little room.

這小房間裡有個顯而易見的變化。

語意用法 a noticeable change 顯而易見的變化；a noticeable improvement 顯而易見的進步。

notorious [noˋtorɪəs]	惡名昭彰的、聲名狼籍的 英解 known widely and usually unfavorably

例 Once known mainly for its natural beauty, Fukushima is now **notorious** as the site of a devastating nuclear accident.

曾以它的天然美景聞名，福島現在以毀滅性的核子意外而聲名遠播。

語意用法 a notorious rascal 惡名昭彰的惡棍。

novel [ˋnɑvl]	新的、新穎的、新奇的 英解 of a kind not seen before

例 France is pushing forward with a **novel** approach: giving away papers to young readers in an effort to turn them into regular customers. （99 指考）

法國正在推動一種新方法，發放報紙給年輕讀者，試圖把他們變成常客。

語意用法 a novel approach 新方法；a novel idea 新觀念。

numerous
[`njumərəs]

許多的、爲數眾多的
英解 being many

例 There are **numerous** reasons to use solar power, but the most important is that it's safe.

使用太陽能有無數理由，但最重要的是它很安全。

語意用法 a numerous army 龐大的軍隊。

nutritious
[nu`trɪʃəs]

有營養的、滋養的
英解 of or providing nourishment

例 Not that I prefer pumpkins for food; but I believe they are somewhat **nutritious**.

不是我喜歡南瓜食品，而是我認為它們蠻營養的。

語意用法 nutritious diet 營養的飲食；nutritious food 營養的食物。

obscure
[əb`skjʊr]

不清楚的、模糊的、朦朧的、隱匿的、無名的
英解 not clearly understood or expressed

例 My girlfriend is into **obscure** 70s South American rock bands.

我女朋友很迷七十年代南美的無名搖滾樂團。

語意用法 an obscure voice 微弱的聲音；an obscure place 隱匿的地方。

obvious
[`ɑbvɪəs]

明顯的、明白的、容易理解的、平淡無奇的
英解 easy to see or understand

例 The most **obvious** one is the importance of teamwork. （98 學測）

最明顯的就是團隊合作的重要。

語意用法 an obvious place 顯眼的地方；an obvious solution 顯而易見的解決方法。

opposite
[`ɑpəzɪt]

相反的、相對的、對面的
英解 being directly across from each other

例 He screamed at the child to stop crying, but of course, that had the **opposite** effect.

他對著小孩大叫不要哭，但當然得到了反效果。

語意用法 opposite to ＋物，表示與某物相反或不相容的。

optimistic
[͵ɑptə`mɪstɪk]

樂觀的
英解 expecting the most favorable outcome

例 They feel **optimistic** about future plans on weight control.（94 學測）

對於未來的體重控制計畫他們感到樂觀。

語意用法 optimistic about ＋事物，表示對某事物感到樂觀。

ordinary
[`ɔrdn͵ɛrɪ]

普通的、通常的、差勁的、平凡的
英解 of common or established type or occurrence

例 Folk tales are usually the stories of **ordinary** people.（91 學測補）

民間傳說往往是平凡人的故事。

語意用法 an ordinary man 平凡的人；an ordinary meeting 例行的會議。

outdoor
[`aut͵dor]

露天的、野外的、戶外的
英解 taking place, existing, or intended for use in the open air

例 The **outdoor** concert was canceled because of rain.（85 學測）

露天演唱會因雨取消。

語意用法 an outdoor café 露天咖啡館。

outgoing
[`aut͵goɪŋ]

外出的、外向的、直率的
英解 interested in and responsive to others

例 He is an **outgoing** and lively person.

他是一個外向活潑的人。

語意用法 an outgoing person 外向的人。

outward
[ˈautwəd]

向外的、外面的、表面的、外界的
英解 of or relating to what is apparent or superficial

例 From all **outward** appearances I seem to have a good life, but I actually have a lot of problems.

從所有表面看來，我似乎過得很好，但事實上我有一堆問題。

語意用法 outward appearance 外觀。

overall
[ˈovəˌɔl]

全面的、從頭到尾的、總的
英解 involving only main features

例 Hiring decisions are based on the manager's **overall** impression of the candidate, not his or her response to any particular interview question.

雇用決策是基於經理對於面試者的整體印象，而不是他或她對任何單一面試問題的回應。

語意用法 an overall estimate 全面的估計。

parental
[pəˈrɛntl]

父母親的
英解 of or relating to a parent or parenthood

例 If you think your **parental** responsibilities end when your child turns 18, you're in for a big surprise.

如果你覺得你當父母的責任在小孩十八歲時就結束，那麼你會大吃一驚的。

語意用法 parental leave 育嬰假；parental control 父母的管控。

partial
[ˈpɑrʃəl]

部分的、偏袒的、偏愛的
英解 relating to only a part

例 Jack made a **partial** payment on the new computer because he did not have enough money for it. （92 學測補）

傑克付了新電腦的部分款項，因為他沒有足夠的錢付清。

語意用法 a partial eclipse 偏食。

particular [pəˋtɪkjələ]	特別的、特殊的、特定的 英解 unique or specific to a person or thing or category

例 When it comes to selecting vegetables, she is quite **particular**.

講到挑選蔬菜，她是很講究的。

語意用法 particular about ＋物，表示對某物是很講究的。

passionate [ˋpæʃənɪt]	熱情的、激昂的、激烈的 英解 having or expressing strong emotions

例 His eyes were full of **passionate** remonstrance.

他的眼裡充滿激烈的抗議。

語意用法 feel passionate 感到激昂的；a passionate speech 激昂的演說。

passive [ˋpæsɪv]	消極的、被動的、順從的 英解 lacking in energy or will

例 Mr. Johnson was disappointed at his students for having a **passive** learning attitude.（95 學測）

強森老師對學生們被動的學習態度感到失望。

語意用法 a passive attitude 消極的態度；passive resistance 消極的抵抗。

patient [ˋpeʃənt]	有耐心的、能忍受的；名詞作病人解 英解 enduring trying circumstances with even temper

例 His train was late, but he was **patient**.

他的火車誤點了，但他很有耐心。

語意用法 patient with ＋人，表示對某人有耐性的。

peculiar [pɪˋkjuljə]	奇怪的、罕見的、獨特的 英解 strange or unusual

例 I heard a **peculiar** humming sound from the pit.

我聽到一個奇怪的嗡嗡聲從地窖傳來。

語意用法 taste peculiar 嚐起來很特別；peculiar smell 特殊的氣味。

perfect
[ˋpɝfɪkt]

完美的、理想的、十足的
英解 having all essential elements

例 Many folk tales are also tall tales—stories of unbelievable events told with **perfect** seriousness.（91 學測補）

許多民間傳說也是誇大的傳說，故事裡十分嚴肅地說著不可置信的事件。

語意用法 a perfect day 完美的一天；a perfect stranger 十足的陌生人。

permanent
[ˋpɝmənənt]

永恆的、永久的、永遠的
英解 existing or intended to exist for an indefinite period

例 We had only planned to be in Paris for a few months, but after six years, we realized our stay would be **permanent**.

我們只計畫待在巴黎幾個月，但六年後，我們了解到我們的停留會是永久的。

語意用法 permanent residence 永久住處。

persuasive
[pɚˋswesɪv]

有說服力的、令人信服的
英解 intended or having the power to induce action or belief

例 Mr. Wang's arguments were very **persuasive**, and the committee finally accepted his proposal.（87 學測）

王先生的論點很有說服力，委員會最後接受了他的提議。

語意用法 persuasive speech 有說服力的演說；find sth. persuasive 覺得某物有說服力。

plausible
[ˋplɔzəbḷ]

貌似有理的、嘴巧的、會說話的
英解 apparently reasonable and valid, and truthful

例 This very simple explanation appeared at once **plausible** and satisfying.

這個簡單的解釋立即顯得振振有詞且令人滿意。

語意用法 sound plausible 聽起來有理；a plausible excuse 貌似有理的理由。

pleasant [ˋplɛzṇt]	令人愉快的、舒適的 英解 enjoyable

例 She had a reputation for being rude to reporters, but she was extremely **pleasant** when I interviewed her.

她以對記者無禮而聞名,但我訪問她時她非常和善。

語意用法 a pleasant evening 愉快的夜晚;pleasant to the eye 悅目的。

plentiful [ˋplɛntəfl]	充足的、富裕的、豐富的 英解 ample, abundant

例 My family didn't have a lot of money while I was growing up, but love and laughter were always in **plentiful** supply.

成長過程中我家不是很有錢,但總是充滿愛和笑聲。

語意用法 a plentiful harvest 豐收;plentiful food 充足的食物。

political [pəˋlɪtɪkl]	政治上的、政黨的、國家的 英解 involving or characteristic of politics or parties or politicians

例 You forget a **political** leader, but you won't forget a robot. (87 學測)

你會忘記一個政治領袖,但你不會忘記一個機器人。

語意用法 a political party 政黨;a political campaign 政治活動。

portable [ˋportəbl]	輕便的、手提的、便於攜帶的 英解 able to be carried or moved easily, esp. by hand

例 Julie wants to buy a **portable** computer so that she can carry it around when she travels. (93 學測)

茱莉想買一部手提電腦,這樣當她去旅行時就可以帶著到處走。

語意用法 easily portable 容易攜帶的;a portable device 可攜式裝置。

positive
[ˈpɑzətɪv]

確實的、絕對的、積極的
英解 characterized by or expressing certainty or affirmation

例 Hanging around people who are **positive** and in good moods is another way to help you find your smile again.（92 學測補）
與積極、總是好心情的人在一起，是另一個幫助你再次尋回笑容的方法。

語意用法 positive thinking 正面思考；positive proof 明確的證據。

potential
[pəˈtɛnʃəl]

潛在的、可能的
英解 possible but not yet actual

例 Stricter measures have been taken to ward off **potential** dangers concerning cigarette-smoking.（87 學測）
已經採取更嚴格的措施來預防吸煙的可能危險。

語意用法 a potential leader 具有領袖潛力的人；a potential dander 潛在的危險。

powerful
[ˈpauəfəl]

強而有力的、有權威的、效力大的
英解 having great power, force, potency, or effect

例 The sun is an extraordinarily **powerful** source of energy.（99 指考）
太陽是一個異常強大的能量來源。

語意用法 a powerful nation 強大的國家；locally powerful 在當地有權勢的。

practical
[ˈprætɪkḷ]

實踐的、實際的、實用的
英解 concerned with actual use or practice

例 The product has to speak to the consumer's needs with both personality and **practical** value.（95 指考）
產品必須在個性和實用價值上呼應消費者的需求。

語意用法 a practical person 務實的人；practical training 實務訓練。

precautionary
[prɪˋkɔʃənˌɛrɪ]

預先警戒的、小心的
英解 taken in advance to protect against possible danger or failure

例 However, he did not expect to use it, and had it ready merely as a **precautionary** measure.

然而，他並沒有打算使用它，擁有它只是作為預防措施。

語意用法 take precautionary measures 採取防禦措施。

形容詞篇

precious
[ˋprɛʃəs]

貴重的、寶貴的、珍貴的
英解 characterized by feeling or showing fond affection for

例 A wise woman traveling in the mountains found a **precious** stone.（97 學測）

一個聰明的女人在山裡旅行時找到一塊珍貴的石頭。

語意用法 a precious moment 寶貴的時刻；precious to sb. 對某人來說很珍貴。

pregnant
[ˋprɛɡnənt]

懷孕的、懷胎的
英解 carrying developing offspring within the body

例 When they awake, all of the women of child-bearing age have become **pregnant**.（91 學測）

當她們醒來，所有已達受孕年齡的女性全都懷孕了。

語意用法 a pregnant woman 懷孕的女人；five months pregnant 懷孕五個月。

present
[ˋprɛznt]

出席的、在場的、目前的、當前的
英解 being here, or at the place, occasion etc. mentioned

例 The **present** economic situation is quite similar to the one we faced in the 1970s.

現在的經濟情勢和我們在一九七○年代面對的很相似。

語意用法 at the present time 現今；past and present 過去和現在的。

prestigious
[prɛsˋtɪdʒəs]

有名望的
英解 respected

例 Four years of tuition and other student expenses at **prestigious** American universities can easily surpass a quarter million dollars.

就讀美國有名望大學的四年學費和其他支出很輕易就可超出二十五萬美元。

語意用法 a prestigious company 有聲望的公司。

private
[ˋpraɪvɪt]

個人的、私人的、非官方的
英解 confined to particular persons or groups or providing privacy

例 As of 1997, the orphanage, which depends on **private** contributions, has saved more than 100 infants. (90 學測)

截至 1997 年,孤兒院靠著私人捐助已經救了超過 100 多個嬰兒。

語意用法 sb.'s private life 某人的私生活;a private school 私立學校。

profitable
[ˋprɑfɪtəbļ]

有利的、營利的、有用的
英解 yielding material gain or profit

例 Selling fried chicken at the night market doesn't seem to be a decent business, but it is actually quite **profitable**. (95 學測)

在夜市賣炸雞似乎不是什麼體面的工作,但實際營利卻很高。

語意用法 mutually profitable 雙方都有利可圖的;potentially profitable 有獲利潛力的。

proper
[ˋprɑpɚ]

適合的、恰當的、合乎體統的
英解 marked by suitability or rightness or appropriateness

例 In Taiwan much time and energy are spent on getting a **proper** education and finding a good job. (91 學測補)

在台灣,很多時間與精力都花在受適當教育與找好工作上。

語意用法 at proper time 在適當的時候;in the proper way 以適當的方式。

prosperous
[`prɑspərəs]

興盛的、繁榮的、富裕的
英解 flourishing

例 Even in the **prosperous** 1990s, the company continued to struggle.

即使在繁榮的一九九○年代，這公司仍然繼續苦撐。

語意用法 a prosperous city 繁榮的城市；economically prosperous 經濟上繁榮的。

protective
[prə`tɛktɪv]

防護的、防衛的
英解 giving or capable of giving protection

例 Typically, an intensely colored plant has more of these **protective** chemicals than a paler one does.（97 指考）

一般來說，色彩強烈的植物比色彩不鮮明的植物擁有更多保護性的化學物質。

語意用法 a protective vest 防彈背心。

proud
[praud]

得意的、自豪的、值得誇耀的
英解 pleased or satisfied

例 She is **proud** of herself for working hard to succeed.（97 指考）

她為自己努力工作獲得成功感到自豪。

語意用法 proud of ＋人事物，表示對某人事物感到光榮。

provincial
[prə`vɪnʃəl]

省的、外地的、地方性的、古板的、偏狹的
英解 of or connected with a province

例 I'm sorry to say that my parents have rather **provincial** views on what they see as their daughter-in-law's responsibilities.

我很抱歉，我父母對於媳婦的責任有比較古板的看法。

語意用法 provincial government 省政府；provincial highway 省道。

provocative
[prə`vɑkətɪv]

挑撥的、激怒的、刺激的
英解 serving or tending to provoke, excite, or stimulate

例 His job as a political columnist is to be **provocative**, not informative.
他身為政治專欄作家的工作是要挑撥、而非告知訊息。
語意用法 highly provocative 挑撥意味很高的；look provocative 看起來是在挑撥的。

psychological
[saɪkə`lɑdʒɪkḷ]

心理的、心理學的、心理學家的
英解 mental or emotional as opposed to physical in nature

例 A trip to the supermarket has now become an exercise in **psychological** warfare.（96 指考）
一趟超市之旅現在已變成一場心理戰的演練。
語意用法 a psychological novel 心理小說；psychological phenomena 心理現象。

punctual
[`pʌŋktʃuəl]

準時的、精確的
英解 prompt

例 Would you rather work with someone who was competent but never on time, or someone who didn't know what they were doing but was always **punctual**?
你比較想和一個能力很強卻從不準時的人工作、還是和一個不知道自己在做什麼卻總是準時的人？
語意用法 Sb. is punctual. 某人很準時。

racial
[`reʃəl]

人種的、種族的、種族間的
英解 of or related to genetically distinguished groups of people

例 Americans with different **racial** and educational backgrounds may vary in their standards of living.（92 學測補）
不同種族與教育背景的美國人可能呈現多樣化的生活水平。
語意用法 racial discrimination 種族歧視。

radical
[ˈrædɪkl̩]

根本的、徹底的、極端的、激進的、與生俱來的
英解 far beyond the norm

例 He came to us because my husband is one of the few **radical** peers.

他朝我們走來因為我先生是少數激進派同伙之一。

語意用法 politically radical 政治上激進的。

rapid
[ˈræpɪd]

快的、迅速的、險峻的；亦作名詞用
英解 done or occurring in a brief period of time

例 Two weeks ago she had never even touched a ukulele, but she's already made **rapid** progress.

兩星期之前她還從未摸過四弦琴，但她進步快速。

語意用法 rapid progress 很快的進展。

rare
[rɛr]

稀有的、罕見的、傑出的、極好的
英解 not widely known

例 When they're told they have a **rare** disease, the first question people ask is "Why me?"

當被告知得了罕見疾病，人們問的第一個問題是：為什麼是我？

語意用法 surprisingly rare 出乎意料地稀有。

realistic
[riəˈlɪstɪk]

現實的、逼真的、實際可行的
英解 showing awareness and acceptance of reality

例 After reading three science fiction novels in a row, I'm in the mood for something a little more **realistic**.

接連讀了三本科幻小說後，我現在比較想讀寫實一點的東西。

語意用法 a realistic plan 可行的計畫；make sth. more realistic 讓某物更實際可行。

regional
[ˈridʒənl]

地區的、局部的、整區的
英解 characteristic of a region

例 I was interested in their **regional** accents.（89 學測）

我對他們的地方口音感到興趣。

語意用法 regional manager 地區經理；regional literature 地方文學。

regretful
[rɪˈgrɛtfəl]

懊悔的、遺憾的、惆悵的
英解 full of regret

例 Management's decision to cut funding for the project only weeks before it was to be completed is truly **regretful**.

管理階層在這專案快完成的幾星期前決定縮減經費，真是讓人遺憾。

語意用法 regretful for ＋事，表示為某事感到後悔。

regular
[ˈrɛgjələ]

規律的、定期的、正常的
英解 normal, customary, or usual

例 The lessons in language laboratories and those in **regular** classrooms did not match.（93 指考補）

語言實驗室的課程與正規教室裡的不符合。

語意用法 a regular meeting 例行的會議；a regular life 規律的生活。

relevant
[ˈrɛləvənt]

有關的、切題的、恰當的
英解 pertinent

例 I've found work experience is much more **relevant** to a salesperson's success than a university degree.

我發現工作經驗和業務員的成功比較有關，而不是學歷。

語意用法 relevant to ＋物，表示與某物有關連的。

reliable
[rɪˋlaɪəbḷ]

可靠的、確實的
英解 dependable

例 Google Earth is a **reliable** research tool.（98 學測）
谷歌地球是可靠的搜尋工具。

語意用法 reliable sources 可靠的來源；a reliable man 可靠的人。

形容詞篇

religious
[rɪˋlɪdʒəs]

虔誠的、嚴謹的、宗教的
英解 concerned with religion

例 In the United States, the only holiday that is both a public holiday and a **religious** holiday is Christmas.
在美國，唯一一個既是公定假日也是宗教節日的是聖誕節。

語意用法 a religious man 信教的人。

reluctant
[rɪˋlʌktənt]

不情願的、勉強的
英解 not eager, unwilling, disinclined

例 Parents are recognizing that films are a chance to persuade a **reluctant** reader to pick up a book and give it a try.（93 指考補）
父母體認到電影是說服一個不情願的讀者拿起一本書試讀的機會。

語意用法 somewhat reluctant 多少有些不情願。

remote
[rɪˋmot]

遙遠的、偏僻的、遙控的
英解 distant

例 Because it's too expensive to run phone lines to extremely **remote** locations, satellite communication is the only option.
由於在極度遙遠的地區裝設電話線很昂貴，衛星通訊就成了唯一選擇。

語意用法 geographically remote 地理位置上很遠的。

repetitive [rɪˋpɛtɪtɪv]	反覆的、嘮叨的 英解 characterized by or given to unnecessary repetition

例 Factory workers who perform a large number of **repetitive** actions are gradually being replaced by robots.

執行大量重複性工作的工廠工人漸漸被機器人取代。

語意用法 endlessly repetitive 無止盡地重複。

resistant [rɪˋzɪstənt]	有抵抗力的、抵抗的、耐⋯⋯的 英解 relating to or conferring immunity

例 She perceived that her will had blazed up, stubborn and **resistant**.

她意識到她的意志燃燒了，固執又反抗的。

語意用法 resistant to ＋疾病，表示對某疾病有抵抗力的。

responsible [rɪˋspɑnsəbḷ]	負責任的、有責任感的 英解 having control or authority

例 Nelson was not a **responsible** person.（88 學測）

尼爾森不是一個負責任的人。

語意用法 responsible to/for ＋人事物，表示對某人事物負有責任。

rough [rʌf]	粗糙的、未加工的、簡陋的 英解 having or caused by an irregular surface

例 The goals of the KPCS are to document and track all **rough** diamonds when they enter a participating country.（96 指考）

KPCS 的目標是當所有未加工的鑽石進入參與國時加以記錄並追蹤。

語意用法 a rough road 崎嶇的路；rough hands 粗糙的手。

rural [ˋrʊrəl]	農村的、鄉村風味的、田園的 英解 living in or characteristic of farming or country life

例 Perhaps that is why in **rural** areas around the world the guitar has been a source of music for millions to enjoy.（92 學測補）

或許那是為何在全世界的鄉村地區，吉他一直都是百萬人享受音樂的來源。

語意用法 rural life 田園生活。

scarce [skɛrs]	不足的、缺乏的、稀有的、珍貴的 英解 rarely encountered

例 The coffee trees that grow the beans are **scarce**.（99 指考）

栽種出這些豆子的咖啡樹很稀有。

語意用法 make oneself scarce 溜走、消失。

secondary [ˈsɛkəndˌɛrɪ]	第二的、次要的、間接的 英解 of the second rank

例 Simon loves his work. To him, work always comes first, and family and friends are **secondary**.（97 學測）

賽門熱愛工作。對他來說，工作總是擺在第一位，家庭和朋友居第二。

語意用法 secondary to ＋物，表示與某物相較下是次要的。

sensible [ˈsɛnsəbl]	明智的、合情理的、明顯的、有知覺的 英解 showing reason or sound judgment

例 If he were more **sensible** he would have become a pharmacist, not a comic book artist.

如果他更明智一點，他會成為一位藥劑師，而不是漫畫書作家。

語意用法 a sensible man 明理的人。

sensitive [ˈsɛnsətɪv]	敏感的、靈敏的、易受傷害的 英解 having the power of sensation

例 Their skin is very **sensitive** to temperature changes.（85 學測）

他們的皮膚對於溫度的改變相當敏感。

語意用法 sensitive to ＋物，表示對某物敏感的。

serious
[ˋsɪrɪəs]

嚴肅的、嚴重的、認真的、需認真對待的
英解 thoughtful

例 The plane landed safely despite what was later described as a **serious** engine problem.

儘管後來被描述成是嚴重的引擎故障，飛機還是安全降落了。

語意用法 sound serious 聽起來很嚴肅、很嚴重；extremely serious 十分嚴重的。

shameful
[ˋʃemfəl]

可恥的、丟臉的、不道德的
英解 deserving or bringing disgrace or shame

例 The government's slow response to the flooding is absolutely **shameful**.

政府對於水災的緩慢回應真是十分丟臉。

語意用法 shameful conduct 可恥的行為。

similar
[ˋsɪmələ]

相仿的、相似的
英解 marked by correspondence or resemblance

例 The Panchen Lamas were chosen in a **similar** way. (93 學測)

班禪喇嘛的挑選方式是相仿的。

語意用法 similar to ＋物，表示與某物相似的、類似的。

simultaneous
[ˌsaɪmḷˋtenɪəs]

同時發生的、同時存在的、同步的
英解 occurring or operating at the same time

例 My daughter can easily carry on three or four **simultaneous** instant message conversations.

我女兒可以很輕易地同時進行三或四個即時訊息的對話。

語意用法 simultaneous interpretation 同步口譯；simultaneous with ＋物，表示與某物同時發生的。

slim [slɪm]	苗條的、纖細的、空洞的 英解 small in width relative to height or length

例 Every time you cross the street there's a **slim** chance you'll be hit by a car.

每次穿越街道，你都有很小的機率可能會被車撞到。

語意用法 a slim girl 苗條的女生。

sociable [ˈsoʃəbl]	好交際的、善交際的、社交的 英解 friendly or companionable

例 If you're not a **sociable** person, advertising is not the industry for you.

如果你不是個善交際的人，廣告就不是適合你的行業。

語意用法 a sociable man 善交際的人。

social [ˈsoʃəl]	社會的、社交的、群居的；亦作名詞用 英解 friendly or companionable

例 Much of your success, both in your work and **social** life, is related to how you listen.（86 學測）

在工作和社交生活，大部分的成功都與你如何傾聽有關。

語意用法 social problems 社會問題；a social gathering 社交聚會。

solar [ˈsolɚ]	太陽的、太陽光的、源自太陽的 英解 of or relating to the sun

例 We can harness energy from the sun, or **solar** energy, in many ways.

（99 指考）

在很多方面我們都可以利用來自太陽或太陽能的能量。

語意用法 solar energy 太陽能；solar radiation 太陽幅射。

solid [ˋsɑlɪd]	固體的、實心的、堅固的、濃密的；亦作名詞用 英解 characterized by good substantial quality

例 After I make my first million, I'm going to buy a **solid** gold toilet.

賺到我的第一個一百萬後，我要買一個實心的黃金馬桶。

語意用法 extremely solid 十分堅固。

sorrowful [ˋsɑrofəl]	悲傷的、傷心的 英解 experiencing or marked by or expressing sorrow especially that associated with irreparable loss

例 He started his speech with the long, **sorrowful** story of his daughter's illness.

他以一個關於女兒疾病、既長又悲傷的故事來開始他的演說。

語意用法 a sorrowful sight 令人心痛的景象。

spectacular [spɛkˋtækjələ]	壯觀的、壯麗的、引人注目的 英解 sensational in appearance or thrilling in effect

例 Because the first movie he directed was such a **spectacular** success, he was immediately offered a contract to direct three more.

由於他導演的第一部電影大獲成功，他立即接獲繼續導演三部電影的合約。

語意用法 spectacular fireworks 壯觀的煙火。

spiritual [ˋspɪrɪtʃuəl]	心靈上的、精神上的、超自然的 英解 intangible

例 Monks and nuns from local temples provided **spiritual** support to victims of the disaster.

從地方寺廟來的僧尼為災難受害者提供了心靈上的支持。

語意用法 spiritual leadership 精神上的領導；spiritual enlightenment 精神上的啟蒙。

statistical
[stə`tɪstɪk!]

統計的、統計學的
英解 of or relating to statistics

例 There is no **statistical** evidence to support the claim that increased airport security has made flying safer.

沒有統計上的證據，支持加強機場安全可讓飛行更安全的主張。

語意用法 statistical analysis 統計上的分析；statistical data 統計資料。

steady
[`stɛdɪ]

穩固的、穩定的、堅固的、鎮定的
英解 fixed

例 The moral lesson is that slow and **steady** wins the race.（98 學測）

寓意是從容而穩定可以贏得比賽。

語意用法 steady progress 穩定的進步；become steady 變得穩定。

straight
[stret]

筆直的、正直的、坦率的、異性戀的
英解 not curved or crooked

例 I asked him why he hadn't finished his chores, but he didn't give me a **straight** answer.

我問他為何還未完成那些瑣事，他沒有直接回答我。

語意用法 straight with sb.，表示對某人坦白不隱瞞的。

sufficient
[sə`fɪʃənt]

充分的、足夠的、能勝任的
英解 being as much as is needed

例 They who act without **sufficient** thought, will often fall into unsuspected danger.

沒有充分思考就行動的人，往往會陷入預想不到的危險中。

語意用法 sufficient evidence 充足的證據；sufficient food 充足的食物。

形容詞篇

suitable
[ˈsutəb!]

適合的、適當的
英解 appropriate

例 Alaska was not a place **suitable** for making a living. （90 學測）
阿拉斯加不是適合謀生的地方。

語意用法 suitable for ＋人或目的，表示適合某人或適合某目的。

superficial
[ˌsupəˈfɪʃəl]

表面的、面積的、外表的、膚淺的
英解 of, relating to, being near, or forming the surface

例 I could only take a rapid glance at the basin whose **superficial** area is two million square yards.
我只能迅速掃視這座表面積達二百萬平方碼的盆地。

語意用法 a superficial wound 表皮上的傷、輕傷；superficial knowledge 膚淺的知識。

superior
[səˈpɪrɪə]

較高級的、較上等的、較優秀的、有優越感的
英解 greater in quality, quantity, etc.

例 The country with the **superior** military does not always win the war.
擁有較優良軍隊的國家不見得總是贏得戰爭。

語意用法 superior to ＋人，表示地位或位階比某人高的。

susceptible
[səˈsɛptəb!]

多情的、敏感的、易受影響的
英解 yielding readily to or capable of

例 Young people are far more **susceptible** to advertising than adults.
年輕人比成年人更容易受廣告影響。

語意用法 susceptible to ＋方面，表示在某方面易受感動的。

symbolic
[sɪmˈbɑlɪk]

象徵的、符號的、象徵主義的
英解 of or relating to a symbol or symbols

例 Everyone in the office showed up to work wearing black, a **symbolic** gesture meant to show management how unhappy they were about not receiving a bonus.

在這辦公室的每個人都穿黑衣來上班，用來作為向管理階層表達因未收到紅利而不滿的象徵。

語意用法 symbolic of ＋物，表示象徵某物的。

sympathetic
[ˌsɪmpəˈθɛtɪk]

有同情心的、贊同的、和諧的、共鳴的
英解 of or relating to the sympathetic nervous system

例 I might be more **sympathetic** to your complaints if you stopped shouting.

如果你停止喊叫，我可能會比較同情你的抱怨。

語意用法 sympathetic to/toward ＋人，對某人表示同情的。

technological
[ˌtɛknəˈlɑdʒɪkl]

技術的、工藝的
英解 based in scientific and industrial progress

例 The telephone is widely considered as the most rapidly evolving **technological** device today.（97 指考）

電話被普遍認為是今日發展最迅速的技術裝置。

語意用法 technological development 科學技術的發展。

temporary
[ˈtɛmpəˌrɛrɪ]

暫時的、短暫的
英解 not permanent

例 Mr. Smith's work in Taiwan is just **temporary**. He will go back to the U.S. next month.（92 學測）

史密斯先生在台灣的工作是暫時性的，他下個月就會回美國。

語意用法 反義字為 permanent 永久的。

tentative
[ˋtɛntətɪv]

嘗試性的、躊躇的、實驗性的
英解 provisional or experimental

例 We haven't confirmed anything yet, but our **tentative** plan is to arrive in Seoul on March 13.

我們還未確認任何事，但我們暫訂會在三月十三日抵達漢城。

語意用法 a tentative plan 暫時的、試驗性的計畫。

terminal
[ˋtɜmən!]

極限的、末端的、終點的、末期的；亦作名詞用
英解 of, being, or situated at an end, terminus, or boundary

例 Immediately after learning that his illness was **terminal**, he started donating large sums to charity.

在得知他的病已至末期後，他很快開始捐贈大筆錢給慈善機構。

語意用法 terminal server 終端伺服器；the terminal stage 末期。

terrible
[ˋtɛrəb!]

可怕的、嚇人的、極差的、嚴重的
英解 very serious or extreme

例 Forty-three percent of all adults suffer **terrible** health effects from stress.
（92 學測）

百分之四十三的成人因為壓力而健康嚴重受影響。

語意用法 look terrible 看起來好可怕；sound terrible 聽起來很恐怖。

terrific
[təˋrɪfɪk]

厲害的、驚人的、非同小可的
英解 very great or intense

例 I think Janice's suggestion to have a barbecue on the roof is a **terrific** idea!

我覺得潔妮絲說要在屋頂烤肉的提議太棒了。

語意用法 a terrific party 很棒的舞會。

thin [θɪn]	薄的、瘦的、細的、稀少的、稀薄的 英解 fine or narrow

例 LCD screens are made up of several **thin** layers of film, glass, and liquid crystal.

液晶螢幕是由幾層薄膜、玻璃和液態水晶製成。

語意用法 look thin 看起來很瘦；incredibly thin 驚人地瘦。

thorough [ˋθɝo]	徹底的、十足的、完全的 英解 carried out completely and carefully

例 As the only person with a **thorough** understanding of the company's computer systems, she felt confident asking for a raise.

身為唯一一個全盤了解公司電腦系統的人,她很有自信地要求加薪。

語意用法 a thorough investigation 徹底的調查。

tolerant [ˋtɑlərənt]	忍受的、寬恕的、有耐性的 英解 able to tolerate the beliefs, actions, opinions, etc., of others

例 If you want people to listen to you, you have to be genuinely **tolerant** of their beliefs as well.

如果你想要別人聽你的,你也必須很真誠地包容他們的信仰。

語意用法 tolerant of ＋物,表示對某物是寬容的。

tough [tʌf]	堅韌的、牢固的、頑固的、強硬的、不屈不撓的 英解 strong or resilient

例 They think that illegal downloading behavior needs **tough** measures to correct. (98 指考)

他們認為非法下載行為需要強硬的措施予以修正。

語意用法 tough wood 堅硬的木頭；act tough 行為舉止很強硬。

traumatic [trɔˋmætɪk]	外傷的、創傷的、精神上有衝擊的；亦作名詞用 英解 of or relating to a physical injury or wound to the body

例 They are formal events in which teens share their **traumatic** experiences.
（99 學測）

那是青少年分享精神創傷經驗的正式場合。

語意用法 deeply traumatic 精神上有嚴重創傷的。

trivial [ˋtrɪvɪəl]	瑣碎的、不重要的、淺薄的、平凡的、輕浮的 英解 of little importance

例 This discovery cannot be treated as a **trivial** finding.（96 學測）

這項發現不能被視為微不足道。

語意用法 regard sth. as trivial 視某物為瑣碎的、不重要的。

truthful [ˋtruθfəl]	誠實的、坦率的、真實的 英解 honest or candid

例 I can assure you that he is a most **truthful** and conscientious young man.

我可以向你保證他是最誠實與盡責的年輕人。

語意用法 truthful about ＋事，表示坦承某事、關於某事是真實的。

typical [ˋtɪpɪk]]	典型的、獨有的、有代表性的 英解 characteristic

例 Mary is a **typical** left-brained learner.（85 學測）

瑪莉是典型的左腦學習者。

語意用法 typical of ＋方面，表示在某方面具有代表性、象徵性的。

ultimate [ˋʌltəmɪt]	最後的、最終的、極限的、最大的、基本的；亦作名詞用 英解 conclusive in a series or process

例 We're planning to visit Bangkok and Kuala Lumpur, but our **ultimate** destination in Taipei.

我們計畫要參觀曼谷和吉隆坡，但我們的最終目的地是台北。

語意用法 the ultimate destination 最後的目的地；the ultimate speed 最大的速度。

ultraviolet [͵ʌltrəˋvaɪəlɪt]	紫外線的；亦作名詞用 英解 of, relating to, or consisting of radiation lying in the ultraviolet

例 Plants make antioxidants to protect themselves from the sun's **ultraviolet (UV) light.**（97 指考）

植物製造抗氧化成分保護白己免於紫外線的傷害。

語意用法 an ultraviolet lamp 紫外線燈。

unanimous [juˋnænəməs]	全體一致的、無異議的 英解 in complete or absolute agreement

例 The vote that elected Eric head of the department was **unanimous**.

選艾瑞克作為部門主管的投票是一致通過的。

語意用法 unanimous about ＋事，表示對某事意見一致的。

unbearable [ʌnˋbɛrəbl]	讓人無法忍受的 英解 not able to be borne or endured

例 Visitors to Bangkok might find the weather, the heat, and floods **unbearable.**（92 指考）

到曼谷的遊客可能會發現天氣、酷熱和洪水都讓人難以忍受。

語意用法 become unbearable 變得讓人無法忍受；absolutely unbearable 讓人完全無法忍受的。

unconventional
[ˌʌnkən`vɛnʃənl]

非傳統的、不合常規的
英解 not conforming to accepted rules or standards

例 She is the most completely **unconventional** person I know.
她是我認識的人裡頭最不合乎常規的。

語意用法 an unconventional approach 打破慣例的方法。

underground
[`ʌndə`graund]

地下的、秘密的、反主流的；亦作名詞用
英解 under the level of the ground

例 **Underground** passageways connect buildings on both sides of the street.
地下通道連接街道兩側的建築。

語意用法 an underground parking lot 地下停車場；an underground station 地下車站。

undetermined
[ˌʌndɪ`tɜmɪnd]

不確定的、未解決的、不果斷的
英解 not yet resolved

例 It is still **undetermined** who will take over for Victoria when she retires.
維多利亞退休後誰來接手仍然懸而未決。

語意用法 look undetermined 看起來不堅決的；remain undetermined 依然未解決的。

unemployed
[ˌʌnɪm`plɔɪd]

失業的、無工作的、閒置的
英解 jobless

例 During a recession, many people become **unemployed** and very few new jobs are available.（92 指考）
經濟衰退時期，許多人失業且新的工作機會很少。

語意用法 become unemployed 變成失業的；make sb. unemployed 讓某人失業。

unfair [ʌnˋfɛr]	不公平的、不公正的、不正當的 英解 not fair

例 It is **unfair** to scare people with a threat.（98 指考）

用威脅的手段來恐嚇人是不正當的。

語意用法 unfair to ＋人，表示對某人是不公平的。

unforgettable [ˏʌnfɚˋgɛtəbl]	難忘的、永誌不忘的 英解 highly memorable

例 The chef added a few drops of lemon juice just before serving and the taste was **unforgettable**.

主廚在菜端上桌前滴了幾滴檸檬汁，嚐起來真是令人難忘。

語意用法 truly unforgettable 實在讓人難忘的。

unique [juˋnik]	特有的、稀奇的、獨一無二的、無可匹敵的 英解 being the only one of a particular type

例 Wright's design put his **unique** stamp on Modernist Architecture's rigid geometry.（93 指考）

萊特的設計在現代建築的精密幾何學上留下獨特的標誌。

語意用法 unique to ＋物，表示對某物來說是特有的。

universal [ˏjunəˋvɝsl]	普遍的、全體的、宇宙的、全世界的 英解 of worldwide scope or applicability

例 The drug problem is **universal**.（90 學測）

毒品問題是全球性的。

語意用法 universal agreement 全體的同意；far from universal 一點都不普遍的。

unknown
[ʌnˋnon]

未知的、陌生的、默默無聞的
英解 not known, understood, or recognized

例 It is held in **unknown**, guarded warehouses where only a few people can see it. (94 指考)

它是在不為人知、有守衛的倉庫裡舉行的,只有少數人可以看到。

語意用法 unknown to ＋人,表示不為某人所知的。

unlike
[ʌnˋlaɪk]

不同的、相異的
英解 different

例 The two paintings are so **unlike** in style that it's hard to believe they were created by the same artist.

這兩幅畫風格如此不同,很難相信是同一位藝術家的創作。

語意用法 unlike accounts of the incident 對於事件的不同描述。

unlikely
[ʌnˋlaɪklɪ]

不太可能的、不像是真的、不可能發生的
英解 improbable

例 It seemed an **unlikely** explanation. (92 指考)

那似乎是靠不住的解釋。

語意用法 an unlikely story 不真實的故事;consider sth. unlikely 認為某物不太可能。

unnoticed
[ʌnˋnotɪst]

未被注意的、被忽視的
英解 not noticed

例 The accident was caused by an **unnoticed** piece of metal on the racetrack.

意外是跑道上一塊沒人注意到的金屬造成的。

語意用法 go unnoticed 未被注意到;remain unnoticed 依然未被注意到。

unpleasant
[ʌnˋplɛzn̩t]

令人不悅的、不中意的、討厭的
英解 not pleasant or agreeable

例 My last visit to the dentist was **unpleasant**, but not especially painful.

我最近一次去看牙醫的感覺不太舒適，但並不特別難受。

語意用法 an unpleasant smell 讓人不舒服的氣味。

unpredictable
[ˌʌnprɪˋdɪktəbl̩]

不可預料的、出乎意料的
英解 not capable of being predicted

例 The weather here is **unpredictable**.

這裡的天氣變幻莫測。

語意用法 totally unpredictable 完全無法預測的。

unrealistic
[ˌʌnrɪəˋlɪstɪk]

不切實際的、非現實主義的
英解 not realistic

例 A common mistake found in parenthood is that parents often set **unrealistic** goals for their children.（95 學測）

身為父母常犯的錯誤就是常常為他們的小孩設定不切實際的目標。

語意用法 an unrealistic dream 不切實際的夢想。

unreliable
[ˌʌnrɪˋlaɪəbl̩]

不可信任的、不可靠的、靠不住的
英解 untrustworthy

例 It's probably OK to drive the car around town, but it's too **unreliable** to take on a long trip.

在城內開這輛車或許還可以，但開長途就不太可靠了。

語意用法 prove unreliable 證實是不可靠的；an unreliable source of information 不可靠的消息來源。

unsolved
[ʌn`sɑlvd]

未解答的、未解決的、未解釋的
英解 not solved

例 Over 90% of home robberies remain **unsolved**.

九成以上的家庭搶案未被偵破。

語意用法 unsolved crimes 未破的罪件；unsolved mysteries 未解的謎團。

unstable
[ʌn`stebl]

不穩固的、不牢靠的、動盪的、反覆無常的
英解 lacking stability, fixity, or firmness

例 It refers to people who are emotionally **unstable**.（97 指考）

它指的是情緒不穩定的人。

語意用法 relatively unstable 相對上不穩定的；mentally unstable 精神上不穩定的。

unsustainable
[ˌʌnsə`stenəbl]

無法支持的、無法維持的
英解 not sustainable

例 Sure, we can all work 14-hour days, but that much overtime is **unsustainable** for more than a week or so.

當然，我們可以一天工作十四小時，但加那麼多班是無法維持超過一星期的。

語意用法 unsustainable situation 無法維持的情況。

unusual
[ʌn`juʒʊəl]

稀有的、奇特的、不平常的、非凡的
英解 peculiar, not normal

例 Australia has lots of very **unusual** animals.（92 學測）

阿拉斯加有很多非常稀有的動物。

語意用法 unusual for ＋人＋ to V，表示某人做某事是不尋常的。

upward
[`ʌpwəd]

向上的、升高的
英解 directed up

例 There has been a consistent **upward** trend in the price of gold over the last few years.

過去幾年金價有持續上揚的趨勢。

語意用法 an upward tendency 上升的趨勢。

urban [ˋɝbən]	城市的、居住在城市的 英解 relating to or concerned with a city or densely populated area

例 Many people move to **urban** areas to have the excitement of city life.

許多人移居到城市地區以便享有刺激的城市生活。

語意用法 urban life 城市生活；urban problems 都市問題。

urgent [ˋɝdʒənt]	緊急的、急迫的、堅持要求的 英解 compelling immediate action

例 It is an old wooden building in **urgent** need of repairs.

這是一間急需整修的老舊木建築。

語意用法 sound urgent 聽起來很緊急；extremely urgent 十分緊急的。

vacant [ˋvekənt]	空的、空白的、空缺的、空虛的 英解 empty

例 The mayor had to step down due to an illness, so the position will remain **vacant** until the next general election.

市長因病必須下台，所以這個職位會空著直到下次選舉。

語意用法 a vacant seat 空位；a job fell vacant 一個職位出缺了。

vain [ven]	自負的、愛慕虛榮的、徒勞的、無效的 英解 characteristic of false pride

例 The captain ordered everything thrown overboard in a **vain** effort to keep the ship from sinking.

船長命令把所有東西丟下船，依然無法阻止船往下沈。

語意用法 vain about ＋方面，表示對某方面感到自負的。

形容詞篇

valuable
[ˈvæljəbl̩]

值錢的、貴重的、有價值的
[英解] having considerable monetary worth

例 Companies that try to save money by using outdated computers are actually wasting their most **valuable** resource: their workers' time.

使用老舊電腦來省錢的公司事實上是在浪費最重要的資源：工作時間。

語意用法 increasingly valuable 越來越有價值的。

---

various
[ˈvɛrɪəs]

不同的、各式各樣的、許多的
[英解] diverse

例 The Virtual Patient can also be used to explore **various** medical situations. (98 指考)

虛擬病人也可以用來探討各種不同的醫療情況。

語意用法 various opinions 各種不同的意見。

---

versatile
[ˈvɜsət̩l̩]

多才多藝的、多功能的、易變的
[英解] having great diversity or variety

例 She is a **versatile** musician who can play many instruments.

她是一個多才多藝的音樂家能演奏多種樂器。

語意用法 amazingly versatile 多才多藝得讓人驚嘆。

---

video
[ˈvɪdɪ‚o]

電視影像的、錄影的；亦作名詞用
[英解] of or relating to television, especially televised images

例 The **video** part of the television broadcast was clear, but the sound was poor.

電視轉播的影像部分很清晰，但聲音很差。

語意用法 video clip 錄影片段；video image 影像。

virtual [`vɝtʃuəl]	事實上、實際的、實質的、虛擬的 英解 being actually such in almost every respect

例 By installing several locks on every door and bars on the windows, he turned his home into a **virtual** prison.

在門上安裝幾道鎖、在窗戶裝上鐵窗，他把他的家變成不折不扣的監獄了。

語意用法 a virtual leader 實際上的領袖。

形容詞篇

visible [`vɪzəbl]	可見的、顯而易見的、明白的、引人注目的、現有的 英解 capable of being perceived by the eye

例 Stocking the most expensive products at eye level helps them sell faster than cheaper but less **visible** competitors. （96 指考）

把最貴的商品放在眼睛平視的高度，有助於它們賣得比那些較便宜、較不醒目的商品好。

語意用法 visible to ＋人，表示對某人來說是看得見的；visible to the naked eyes 肉眼可見的。

visual [`vɪʒuəl]	視覺的、可被看見的、栩栩如生的 英解 relating to or using sight

例 Boys, in contrast, showed an early **visual** superiority to girls. （93 學測）

相反的，男孩的早期視覺表現優於女孩。

語意用法 the visual arts 視覺藝術；visual instruction 視覺教具。

vital [`vaɪtl]	生命的、維持生命所需的、極其重要的、攸關生死的 英解 essential to maintain life

例 The decomposers are a **vital** link in the natural cycle of life and death.
（88 學測）

分解者是生死自然循環的重要環節。

語意用法 vital to/for ＋物，表示對某物來說極為重要的。

voluntary
[`vɑlən͵tɛrɪ]

自願的、自發的、有自由意志的
英解 done or undertaken of one's own free will

例 My supervisor said attending the company's sports day was **voluntary**, but I got the impression it would look bad if I didn't go.

我的主管說參與公司的運動日是自發性的，但我覺得如果我沒去場面會很難看。

語意用法 a voluntary helper 自願的援助者；a voluntary army 志願軍。

vulnerable
[`vʌlnərəbl]

易受傷的、有弱點的、難防守的
英解 susceptible to attack

例 In fact, the infant is the most **vulnerable** member of society to this chemical. （92 學測補）

事實上，對這化學物來說嬰兒是社會中最脆弱的成員。

語意用法 vulnerable to ＋物，表示對某物來說是脆弱的。

wayward
[`wewəd]

任性的、剛愎的、倔強的、難捉摸的
英解 resistant to guidance or discipline

例 My wife is in a **wayward** mood today.

我太太今天的心情難以捉摸。

語意用法 a wayward child 任性的小孩。

wholehearted
[`hol`hartɪd]

全心全意、全神貫注、真摯的
英解 with unconditional and enthusiastic devotion

例 You have our **wholehearted** support for your new project.

你的新專案有我們全心全力的支持。

語意用法 a wholehearted friend 真誠的朋友。

widespread
[`waɪd͵sprɛd]

普遍的、廣泛的
英解 extending over a wide area

例 The practice of the dowry in India is still **widespread**. (98 指考)

嫁妝這項慣例在印度仍然很普遍。

語意用法 widespread among ＋族群，表示在某族群是很普遍的。

willing [ˋwɪlɪŋ]	樂意的、願意的、心甘情願的 英解 disposed or inclined toward

例 He was **willing** to make new changes. (96 指考)

他樂意做出新改變。

語意用法 willing ＋ to V，表示自動、樂意去做某事。

wise [ˋwaɪz]	有智慧的、聰明的、博學的 英解 having or prompted by wisdom or discernment

例 The **wise** woman generously opened her bag to share her food with the traveler. (97 學測)

這個聰明的女性慷慨地打開她的背包將食物與這名旅行者分享。

語意用法 a wise leader 有智慧的領導者；a wise plan 聰明的計畫。

wonderful [ˋwʌndəfəl]	極好的、精彩的、非比尋常的 英解 extraordinarily good or great

例 There was once a man in Puerto Rico who had a **wonderful** parrot. (87 學測)

在波多黎各，曾有一個人養了一隻非比尋常的鸚鵡。

語意用法 weird and wonderful 古怪卻美好的。

worldwide [ˋwɜld͵waɪd]	普及全世界的、世界性的 英解 universal

例 Very few products ever achieve **worldwide** success.

很少產品獲得世界性的成功。

語意用法 worldwide crisis 世界性的危機。

| **worth**
[wɝθ] | 值得的、有價值的；亦作名詞用
英解 meriting or justifying |

例 We considered opening a branch office in China, but concluded that it wasn't **worth** the trouble.

我們考慮在中國大陸開設分公司，但後來認為不值得費這個力。

語意用法 worth + Ving，表示值得做某事。

| **youthful**
[ˈjuθfəl] | 年輕的、富青春活力的
英解 suggestive of youth |

例 Voters elected him despite his many **youthful** indiscretions.

儘管他年輕時有許多鹵莽的行為，選民還是投票給他。

語意用法 youthful days 年輕歲月。

| **zigzag**
[ˈzɪgzæg] | Z 字形的、鋸齒狀的；亦作名詞用
英解 travel along a zigzag path |

例 It swims away in a **zigzag** path.（93 學測）

牠以 Z 字形路徑游走。

語意用法 a zigzag path 曲折小徑；a zigzag line 鋸齒形的線。

副詞篇

▶ ▶ ▶ Adverbs

afterwards

barely

mainly

besides

otherwise

furthermore

absolutely
[ˈæbsəˌlutlɪ]

絕對地、完全地
英解 completely and without qualification

例 It was an obvious conclusion, but it was **absolutely** wrong.

這是一個顯而易見的結論，但卻完全錯誤。

語意用法 用於口語有「對極了、正是如此」的意思。

accordingly
[əˈkɔrdŋlɪ]

照著、因此、於是
英解 because of the reason given

例 **Accordingly**, anyone who wishes to love and be loved will want to establish lasting relationships.（86 學測）

因此，每個期待去愛並被愛的人都會想要建立長久的關係。

語意用法 accordingly 通常置於句首，表示之前的原因導致後面的可能結果或做法。

afterwards
[ˈæftəwədz]

事後、隨後、往後、以後
英解 subsequently

例 It's far better to think twice of it now than **afterwards**.

現在多想想比事後再想好。

語意用法 afterwards 表示往後的時間，此處與 now 相比較。

altogether
[ˌɔltəˈgɛðə]

全然、全部、總之
英解 completely

例 There are **altogether** 154 foreign students in this university, representing a total of thirteen different countries.（92 指考）

這所大學裡全部有 154 名外國學生，分別代表總共十三個不同的國家。

語意用法 altogether 表示全部合起來，通常放在 be + altogether，或是句首或句尾。

backwards
[ˋbækwədz]

向後、逆向、往回

英解 at or to or toward the back or rear

例 Amy turned and walked **backwards** as she left.（92 學測補）

艾咪轉身向後走，離開了。

語意用法 放在動詞之後，表示向後的動作，如 play backwards。

barely
[ˋbɛrlɪ]

幾乎沒有、勉強、貧乏地

英解 only a very short time before

例 I always have trouble reading my daughter's letters because her handwriting is **barely** legible.

我讀我女兒的信總是有困難，因為她的字跡實在難以辨識。

語意用法 be + barely；barely +一般動詞。

beforehand
[bɪˋforˌhænd]

事先、預先、提前

英解 in advance

例 My grandmother likes to surprise people. She never calls **beforehand** to inform us of her visits.（93 學測）

我奶奶喜歡給人驚喜，她從不事先打電話通知我們她要來訪。

語意用法 動詞 + beforehand，表示先做這個動作。

besides
[bɪˋsaɪdz]

除此之外

英解 making an additional point

例 **Besides**, one of his hands should bear a mark like a conch-shell.（93 學測）

除此之外，他的一隻手應該配戴像是海螺商標的標誌。

語意用法 放在句首單獨使用，如本句，表示除了前面所說的之外。

closely [ˈkloslɪ]	接近地、緊密地、親密地、嚴格地 英解 in a close relation or position in time or space

例 We **closely** followed the advice in your article.（98 學測）

我們嚴格地遵循您文章上的建議。

語意用法 closely ＋動詞，表示仔細地做這動作、或是緊緊地做某動作。

drastically [ˈdræstɪk]ɪ]	大大地、徹底地、激烈地 英解 in a drastic manner

例 This does not stop the discoloration, but will **drastically** slow the process.

這不能阻止褪色，但會大大地減緩過程。

語意用法 drastically ＋動詞，表示徹底進行此動作。

furthermore [ˈfɝðɚˋmor]	此外、再者、而且 英解 in addition

例 **Furthermore**, the city also planned to sue him for a quarter of a million dollars.（83 學測）

此外，這座城市還打算起訴他二十五萬美元。

語意用法 furthermore 通常放句首，表示此外、進一步。

likewise [ˈlaɪkˌwaɪz]	同樣地、也 英解 similarly

例 Oolong tea is prepared **likewise**, but without the fermentation time.

（95 學測）

烏龍茶的製作過程相同，但沒有發酵的時間。

語意用法 放在動詞之後，表示同樣進行的動作。

mainly [ˈmenlɪ]	主要地、大部分地 英解 for the most part

例 This was done **mainly** to convince people that the priests were powerful.

（92 學測）

這麼做主要是為了使人們信服祭司的力量強大。

語意用法 mainly ＋動詞，此處為被動：be ＋動詞 -ed mainly。

meanwhile [ˈminˌhwaɪl]	在這期間、同時 英解 during the intervening time or period

例 **Meanwhile** he did what he could.

同時他做了他所能做的。

語意用法 放在句首，表示與前面動作同時進行的動作。

merely [ˈmɪrlɪ]	只是、僅僅、不過 英解 only

例 Bob refused to be taken to the hospital, insisting that his wound was **merely** a scratch.

鮑伯拒絕上醫院，堅持他的傷口只是輕微抓傷。

語意用法 merely ＋一般時間或金錢，表示僅僅。

moreover [morˋovɚ]	此外、並且 英解 furthermore

例 Students cannot afford the tuition increase, and they would, **moreover**, refuse to pay it even if they had the money.

學生負擔不起上漲的學費，此外，即使他們有錢也會拒絕支付。

語意用法 放在句首，表示進一步、而且。

neither [ˈniðɚ]	也不、兩者無一 英解 not in either case

例 He was **neither** good nor evil.

他不善良也不邪惡。

語意用法 neither 用於相對的否定句；neither ... nor 表示兩者皆不。

nevertheless
[͵nɛvɚðəˋlɛs]

然而、不過、仍然
英解 however

例 **Nevertheless**, the results of his listening did not make him popular.
（88 學測）

然而，他傾聽的結果並沒有讓他受到歡迎。

語意用法 轉折用語，放在句首，表示後面的動作與前面不同。

otherwise
[ˋʌðɚ͵waɪz]

不同地、除此之外、否則、不然
英解 differently

例 Jeff's jokes enlivened what was **otherwise** a boring budget meeting.

傑夫的笑話讓原本無趣的預算會議變得生動。

語意用法 與祈使句、假設法連用，放在句首，表示不如此做，就會如何如何。

rather
[ˋræðɚ]

相當、頗、寧可、而非
英解 somewhat

例 Another moral which also means a great deal is "competition against situations **rather** than against rivals." （98 學測）

另一個很有意義的寓意是「反抗局勢而非反對敵手」。

語意用法 A rather than B，表示寧可是 "A" 而不是 "B"。

therefore
[ˋðɛr͵for]

因此、因而、所以
英解 thus

例 Mr. Mooney did all the work, and it is **therefore** Mr. Mooney who should receive all the credit.

莫尼先生做了所有的工作，因此，所有的功勞都該歸他。

語意用法 therefore 表示因此，可放在句首，或主詞＋ therefore ＋動詞。

374

undoubtedly [ʌn`dautɪdlɪ]	毫無疑問地、肯定地 英解 certainly

例 Your mother is **undoubtedly** a very generous woman.

你母親無疑是個非常大方的人。

語意用法 undoubtedly ＋形容詞，表示此事毫無疑問。

wholly [`holɪ]	完全地、全部 英解 completely, totally, or entirely

例 He had been so **wholly** unprepared for what he heard now.

對於他現在所聽到的他完全沒有心理準備。

語意用法 not wholly ＋動詞，與否定語連用時表示部分否定，即表示非全部。

widely [`waɪdlɪ]	廣泛地、大大地 英解 extensively

例 As computers are getting less expensive, they are **widely** used in schools and offices today.（94 學測）

隨著電腦越來越便宜，現在學校與辦公室都很普遍地使用電腦。

語意用法 be ＋ widely ＋ p.p.，表示某動作被廣泛運用。

副詞篇

其他詞性篇

▶ ▶ ▶ Others

underneath

through

unless

towards

whenever

throughout

although [ɔˋðo]	雖然、儘管、然而 英解 even though

例 **Although** he is a chef, Roberto rarely cooks his own meals.（94 學測）

雖然羅伯托是一名主廚，他鮮少自己做飯吃。

語意用法 although 引導的副詞子句通常置於主要子句前，表示雖然、儘管。

beyond [bɪˋjɑnd]	越過、超出範圍、超脫於 英解 on the other side of

例 It seemed to me that the management had gone **beyond** their legal right in making this order.（90 學測）

在我看來，發號這個命令已經超出管理階層的法律權限。

語意用法 beyond ＋名詞，表示超過某些事，如：beyond my control，表示超過我能控制的。

through [θru]	通過、穿過 英解 in one side and out the opposite or another side of

例 I've lost nearly 20 kilograms so far **through** hard work and determination.

藉著努力和決心，我目前瘦了將近二十公斤。

語意用法 through ＋事、物，表示透過某件事或某物。

throughout [θruˋaʊt]	遍及、貫穿、從頭到尾 英解 all through

例 Recent studies show that levels of happiness for most people change **throughout** their lives.（96 指考）

最近的研究指出，大部分人的快樂指數隨著他們的一生改變。

語意用法 throughout ＋事、物，表示整件事從頭到尾。

towards
[tə`wɔrdz]

朝向、將近、對於
英解 in the direction or vicinity of

例 After you come out of the subway exit, walk **towards** the large blue building—that's the bus station.

你走出地下道出口，朝藍色大樓的方向走，那就是公車站。

語意用法 不含到達終點的意思，只表示往一個方向。

underneath
[ˌʌndə`niθ]

在其下
英解 under, below, beneath

例 He distrusted banks and chose to keep his savings in an old cardboard box **underneath** his bed.

他不信任銀行，選擇把他的積蓄放在老舊紙盒置於床下。

語意用法 在某件事之下，放於句首，也可以 underneath ＋物。

unless
[ʌn`lɛs]

除非、若非
英解 except under the circumstances that

例 In Samoa a woman is not considered attractive **unless** she weighs more than 200 pounds.（94 學測）

在薩摩亞，一個女人除非體重超過二百磅否則是不會被認為有吸引力的。

語意用法 unless ＋狀況，表示除非是某狀況。

whenever
[hwɛn`ɛvə]

每當、無論什麼時候
英解 at every or any time that

例 **Whenever** a Dalai Lama died, a search began for his reincarnation.（93 學測）

每當達賴去世，就會開始尋找他的轉世靈童。

語意用法 whenever ＋人＋動詞，表示每當某人做某事。

其他詞性篇

379

wherever
[hwɛrˋɛvɚ]

無論去到哪裡
英解 in or to whichever place or situation

例 **Wherever** you go, there are buildings in Romanic, Baroque, and Rococo styles that were popular hundreds of years ago.（97 學測）

無論你走到哪兒，都有流行了幾百年的浪漫主義、巴洛克以及洛可可風格的建築。

語意用法 wherever 與 whenever 用法同，表示地方。

whichever
[hwɪtʃˋɛvɚ]

無論哪個、無論哪些
英解 whatever one or ones

例 But **whichever** of these we prefer some difficulty will arise.

無論我們偏愛哪一個，都會造成一些困難。

語意用法 whichever 指的是事物的選擇。

whoever
[huˋɛvɚ]

無論誰、到底是誰
英解 whatever person or persons

例 **Whoever** told you that you could sing was just trying to be polite.

無論是誰說你會唱歌，都只是客套而已。

語意用法 whoever 表示人的選擇，任何人皆可。

within
[wɪˋðɪn]

在某範圍內、不超過
英解 in the inner part or parts of

例 After all, you must live **within** a limited budget.（95 學測）

畢竟，你必須以有限的預算來過活。

語意用法 within ＋事物，在某事物的範圍內，如：within a speed limit 在速限內。

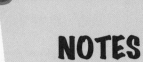

NOTES

NOTES

NOTES

國家圖書館出版品預行編目資料

改變一生的大考單字課 / 陳超明作. -- 初版. -- 臺北市：
貝塔出版, 智勝文化發行, 2011.06
　　面：　公分

　ISBN: 978-957-729-837-9（平裝附光碟片）

　1. 英語　2. 詞彙

805.12　　　　　　　　　　　　　　　　100007652

改變一生的大考單字課

作　　者 / 陳超明
文字整理 / 巫立文
執行編輯 / 陳家仁

出　　版 / 貝塔出版有限公司
地　　址 / 台北市 100 館前路 12 號 11 樓
電　　話 / (02) 2314-2525
傳　　真 / (02) 2312-3535
客服專線 / (02) 2314-3535
客服信箱 / btservice@betamedia.com.tw
郵撥帳號 / 19493777
帳戶名稱 / 貝塔出版有限公司

總 經 銷 / 時報文化出版企業股份有限公司
地　　址 / 桃園縣龜山鄉萬壽路二段 351 號
電　　話 / (02) 2306-6842

出版日期 / 2011 年 6 月初版一刷
定　　價 / 400 元
I S B N / 978-957-729-837-9

改變一生的大考單字課
Copyright 2011 by 陳超明
Published by Beta Multimedia Publishing

貝塔網址：www.betamedia.com.tw

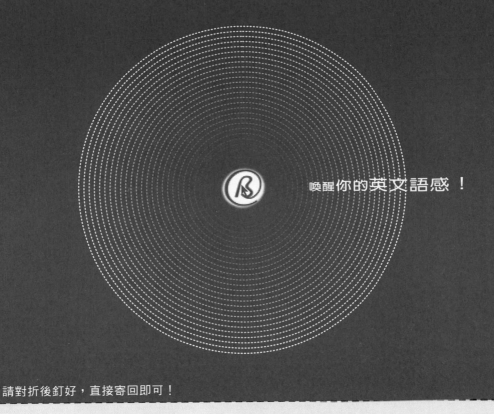

喚醒你的英文語感！

請對折後釘好，直接寄回即可！

100 台北市中正區館前路12號11樓

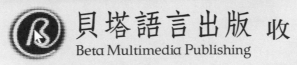 貝塔語言出版 收
Beta Multimedia Publishing

寄件者住址 □□□

貝塔語言出版
Beta Multimedia Publishing

讀者服務專線 (02) 2314-3535　讀者服務傳真 (02) 2312-3535
客戶服務信箱 btservice@betamedia.com.tw
www.betamedia.com.tw

謝謝您購買本書！！

貝塔語言擁有最優良之英文學習書籍，為提供您最佳的英語學習資訊，您填妥此表後寄回（免貼郵票），將可不定期免費收到本公司最新發行之書訊及活動訊息！

姓名：＿＿＿＿＿＿＿＿＿　性別：□男 □女　生日：＿＿年＿＿月＿＿日

電話：（公）＿＿＿＿＿＿（宅）＿＿＿＿＿＿（手機）＿＿＿＿＿＿

電子信箱：＿＿＿＿＿＿＿＿＿＿＿＿＿＿＿＿＿＿＿＿＿＿

學歷：□高中職含以下　□專科　□大學　□研究所含以上

職業：□金融 □服務 □傳播 □製造 □資訊 □軍公教 □出版
　　　□自由 □教育 □學生 □其他

職級：□企業負責人 □高階主管 □中階主管 □職員 □專業人士

1. 您購買的書籍是？＿＿＿＿＿＿＿＿＿＿＿＿＿＿＿＿

2. 您從何處得知本產品？（可複選）

　　□書店 □網路 □書展 □校園活動 □廣告信函 □他人推薦 □新聞報導 □其他＿＿

3. 您覺得本產品價格：

　　□偏高 □合理 □偏低

4. 請問目前您每週花了多少時間學英語？

　　□不到十分鐘 □十分鐘以上，但不到半小時 □半小時以上，但不到一小時
　　□一小時以上，但不到兩小時 □兩個小時以上 □不一定

5. 通常在選擇語言學習書時，哪些因素是您會考慮的？

　　□封面 □內容、實用性 □品牌 □媒體、朋友推薦 □價格 □其他＿＿＿

6. 市面上您最需要的語言書種類為？

　　□聽力 □閱讀 □文法 □口說 □寫作 □其他＿＿＿

7. 通常您會透過何種方式選購語言學習書籍？

　　□書店門市 □網路書店 □郵購 □直接找出版社 □學校或公司團購 □其他＿＿

8. 給我們的建議：＿＿＿＿＿＿＿＿＿＿＿＿＿＿＿＿＿＿

＿＿＿＿＿＿＿＿＿＿＿＿＿＿＿＿＿＿＿＿＿＿＿＿＿＿

＿＿＿＿＿＿＿＿＿＿＿＿＿＿＿＿＿＿＿＿＿＿＿＿＿＿

喚醒你的英文語感！

Get a Feel for English !

喚醒你的英文語感！

Get a Feel for English !